PRAISE FOR

"MY BEAUTIFUL SIN ... sexy book in this brilliant series! ... I can't wait to see where this story will take us in the final book. And can someone please get Netflix on the phone for this already!!!????" *BJ's Book Blog*

"J. Kenner knows how to deliver a tortured alpha that everyone will fall for hard. Saint is exactly the sinner I want in my bed." *Laurelin Paige, NYT bestselling author*

"J. Kenner has done it again! Fans of her Damien Stark series are going to totally fall for Devlin Saint in this sexy, compelling page-turner." *NYT Bestselling author Carly Phillips*

"This story ticked all my boxes, I swooned, I sighed, and at times I held my breath as Devlin and Ellie push trust and love to the limits, the chemistry is sizzling, the characters loveable and I can't wait to see where we go with book 2 in this series." *Thelma and Louise Book Blog*

Also By The Author

THE STARK SAGA
novels
release me
claim me
complete me
anchor me
lost with me
novellas
take me
have me
play my game
seduce me
unwrap me
deepest kiss
entice me
hold me
please me
indulge me
delight me
cherish me
enchant me

STARK SECURITY
shattered with you
shadows of you-short story
broken with you
ruined with you

SEE MORE TITLES AT WWW.JKENNER.COM

MY BEAUTIFUL
SIN

NEW YORK TIMES BESTSELLING AUTHOR
J. KENNER

M&O

My Beautiful Sin Copyright © 2020 by Julie Kenner

Cover design by Michele Catalano, Catalano Creative
Cover images from Deposit Photos- Syda_Productions (fireplace), Imaginechina-Tuchong (bed), and Shutterstock - Ligak (negligee)

ISBN: Digital: 978-1-949925-91-3
Print: 978-1-949925-92-0

Published by Martini & Olive Books
V-2020-11-25P

CHAPTER ONE

D evlin Saint propped himself up on his elbow and gazed
down at the naked woman sleeping beside him, her pale
skin illuminated by a shaft of moonlight, her soft brown waves
fanned out on the white pillow.

Gently, he ran his hand over her bare shoulder, then down
her arm, relishing her heat and the softness of her skin beneath his
palm.

His.

The word flashed neon in his mind, and he had to bite back
an ironic chuckle. He hadn't felt possessive of a woman since his
first love, and he'd been a different man then. A different name. A
different look.

In the years since he'd left Alex Leto behind and become
Devlin Saint, the women in his life had been disposable, and he'd
never expected that to change. There was no woman who had
charmed or challenged him. No woman who'd made his heart
sing. Not a single female for whom he'd felt even remotely possessive. Only that first, lost love.

The same woman who, through some miracle he didn't
deserve, was now curled up beside him, her soft skin teasing his
senses as his mind struggled to believe that she was his again after

all this time. That somehow, despite who he was and what he'd done, she believed in him enough to fight her way back into his life.

His El. His love. His light.

She'd been his heart all those long years ago. The best part of him. The part that made him want to be a better man.

The part that he'd clung to and cherished and tried to keep alive during the hellish years after he'd walked away.

He hadn't wanted to leave her, and looking at her now, he couldn't remember how he'd ever found the strength. Except that he'd had to. There'd been no other choice. It hadn't been about him, but about her. About keeping her safe. Because being aligned with him in those cold, dark days would have been no life at all.

And now? The voice in his head was harsh. *Is it really so different now?*

With a sigh, he slipped from the bed, careful not to wake her. He crossed to the sliding door and looked out toward the moonlit ocean. The night was quiet, peaceful, and he embraced it, knowing better than most that such moments were all too rare.

Then he turned to look back at Ellie, enjoying the way the moon's kiss set her skin aglow. For as long as he'd known her, she'd burned from within, as wild and bright as a living flame lighting his way.

Christ, she was everything to him.

Slowly, so as not to wake her, he returned to the bed and slid in beside her, his fingertips once again drawn to her soft curves.

Damn him for ever leaving her. And damn him now for fighting for her. For claiming her. For drawing her in instead of shoving her away when he'd had the chance, not to mention the strength.

But he couldn't bear the thought of being without her. So he'd allowed her into his orbit, knowing damn well that was a dangerous place to be.

He was a selfish bastard, but how could he push her away

when he finally understood how dead he'd been inside for the last ten years? She'd brought him back to life. She made him whole.

He'd told the truth when he'd sworn to protect her. He only hoped that he could. Because the wolves were circling. Soon, they'd attack, letting loose a swarm of secrets he'd tried to keep contained. Secrets he kept hidden from the world. From the public that thought of him only as a reclusive and intriguing phil- anthropist.

And, yes, secrets he still hid from El.

Not paltry secrets like the identity of his father or even the truth surrounding the death of her uncle. But bone-deep confi- dences and dangerous lies.

His biggest fear was that once revealed, he'd lose Ellie all over again.

For now, though, she was his, and his secrets were safe.

And Devlin was going to do his damnedest to make sure it stayed that way.

CHAPTER TWO

I wake to the feel of Devlin's body pressed against mine, his heat burning through me. I don't move, just breathe in, enjoying this still-new sensation of having the man I love so deliciously close.

I don't know what time it is now, but wide shafts of light slice the room, squeezing in through the gaps in the drapes that block the eastern-facing windows. My eyes are only half-open, my mind still fuzzy with the remnants of lust and heat as I watch the tiny flecks of dust dancing in the sunshine.

I'm guessing that it's past ten, and though I know we should both get out of bed, I don't want to. I want to stay here forever, safe in Devlin's arms, well away from the grasping claws of the outside world.

You're in over your head. Find the truth. Don't trust anyone.

The memory of the text I received last night sends a chill through me. I hadn't shown it to Devlin. I'm not sure if I wanted to protect the sensual intimacy of our night together or if I was afraid of what I'd see on his face—the things he might feel compelled to tell me. And the shadow of the secrets he's withholding.

After all, everything I'd learned recently nearly broke me.

The knowledge that he's the son of one of the most notorious criminals to ever walk the earth was bad enough. But when I learned that it was Devlin who'd killed my uncle Peter all those years ago, the ground had fallen out from under me.

It had taken long talks and even longer forays deep into my own soul to accept the truth, understand his motivations, and not only forgive him, but realize how deeply I need him. I'd run back to him with a change of clothes and the determination to convince him that everything could be right between us.

Then that text arrived.

What if there's another horrible revelation? Maybe I can face it now, in the morning light. But last night? With candles and kisses, and the fervor of reconciliation?

No way—that hadn't even been an option.

So instead of sharing the text, I'd shoved down my fears.

I haven't even considered the possibility that the vague language refers to something other than Devlin. Of course it's about him.

He told me straight out that he's still clinging to secrets. But secrets are slippery. It's rare that they are truly secure. Someone else knows what he's trying to hide.

But whether this text was meant as a warning or a threat, I don't know. Either way, it was meant to divide us, Devlin and me.

I won't let it, though, and now I draw strength from the knowledge that I know this man. The real man, not merely the picture he paints for the world.

Except that's not entirely true, and I tremble. Not because I know the secrets he's keeping, but because I fear that he loves me enough to walk away if those secrets put a target on my back. He did it once already, after all.

That certainty weighs on me, and I close my eyes, longing for the return of sleep. I want to wake up again, only this time with no memory of the text. I want it to be nothing more than the remnant of a nightmare. Something I can ignore.

Something I don't have to tell him.

As if the mental storm in my head has awakened him, his hand slides along my thigh, rising higher until he's caressing my hip. His lips brush the nape of my neck, and my body immediately responds, my nipples going hard, that insistent pulse between my legs increasing.

Without a word, I roll over and find his chiseled face smiling back at me. His chin-length dark hair frames his face, and his eyes —sandy brown at the moment—watch me with such tender intensity that my heart actually aches.

We've been through so much in such a short time. Secrets, lies, promises. His revelations had both scared and horrified me, but I'm still here, despite Devlin trying his damnedest to push me away.

Now, someone else is pushing, suggesting even darker secrets. But it doesn't matter. I'm fighting back against that someone, too.

I've gone from hating Alex Leto for walking away from me all those years ago, to loving Devlin Saint with an intensity so deep I know that I would sacrifice anything to keep him near me. There is darkness around him, true. But I like to think that I'm the light he needs in his life.

I know for certain that he's what I need in mine. And I'll be damned if I'll let random, anonymous threats shake my faith in him.

He studies my face, and the silence that still lingers between us seems thick with possibility. I don't break it. Instead, I use my forefinger to gently trace the scar on his face.

It's not a scar he had in our youth, and though he has yet to tell me the full story of how he got it, I know that it's a mark of the man he is now. It bisects his right brow, then continues down his cheek, the offending blade having thankfully spared his eye.

It terminates on his upper lip beneath the close-trimmed mustache that I brush lightly before cupping his jaw with my hand, enjoying the sensation of his rough beard against my palm.

He'd been clean-shaven when we were young, but he'd been a

different person then, too. And honestly, I can't complain. The Alex Leto I'd loved then could turn heads, no doubt. But Devlin Saint is the full package. He's confidence, control, and a hint of danger all wrapped up in a man who must have been designed by the gods on a particularly good day.

Best of all, he's mine.

"Hi, there," I say, my voice the barest hint of a whisper.

He doesn't respond. At least not with words. Instead, he rolls us over so that I'm on my back and he's straddling me, his hands sliding up my body as he lowers his mouth to mine.

The kiss is slow and deep, and I want to melt into it. Into *him*. I spread my legs, wanting everything he is willing to give, then cringing when I remember. "Wait," I whisper, tightening my grip on his shoulders. "Do you have a condom?"

He hesitates a second too long before stretching his arm out to pull open the bedside drawer. He may not have even realized he hesitated, but I know he did. And I know why.

We'd forgotten about protection last night. Which isn't a huge problem since I've got an implant. Except that before Devlin, I wasn't exactly playing it safe. I haven't played it safe in years. On the contrary, from fast cars to anonymous fucks, I've spent much of the last ten years standing at the edge of a metaphorical volcano, daring the world to push me in.

I hadn't feared death; I'd danced with it, tempting it to claim me the way it had my entire family.

Now, though, I understand fear.

Now, I have something to lose. It's been a while since I've been tested, and the thought that I might pass something horrible on to him haunts me.

But from Devlin's perspective ... well, he probably assumed I didn't press last night because we're truly, finally together. So what must he think it means for me to ask now?

He says none of that, though. Instead, he sheaths himself then flashes me a humor-filled grin as he says, "Take two."

I laugh—probably more than the joke really called for—and hook my arms around his neck. "Kiss me," I murmur. "Make love to me."

"Baby, that's exactly what I have in mind."

We're both beyond ready, as if our naked limbs tangled in sleep had been foreplay enough. I arch up, silently begging him to enter me, wanting nothing more than this man, his hands on me, his cock inside me. It's fast and urgent, both of us spiraling upward in a frenzy of heat and need.

Soon, I'm gasping, on the cusp of going completely over.

"Now," he says. "Come for me now, baby."

It's a command I can't disobey, and my body breaks apart, my core tightening around him, taking him over the cliff with me as we fall off into space, tumbling over and over until we are spent and gasping, locked in each other's arms as sunshine fills the room, welcoming us to the day.

I stretch languorously as he moves off of me and deals with the condom. "That was so much better than an alarm clock," I say.

"Such high praise." I hear the tease in his voice as his fingers stroke my hair. "Do you want coffee?"

I start to sit up, "Always," I say. "I'll go start some."

He shakes his head, then bends over to kiss me lightly on the lips. "No, stay where you are. I like the thought of you staying in my bed as long as possible."

I lift a brow and lean back. "Waiting on me? I could get used to this."

"That's the idea." He winks, and I laugh. Then I simply sit there and enjoy the view as he gets out of bed and pulls on a pair of sweatpants that he'd left hanging over the back of the chair.

He turns from me as he heads to the door, and I watch that perfect ass move away from me. I sigh happily. I never thought that he would be mine again, not after all we'd lost when we were young.

A fist tightens around my heart, and I can't hold back the swell of fear that once again it's not going to last. That what we found isn't permanent. That all the dark shadows of our youth are going to swarm back in to haunt us, and that all my qualms about returning to Laguna Cortez are finally going to come true.

I'd left Manhattan and returned to my hometown with an assignment to write an article about the Devlin Saint Foundation and my own plan to research the circumstances surrounding the murder of my Uncle Peter a decade ago. But though I'd grown up here, returning was like coming home to hell.

This town held so much loss for me. My mother died in a car wreck, my father was brutally murdered in the line of duty. And then my guardian, Peter, had been assassinated by a single shot to the head, leaving me lost and alone.

The night that he died had been the first time that his assistant, Alex Leto, and I had made love, both of us surrendering to grief and loss and lust.

I'd been seventeen, he'd been almost twenty, and the heat that had been burning between us had finally reached a boiling point. He'd filled me up and sent me reeling. He'd helped me forget about the horror of my uncle's death, at least for a few precious moments.

He'd soothed me, and he'd told me with words and his body how much he loved me.

Then he ripped me to shreds. Because that was the last time I ever saw Alex Leto.

When I came back to Laguna Cortez ten years later to research those two stories, it wasn't Alex I found, but Devlin Saint. A new man, a different man.

A man who swore he would have nothing to do with me because of his dangerous past. And yet here I am in his bed, exactly where I intend to stay.

You're in over your head. Find the truth. Don't trust anyone.

The vile words fill my head once again, and I reach for my

phone, determined to see them in black and white. To change the memory from emotion to nothing more than evidence.

Whoever sent these words hadn't broken into my home or assaulted me on the street, and yet the message seems just as invasive. It was sent with the intention to wound me, and the arrow has undeniably hit home.

Of course, I could be wrong about the text's meaning. But if it's not about Devlin and the secrets that surround him, then I really am at a loss. And if it is about him, then he and I have much more to face than simply moving past the ghosts of our youth.

By the time he comes back to the room with two steaming mugs of coffee, I'm sitting up in bed with my arms around my knees. Since he immediately frowns, I assume my expression isn't what he'd expected after a delicious morning in bed.

He puts the coffee on the table then sits on the edge of the bed. "What's wrong?"

I hesitate, knowing that if I open this door, I'll be fueling his fears that he and his secrets are a danger to me. But at the same time, if I stay quiet, whoever sent this has already won, simply by driving that silent wedge between us.

So I draw in a breath, meet his eyes, and say, "We need to talk."

His mouth quirks, and that bisected brow rises. "Tired of me already?"

I laugh, and it feels like a pressure valve has opened. "I need to show you something," I say, picking my phone up from where it sits beside me on the mattress.

His expression turns serious. "What's going on?"

"I should have showed you this last night, but I didn't want..."

I trail off with a shrug, knowing that he'll understand. It was our first night back together. He has to know that I wouldn't have wanted to bring anything horrible into this room with us.

But now I unlock my phone and pass it to him. As he reads the text, I watch his face, searching for a hint of worry or anger or confusion. But there's nothing. And once again I'm reminded of who Devlin Saint really is. He's an invention. An enigma. A man with a dark and secret past. A boy who had to learn how to hide not only himself but also his emotions in order to grow into the man he's become.

And though I know he trusts me, I can't deny the small stab at my heart when I see that right now, he's hiding those emotions from me.

I can read nothing in his eyes when he lifts his face to mine. "I assume you don't know who this came from."

"No. I looked up the number but there's no info. I'm guessing it's a burner—I may see if Lamar can dig deeper," I add, referring to my friend who's a detective.

"No. I can handle it. I have resources."

I nod, not surprised that he doesn't want Lamar involved. Not only does Lamar not know about my past with Devlin, but whenever they're together, I feel the undercurrent of tension. They're both protective of me, neither fully trusts the other, and I'd just as soon not be in the middle of that any more than I have to be.

As for Devlin having resources, that makes sense, too. After all, his foundation not only helps with the rehabilitation of victims of all sorts of crimes, but it also provides support for and access to paramilitary organizations who can assist with rescue missions. So even if the DSF doesn't have a department that can trace back the number, I'm sure he knows someone who can.

"Fine," I say. "No problem."

He reaches for my phone, but I pull it back. "I'll give you the number on one condition. Anything you learn, you tell me."

He hesitates, then nods as I text the number to him. When I look up, his expression is harsh, and he stands, running his fingers through his hair as he paces the large bedroom, an icy fury building around him.

"This is the way it will always be, isn't it?" His voice is tight. Controlled. "My past following us. My secrets threatening to come between us."

I slide out of bed as well, grabbing the T-shirt that he didn't put on and tossing it over my head. I don't know why I feel the need to be clothed around him right now, but I do. And once the shirt is hanging mid-thigh, I move into his arms.

"No." I shake my head firmly "It's an annoyance. It's an intrusion. It's a threat. But it's not coming between us."

For a moment, I see nothing on his face. Then the light of a smile blooms in his still-brown eyes. He's not yet wearing the green contacts that are part and parcel of the man he has become. Right now, he's a little bit Devlin and a little bit Alex, and I wrap my arms around him, holding tight to both sides of the man I love.

"I bet it's from someone who doesn't realize that I already know who your father is." I tilt my head up, then see him nod slowly, as if considering that possibility. I'm almost positive I'm right, because what else could it be?

"I suppose it must be. But I honestly don't know who."

I haven't got a clue either. "There must be people out there who've learned the truth about who you really are. Maybe they're laying low and biding their time."

I watch as his demeanor shifts from neutral to ice cold. And once again, I get a hint of how dangerous this man can be.

When he remains silent, I press. "Who other than Anna, Tamra, and Ronan know you used to be Alex?" Ronan Thorne is his best friend, with whom Devlin served in the military, having enlisted as Alex after he ran from his father.

As for Tamra Danvers, she knew his mother and sought him out after she died when Alex was still young and essentially held hostage by his father, a notorious crime lord known as The Wolf. She's watched over him for years, even coming to Laguna Cortez when he did. She worked in community relations at the police department at the same time I was interning there during high school.

I'd adored her back then and still do now that she works as the Devlin Saint Foundation's publicity director. Both Devlin and I trust her completely. In fact, she's the one who held my hand the most in the days after I found out that it was Devlin who really killed Peter, and I'm forever grateful to her for helping me find my way back to him.

Anna Lindstrom, the third of the trio closest to him, now works as his assistant. Just a couple of years older than Devlin, she grew up on the Wolf's Nevada complex with him. She's also the first girl Alex slept with, and she's curvy and gorgeous. The first time I saw her in a slinky silver dress, I wanted to claw her eyes out. We're friendly now, but I have to confess that some jealousy still lingers.

That, however, is on me. She's loyal to a fault, and I can't imagine she would ever hurt Devlin.

Still, there must be others. "You told me that even though you weren't in Witness Protection, you had government help setting yourself up as Devlin Saint after your father was killed."

He nods. "In exchange for information about the spider web of his operation, yeah."

"Well, those people know the truth. And there must be people who surrounded them who do, too. A clerk. A transcriptionist. Someone who didn't think you deserved to start fresh, not with a father like that."

His face hardens, and I wish I could call back the words. Because I know that part of Devlin really does feel that way—that he doesn't deserve this new life, because he's been tainted by his dad. And by his own actions, too.

I take his hand and hold it firmly. "It isn't true. It isn't what I believe. But someone might. And if they've been watching you, waiting for an opportunity…"

I trail off, and he nods. "It's a possibility," he concedes. "I'll look into it."

I frown, still thinking. "Maybe someone from those days thinks that you're running an illegal enterprise through the foundation—the sins of the father," I say, my voice as harsh as his expression. The possibility doesn't sit well with me. I don't believe it, but I can't deny that someone might. The Devlin Saint Foundation is a highly renowned philanthropic organization that has risen to a place of prominence in the five years of its existence. Which means it's attracted a lot of attention.

"The DSF grew quickly, and you funded it with your father's money," I continue, thinking out loud. He'd inherited a significant chunk of his father's fortune simply because there'd never been enough proof for the government to legally attach those funds.

"Because I wanted to clear the taint on those dollars. Do good rather than ill."

"I know that," I say. "But people see what they want."

Again, I think about Ronan. They've been friends since Devlin's time in the military, and now Ronan is loyal to the DSF, working with Devlin on many worthy causes. But I can't help but wonder who he was before. Was he jealous of Devlin's sudden fortune?

In the service, they were surely equals. But now Devlin is the name and face behind a world-renowned organization. Does Ronan applaud Devlin's efforts because he believes in them? Or because he's biding his time to render Devlin's comeuppance?

I force myself to shake off the suspicions. I like Ronan—I do. But there's no denying that he rubbed me the wrong way early on, suggesting it might be better for me to walk away rather than be a "distraction" to Devlin.

Yeah, well, fuck him. I'm happy to distract.

But probably best if I don't let my irritation morph into a completely unsupported accusation.

"You thought of something?"

I look up to see Devlin watching me, so I shake my head. "No. Not really." I manage a thin smile. "I was hoping for inspiration, but nada. You're going to talk to your old contacts? Maybe see if there's someone from your past who's been paying too much attention to you?"

"Believe me, I'm going to pursue this. I don't like threats, and I like them even less when they're aimed at you."

"Can't argue with that," I say. "I'm going to see what I can find out as well."

"Just leave it be," Devlin says. "I'll see if there's any relevant chatter. But I don't want you poking around. Someone sent you a warning. That means there may be danger."

"Oh, please." Danger doesn't scare me, but losing him does. And if he thinks I'm going to just sit around...

I square my shoulders and meet his eyes. "Someone seems to think that you've resurrected your father's empire. And I have an interest in helping you prove that's not true."

"That's not your—"

"More than that," I continue, cutting him off as my temper rises. "The text came to me, remember? Hell, you're not even named. Maybe it has nothing to do with you. But if someone is sending me threats, I'm damn well taking steps to protect myself. So don't tell me what I can and can't investigate. In case you've forgotten, investigating is my job. Reporter. Remember? With bonus points for the police background."

I see the irritation wash over him, and steel myself for an argument.

"Reporter?" he snaps. "Are you actually telling me that this is something you're going to report?"

I wince. "Of course not. My point is that I have skills. And I intend to use them."

"Dammit, El, you need to stay away from this. From bumping up against any lingering remnant from my father's enterprise."

"I'm not a child, Devlin. This is my—"

"For fuck's sake," he snaps. "I'm not playing protective caveman here. But I need time to talk to my sources quietly. You start digging, and you're going to let whoever sent that note know that they've struck a nerve."

I'd been about to speak, but that silences me. He's made a good point. Just not the point he thought he was making.

He's right that if I start looking around, the sender will know I'm interested, and the odds are that they're arrogant enough to believe they can win me over. And that means that a few inquiries may be just the lever I need to start an avalanche of information.

"Fine," I finally say, coolly. "You may be right."

But what I don't do is agree to lay low.

CHAPTER THREE

D evlin caught the back of her T-shirt as she started to move past him, pulling her to a stop. "Have you forgotten how well I know you?"

She looked over her shoulder, her whiskey brown eyes pointedly fixed on his hand knotted in the gray Army Special Forces Tee. "Problem, Mr. Saint?"

"You need to drop this, Ellie. Let me handle it."

"Hmm." She looked him up and down, a cool gaze so different from the way she usually looked at him. He was certain it was the look she'd used when she'd been in uniform—hell, it was probably part of her uniform. The key component in her transformation from petite woman to hard-ass cop.

Now, he assumed it was the look she used when interviewing a recalcitrant source. It wasn't a look he'd expect in a bedroom, but he couldn't deny that he liked it. She was strong, and always had been.

But she was stubborn, too, and it was at times like these when that trait could be a real pain in the ass.

"You're the one who said I have people I can talk to," he pressed. "Let me do that."

"I have people, too," she retorted. "And, to once again point out the obvious, the message came to me. There's a chance it has nothing to do with you."

"Bullshit."

Her shoulders sagged, and when she said, "Goddammit, Devlin," he thought he'd won, but then she bent forward, tugged her head and arms out of the shirt, and continued on toward the bathroom, completely naked with him holding the shirt.

"El—"

"We're not having this argument," she said. "You want to keep me here, fine. You're bigger than me. Hell, use the damn shirt and tie me to the bed. But barring that, I'm going to do what I think is best, and you can do the same. And what *I* intend to do is identify the fucker who's sending me anonymous notes like that's going to scare me."

She turned again and disappeared, slamming the door behind her. He started to follow, but stopped, opting to calm down before he did. She was strong-willed, and so was he, and God knew she didn't back down from what scared her. On the contrary, she faced it dead on.

He should have known better than to try to persuade her to back off because she might stir up a hornet's nest. Ellie poked hornets' nests just to feel the rush. And he understood why better than anyone.

The trouble was, she didn't understand how large and how dangerous this particular nest could be. His world was precarious and there were many people who would like to see him fall. She poked in the wrong place, and she could end up trapped inside a deadly swarm.

So many secrets. So many lies.

He told himself over and over that the less she knew, the safer she was. Because the more thread she had, the more she would pull, and the more likely it was that his world—and the world they wanted to build together—would unravel along with them.

She might not fear those dangerous places, but he did.

He hadn't before. Until she'd re-entered his life, he'd been more than willing to flip danger the bird. Because what did he have to lose?

Now he was vulnerable, where before he'd been steel. Now he had a soft spot. And God knew he would kill anyone who hurt his El.

He wanted to tell her everything. Wanted to hold her close and watch as she curled up against him, her eyes shut as she took in all of his secrets. He had a fantasy that she would understand. That everything he did, everything he was, would make sense to her.

But he couldn't quite believe it.

Honestly, he was terrified.

There. As simple as that.

He hadn't felt real terror since the day he'd run from his father, but Ellie had brought it back into his life. Because of her, he had something to lose, something to risk.

More, he had something to protect. And that's what he was doing, even if part of it meant that he was protecting her from him. From the dark places in his soul that, if she could see, would cast him in an entirely different light in her eyes.

Shit.

Without even realizing that he was on the move, he'd reached the door and thrown it open. She was in the shower now, the outline of her body visible through the steamy glass. The room was lit only by a tinted skylight, making the scene before him look like one from an erotic movie.

Despite his irritation, he felt his body go hard. Despite? Hell, maybe it was because she frustrated the hell out of him. He wanted to claim her again. Bend her to his will. Feel like maybe— just maybe—he had some iota of control over the maelstrom that was beginning to swirl around them.

And if that really did make him a goddamn caveman, well, so be it.

Her head was tilted back, her face in the spray, and she hadn't noticed him enter.

He untied the sweats and let them drop to the floor, then kicked them aside. He was already hard, and he couldn't even see her clearly. He reached down, slowly stroking his cock as he watched her. Had there ever been a moment in his life when this woman hadn't turned him on? She'd been only sixteen when they'd met, and the impact of seeing her that first time had been like a kick in the gut.

She was his weakness, he knew that, and he didn't like being a weak man. But it was worth it because she was his.

No matter what, she was the manifestation of everything he had fought for in his life, everything he was still fighting for, love and goodness and hope and a future. All wrapped up in one woman who belonged to him. A woman he would always fight for, even if it meant fighting her.

He crossed the steam-filled room and slid the shower door open, startling her. Then he looped an arm around her and tugged her toward him just as she was sagging with relief after that initial surprise.

"Dev—" she began, but he silenced her with a punishing kiss, then released her long enough to press her against the black tile wall, one arm caging her in place as the fingers of his other hand slipped between her legs. She was so damn slippery, and her lips parted in a soft moan that shifted into a gasp as he thrust two fingers inside her while pressing the pad of his thumb against her clit.

"If this is how you act when you're pissed," she murmured, "I'm going to make it a point to keep irritating the hell out of you."

He bent forward and nipped her ear. "Sweetheart, I'm barely irritated. You haven't seen me pissed. I doubt you really want to."

He pulled back long enough to see her face, expecting a lashing from her sharp tongue. Instead, all she said was, "Ditto."

He couldn't help it. He laughed.

"I'm only doing my job," she said. "And someone sent that message to me. I want to know who. And why. Why does someone want to scare me off you? Why should they even care

about us? For that matter is it about us? Or is it about what I am—
a reporter—and who you are? Is someone trying to position me to
expose you? Or is there something bigger going on here?"

She reached down, holding his hand more firmly in place,
then holding his eyes as she ground against him, her mouth
parting as a tremor cut through her. "Maybe they think I'm their
ally. That I'm just using you to get what I want."

"And what's that?" His cock was so hard he could barely form
words.

"Maybe I want the danger," she said. "Maybe I just want a
good fuck."

"Well," he said casually, "who doesn't? But, sweetheart, if it is
danger you're craving, you need to back away. Because you may
not like what you find."

She lifted her chin, her eyes flashing. "Won't I?"

His heart pounded in his ears as if his blood was screaming at
him to tell her. To tell her every goddamn thing. But all he said
was, "Do you think I can stand to lose you again?" He moved his
fingers inside her, gratified when she writhed against him and bit
her lower lip in an obvious effort to keep from crying out.

He bent to kiss her, his cock so hard now he thought he would
explode. He wanted to flip her around and take her from behind,
the weight of her breasts filling his hands as he sank deep
inside her.

But when he started to pull his hand free, she caught it, then
met his eyes and shook her head. "The only way you can lose me
is if you're the one walking away," she said. "And just for the
record, no matter how much I might want to feel you inside me
right now, there is no way in hell you're going to fuck me into
submission."

She ducked under his arm and moved nimbly to the shower
door. "I have work to do now," she said. "And, I think, so do you."

CHAPTER FOUR

"Ellie?" Brandy's voice pierces the quiet hallway.

"Yeah, it's me," I shout, kicking off my shoes.

"What the hell?" she asks, appearing around the corner in pajamas and an apron. Her blond hair is now tipped in blue, the pink apparently abandoned. Jake bounds into the hall at the same time, and I bend down to rub the scruff of his neck as he whines and writhes with pleasure. A tawny Labrador-mutt mix, Jake is almost eleven years old, but still convinced he's a pup.

"Jake, cushion," Brandy says, then strokes his coat as he obediently heads for his giant pillow by the patio door. She returns her focus to me. "Why aren't you still at Devlin's having wild make-up sex? Or do you need more clothes? I was assuming clothes really weren't an issue..."

She trails off with a sly wink, and I roll my eyes. "Cute," I say, "but I came home to see you. And because Devlin has meetings all day. I mean, the man runs a multi-billion dollar philanthropic outfit. You'd think he could shift his schedule, right?"

"It's a screwed-up world."

"It really is." I sniff the air. "If those are muffins, then you can have the honor of lifting my spirits."

She shakes her head in mock exasperation. "You're practically walking on air. Whether he has a meeting or not, your spirits are just fine."

"Yeah," I admit, following her to the kitchen, "they are. And they'll be better when you pass me one of those." Brandy is a whiz in the kitchen. And at the sewing machine, too. She's carving out a solid career with BB Bags, the business she started on Etsy to sell her oiled canvas totes and purses.

Now, she's in several local boutiques, not to mention some seriously trendy shops in Los Angeles. But I swear she could have just as easily opened a bakery and have a line out the door every day. She's tall and thin, and I swear she can eat everything she bakes and never see it on her hips. Me, I'm only five feet, five inches, and I'm risking a new jean size every time I indulge. But it's a risk worth taking.

"Banana nut," she says going around the counter to put one on a plate for me. "Pretty basic. Sorry."

"Are you insane? That sounds incredible." It's still hot from the oven, and I peel the paper off, careful not to burn my fingers.

"So?" She starts to peel her own muffin. "What they're saying is true? It all worked out? You and Devlin are back together, even though you're not at his place this very minute having make-up sex?"

"Trust me," I say. "There has been much make-up sex. And Back Together sex. And He's Just So Hot and Tempting sex."

"That's a lot of sex for less than twenty-four hours," she notes.

I make an innocent face. "You think so? Because if it wasn't for those meetings, I could have gone on and on and on and on and—"

She tosses up a hand, cutting me off. "I get the picture. And I'm very happy for you and your still-unsatisfied libido."

I'm about to ask about the new guy she's been seeing, Christopher, and the state of her libido, but something she said earlier strikes me. "What did you mean by *they're saying*? Who's saying what?"

She's just taken a huge bite, and now she hurries to chew and swallow as she aims a *duh* look my way. "The tabloid chasers. The Insta-hounds. The Tweeters." I must look blank, because she rushes on. "You didn't see them here? Or outside of Devlin's place? I figured you had to run the gauntlet to get to the front door."

I shake my head, and she gapes at me as if amazed at my cluelessness. Then she pulls out her phone. She taps a bit, then passes it to me so I can scroll through a gazillion hashtagged images that run the gamut from yesterday—with me rushing out of Brandy's house and into Devlin's—to this morning with Devlin kissing me in his doorway less than an hour ago. As I'm looking, another pops up with me right here, shoving my key into the lock, blissfully ignorant of everything around me.

"I can't believe I didn't notice I was being watched." I aim a frown toward Brandy. "Some cop, huh?"

"Former cop," she says, and I'm about to point out that a reporter should keep a watchful eye, too, when she continues. "And to be fair, it's not like they're obvious."

She goes to the small kitchen window that faces the front yard. "That green Toyota's been there since before you left yesterday. And the driver's so slunk down he's totally hidden. See?" she asks as I slide off my stool and come up behind her. "And that red Subaru was gone for a while. I think it must have followed you to Devlin's last night, then come back today. But it's not like either of those cars is out of place. The street is packed."

She's right about that. Some of the neighborhoods lower in the hills have parking that is only reserved for the residents. This street is far enough away from the Arts District that the city assumes the tourists won't be a pain and monopolize the street parking. They might be right, but whether it's locals or tourists, there's rarely a curbside spot in this neighborhood, and the various vehicles just fade into the scenery.

I head back to my stool, still carrying Brandy's phone. There are a zillion comments on the various posts, and I'm not inclined to read through them all. Instead, I slide the phone back across the counter to her. "So what's the consensus?"

"Well, yesterday it was that you were storming over there to give him a piece of your mind—and no, there wasn't any speculation about what exactly you were pissed about. But now it's turned around, and everyone's saying how you two are back together. Most folks think that's great, but there's a lot of *damn, the hottie is off the market* chatter, too. So those folks think you're a dream-crushing slut-puppy."

"Fame is a fickle bitch," I say, making her laugh since we both know that the spotlight is the last place I want to be. "Still, it could be worse," I continue. "Considering who Devlin is, they could be getting in our face every time we're in public. So far, they've been pretty invisible. Hell, I didn't even know anyone was watching us at the track until that picture turned up."

Early on, there'd been a few snaps here and there of Devlin and me together, but most of the posts said nothing more enticing than that I was a reporter who used to be a Laguna Cortez local, and I was writing an article about the DSF. It wasn't until Devlin took me on an overnight trip to a desert racetrack that the media started paying attention. We'd made the mistake of sharing a deep, bone-melting kiss on the steps leading up to our trailer. After that, goodbye privacy, hello public eye.

Now I'm the girl who pulled the very eligible and enigmatic Devlin Saint off the market.

And that must have pissed some people off.

I frown, thinking of the mysterious text as I consider that.

"What?" Brandy asks, obviously noticing my change in mood.

"Take a look at this," I say, then pull up the text and pass her my phone.

"You're in over your head. Find the truth. Don't trust anyone." She reads it aloud, then meets my eyes. "Well, that's super creepy. Who sent it?"

"Your guess is as good as mine." I smoosh some muffin crumbs under my finger, as if I were squishing the bastard who's taunting me. "I'm assuming someone who doesn't realize I know who Devlin's father is. But maybe it's about something else entirely."

Her brow furrows. "Like what?"

I hesitate, but Devlin has never asked me to hold back around Brandy. He understands that I need someone to talk to. And right now, I need someone more than ever.

I draw in a deep breath, then lay it out for my bestie. "Devlin told me he has more secrets. But he also said he's not going to tell me. Not ever."

She tilts her head and stares me down. "Seriously? And you were okay with that?"

"Yes. No. I don't know." I drag my fingers through my hair. "It was like he was warning me off, but I can't walk away again, Brandy. I can't."

"I know." Her voice is gentle. "I get that. But still, if he has secrets that are going to put you in the crosshairs for creepy messages, then it's only fair he tells you the damn secret."

I almost smile. Brandy's not big on cursing, so the extra punctuation only underscores how indignant she is on my behalf.

"Not arguing," I assure her. "And I don't believe he'll keep his secrets forever. That's just not *us,* you know?"

"This is all new, Ellie. He's not Alex, remember? You're working from a completely different *us* now."

I don't answer, because she's right, and my chest tightens in response to the truism.

Brandy frowns, then passes me another muffin, like it's a consolation prize. "You're probably right. After all, the man is head over heels. He wants to protect you now, but he'll tell you eventually."

"Maybe. Probably. I don't know." I shake off the melancholy. "It doesn't matter, anyway. The point is this might not be about his dad. This might be about those secrets."

"I get that. But what good does it do if you don't know what the secrets are?"

"It doesn't matter. The secrets themselves aren't relevant."

"Then what is?"

"Who else knows them."

For a moment, she looks confused. Then her face clears. She circles the bar and comes to sit beside me, swiveling her stool so she can face me. "You're saying someone sent that text to scare you off. Someone who knows the rest of Devlin's secrets and doesn't want you to learn them?"

"Pretty much."

"Okay, maybe. But how will you ever figure out who?"

I meet her eyes. "I have an idea already."

Her brow furrows. "Who?"

"Ronan Thorne." Considering how much Devlin relies on him, I feel a little disloyal saying the name, but I can't shake the sense that something is up with him. And one thing I always do is trust my instincts.

Brandy frowns. "But they're total buds."

"All the more reason. They had each other's back in the service, so he's going to have Devlin's back now, right?"

"I guess, but this—"

"He doesn't trust me."

She sits up straighter. "What are you talking about?"

"Or, I don't know, maybe he simply doesn't like that I'm a reporter." I drag my fingers through my tangled waves. "All I know is that he tried to warn me off Devlin early on. Said I was a distraction."

"Ohhh." She draws out the word as she nods her head. "Distracting him from all that other secret stuff he does."

"That's what I'm thinking. And he was in Vegas when Devlin and I were, too. They were talking in the lobby bar super late. And when I went down to join them, Ronan didn't seem happy to see me."

"Maybe you interrupted an important meeting. Or maybe he's protective of his friend. Like the way you and I watch out for each other."

"Maybe," I concede. "But it feels like more than that."

"Okay, so you work backwards. What could the secret be? Something that affects them both, right? Not their military service, because that's over. But there's foundation stuff, right?"

"Exactly. But what? The foundation supports a lot of causes. I know about how it helps trafficking victims, but that's only the tip of the iceberg."

"But Ronan was in Vegas, and that's where that rehab center is for the victims. Maybe something there?"

"Possibly," I say. "But it's a quick trip. He could have come to Vegas simply because he needed to talk to Devlin."

"Are you going to try to figure it out?"

I swallow, unsure. Devlin's made it clear that he intends to hold his secrets close, so poking around trying to uncover them would surely be a breach of the relationship rules. At the same time, I want to know what that text means, and unless I know what the secret is, how can I figure it out?

"*Shit*," I say, making Brandy frown. "Of course, the text is about some other secret. If it wasn't, why would Devlin be so insistent that he be the one who investigates?"

Brandy laughs. "Now you're overthinking," she assures me. "You may be right. Or it could just be that Devlin's a protective guy who's used to being in control. It must be making him crazy knowing that some jerk is sending you cryptic messages. Of course, he wants to find out who's behind it. The man's your white knight, after all."

"Tarnished knight," I say with a smile, remembering what Devlin had called himself.

"Huh?"

"Never mind. The point is, you're right." I squeeze her hand. "Thanks. I'm going to take it one step at a time and wait to see if Devlin learns anything about the sender's identity."

"Good for you."

"What about you?" I ask as she slides off the stool and goes back around the island and into the kitchen. "On the boyfriend front, I mean?"

"Me?" Her voice squeaks a little, which tells me everything. Or, at least, it tells me a lot.

"Spill it," I say, rising up off my stool to grab yet another muffin despite her feeble attempt to slap me away. "Is there something new on the Christopher front? Oh my God, did he stay over last night?"

She hadn't said a word to make me think that, of course, but I can tell that something has shifted between them from the way her cheeks flush pink. Now, she says, "*No.* Well, okay, yes. But we didn't—you know." Her cheeks bloom all the way to red. "But I want to," she adds, her voice such a low whisper I can barely make out the words.

My heart squeezes with worry. "Are you sure?"

The blush deepens. "He's sweet, and he hasn't pushed me. I mean, he wants to—we've talked about it. But he gets that I want to take it slow." She shrugs as if it's no big deal, but of course it's a huge deal. "He's a really good guy, you know?"

"From everything you've told me and everything I've seen, the man's a freaking prince. But does he know why you're taking it slow?"

She shakes her head. "God, no." She hugs herself. "I mean, he obviously knows I have issues, and I've kind of suggested that I was in a bad relationship."

"Brandy..."

"I know—"

"Do you? Because if you're really serious about him, you need to tell him everything."

"I *know.* It's only that I have a hard enough time talking about it with you. But I really do get it. I want to tell him. I think he's the first guy that's ever mattered to me enough to tell. But I'm scared it'll mess everything up."

"Yeah," I say, my heart aching for her. "But if you want something real between you two, you're going to have to tell him at some point, right? Better to talk now. Wait too long, and it'll just get harder."

"I suppose. And I really do plan—*oh, shit*. The second batch." She whirls away from me, and I look down to hide my expression, all my attention on my muffin.

I don't blame Brandy for being scared to talk about what happened to her. After all, like me, she's almost twenty-nine. Unlike me, she's only slept with one guy, not counting the bastard who stole her virginity, and it didn't go well. Conversations about sex with men aren't high on Brandy's skill set. For that matter, neither is picking guys who will be sensitive to what she needs.

She's gone out with a few she genuinely liked, but so far none who were inclined to stick around when they realized sex might be a long time coming.

The world really isn't a fair place. I've known that my whole life. Brandy's known it since our senior year. And both of us have been at the receiving end of that basic reality more than our fair share. Which, I guess, proves the point.

I pull off a piece of muffin and pop it in my mouth, savoring the sweet, nutty flavor. Brandy's my best friend, and one of the nicest people I know, so I hate that she's had such shitty luck with men. Maybe it's the law of averages, but I can't believe there aren't more men out there who are not only willing to wait, but are also sweet in bed.

Maybe Christopher really is the guy. If she's getting that serious about him, I hope so; I hate the thought of her getting hurt again. And the truth is, they really don't know each other that well yet. He's a novelist who came to town to do research for his next thriller. I met him in the Research Room at the Devlin Saint Foundation. About the same time, he met Brandy by accident, which means they've been seeing each other for about five minutes in Relationship Time. I'm not even sure where he actually lives, only that he's staying at an Airbnb while he's in Laguna Cortez.

He's smart and sweet and seems to truly care about Brandy. I see that clearly enough, and I know that she does, too, and yet she's still holding back. Understandable, I suppose, considering she was practically unconscious her first time after an asshole at a party slipped her a date rape drug. As if that wasn't bad enough, she ended up pregnant, which sent her parents over the deep end and the baby into an adopted home.

Traumatic as hell, and so I get why she doesn't want to talk about it. But if she holds onto that secret for too long, I'm certain it'll drive Christopher away. After all, some secrets between couples are okay. But when the secret is big—when it's the kind that can truly impact a relationship—well, then silence isn't a neutral issue. It becomes a real obstacle in the relationship.

I frown, realizing I'm no longer thinking about Brandy. My thoughts have instead turned to Devlin. He flat out told me that he has secrets. *There will always be secrets between us,* he'd said. *You should have stayed away.*

He told me he was a dangerous bet, but he never expected me to run. Not really. That much I'm sure of. Because Devlin knows me. He's seen my demons, and he knows that danger doesn't scare me.

No—that's not true. It *does* scare me. But that's the thrill. That's the rush, all the more potent because I never expect it. Danger stole my whole family from me, and yet I'm still here.

I'm not the girl who flirts with danger. I'm the woman who tells danger to go fuck itself.

I shiver, not liking this dark direction of my thoughts. What I feel for Devlin is real—*it is*. It's not some fucked up manifestation of survivor's guilt. I know that. I believe it. I love him, and I'm falling deeper every day.

But how deep can the roots of our relationship really go when I know that he's not only been keeping secrets, but that he never, ever intends to reveal them to me?

CHAPTER FIVE

"So we're meeting tonight, right?" I ask a few hours later as Brandy frowns at her reflection in the hall mirror. "You, me, and Lamar for drinks at five?"

"That's the plan," she says. "As long as it's only us playing catch-up and not the two of you organizing my love life."

"Cross my heart," I say, miming the action as I speak the words. "You sure you don't want to talk more?" She'd deftly shifted the conversation after rescuing the second batch of muffins, and since my thoughts had turned far too deep and disturbing, I hadn't pressed the issue. Now, though, I'm having friend guilt.

"With you, maybe, later. But as much as I love Lamar, I don't want him being my relationship guru. Just my drinking buddy."

I laugh, because I can't argue with that. "Fair enough. I'll shield you from questions about Christopher, and you do the same for me with questions about Devlin."

She makes a face. "I'll wear my favorite fire-retardant outfit."

"Not funny."

"Oh, I think it was," she teases. "At least a little."

She smirks, and I frown. We both know that Devlin isn't on Lamar's Favorite People list. Or, more accurately, he's not on

Lamar's Favorite People for Ellie list. Lamar and I have been friends since we were cadets at the Irvine Police Academy. I'd been the only female and he'd been the only black cadet, and we'd bonded immediately. And though there's never been anything romantic between us, we're both protective of each other, and Devlin has picked up on that.

A long time ago, Lamar had a semi-crush on me. More of the *let's be friends with benefits* variety than the *let's start a relationship* kind. Sometimes, he'll still tease me about hooking up, but not in a serious way. I'm sure he'd still go for a friends with benefits fling, but that's because he has no problems mixing casual sex with friendship. I do, though, and I put the brakes on that possibility years ago. Because while he may be able to sleep with someone and stay friends, I fuck and bolt.

Or I used to. Devlin is the only exception to my rule. Probably because it was my past with Alex that set that particular rule in motion.

Now Lamar's like Brandy. A close confidant. Unlike Brandy, he doesn't know that Devlin used to be Alex Leto. Which means I have to watch myself around him, which I hate. But at the same time there's no way I'll break Devlin's confidence. I might harass the shit out of him to give in and let me tell Lamar, but I absolutely won't undermine him.

In fact, Lamar may never learn the truth. Because unlike Brandy, Devlin doesn't trust him. That, however, is Devlin's problem. I can count on two fingers the close friends I have, and while I'll keep Devlin's secret, there is no way I'm ditching a friend just because my boyfriend is jealous.

"Cask & Barrel at five, right?" Brandy asks.

I nod. "Perfect."

"Cool. Would you put Jake in his crate when you leave? I need to get out of here or I'll be late."

I nod in assent, and she reaches down to stroke Jake, who's sitting still, remarkably well-behaved in the hallway.

She twists around, obviously searching for her keys. "What

are your plans?" she asks, finding them not on the hall table, but deep in her tote.

"I'm going to drop by the station and see if Lamar can help me with some research about Peter. But before that, I'm going to call Roger and see if I still have a job."

She'd taken a step toward the door, but now she freezes. "You're moving back to New York?"

"No, no." I made the decision to stay in Laguna Cortez with Devlin, and I'm not changing my mind. But I love my job, too. And if I can finagle a way to keep it, well, then I'm more than willing to beg.

"Good luck," Brandy says when I tell her as much. She gives me a hug, rubs Jake's head, then hurries outside, slamming the door behind her.

With Jake at my heels, I head back to my room and settle on my bed. Jake flops in the sunny spot by my window as I slip on my headphones and dial the number for *The Spall Monthly* in Manhattan. "Hey, Brenda," I say, when the receptionist answers, "it's Ellie. Is Roger around?" Roger Covington is my editor, and we haven't talked since he killed my profile of the DSF after learning that Devlin and I are involved. Add in the fact that I told him I'm staying in California, and I'm not sure where our friend-ship stands, much less my job.

"He's in the staff meeting," Brenda says, and I do a mental head-thwap, having forgotten the time difference. "But they're almost done. Do you want to hold? Or I can have him call you back."

I glance at my watch. If Roger's on form—and he always is—they'll wrap promptly in seven minutes. "I can hold," I say, then settle in to listen to the classical hold music as I rummage in the floor of my closet for the box of my mother's journals.

I'm willing to give Devlin twenty-four hours to see if he can learn something about the text. But I'm not willing to step back on learning more about Uncle Peter.

My first hint about Devlin's true identity as the son of the notorious crime lord known as The Wolf came not long after I'd skimmed one of these very journals. I'd been a tiny thing at the time of the entry, and Mom was concerned about the kind of business her brother, Peter was in.

With me and Mom in the car, he'd gone to see the mother of a boy named Alejandro, who Peter had said was his boss's son.

Soon after I read the entry, I made the connection. Peter worked for Daniel Lopez, aka The Wolf. Alex Leto was Alejandro Lopez, The Wolf's son. And Alex had become Devlin.

It was a huge revelation at the time. Now, that I've learned the deeper truth, it's only part of who Devlin is—and was.

For years, I hadn't had the heart to read my mom's words, too afraid that I'd be so consumed by grief that I'd get dragged down into the dark. I only started flipping through the pages when I began researching the article about Uncle Peter.

I came back to Laguna Cortez because new evidence had turned up after his death, and I soon learned that Peter had been in tight with The Wolf. And when he'd started skimming off money, The Wolf had ordered him killed.

I'd wanted to know how a seemingly upstanding man from a solid, middle-class family could have gotten sucked so deeply into an organization like The Wolf's. But Peter died over ten years ago, and with no one else alive in my family and no other solid leads, I'd turned to my mom's journals.

My first foray into my mother's words had been limited, though. I'm not sure if it felt wrong to read her private thoughts or if I was afraid of crossing that black curtain of grief. Now, though, I want to know more. I want to learn what had troubled my mom about Peter, but I also want to learn more about the woman who loved me and was taken from me.

My mother didn't label the spine of her journals, but one is only three-quarters filled out, and so I assume it's the last of the books. With my heart pounding, I flip backwards to the final entry.

. . .

Charlie did it again. He promised he'd be home in time for dinner with me and Ellie. He hasn't read her a bedtime story in a week. I know he loves both of us, but why can't he understand that he needs to show it, too?

Forgive me, diary, I'm just griping. He's a good man. A good provider. And I know he's busy with so much responsibility, but even so...

I tried to call Peter to talk to him about Charlie. I know I should keep my marital issues to myself. But all my life, Peter has been my confidant. I know he's still upset with me, but I had to talk with him. He didn't answer the phone, though. I left a message, because maybe he's screening calls. I told him to call me in an hour, because I need some air. I'm going to go take a drive. Hopefully Lisa can babysit for an hour or so. Ellie's asleep, so doing her homework here is pretty much the same as doing it across the street at her house.

Maybe I'll pick up a few more things for Ellie's party tomorrow. Then it doesn't seem like I'm escaping because I'm feeling alone and frustrated by the men in my life.

How is it that my baby is almost four!!??!!

Just called Lisa, and she's on her way over. How lucky am I to have such a responsible high school kid right across the street?

My next entry will be much less whiny. Maybe I'll even buy a bottle of wine and seduce my husband. Give him a reason to get home early. I think I like that plan...

I close the book, shaking. *Ellie's party tomorrow*. She'd written this the night she was killed. The night that her car had gone over one of the cliffs, taking a chunk of the metal guardrail with it and killing my mother instantly.

Had that been part of the reason that Peter left Los Angeles and moved to Laguna Cortez? Had he felt guilty for missing my mom's call—or, worse, for ignoring it?

And why was he upset with her? I know they'd been close their entire lives. My dad and Uncle Peter told me as much. So what could she possibly have done that made him want to ignore her?

I pull my knees up to my chest and hug my legs. From the earlier diary reference, I know that Peter wasn't living in California when I was two. But he must have had work in Los Angeles because Mom and I had gone up to visit him, and I know he moved there later.

She'd been worried about him in that first entry I'd read, writing that Peter was involved in the kind of business that the wife of the Chief of Police probably shouldn't know about.

Did she know something concrete? Or did she just have a vague feeling? And what had changed between then and my fourth birthday? Why had Peter moved to LA?

I don't know any of those answers, but I damn well intend to find out.

Especially since poking around in Peter's past just might shake a few things loose—including the identity of whoever sent me the text.

———

After another five minutes on hold, I'm considering hanging up, getting a coffee, and trying this call later. I'm just about to do that, when the hold music stops abruptly, and Roger comes on the line.

"I was expecting you to call me back," he says. "Should I assume that the days of silence mean I'm down one reporter? Not to mention someone to split cheese fries with from Freddie's?"

I grin, my stomach growling at the memory of the incredible fries from the deli two blocks from the office. I'm also smiling because if he's teasing me about fries that means I haven't turned a friend into an enemy.

"I guess we were at cross-purposes. I was waiting for *you* to call *me*."

In addition to the DSF profile, I'd left Manhattan so that I could investigate Peter's death and, possibly, turn my research into a story for *The Spall*. But when the news of my relationship with Devlin leaked to the press, Roger pulled me off not only the profile, but also the story about Peter.

I clear my throat. "After I dropped the bomb about staying in Laguna Cortez, I figured you'd have to do some thinking. And if you were thinking that the magazine still wanted me, then you'd have to do some negotiating with Franklin." Franklin Coates is the magazine's publisher, which means he's the guy who ultimately holds my paycheck in his hands.

"I do want you," Roger says, "and Franklin's willing to let you work remotely. I won't say that we over-reacted—getting involved with Saint while writing a profile about him and the foundation was a lot of things, bad judgment included."

"I know. I—"

"But everyone makes mistakes, and Franklin and I both know you're an excellent reporter and an asset to *The Spall*."

A steel band around my heart loosens, and I suddenly realize how much I hadn't wanted to not get fired.

"Thank you. Roger, that means so much to me. I—"

"We're going to run the profile," he says, and my entire body goes limp with relief.

"That's great news. The foundation does such good work, that—"

"No byline," he says, and I cringe. "I'm sorry, kid, but under the circumstances, it's best for the profile on the Devlin Saint Foundation to be published without a reporter's name."

I almost argue, but I know it's futile. And, hell, they're probably right. I genuinely believe in the work Devlin's foundation does, and I'd hate for the fact that we're together to confuse the message.

"Fine," I say. And then, because I'm afraid that came out too curt, I add, "Thank you."

"We want to keep you, kid. You're an asset. Can't give some West Coast rag the chance to snatch you up."

"What about my piece on corruption inside the New York transit—"

"Not your story anymore."

I clear my throat but say nothing. I can hardly expect the magazine to pay for me to take the red-eye back and forth for research.

"Corbin will be taking over all your New York-based articles."

"Great," I say, that one little word holding a bucketful of vitriol.

"Tell me how you really feel," Roger says, and I grimace. Corbin Dailey and I have a firmly established mutual destruction policy. I hate him because he's an arrogant, backstabbing prick with no flair for the written word. He hates me because I know it.

"You can't possibly have expected me to be happy about that."

"No, and it was Franklin's call. If you want to consider it a punishment, I won't correct you."

"Fine. Fine. Do you have any actual good news for me?"

"Other than continuing to draw a paycheck?"

I rub my temple. "Funny. I was hoping we could talk about the Peter story. I'm still planning on writing it, and I'm going to publish it somewhere. So if—"

"Whoa, whoa, whoa. I talked with Franklin about that, too."

"Oh." I sit up straighter. "And?"

"We still want to run it. *With* a byline. We think having your name on it would be an asset. A personal essay with solid reporting to underscore the emotional parts. What do you say?"

What I want is to squeal with joy because it's perfect, and I tell him so.

"Then keep me posted. I'd like it to run next month, but I have a feeling you're going to need more time to dig."

"You're right about that. In fact, I'm about to head to the police station right now. I'm hoping Lamar can spare some time to help me with a couple of interviews." I want to talk to Peter's business contacts in Laguna Cortez. And I want to start tracing back to his contacts in LA.

"Detective Gage? The one who came to the office about a year ago?"

That summer, Lamar had flown to New York for a long theater weekend, and I'd taken him to the office to show off my editor and my desk with the same kind of glee that he shows his badge to elementary school kids.

"Give him my best," Roger says.

"Will do," I say, before ending the call with a fresh burst of enthusiasm. After all, not only am I no longer in employment limbo, but I've got a legitimate, work-related reason to do all the research that Devlin wants me to avoid.

CHAPTER SIX

L amar's interrogating someone when I arrive. I'd called ahead to make sure he wasn't in the field, and since I'm not only expected but also a bit of LCPD royalty, I'm escorted in and permitted to sit in observation watching Lamar do his thing.

It's a nice perk, but all in all I'd rather my father—the former Chief of Police—not have been killed in the first place. His death had left me with Chief Randall and his wife Amy as my guardians during that nether period between Daddy's murder and me bailing on my last year of high school.

I don't think about that now, though. Instead, I entertain myself by watching Lamar, whose ability to shift seamlessly between good cop and bad cop makes him a formidable interrogator.

Today, he's doing his rendition of a burnt-out bad cop, and the way he verbally lashes out at the suspect combined with his don't-give-a-fuck posture is a dead-on perfect performance.

The subject in the chair seems to think so, too, because the more Lamar goes on, the twitchier he becomes. By the time an hour's passed, the guy is ready to share all he knows about how his landlord set fire to the laundry room, apparently betting that an insurance payout was more likely than an arson conviction.

"Not bad," I tell Lamar, after he enters the observation room to a round of applause from me and a handful of uniformed officers who've also been enjoying the show.

"By the way, where's Endo?" I ask, after I've followed him back to his very cramped broom closet of an office.

I've only met his partner, Benton Endo, once. I'd flown from New York to San Diego to do research on a story, and the two had driven down to meet me for dinner.

"Thought I told you. I'm flying solo until he gets back. Paternity leave. Three months at home changing diapers." He flashes a grin. "Poor bastard."

"Don't even. I bet you swing by at least twice a week so that the baby knows Uncle Lamar."

"Damn," he says. "It's like you know me."

"In all your annoying glory. Tell him and his wife congrats from me. And as for flying solo, it didn't look like you needed him today at all. But I think I saw a bit of *Our Suburbia* when you were working that suspect."

He winces. "Now you're just being cruel."

"Hardly," I counter, my voice laced with a tease.

Our Suburbia was the most popular of the shows from Lamar's days as a child actor. Not only had it been a big hit twenty years ago, but so had Lamar, who'd played the second youngest brother. I never watched the show as a kid, but after meeting Lamar, I'd made it a point to binge every episode.

"That show was pure art," I add.

"Love you, too, Sherlock," he says dryly.

"You're the best, Watson," I counter, both of us using the names we adopted for each other years ago. "Honestly," I add, "I think we need to make a night of it. A DVD set of Lamar's Greatest Hits, pizza, liters and liters of wine. You, me, Brandy, Devlin. It'll be—"

I cut myself off when I see his face go hard. That's when I remember I haven't told him everything. I've been living on Ellie Time, and to me it feels as if Devlin and I have been back on an even keel for months. But the truth is that I was coming to terms with never seeing him again just a few days ago, and it's only been one night since I've wrapped my head around the inescapable truth that I not only believe in him, but I'm committed to working on *us*.

Lamar, however, has been privy to none of that.

Which is why I sit, then nod for him to do the same. "It's all good," I say. "We're back together."

"What part of that is good?"

"Lamar—don't."

He sucks in air through his nose, then runs his hand over his close-shaved hair. When we first met, he'd told me that in the three years between his TV career and becoming a cop, he'd worn dreads. Then a mugger in San Francisco had grabbed his hair, beat the shit out of him, and stolen his wallet.

That horrific encounter had inspired him to not only cut off the dreads, but pursue the law enforcement career that he'd been thinking about ever since he'd played a teen gang member in a movie. He once told me it was total shit as a film, but life-changing in its inspiration.

I'd thought the story was great—and resolved to always wear my hair up when I was in uniform. Just in case the bad guys got any ideas.

Now, he studies me, his eyes narrowing. "You're sure?" he presses. "This is what you want? Devlin is *who* you want?"

"Yes," I say, and that single word is the product of great restraint. I want to tell him everything, but of course I can't.

Lamar sees the projection of a man that Devlin has meticulously built over the last five or so years. A reclusive man with billions to his name who started a charitable foundation. A hard, private man known to sleep around, but eschew any long-term commitments. A man who supports his community, sure. But not the kind of guy you want your best friend hooking up with. I get that.

"I just worry," he says.

"You don't have to," I counter. "And we don't need to talk about it, either. I'm not here for relationship counseling." I shift in my chair. "Are you still free to come with me on these interviews?" When we'd talked earlier, his day had been wide open.

He winces. "Sorry, Sherlock. I can do one in town, but if you still want to drive to LA, I'll have to pass. Turns out I've got a witness coming in a couple of hours."

I'm disappointed, but I nod. I'd hoped to poke around in Peter's life before my mom's death, trying to get a sense of what he had his hands in even before he moved down to Laguna Cortez to help my dad raise me.

But there's plenty to learn about Peter during his Laguna Cortez years. And, besides, I have another errand I want to squeeze in today. So I nod and assure Lamar that's fine.

"Tomorrow should work," he tells me. "I've got the day off, and I'm willing to give up my leisure time for you. Assuming the magazine's paying for lunch."

"I think it's the least *The Spall* can do for both of us," I assure him.

I pause as we head out for today's interview, a new thought hitting me. Lamar looks back over his shoulder, his brow raised in question.

"Problem?"

I shake my head. "Nothing. Something just occurred to me. But—never mind."

"Seriously? You're going to leave it at that? You know that only makes me more curious."

I laugh. "It's nothing. Probably nothing." I draw a breath, buying time. I should make something up. I shouldn't ask what I'm thinking about asking.

But, of course, I do. "Okay, here it is. How well do you know Ronan Thorne? You told me you met him at one of the DSF functions, but have you guys hung out? Or do you just bump into each other now and then?"

His brow furrows, but he takes the question in stride. "Honestly, I barely know him. He's friends with Saint, though." He cocks his head as he looks at me. "Not sure what kind of a man that makes him."

"Give it a rest. And while you're resting, could you look into him for me?"

He pauses as we reach the plaza outside the LCPD. "Why? What's going on?"

No way am I telling Lamar about the text and the threat. It would worry him too much, and I don't want him poking around, learning things about Devlin that neither Devlin nor I are ready to share. So instead I tell him the truth—just not the whole truth. "He basically told me that I shouldn't be with Devlin," I say. "And he was in Vegas when I went on that trip with Devlin, too. Didn't seem too keen to see me there."

"Apparently Ronan and I have more in common than I thought."

"Lamar..." I'm sure he can hear the frustration in my voice. He and Brandy are my best friends. I want him to get along with the man I love.

"Fine, fine. What is it you're looking for?"

"He probably just rubs me the wrong way," I admit. "But I can't get over the feeling that he's hiding something. I want to know what it is."

When Ronan had first suggested I back off, I thought he was trying to protect Devlin's heart. But then a horrific criminal named Lorenzo Bell was assassinated in Vegas when Devlin and I were in town, shot at point blank range by an unknown assailant.

Ronan wasn't supposed to be there, and yet Bell had been killed the same night Ronan coincidentally arrived in town. Now, I can't shake the suspicion that Ronan wanted to sabotage my relationship with Devlin so that a nosy reporter wouldn't be poking around.

That, however, isn't something I'm willing to share with Lamar. Not without proof. So all I say is, "Will you?"

"What am I looking for?"

"I don't know. Anything that makes your brows rise. Like that," I add as his brows go up.

He smirks, then schools his face back to stern. "That's a pretty broad assignment. But I suppose I could do a basic background check and see if that leads anywhere. Honestly, I like the guy. I don't think I'll find anything."

I shrug. "If you don't, that's great. It's not as if I'm hoping to learn that Devlin's closest friend is dirty."

That's the truth. Ronan might rub me the wrong way, but Devlin has been betrayed enough. I don't want Ronan to be a member of that small but dangerous club. But I do want answers.

I'm not worried about Lamar stumbling across Devlin's connection to the Wolf. That's buried deep. And although Devlin has told me that Ronan knows the truth about Devlin's parentage, I'm sure there's no straight link between Ronan and The Wolf. After all, Ronan and Devlin met in the military, and that was after Devlin had broken with his dad.

Because I'm certain of that, I feel no guilt at all.

Or, at least, not much.

"So will you look?"

He lifts his hands as if in surrender. "I guess I have to."

I grin, understanding. Years ago, we promised to always have each other's backs. "Love ya, Watson."

"Back at you, Sherlock."

That settled, we head toward the SeaSide Inn. We decide to walk, even though it's quite a trek. But the day is beautiful, and if time gets tight, he can always take an Uber back to the station.

"What do you think you're going to learn?" He poses the question between the various restaurant choices I'm throwing out for tomorrow.

"You mean now? At the hotel?" Peter used to own the inn, and I explain that I'm hoping the current owner—who was the manager back when I was a kid—might know something about Peter's less-than-legitimate activities.

"If he does, it's probably because he was dirty, too. In which case, he won't say a word."

"Maybe," I concede. "But I have to ask the questions. You know how it works. You don't have a lead until you have a lead. Right now, I'm sifting through sand."

"Anything in your mom's diaries?"

"About the hotel? No, but there wouldn't be. Peter didn't move here until after Mom died. He came to help Dad take care of me."

"Right," Lamar said. "So not much use for this article, huh?"

"Maybe more than I expected." I say, realizing I never told him about the journal entry I'd found when Devlin and I were in Vegas. "My mom wrote that she was afraid Peter was mixed up with the kind of people a cop's wife really shouldn't know about."

"You think Peter was already working for The Wolf? Even back then?"

I nod. "And there's another entry I found from right before she died. Peter was upset with her. I need to skim back to see if I can find out why, but my guess—"

"—is that she was prodding her brother to get the fuck away from The Wolf."

I grimace and nod. "Or out of the business. I don't know if she ever knew specifically about The Wolf." I pause on the sidewalk, forcing Lamar to take a step backward.

"What?"

"It just doesn't make sense. My mom had a great family. Small, yeah. And her parents died young, but still great." All of my grandparents are gone, actually, taken by various illnesses instead of the unexpected tragedy of my mom and dad, but leaving me just as alone. "I mean, Peter was comfortable. And I know he had decent money because he and Mom both inherited when their dad died. So why shift out of that comfortable world into the dangerous life that killed him?"

"Can't answer that, but I see it all the time. Maybe it started as thrill seeking and he got in over his head. Maybe he felt helpless and wanted power. Maybe he was simply wired wrong."

I shake my head. "Not the last. He was good to me. Solid. He had to put up with a grieving teenager, and he rose to the task. He loved me, but he still did all that stuff. And I'm afraid—"

"What?"

"I'm afraid of the way I'm going to feel about him once I know the whole truth."

He takes my hand and squeezes it. "No matter what, he was still a man who loved you. Flawed, maybe. Screwed up, probably. But he was there when you needed him."

And that, I think, is what I have to hold on to.

CHAPTER SEVEN

The SeaSide Inn sits on the Pacific Coast Highway almost directly across from where the Devlin Saint Foundation now stands. Back when Uncle Peter used to own the Inn, the DSF's location was a weed-covered vacant lot that folks used for illegal beach parking.

Peter and I often walked here from his house, one of the few in Laguna Cortez that is on the ocean side of the highway. I even helped him fix up the Inn. Or, at least, I painted a few walls. Mostly, he was giving me busy work, as the actual contractors did the heavy lifting. But I remember feeling important, and I've always liked this cute little hotel.

The part that faces the highway isn't anything particularly special. It's welcoming, sure, but mostly functional with a circular driveway and a porte-cochere that allows guests to valet park without blocking traffic on the Coast Highway. Once inside though, the hotel has a charming Mediterranean vibe. It's designed as a square, with the four sides comprising the halls leading to the various rooms.

The middle of the square is a sunny atrium, with a small pool, outdoor seating, and a full-service bar that draws both hotel guests and locals.

The reception desk is the first thing we see when we walk through the main glass doors. When I was young, the manager was a man named Taggart. I never knew his first name, and though I could have looked it up before making this trip, I didn't bother. He's not at the front desk right now, though it wouldn't be unusual for him to still be working here. After Uncle Peter's death, I learned that he bought the hotel, and I don't see any reason why he would have sold it. After all, tourism in Laguna Cortez is still going strong.

It makes sense that he wouldn't be at the front desk though. He's the owner now not the manager, and the woman I see there is about my age. I glance at Lamar, who takes the hint and approaches first. After all, he's deliciously good-looking, and I'm all for smoothing the way with a witness. She looks up as we approach and smiles in greeting.

"Are you checking in?" She has deep set eyes, light brown skin, and a hint of an accent. Central Mexico, I think, though I'm not positive. She wears a white shirt under a blue blazer with a gold nametag that says, *Reggie*. Her hair brushes her shoulders. It's completely straight, dark brown accented with streaks of cobalt blue. She has a wide and friendly smile and I notice that she wears no rings. Single then. Maybe the Lamar move will turn out to be the right one.

"We were hoping to speak to Mr. Taggart," Lamar says. "He's the owner, I believe?"

"Is there a problem? I'm the manager."

"No problem. We were hoping to ask him a few questions about the man he bought the hotel from."

Her attention shifts from Lamar to me, and I can't help but think that her reaction is surprise. "Oh," she says. "Mateo Taggart is my father. But he's not here. He had a stroke about three years ago. He lives in a nursing home now."

"I'm sorry to hear it," Lamar says. "Do you think we could visit him there?"

"You could. But I'm afraid he's not himself. The odds that he would remember anything from that long ago—or for that matter be able to carry on a coherent conversation with you—are slim."

She blinks, and I get the impression she is trying to keep herself together. I wonder about her relationship with her dad. About whether or not it hurts worse to lose a parent in that way, slowly through illness or a failure of mental capacities, than it does to have them taken away from you completely at a young age.

I take a step closer, struck by the fact that she seems so familiar. I wonder if we've seen each other before. "Did you go to high school in Laguna Cortez?"

Her eyes widen in surprise.

"I'm sorry. It's just that you look familiar."

"Oh. No, I didn't grow up here. My parents divorced when I was young. I lived with my mother. I moved here about six years ago to help my dad with the place." She makes a face. "And because I couldn't decide what I wanted to be when I grew up. Dad always said the hotel would be my inheritance, so I should learn to manage it." She sighs. "Guess I got my inheritance early."

"I'm sorry about your dad," I tell her. "But I bet it comforts him to know the hotel's in your hands."

"Thanks. That's sweet." She taps the edge of a stack of promotional postcards, straightening them. "So, what is it you think my dad might be able to help you with?"

"Peter White," I say. "He was my uncle, and he was killed when I was seventeen. I'm just trying to find out more about him. You know, fill in the gaps in my personal history, and understand why he might've been killed. The murder was an odd one."

"I know the name. He's the man my father bought the hotel from, right?"

I nod.

"I'm sorry, but that's all I know. I don't even think we have any documents or notes that Mr. White left for my father about managing the business. I assume you've talked to the police."

"Of course, but this isn't really about solving his murder. This is more about me understanding the man that he was."

"I get that. I've been packing up a lot of my father's things over the last few years, sorting through them, learning a bit about his life. Again, I'm sorry for your loss. I wish I could help."

"Well, thank you for your time," Lamar says. He glances at me, and I nod. As far as I can tell, there's nothing else to learn here. We say our goodbyes, then head out.

Once we're on the street, I pull Lamar to a stop. "She didn't look familiar to you?"

Lamar shakes his head. "No. Trust me. I would remember her."

I roll my eyes.

"Speaking of good-looking women..." He trails off with a nod to the DSF across the street. "Mind if we pop in?"

At first, I'm confused by the question. Then I remember Tracy Wheeler, currently interning at the Devlin Saint Foundation. The same Tracy who turned Lamar's head when we went to the gala together not so long ago. "You are such a manwhore."

He manages to look innocent. "I don't know what you're talking about."

"Millie already texted me. You sent her a text asking if she wanted to join us for lunch tomorrow in LA." Millie is a friend from our days at the Irvine PD. She quit not long after we joined up in order to go to law school. Now she's an Assistant US Attorney based in LA.

"She can't, by the way," I continue. "She's prepping for trial. But she said she was excited you asked." I cross my arms over my chest. "She's a friend. Don't toy with her. Tracy either. I like them both."

He holds up his hands. "Whoa. I'm not looking to hurt anybody. But if I like someone and they like me..." His smile widens. "And, honestly, what isn't there to like?"

I try to keep a straight face, but end up laughing. "Manwhore," I repeat. "And don't think the fact that I'm laughing diminishes my message. Hurt either of them, and I'll have your balls in a sling."

"Noted," he assures me. "My balls and I will be on their best behavior."

I shake my head in exaggerated exasperation. The truth is, I *do* hope he finds someone, I'm just afraid that in his search, he's going to end up hurting one of my friends. It's not an unreasonable fear. I've never seen Lamar get serious about anyone. He's dated a number of women and men in the time that I've known him, always nice people, usually fun, usually smart. The kind of people that I could see him being happy with on a long-term basis. Yet for some reason, it never works out.

I don't know why, and it makes me worry. I love him dearly, but I also know that I don't completely understand him. One of these days, I'd like to. But until then, we continue to muddle along.

"Don't break Tracy's heart," I order as we reach the DSF's main entrance.

"I wouldn't dream of it."

I'd like to give him a sterner warning—after all, I feel a bit protective of Tracy since she works for my boyfriend—but he's already opened the door for me. I enter, pausing for a moment to take in the familiar interior, so stunning in its simplicity of stone and steel.

I cross to the reception desk where Paul, the same man who greeted me the first day I arrived, still sits. He looks up now with a smile of welcome. "Ms. Holmes. Shall I let Mr. Saint know that you're here?"

"It's Ellie, Paul. And sure, that would be great. But let him know that it's no big deal. We actually came to see Tracy, so if he's busy, he doesn't need to come down."

"I'll let him know. And I'll buzz Tracy."

I thank him, and Lamar and I wander toward the wall of windows that opens onto an outdoor seating area. These walls are meant to be pushed completely aside, disappearing like pocket doors into the structure to make an indoor-outdoor entertaining area. The foundation holds a lot of fundraisers, and with the view of the Pacific beyond the flagstone patio, you couldn't ask for a better location.

Lamar leaves me to run to the men's room, and I'm watching the ocean when Tracy comes up behind me.

"Hey!"

I turn, then find myself engulfed in Tracy's hug.

"It's great to see you," Tracy says, stepping back. She wears her hair in a close-cropped afro which accentuates her high cheekbones. "What's up?"

"What's up is that you have an admirer," I say. "I'm here with Lamar. He wanted to pop in."

"Oh." A smile tugs at her mouth. "Well, that's nice, isn't it?"

I consider warning her. Telling her that Lamar never seems to gets serious. But I keep quiet. After all, I'm the last person who should be giving dating advice. Besides, every time Lamar makes a comment about my relationship with Devlin, it just pisses me off. "Have you guys been seeing a lot of each other?" I ask instead, as Devlin's assistant, Anna, hurries toward us.

Tracy shakes her head. "We see each other around our building, but not that much. Our schedules are pretty different. But," she adds with a lilt in her voice, "we've been doing a lot of texting. He's sweet."

"Yeah," I say honestly. "He is."

"Are you talking about Lamar?" Anna asks. "I saw him upstairs. He was coming up as I was coming down."

I frown, wondering why he didn't pop into the first floor men's room. Not that it matters, and the thought leaves my head as Anna reaches out to take my hands. She's a stunning redhead, with vivid blue eyes and perfectly clear skin. It's a rare combination—the hair and the eyes—a fact I'd learned when I did a piece on recessive genes my first year at *The Spall*. Rare or not, the bottom line is that Anna turns heads, and I'd been jealous as shit the first time I saw her at Devlin's side.

Now that I know they're just friends, I've grown to like her. But I still look like a short, plain kid playing dress up next to her curvy, movie star looks.

"I'm *so* glad to see you. I was going to call you today and tell you how happy I am. Devlin told me you two worked things out. I'm thrilled for you both. I was so worried," she adds, stepping back and looking me up and down. "But here you are, glowing."

I laugh, embarrassed. I've never been great at being in the spotlight. "I'm not."

"You are," Tracy says, and I reluctantly concede the point.

As an intern, Tracy's new at the DSF, and not in Devlin's circle of friends. Anna, however, has known him since childhood, and is perfectly aware that he used to be Alex Leto, aka Alejandro Lopez. What I don't know is if she or Ronan know the truth about who killed Peter. Probably not—why would they? It's not as if Devlin would have wanted to advertise the truth back when he was still Alex. Or why he'd feel the need to spill his secrets later when he founded the DSF. Tamra knows—but that's because she was like a surrogate mom to him, and he told her the whole story after the fact.

"—way down."

"Sorry?" I look up, realizing that I'd zoned out and entirely missed something Anna was saying.

"I said he was in the middle of something when Paul buzzed. But he should be down any—oh, there he is. Perfect timing."

"For both of us," Tracy adds, leaning over to whisper in my ear.

I don't know what she means until I turn and see Devlin descending the stairs with Lamar right beside him. Devlin's in a gray suit with a pale blue shirt. His hair is swept back from his face, and the dark rim of the glasses he wears as additional camouflage only make him look even more the corporate warrior.

Warrior, indeed, I think. His posture is tense, his mouth set firm, his every move precise. He's moving with Lamar, but they're not talking, and the air between them seems to shimmer with meaning.

I don't know what happened between the two of them, but I can read the room easily enough.

And what I see tells me that Devlin is pissed as hell.

CHAPTER EIGHT

When Devlin and Lamar reach the main floor, Lamar extends his hand to shake. But Devlin is already on the move, and he simply brushes Lamar's shoulder in a silent indication that it's time for them to come join us. I can't tell if it's an intentional slight, or if he didn't see Lamar's hand in the moment. I hope it's the latter, but I fear it's the former.

When they reach us, Tracy moves forward to meet Lamar, so I don't have the chance to ask him what that was all about. Devlin comes straight toward me as Anna melts away, presumably to go back upstairs and take her place at the command center for Devlin's office.

I move back, further away from Lamar and Tracy, then whisper, "What the hell?"

His voice is tight as he says, "Your friend had a message to deliver."

"Oh?"

"If I hurt you, he's going to squeeze the life out of me."

I almost laugh. I don't doubt Lamar's talents as a police officer, but the thought that he would be able to bring a man like Devlin to his knees is amusing. What I do, though, is wince. "I'm sorry."

"Unless you sent him on that particular mission, you don't have anything to be sorry about. Detective Gage, however, has plenty to account for."

"Devlin, don't—"

"He's your friend, so I'm cutting him some slack." His voice is as sharp as a blade. "But the next time he comes into my place and proceeds to lecture me about—"

"What?" Since he cut his words off so sharply, I twist around, wondering if Lamar or Tracy has approached. But we're still alone and out of earshot.

Devlin shakes his head, his features softening as he says, "Fuck, I'm sorry. He's just looking out for you. I know it. It's fine."

"It doesn't sound fine."

He runs his fingers through his dark hair, unintentionally releasing most of it from the leather tie that holds it back. "It is. Truly. I'm sorry."

I study him, knowing that he's jealous of the friendship Lamar and I developed in the years that Devlin and I were apart. Years we can't ever get back. And that's why I decide that it's the better part of valor to say nothing more than, "Thanks."

"I don't know what you're thanking me for, but you're welcome." He studies me for a moment, then frowns as he grips my elbow. "Come with me."

I hesitate, but Lamar has caught up with Tracy, so I don't object when Devlin leads me outside and into a small alcove out of sight from the massive windows that provide foundation visitors with a view of the ocean.

"What are we—" But my words are cut off by a bruising kiss, hot and demanding. I melt against him, my body firing instantly as I crave more.

"Careful," I gasp when he lets me up for air. "Get me too riled up, and you're going to have a hard time slowing this party down."

"With you, I never want to slow down."

I hook my arms around his torso and press close enough that I can feel his erection. "I like the sound of that. The feel of it, too."

"Naughty girl."

"For you? I'll be as naughty as you want."

With an unexpected ferocity, his hand fists in my hair and tugs my head back. I gasp, not from pain but from the unexpected motion and from the wild intensity I see in his eyes.

"You're mine," he growls, and I melt a bit at the possessive tone. "Say it."

"I am. Of course, I am." I flash a smile, realizing he doesn't yet know my big news. "I'm even officially staying in Laguna Cortez."

His brow furrows as he releases his hold on me. "Officially?"

I nod. "I was going to stay anyway, obviously, but now I can stay with a paycheck. Roger told me that I can work from the West Coast. I'm even keeping most of my stories, except for the ones that are New York based. My arch nemesis is getting those." I wrinkle my nose.

A smile tugs at the corner of his mouth. "I didn't realize you had an arch nemesis."

I lift a brow. "Doesn't everyone?"

"Touché." His voice is light, but I see a shadow cross his face. I think of that horrible text and regret the joke. Then the moment passes, and he clears his throat before saying, "So tell me more."

"That's pretty much it. I'm still on payroll, only I'm working from here. They're going to publish the profile on the Devlin Saint Foundation—you're very welcome—but I don't get a byline."

He winces. "Oh, baby, I'm sorry."

"No. It's okay." I squeeze his hand. "Considering the trade-off is you, I have no objection. Besides, I thought about it, and I don't want the fact that we're together to suggest any sort of bias in the article. I want readers to see the DSF and understand it for what it is. Because it's a really special organization, and the work you do is important."

"It means a lot to hear you say that."

"I'm only saying what's true. But that's the beauty of it. It doesn't matter how much it means to you or me. What matters is what it means to all the people the foundation helps."

He swallows, then gently lifts my hand and kisses my palm. "Yes," he murmurs, his voice heavy with emotion. "Exactly that."

"And I do still get a byline," I tell him. "Just not for that article."

"A new assignment?"

I hesitate, because he won't be releasing balloons about this one. "They want me to do the article on Uncle Peter after all."

His expression goes totally flat. "Do they?"

I manage a laugh. "Don't get too enthusiastic. Besides, it's good. This way all the research I want to do for myself comes with a paycheck."

He says nothing, and so I barrel on.

"It's going to be a more personal piece. Almost an essay about my journey to figure out what happened to Peter. The arc of his life into and out of The Wolf's fold."

He rubs his temples. "Ellie—"

"I know you don't like the idea, but too bad. I'm going to find answers. I want to know about my uncle. About what he was involved in. I want to know how he went from being the man he was to the man he became."

"I get that, but, baby, it's only going to hurt. And the more you learn about how deep he was in my father's organization will be like salt in a wound." He takes my hand. "I don't want you hurt like that. Not when you don't need to be."

"I know. And I know Uncle Peter and his connection to The Wolf overlaps you."

"That's not what I'm trying to—"

"But you have to know that I would never put anything in that article that reveals who you are. Or even hints. Hell, I don't even need to mention you."

"We've talked about this. I still don't like it. There's no upside to poking around in the past, Ellie. It's never a good idea to dig up skeletons."

"That's my job, Devlin." My voice is hard. "I dig up skeletons. It comes with the territory."

"To find answers that affects the now. That's what a reporter does. But you'll never truly have answers with Peter because Peter's not around to give them to you."

I yank my hand out of his. "Stop telling me how to do my job. I get you don't like me poking around in areas that might overlap with your dad, but you're going to have to get over it. And I also know that I may not be able to learn what was in Peter's head, but there are still facts I can learn. Facts I need to learn."

He frowns. "Like what?"

"Little things. Like why he was mad at my mom right before she died. And whether or not that was part of why he moved here to help take care of me. Was it guilt? Did he believe she'd been driving too fast, thinking about some fight they had? Was that why her car went over?"

His expression is beyond sad. "Baby, no. You'll never find those answers. There's no one who can tell you."

"I still have to ask the questions," I say. "It's like a prayer, you know? It's my way to honor them."

He draws in a breath, then lets it out slowly. I assume he's gathering his thoughts for another objection, but instead he just says, "Okay."

"Okay?"

He nods and repeats himself, only this time with a smile. "Yes, okay Not that it matters," he adds. "I know you're not asking permission, just keeping me in the loop."

My heart twists a little. He's right, and I'm glad he understands that.

He gives my hand another squeeze. "Is that why you came by? Or am I forgetting a lunch date?"

"No, no. Lamar wanted to see Tracy. You're just a perk."

"For me as well." His hand is still holding mine, and I'm hyperaware of the way that his thumb grazes the skin on the back of my hand. "So, what are you going to do now?"

"He's abandoning me for his job. I was thinking I might try to meet up with a few more of the people that Uncle Peter dealt with." What I don't tell him is that I've got a personal errand to run, too. The kind that makes my stomach twitch with nerves, but I know I have to go through with it.

"More? Who've you seen already?" The words are seemingly casual, but I hear the edge to them.

"No one, really. It didn't pan out. We started at the SeaSide Inn," I explain. "It turns out the owner had a stroke. He's in a nursing home. His daughter manages the property now, but she doesn't really know anything. So that was a dead end."

"I knew about Mr. Taggart, of course."

For a moment, I'm confused. Then I remember. "That's right, guests at the foundation usually stay at the Inn, don't they?"

"There are a number of hotels around town that we suggest, but we have a particularly good relationship with the folks at SeaSide, yes. Mateo Taggart was a genuinely nice man. And Regina's a very competent manager."

"Was she at the gala?"

His brow furrows, then he shakes his head. "Not that I recall. She would have been invited, of course. But I think she was out of town. Why?"

"I don't know. She just looks familiar." I shrug. "No big deal. She probably reminds me of someone else."

"Well, if you do know her, I'm sure you'll remember." He says this in an offhand way, as if it doesn't really matter. Which, of course, it doesn't. "And what are you doing this evening?"

"I'm having drinks with Brandy and Lamar. Then I thought I'd go to my boyfriend's house and make him dinner." I wait a beat, then add, "Unless you'd rather I go to your place."

He flashes a cocky smile, then pulls me close, hooking his arms around my waist. "You're asking for it."

"With you? Anything, any time."

"I like the sound of that," he says. "But I have a meeting tonight."

"No big deal." I keep my voice perky even though I'm disappointed. "I'll just make another date with one of the many men I keep on a leash."

He makes a growling noise, and I laugh. "Call me when you get home?"

"You could be waiting for me," he suggests. "Preferably in my bed. Ideally naked."

"I could, but I'm staying at Brandy's. I think it's best that I continue to stay there, don't you? Whoever's watching us probably shouldn't believe that despite the warning, I'm still so comfortable with you that I've moved in."

He nods. It's clear, however, that the mention of my secret correspondent disturbs him.

I can't say I blame him. It disturbs me, too.

CHAPTER NINE

I'm not doing more interviews today, and I feel a little guilty about the tiny lie I told Devlin. But I console myself with the fact that I told the literal truth. I said I was *thinking* I might try to meet up with more of Peter's contacts. And here I am, totally thinking about that. Thinking about anything, actually, other than the fact that my feet are currently in stirrups as a nurse with a kind face takes a vaginal swab.

It's not until she stands up and smiles warmly at me that I realize my facial muscles are practically frozen into a horrible grimace.

"It wasn't that bad, was it?"

"That depends. Is it over?"

A smile flits over her face. "All done. You can get dressed now."

I pull my feet free and sit up. "When will I know?"

"I can't promise, but we've been getting results from the lab pretty quickly. You might hear back as early as tomorrow afternoon. But it could take up to seventy-two hours."

I wince, hating the thought of waiting. But it's not as if someone wrestled me to the ground and stabbed me with an infected needle. I did this to myself, and I can suck it up. "Right,"

I say. "Okay." I keep my fingers pressed to the cotton ball and tape on my arm from the blood the phlebotomist already drew. "So, if I don't hear by then, I should call?"

"Of course. But in the meantime, try not to worry. Worry won't change anything. And here," she adds, handing me a plastic bag with pamphlets and condoms. Like a party favor.

I thank her and assure her I'll do my best not to worry. But I *am* worried. Hell, I have reason to be. Over and over again, I've battled my demons by using myself as the weapon. It's not as if my modus operandi is a secret. It's not as if it was something I'd been doing unawares. Fucking a guy in a parking lot or alleyway wasn't something I checked out for. On the contrary, it was sharper than life, blindingly brilliant, and utterly meaningless. It was a battle. A statement. An escape.

Most of all, it was guilt. Because each and every one of those encounters could have been the last. The last fuck, the last kiss, my very last breath. I was risking everything from disease to psychos. *Survivor's guilt.* That's what they call it. I know, because a shrink once told me. I flirt with danger, because deep down I can't believe that I'm still living when my entire family is dead. Because what the hell makes me so damn special?

For years, I've chased danger and it was okay. Because at the end of the day, I didn't care about the outcome. Survival simply meant that life had more chances to kick the shit out of me. And death—well, that would repair the status quo, right? But now—

Now I have Devlin. And I want to have him fully. Completely. I don't want to have to wear a condom. I don't want that physical reminder of my past bad behavior between us.

Most of all, I want him to be safe, because I can't stand the thought of losing him. Either because I'm taken from him, or because he's taken from me. And I know that I will do anything—anything—to keep us safe and whole and together.

Steeling my shoulders, I get dressed and pay, then step out of the clinic into the bright light of day. It was the closest walk-in clinic I could find, and even though it was perfectly clean and sterile, I feel a little squidgy, which is foolish since testing is the smart thing, not the stupid thing. I wonder how many people like me don't get tested because it feels so awkward to go into one of these places, like it's a reflection of your own mistakes. But I'm glad I came, because Devlin is worth it. And I guess I am, too.

His name is on my mind as I lift my head and put on my sunglasses, and for a moment I think that I'm only imagining him standing there at the end of the walkway that runs from the street to the clinic's door. Then my chest tightens, and I realize that it really is him. A hot rush runs through my body, a mix of shame and horror and anger. I let the anger fuel me, as it's the emotion I'm the most comfortable with, and I rush forward, my hands clenched at my sides.

"Are you seriously tracking me?" My voice is heavy with indignation.

Last night, we set up our phones to share each other's locations. With the social media interest in our relationship, Devlin thought it made sense. And in light of the creepy text message, there's no denying that he's probably right, and for more nefarious reasons than tabloid interest.

But I never in a million years expected him to spend his day monitoring where I go.

He holds up his hands, looking chastened. "It wasn't like that, I promise. You said you were going on interviews, and I wanted to drop a file by."

He hands me a thick manila envelope I hadn't noticed that he was holding. "I had Anna pull together as much information on Peter's various business interests as we have in the foundation's records, then cap it off with whatever else she could find online. Some of it you probably already have, but I thought you might want to see if there were any names in there that you could get in touch with today. I meant to give it to you while you were at the DSF, but to be honest, after Lamar's little chat with me, it completely slipped my mind."

"Oh." Considering he's not exactly gung-ho about me poking

around in Peter's life, I'm a little surprised he's helping me. But maybe he figures the more he helps, the sooner I'll finish. "Well, thank you. But I hardly see the reason to track me all over town. I mean, tomorrow would have been—"

He lifts a hand, cutting me off. "I looked to see if you were in walking distance," he says. "Nothing more. And I wouldn't have come at all, except that the map only says this is a medical clinic. You were supposed to be interviewing associates of Peter's, and I didn't think they would be doctors. Although, I suppose he might have been trying to move pharmaceuticals. Bottom line, I thought maybe you'd been hurt. I thought this might have been an urgent care clinic. And when I called and you didn't answer ... well, I needed to come see for myself."

I check my phone. Sure enough, he called twice while I had it on silent.

I take a deep breath and close my eyes. I want to stay mad at him, because it will shield my own embarrassment, but everything he says makes sense, and I do appreciate it. So I pull up my big girl panties, smile, and shove my hands deep into the pockets of my jeans.

"Yeah, well, it's—" I clear my threat. "We didn't use a condom. And I—I just wanted—I mean, if I gave you— Oh, hell," I blurt. "I just had to know."

I'm relieved to see that he doesn't look shocked or terrified. On the contrary it's obvious that he understands fully what I'm saying. "I thought it might be something like that," he says, taking a step closer. "This morning, you were playing it a bit coy. You either had something else on your mind or you were doing your best to keep me hard with anticipation."

I laugh. "Well, that's a good plan. And we do know how much you get off on anticipation. But, no. I—oh God, Devlin, what if I fucked it up for us? I've been so stupid."

"No. You haven't." He reaches out and strokes my cheek, and I can't quite meet his eyes. He has to use his fingertip to tilt my head up. "Baby, do you have any idea how much this means to me? The fact that you're doing this now, because of me?"

"Well, of course I'm checking because of you. Who else?"

"Oh, El." There's laughter in his voice as he bends and kisses my forehead, then pulls me close, crushing me against his chest as he wraps me in his arms. I pull my hands free and hold him close, too. "Whatever the result, we'll be fine. And I'm glad you came. Because I want all of you. As soon as we know, I want every single bit of you, and I don't want a barrier between us."

My eyes prick with tears. "But what if—"

"No. No what ifs. We'll deal with things as they come. And until then..."

"What?"

"How about I take you to dinner tonight? A proper date."

I melt a little. "You said you had plans tonight."

"Rescheduled."

"Oh." I exhale, knowing I can't say yes. "I'd love to, but I made plans."

His bisected brow rises. "Another boyfriend?"

"A wild three-way," I counter. "Me and Brandy and Lamar. We decided to extend our drinks into dinner. I set it up after you said you were busy."

A muscle in his cheek tightens, but to his credit he doesn't say anything.

"We haven't spent a lot of time together," I point out. "The three of us, I mean. I've either been with you, or I was in a shit mood."

"Because of me," he adds, with enough humor that I know he's not annoyed.

I shrug. "Yeah, well, the bottom line is we're getting together tonight. You can amuse yourself?"

"I think I can manage. I need to check in on something at The Phoenix, anyway."

"You're going to Vegas?" Considering he has his own fleet of jets, it's not an off-the-wall possibility.

"No. I think the power of the internet will suffice. But I need you to do one thing for me."

"Sure. What?"

"Kiss me. Tide me over until I see you tomorrow."

"With pleasure," I say, as move closer, then rise up onto my toes, not even caring if someone snaps a photo. I hold onto his shoulders as my mouth closes over his, and as he pulls me close and kisses me hard, all I can think is that despite having one of the most miserable childhoods imaginable, I seem to have finally earned a little bit of happiness.

CHAPTER TEN

Since I still have plenty of time before I'm meeting Brandy and Lamar, I sit in Shelby, the dark blue 1965 Shelby Cobra that's only been pushed out of the number one spot in my life now that Devlin's in the picture, and flip through the file that Devlin gave me. My eye immediately notices a reference to Cotton Building Supply, a place that is already at the top of the list I've been compiling of businesses Peter worked with on a regular basis.

In the days after I learned that Devlin—*Alex*—had killed Peter, I'd forced myself to do some actual work. If I couldn't heal the ache in my heart, at least I could try to ignore it. Mostly I didn't succeed, but I did manage to sort through some boxes of old records.

With Peter's death, Chief Randall and his wife Amy stepped in as my guardians. They'd hired a lawyer to wrap up Peter's construction business, boxed up all the business files, and stuck them in storage in case I ever wanted them. I'd brought a few of those boxes home, and as my numb brain pored over paperwork, I'd realized two things. First, that my uncle was smart enough to keep very clean books. There was nothing in those papers that indicated any ties to The Wolf, to drug money, to anything unto-ward at all.

And second, that Uncle Peter had business connections in Laguna Cortez long before he moved here to look after me. That was about all I could manage, though. Digging deep just made me remember the man, his death, and Alex—the boy who had pulled the trigger.

I close my eyes, warding off the shadow of those days that seem so long ago, but were really only so many yesterdays. Devlin and I are past it now, but that doesn't mean it wasn't a wound. It was. It's just scarred over. And that's the interesting thing about scars—the healed area ends up a lot tougher than the original skin.

I guess that's why I can look now. Why I'm heading out to chase leads from both Devlin's and Peter's records, including Cotton Building Supply, a business Peter frequented when he was based in LA and then later in Laguna Cortez.

Cotton Building Supply is located inland, past the Five, and though it's technically within the Laguna Cortez city limits, this definitely isn't the part of town that goes on postcards. The opera-tion is the low-overhead kind, with a shack that fronts a lumber-yard that seems to get more intense the deeper you go, so that the area closest to the street is for the DIY crowd, and the stuff in the far back is for the commercial clients.

I only see one employee—recognizable by the brown vest and brass nametag—and since he's inside ringing up a customer, I wander the DIY area, thinking about what I could do with the house I own here once my tenant moves out. I've never lived in the house as an adult, but it was my childhood home until my father died. I inherited it, but Uncle Peter managed it, renting it out and using the income and my dad's life insurance policy to pay off the mortgage and then putting the income away for me. It's not a lot, but it made a nice dent in my Manhattan expenses, that's for sure.

Right now, I don't have any expectation that my long-time tenant is going to give his notice. But I do know that his current lease ran out a few months ago, and he hasn't yet renewed. He's told the management company that he wants to be "flexible," and so he's currently month-to-month.

All of which is fine by me, but at the same time, part of me wants him to just go. I'm enjoying living with Brandy, but I miss having my own place. And the truth is I can't stay with Brandy forever. She doesn't own her house, and she doesn't rent it. Instead, she acts as a caretaker for the mostly-absentee owner whom she calls Mr. Big.

Originally, I was only planning on being in Laguna Cortez temporarily, so bunking with Brandy was no big deal. Now that I'm staying, I need to make some decisions.

Even with Devlin in the mix—and he's very much in my mix —I'm thinking about looking for my own place. Maybe a guesthouse or a rental in Lamar's condo building. Someplace where I have my own space as Devlin and I grow in our relationship. Other than rooming with Brandy in college, I've been on my own all of my adult life, and it's weird to feel like I'm camped out in someone else's nest.

I push the thoughts out of my head—it's not something I plan to deal with today—and I wander back inside, hoping that the guy on duty is free now. Luck is with me, and he lifts a hand as I enter.

"I was just coming to look for you," he says. "Sorry for the wait. How can I help you? Let me guess," he continues without a pause. "You're thinking about adding a patio to your house."

"No, but it's not a bad idea. My name's Elsa Holmes. I'm a reporter with *The Spall Monthly*."

"Right. Right. I've heard of you."

"The magazine, you mean?" Even folks who only read magazines like *People* and *Entertainment Weekly* have usually heard of *The Spall*, since it's right there next to *The New Yorker* and *The Atlantic Monthly* at grocery store checkouts. But it's a rare person who actually knows the names of individual contributors.

"Huh? Oh, no. From Instagram. You're the gal's scre—*dating* Devlin Saint, right?"

I manage not to cringe. "Right on both counts," I say with so much enthusiasm that he actually blushes.

"Sorry, sorry." His pale face is covered with red blotches. "I don't know why they let me out in public. Honestly, I have no filter."

I laugh, deciding I like this guy. "It's okay, really."

"Right." He wipes his palms down the front of his jeans. "So, you're a reporter. And you're talking to me, why?"

"I'm doing an article on my uncle. It's a profile piece," I explain, "and I'm trying to track down people he knew before he was killed."

"Oh, wow. I can't think of anyone I know who was killed. What's his name?"

"Peter White, and I doubt you knew him. He died about a decade ago. But he did business here. I think he dealt with the previous owner, Mr. Cotton."

"Right." He nods slowly. "Oh, I'm Tom, by the way." He points helpfully to his nametag. "My brother owns the place now, but I'm guessing you knew that."

"I pulled up the public records online," I say. "He bought it about six years ago, right? I was hoping that maybe he kept in touch with Mr. Cotton—Harold. Maybe they were friends, or maybe your brother had his contact information. I haven't spent too much time looking, but nothing popped up in my initial search."

"That's probably because his name wasn't really Cotton. It was Longfeld. Harold Longfeld. Cotton was his mother's maiden name and I guess her family owned this land generations ago. He used the name because—well, honestly I don't know why he used it, but he even signed legal documents as Cotton."

"Thanks," I say. "You just saved me a few hours of research." I would have gotten there eventually, but this is why going out into the field is never a bad idea. "So why did he sell?"

"I didn't pay much attention at the time. I was in college then and only working here on weekends, but my brother talked about it when I was home visiting family, so I got some of the story even though his wife hates when he talks about work. I mean, they fight and fight and—"

"That must have been rough," I say, hoping to get him back on track. "What did he say about Mr. Cotton? Or, Mr. Longfeld, I mean."

"Right, right. Yeah, so I guess Cotton was charged with embezzlement and money laundering. A whole big thing. Woulda been charged as Longfeld, though, so probably why you didn't know about it. You didn't know, did you?"

I shake my head. "Do you know any details?"

Tom shrugs. "Not really. Just that the charges didn't stick. That's when he was selling to my brother. I remember because he was afraid Longfeld would pull out of the deal, but he didn't." He shrugs. "Obviously."

"Is Longfeld still around? Do you have an address?"

"Ain't hard to find. Turns out he ended up in prison anyway."

I frown. "What for?"

"DUI. He killed some lady. I got a friend in the DA's office who told me the story. Knew there was a connection between Longfeld and Buddy. That's my brother. Guess he figured I'd want to hear the gossip."

I nod slowly. "There would have been a trial," I say, thinking out loud.

Tom shakes his head. "No, he pled guilty. Practically on the spot my friend said. Seems he'd been giddy when he beat the financial charges. But when he killed that woman, something snapped. Didn't even try to plea bargain. Said he deserved what he got, and not just because of that woman."

"*Not just because of that woman,*" I repeat. "Any idea what he was talking about?"

"Personally, no. But I asked Buddy. He said there'd been rumors about Cotton running his business on the dirty side of things. Like he had ties to some big crime boss. The Lion? The Jackal? I can't remember."

My gut tightens. "The Wolf?"

He nods slowly. "Yeah. Yeah, I think that was it." He shrugs. "Anyway, I remember thinking it all seemed very *Sopranos*." Another shrug. "Not much help. Sorry."

"No, actually that's useful. I appreciate your time." I pull Devlin's list of Uncle Peter's old contacts out of my bag. "Any chance you know any of these folks?"

He skims over it, but shakes his head. I'm disappointed, but not too much. After all, Tom gave me more than I'd expected, including Buddy's contact information in case I want to talk to him, too.

I still have a few hours before dinner, so I hop back into Shelby, then open her up on the wide inland roads as I head back toward the picturesque side of town. When I reach Sunset Canyon Road, I floor it, then whip onto the tiny, winding streets that curve around and down like a twisting, meandering river until they hook up with Pacific Avenue right at the base of the hill that leads up to Brandy's house. And, further, up to Devlin's.

This is the long route, but I don't care. Opening Shelby up on these roads is a pleasure. The wind in my face, the roar of her motor surrounding me. The danger of the sharp curves and narrow lanes. My blood pounds and my skin tingles, and it's only when I make that final turn toward the Arts District that I realize why the feeling is so familiar. Because it's the same rush I feel in Devlin's arms. That heady sensation of being fully present and utterly alive.

Smiling, I turn to the right, putting the hill at my back and aiming Shelby toward the ocean. I miraculously find street parking with time left on the meter, and I gather my things and head to Brewski, figuring I'll grab a coffee, go over my notes, and see if I can luck out and arrange to see Mr. Longfeld later this week.

I sip a latte as I work, and by the time I need to cross the street and head to the Cask & Barrel to meet Brandy and Lamar, I've not only organized my notes, I've got an actual appointment tomorrow with Mr. Longfeld. Turns out he served time for the DUI, just like Tom said, but he also got early release based on time served and good behavior.

Now he's living in Los Angeles and working as a stock clerk in a mom-and-pop grocery store in Panorama City, deep in the San Fernando Valley. Since Lamar's a Beverly Hills brat who thinks the Valley is one of the seven circles of hell, I plan to wait until we're en route to tell him our destination.

The Cask & Barrel is on the same block as Brewski, but on the north side of the street. I forego the crosswalk and dodge cars as I aim myself in that direction. Although the restaurant wasn't around when I was a kid, Brandy and I have been to it a couple of times since I've come back, and I've started to think of it as our go-to place.

I'm about to pull open the door when I hear Brandy squeal. I turn to find her flying toward me, her arms outstretched. She grabs me in a rib-cracking hug, towering over me by almost seven inches. I bite back a happy laugh. "You freak. What's with the massive PDA? I just saw you this morning."

"I'm excited we're finally all three having drinks together. And dinner. Food to sop up the alcohol." She waggles her brows and I have to laugh. Brandy is a very conservative drinker, so I'm both amused and suspicious.

"Does this anticipation of drinks and conversation have anything to do with Christopher? Did you change your mind? Do Lamar and I get to offer all sorts of unsolicited relationship advice, after all?"

She rolls her eyes. "What? I can't be excited about hanging with my besties? Speaking of, where's Lamar?"

I glance up and down the street. "He's late."

"Only by a minute. Or maybe he's already in there."

As if in response, both of our phones chime. I'm pulling mine out of my back pocket as she shakes her head, holding her phone toward me as she says, "Don't bother. It's to both of us."

Table near the window. Get in here and quit gossiping about how handsome I am.

We both turn, find the window, and blow him a kiss. Then, laughing as if that was the funniest thing in the world, we turn back to the door. I'm about to pull it open when I see Christopher walking up the street, his long legs eating up the sidewalk and his golden hair gleaming in the streetlights that are coming on as dusk falls.

I glance at Brandy, who looks sheepish. "I hope you don't mind. I told him we were going to dinner, and he really wanted to come."

I like Christopher just fine. But that doesn't mean I want him here tonight. This was supposed to be our time, and that thought must show on my face, because Brandy frowns, and says, "Oh, dammit, I'm so sorry. I'll tell him it's not going to work out."

"It's just that Devlin's evening freed up, but I told him not to come since it was only the three of us."

"I'm an idiot. I should have asked. Of course he and I will see each other later. I'll have him come to the house sometime tomorrow. Which reminds me, why aren't you sleeping at Devlin's? Your text said you'd be home tonight." She frowns. "Everything was okay with you two this morning. It's still all good, right?"

"Perfect," I assure her.

"Okay, then." She glances toward Christopher. "I'll go take care of it."

I reach out and take her hand, giving it a gentle squeeze. "Thanks." There's a lot of reasons why Brandy is my best friend, not the least of which is because she's a genuinely good person. Mostly it's because she understands me. And despite all of my faults, she loves me.

"I'm going to go in and appease Lamar," I say. "See you in there?"

"Order me a glass of red," she says, then hurries off to meet Christopher, who's paused a few feet away, probably picking up on the fact that we were discussing him.

I feel a little guilty, but not enough to invite him, so I push the feeling away and go inside. The place is bustling, and I wedge myself through to the table that Lamar's managed to snag and pull out one of the chairs.

Lamar's already ordered potato skins and bacon-wrapped shrimp, so we pig out on appetizers and wine, then order more when Brandy joins us. The conversation is easy and random, and I'm in a giddy mood that has nothing to do with the two glasses of Pinot Noir I've downed.

The waiter has just taken our dinner order when Lamar sits up straight, his brow furrowing as he leans forward, clearly trying to see something in the dark. When he sits back, I can feel the irritation coming off him in waves.

"What is it?" But even as I ask the question, I'm turning around in my seat. And in the same moment that Brandy mumbles *oh,* I see him in the doorway.

Devlin.

CHAPTER ELEVEN

I whip back around to look at Brandy. "I swear I didn't invite
him." Even though that's true, I still feel guilty for sending
Christopher away, which is ridiculous and only makes me more
irritated with Devlin.

Her eyes are wide as she nods. "Yeah, well, he's still here."

I scowl, because she's right about that. "I'll be right back," I
mutter as I push back from the table. I have a feeling it's not a
coincidence that he showed up here.

He's heading our direction, his expression flat. I don't know
why he's here, but I know he's pissed.

Guess what? So am I.

I hurry to meet him and grab his elbow, noting that he's practically vibrating with irritation. "What's wrong? Why the hell are
you here?"

"I have a few things I want to discuss with the detective." His
voice is tight. Clipped. And very scary. "No time like the present,
right?"

I have absolutely no clue what's going on in his head, but
something has obviously pushed his buttons. He takes a step
toward our table. I see Lamar flinch—just the slightest reaction,

but I know my friend well, and he doesn't look confused. On the contrary, he looks guilty.

Well, *fuck*.

I grab Devlin's elbow and tug. "Outside," I say, starting to steer him toward the door. He resists, though, his eyes hard. But not on me. No, he's looking over my shoulder to Lamar, who's manned up and is now staring back daggers.

I fight the urge to lash out at both of them. I don't know what is going on, but I have no doubt they are both equally to blame.

"Outside," I say again to Devlin. "And if you fight me or him, you know damn well that all of our pictures are going to end up in the news tomorrow. And I don't mean the *Laguna Leader*," I add, referring to the town's tiny excuse for a newspaper.

When Devlin stands firm, I step even closer, breathing in the scent of musk and fury. "Do you really want this bullshit all over social media? I don't know what's going on, but you need to think about that. Now come with me, dammit. Let's talk outside."

I think he's going to continue to ignore me. Then he nods, a curt, quick motion, before deliberately turning away from the table where Brandy remains sitting, staring at us, while Lamar stabs at his appetizer, pointedly not meeting my eyes.

I follow him outside, and as soon as we're away from the door, I round on him. "What the fuck, Devlin?"

Rather than answer, he takes my elbow and tugs me further down the sidewalk, pushing me into the alcove of a closed lingerie store. My back is against the door, and he stands close enough that I can feel the fury coming off him in waves. I fight the urge to reach out and touch him, afraid that just that simple contact would be enough to spark an explosion.

Instead, I draw a breath and square my shoulders. He's not the one with the right to be pissed—I am, and I lift my chin to look him square in the face. "I made Brandy send Christopher away because it was supposed to just be the three of us," I continue, before he can speak. "And I really don't appreciate—"

"This isn't about you," he snaps, cutting me off. "That son of a bitch has been digging around in my past, trying to get information on my military service record."

"Oh." I frown. I didn't know this. And it pisses me off, too. I asked Lamar to find out about Ronan, but I damn sure didn't expect him to take that as *carte blanche*. If Lamar was going to look into Devlin, he should have told me. And the idea that he's poking around about my boyfriend behind my back doesn't sit well with me at all.

"I didn't know." I don't tell Devlin that I'm pissed, too. Right now, the thing to do is keep him calm, because I really don't want him going back in there and confronting Lamar. Not in public. And definitely not until I've had a go at him first.

I reach for his hand, relieved when he returns the gentle pressure. "You found this out when you were talking to your connections," I say. "Investigating who might have sent me that text."

He nods.

"Did you find out anything? Has anyone been making inquiries about you?"

His expression is hard as stone as he says, "Only Lamar."

I let that one roll off me, not just because I want more info, but because I want to give Devlin time to cool off. "What about the phone? Did you get any info about the number they texted from?"

For a second I think he's going to argue and force this conversation to stay on Lamar. Then he says, "We recovered the phone. A burner. It had been used once—to send that text. No fingerprints, no identifying marks."

"Oh." I'm taken aback. That wasn't something I'd expected. "How'd you manage that?"

"Are you familiar with Type-O SMS messages?"

I shake my head.

"In a nutshell, it's a way to ping a phone and track the location. It only worked because whoever sent that message had fully charged the phone and hadn't shut it off before tossing it. My people sent the message to the number and from there we were able to find the phone."

"That's easy."

He laughs. "Not really. I left out the part about searching trashcans and gutters. It took most of the day, but the team found it."

"I'm impressed," I say, and I mean it. When Devlin took me to Vegas, I'd gotten a sense about how much more he and the foundation do than simply providing money to victims of organized crime, but this is the first time I realize that the DSF has an investigative arm as well. I'm not surprised—Devlin's the kind of guy who jumps all in—but I am surprisingly moved, and I think it's because that's one more thing that he and I have in common. That need to dig for and find answers.

"So what now?" I ask, but I already know the answer.

"That phone's a dead end."

"Which means that we're out of luck until I get another text."

He nods, and I'm grateful he doesn't offer a platitude, suggesting that maybe another text won't come. We both know it will.

He reaches for my hand and pulls me close. "There is one other lead," he begins. "Whoever sent that text thinks there are facts about me you need to learn. Which means the texter is gathering information, probably intending to send you specific dirt with the next text."

"But I already know how dirty you are."

The words are intended to make him smile, but all I see is a shadow in his eyes, and I remember what he told me before—*There will always be secrets between us. Things I'm not willing to talk about. Not ever.*

I shake my head. "It doesn't matter," I say automatically, but I can't help but wonder if it does.

"Other than me, who would do anything to protect you? Who'd challenge me—investigate me—if he thought you were going to disappear in the quicksand."

For a moment I simply stare. Then I yank my hands out of his, shaking my head as I whisper, "No. No way did Lamar send that text. That's not possible."

"Oh, I think it is. He's the—"

"No," I say more firmly. "Absolutely not. There is no possible way." I draw a deep breath and continue. "I trust Lamar with my life. And he didn't even know we were back together last night. Even if he did, he'd never send that kind of a text. If he has a problem with you—which he does—he'd tell me straight out. Which he has."

At that, Devlin smiles, albeit only a little. And it's a cold, scary kind of smile.

"And there's no point in Lamar sending a text, because there's no need," I continue. "He already has my ear. But you know what?" I add, taking his hands as I move closer. "I'll tell you who we need to look at."

His eyes narrow. "Who?"

"Just how well do you know your buddy Ronan?"

"No."

That's all he says. Just that one, tiny word. As if that's enough to erase all my fears and suspicions. Not to mention all the hints that Ronan isn't as clean as the driven snow.

"That's it?" I counter. "Objection, your honor. I'd like to see some evidence."

"It's not Ronan. I'm certain."

"Well, then I guess we're both certain. It must be somebody else."

He exhales loudly, clearly annoyed. But that's fair. I'm annoyed too.

I decide to try again. "Look, Lamar knows that telling me you're dangerous isn't going to scare me away. So he wouldn't bother sending texts. He knows me too well. But Ronan doesn't know me at all."

"Oh, I think he has a pretty solid picture," Devlin says. "But the bottom line is that I *do* know him."

"Oh, do you? So that means that you already know he doesn't like that we're together. That he thinks I'm nothing but a distraction."

"He what?"

"You heard me."

I watch his face and see just a flicker of something that looks like fury before it goes completely blank.

"He didn't send that note."

"Goddammit, Devlin..."

"Do you trust me?"

I meet his eyes as I cross my arms over my chest. "Do *you* trust *me*?"

"I do," he says easily. "But I think your perspective is tainted by friendship."

"And yours isn't?" I frown, remembering my earlier question. "Does Ronan know about Peter? For that matter, does Anna?"

His head snaps back, but he recovers quickly. Still, it's enough to confirm that the question surprised him.

"I know Tamra does," I say. "But I don't know about them."

"They know," he says simply.

"You trusted them with that big a secret because you knew what kind of people they were."

"Ronan, yes. With Anna, it was different. She knew what I'd been ordered to do before I did."

"Oh." I frown as I rearrange things in my mind. "So she—"

"My father sent her here with the order for me to kill Peter. And after she told me, that's when she ran for Chicago and enrolled in Northwestern. It was the final straw that made her escape my father to try to start a new life. As for Ronan, he was there when Alex became Devlin. He was my friend, my confidant, and my brother in arms. I—"

"Trusted him," I say softly. "I get what you're saying. But it's the same with me and Lamar. And it's not just trust, Devlin. You can talk to them—I mean really talk. Nothing's changed now that

I'm in your life. But for me it has, because I can't talk to Lamar anymore. Not really."

I hadn't expected to say any of that. Hell, I'm not even sure I was aware I was feeling it. But the words pour out, almost choking me with their power. I still have Brandy, but gaining Devlin means I lost Lamar. He's still in my life, of course, but only in the censored version.

I watch as irritation flickers over his face. Then he draws in a breath, and slowly nods. He bends forward and presses a soft kiss to my forehead. "I'm sorry," he says. "I'm not used to..."

I wait, but apparently he's not going to finish that sentence. "Used to what?"

"To being with a woman who matters to me. Come on."

My heart is swelling so much it takes me a minute to realize that he's tugging me back toward the Cask & Barrel. "What are you doing? I told you it's just the three—"

"Trust me," he says, then pulls open the door. I want to object, but I do trust him, and I want to make sure he knows that. So I draw in a breath, hope Lamar and Brandy aren't going to lose their shit, and follow him inside.

He pauses inside the doorway, then cuts a path through the crowd. Some of the patrons turn and look, pointing and taking pictures. Devlin Saint is a known quantity—and mostly known as a recluse. The fact that he's out—and with the woman who's supposedly pulled him off the market—is enough to make the photo hounds perk up and start snapping.

"Hello, Instagram," I mutter as Devlin barrels on.

Brandy's got her back to the room and is deep in a story, her hands moving as she describes either making muffins or a purse—or possibly petting Jake. Lamar is laughing, but the sound catches in his throat when he sees us.

"Saint." The word is flat. Emotionless.

Brandy twists around, her eyes wide with surprise before cutting to me. I see the question—and the accusation—and I can only shrug and raise my hands and hope that whatever Devlin says now will get me out of the doghouse with my friends.

Lamar and Brandy exchange surprised glances as Devlin settles into the four-top's empty chair. I follow his lead and slide into mine.

"You know about Alex?" Devlin asks, his attention on Lamar.

Lamar's brow furrows, but to his credit, he rolls with it. "I never knew Alex, but Ellie told me about him. Back when we were in the Academy, we exchanged notes on our past relationship disasters."

I see Devlin wince, but I can't tell if Lamar notices or not.

"Right. Well, I think it's only fair that you know the truth. I'm Alex."

"Oh."

I can tell right away that Lamar's response is only perfunctory. He has no idea about the magnitude of what Devlin just said. Then his eyes widen and he says, "*Oh,*" and I realize that it's all clicked. "Why are you telling me—"

But Devlin cuts him off by sliding back his chair. He leans forward and lowers his voice so that there is no chance of anyone overhearing. "She trusts you. That means I trust you." He looks between me and Brandy. "Tell him the rest of it."

I see Brandy's eyes widen, reflecting my own surprise. "Everything?" she asks. "I mean, not that there's anything shocking," she adds, as if to cover a faux pas.

Amusement flickers across his features, but his attention stays on Lamar as he stands. "Everything. And then if you have questions, ask Ellie. If she doesn't know, ask me. Don't poke around in my life. Trust me when I tell you that isn't a good idea. I don't appreciate it, and more importantly, there are people who worked very hard to make me who I am. And they don't appreciate it either."

"What the—?" Lamar says, but Devlin is already striding toward the door. I glance between my friends and him, then lift a finger in a *just one sec* sign as I hurry outside after my boyfriend, feeling just as bewildered as my friends.

I get caught in a crowd of college kids, and by the time I get to the door, I'm afraid he'll have already disappeared. But he's on the sidewalk waiting for me, and seeing him standing there in the soft glow from the restaurant's windows, I melt a little.

"You did that for me."

The hint of a smile flickers across his lips. "I think you already know there's very little that I wouldn't do for you."

"But—"

"No." He presses a fingertip to my lips. "You were right. I can talk about my world, my life, my past, and my present with so many people, even despite all the secrets I'm keeping. You only had Brandy."

"Not only," I tell him. "I have Tamra. And Anna. I'm enjoying getting to know her."

"I'm glad you feel that way, but it's not the same, and I know that." He slides his arms around my waist, and I tilt my head back to meet his eyes. "I don't want to be a negative in your life," he says.

"You couldn't ever—"

"Yes, I could. And that's exactly what you were telling me earlier. If I walk into your life and suddenly you have to change the way you talk to your closest friends, then I've taken something from you whether I meant to or not. And that's not acceptable."

"You took a risk telling him."

"No, I didn't. You trust him, remember?"

I laugh, then nod. "Yeah, I do." I rise up onto my toes to kiss him. "Thank you."

"You're very welcome."

"Okay. Well, I guess I'm going to go back in there and finish my dinner and field a dozen questions. And I'll see you tomorrow, Mr. Saint."

"Come to my place later."

I shake my head, grinning. "No."

"All those points I just won?"

A bubble of laughter explodes from me. "Don't even try guilt."

"I have a full box of condoms."

"No," I repeat, but I'm having a hard time not laughing.

"But you want to."

"I do," I admit.

"So you're punishing me."

"No way," I tease, my voice singsong. "I'm giving you what you like best. Anticipation."

He leans forward and whispers. "In that case, I'll have to make sure it pays off when I see you next."

Then he turns and walks away. I watch him go, only to have my breath catch in my throat as I see a familiar figure in a doorway across the street.

Regina Taggart.

I tell myself it's a coincidence. But as I watch—as her body turns while she watches Devlin walk to his car—I can't help but fear that I'm wrong.

We end up getting the rest of our food to go since we can't risk being overheard. Lamar heads out first, leaving Brandy and me to take care of the check. He's parked about two blocks away, so that's fair, and the plan is that we'll meet at Brandy's place. As soon as we've taken care of the bill, we head out onto the street with the take-out bags.

"You could've gone with Lamar," I point out. She'd walked to the restaurant and is now hitching a ride back with me. "You'd already be there by now, getting us all set up and ready to eat."

She shoots me a sidelong glance. "Right. Because we have absolutely nothing to talk about." I shrug as she continues. "Are you sure we're understanding Devlin right? Maybe he was drunk? Maybe he was being ... I don't know, *stupid*."

I circle Shelby and pause at the driver's side door. "No, we understood right. As for him being stupid..." I trail off, because I want to believe in both Devlin and Lamar, but I can't deny that the door Devlin opened scares me.

Brandy lingers at the passenger side of the car. Then she pulls open the door and slides in. I do the same, settling in behind the wheel. "I don't get it," she says. "I mean, Lamar is a cop."

"Yeah," I say. "I noticed."

She tilts her head as if in admonishment. "Don't be glib about this."

I take a deep breath and try to relax. "I promise you, I'm not being glib. I'm trying to process everything. I trust Devlin. And I trust Lamar. And I want this. I want to be able to talk to him. Is that so bad?"

"Of course not! It's just, well, you realize there's no statute of limitations on murder, right? Surely, Devlin didn't really mean you should tell Lamar *everything*."

My stomach twists unpleasantly, and for a moment I think I might be sick. But I square my shoulders, because I believe what I told her. I do trust Devlin. And I do trust Lamar. And I know that they both love me, and that neither of them would hurt me. But, yeah, I'm scared, and I tell her so.

"So, what are you going to do?"

I draw in a deep breath then let it out slowly. "I'm going to tell Lamar the truth, just like Devlin said." I shift more in the seat so I'm looking at her directly. "It'll be okay. Don't you think it will be okay?"

I can see from her face that she's unsure, but then she slowly nods. "Yeah," she says, not entirely with conviction. "Of course it will. Lamar would never hurt you, and he knows that screwing with Devlin would do exactly that. Friendship tops everything, right?"

I nod, because she's right. But I also hear what she doesn't say —but does *everything* include the law?

I answer the unspoken question aloud. "Yeah, friendship wins. It has to."

I turn forward and grip the steering wheel, wondering how much I truly believe what I said. Do friendship and love and family always win? If I had known what Uncle Peter was doing all those years ago, would I have stayed quiet? After all, I've stayed quiet about the fact that Devlin killed my uncle.

It's different, though. What Devlin did was shocking, but understandable. He killed to save me. That's an easy call, and I don't feel any guilt holding onto that secret.

Peter, though...

He was stealing money and getting people hooked on drugs. And he was doing all of that for no reason other than his own profit.

Still, I'd loved him. Would I have turned him in? Or would I have kept his secret?

I don't know, and my uncertainty bothers me. Thankfully, it's not a question I have to face. Uncle Peter is dead, and exposing those secrets now doesn't bother me.

The bigger question for tonight is how will Lamar feel once he knows the truth. Will he protect Devlin's secrets, knowing that it would destroy me if he revealed them? Or will the oath that he took as a police officer take precedence?

Devlin's surely thought about that, too, and I know that he must believe my friendship is strong enough with Lamar to ensure that he'd never do anything to hurt me, including revealing a crime. So how is it that I'm suddenly doubting? How is it that I'm suddenly scared?

It's a rhetorical question, of course. I'm scared because even though I know Lamar well enough to know how he's going to react, until the moment he tells me it's okay, there's always the chance that everything will go south.

Brandy seems to realize that I'm lost in my own thoughts and says nothing during the short drive back to her house. Lamar knows the key and alarm code to her place, so he's already inside when we get there. I see him, and my stomach curdles when I realize that I can't read his expression.

Then he smiles at me and holds out his arms and holds me close, giving me a hug. "I don't know what it is you're going to tell me, but you know it's going to be okay, right?"

"Yes," I lie. "I know."

Brandy's right behind me, and she quickly moves to the kitchen and starts plating all the food we brought in from Cask & Barrel.

"So, are you going to make me guess what this is all about?" Lamar asks. "Or are you going to dive in?"

"I thought I would stall until we had food. And possibly lots of alcohol."

Lamar chuckles. Then he settles himself on one of the barstools across from where Brandy is bustling like someone who needs to stay in motion in order to prevent the apocalypse. I hop onto the stool next to him and try not to fidget.

"All right," I say, but then don't know how to continue. There's too much to tell him and I don't have any idea where to begin. Finally, I decide that the only way to go forward is to start with the worst and work backwards.

I'm about to do that when I realize that's a stupid approach and starting with the worst would just freak Lamar out. So, I tell him about how Alex disappeared the night Uncle Peter died, which is something he already knew, and I figure it's a good way to ease him into the story.

"You know all that, of course. How he left and broke my heart."

"Which is one of the reasons that I've always thought Alex was a bastard. And now that I know he's Devlin, it all sort of fits together."

I almost snap out a defense of Devlin, but then I notice the slight curve of his mouth. He's teasing me to make this easier, and that simple knowledge lifts a huge weight from my shoulder.

"Right. Okay. Well, the reason that he had to disappear is that he's really Alejandro Lopez. Do you know who that is?" It's a foolish question, because I can already see the answer in Lamar's eyes.

"Devlin Saint is The Wolf's son?"

I nod. "And after Uncle Peter was killed, he ran. That's when he joined the military." I don't say that Devlin's the one who pulled the trigger. Not yet.

In the kitchen area, Brandy is practically buzzing with anticipation, as nervous as I am about what Lamar's ultimate reaction will be.

Right now, he's calm, his expression pensive, as if he's fitting the puzzle pieces together. "So, he became Devlin Saint in order to hide from his father?"

"Yeah. And after his father died, he inherited everything that the government couldn't take. He also inherited a lot of money from his mother. His mom's family wasn't dirty, so he used that money to live on, and he put everything he inherited from his dad into the foundation."

"He wanted to make the bad money good."

"Exactly," I say, thrilled that he got there before I pointed it out.

"And you didn't know any of this?"

"Back then? No. All I knew was that my boyfriend disappeared."

"What about when you came back? Had you learned about Devlin then?"

I shake my head. "Not at all. You know exactly why I came back. Because Chief Randall told me that the guy who confessed to Uncle Peter's murder couldn't have done it. And that lifted the veil on the fact that Uncle Peter was somehow tied to The Wolf."

"So when did you learn that Devlin was Alex? I mean, you also came to write a profile on Saint and his foundation. I know you, remember? You would have done your research before. Seen pictures of him."

"True enough. But he doesn't look like Alex anymore. He had

some surgery, he changed his hair, he wears contacts to change the color of his eyes. And apparently the scar—"

I frown, since I still don't know exactly how he got the scar. Just that he was at the wrong end of a knife. "I'm assuming it was from his time in the military."

Lamar nods. "Okay. Go on. Does he know who really killed Uncle Peter?"

Across the bar, Brandy chokes on her sip of water, then holds up a hand in apology.

I keep my focus on Lamar and take a deep breath. "The truth is ... well, the truth is that Uncle Peter was stealing from The Wolf just like we thought. And—and so The Wolf arranged it. Uncle Peter's death, I mean."

"Right. That much, I knew."

I nod, then glance at Brandy before drawing in a breath as I turn my attention back to Lamar. Can I do this? Can I really burden him with this knowledge? If I don't tell him, will it taint our friendship?

More importantly, what will it do to him—a cop—if I do?

Lamar's brow furrows. "You're telling me that Devlin knows who The Wolf hired."

I force myself not to look at Brandy, then I swallow and say, "I'm not *telling* you anything."

He almost smiles. "No. I guess you're not. *Shit.*" He runs his hands over his shaved head. "If he knows, why the hell hasn't he told Chief Randall? Because then he'd have to reveal how he knows," he continues, answering his own question. "And that would mean revealing who he is now. *Fuck.*"

I swallow, then force myself not to lean back when he turns his narrowed gaze on me. "But he's told you," Lamar says, his words coming slowly as if he's a freshman trying to talk his way through a calculus problem. "He must have because that's not what you're investigating. You're looking into the *why* behind what Peter did. Not the question of who shot him. You. His niece. And you're not even looking anymore."

"That's not the point of the article," I say.

"No," he agrees. "You're doing your family piece. A story of how it all went wrong."

I glance toward Brandy; I can't help myself.

Lamar doesn't notice, though. He's still working through his thoughts, and I can't think of a way to distract him.

"For as long as I've known you," Lamar says, "you're like a dog with a bone. Your editor may want the touchy-feely story, but you want answers. And when you first came to town, you wanted to know who the real killer was. But now you're not looking anymore."

"What would be the point?" I ask. "You know as well as I do that the odds of getting a conviction when someone else has already confessed or been tried. It's rare to never."

"Maybe. But you'd still want to know, and yet you're not looking. That means Devlin told you. So then the question is why aren't you pursuing it? Is the killer dead? If so, why haven't you told Chief Randall. Or me, for that matter?" He starts to pace, the tension in his body coming off him like waves. "Instead, you're holding it close because Devlin told you to. Or else he—"

His eyes go wide, and his body straightens. "Oh, fuck me. Ellie, what the hell? You're telling me that Devlin Saint killed your uncle?"

A cold chill runs over me. "I *never* said that."

He closes his eyes, draws a breath, then opens them again. "He told you to tell me everything. So why did you leave that part out? I mean, Brandy already knows, right?"

This time, I don't even try to hide the fact that I'm looking toward Brandy. She nods, but I've already made up my mind. "Yeah," I say. "She knows."

"You didn't tell me because you didn't want to burden me. Even though Saint told you to. He said to tell me the rest of it."

I lift a shoulder in silent acknowledgement, and he nods, obviously still processing everything.

"So tell me the rest. Like how the hell you can possibly be okay with this. I mean, your boyfriend murdered your uncle."

I shake my head. "I never said a word about Devlin killing Peter. But you and I know that if he did, there would only be one reason for it, and that's if he was protecting me."

Lamar nods slowly. "His father gave him an ultimatum. Take out Peter or watch his girlfriend get blown away."

"Defense of others," I say softly, wishing that Lamar understood. That he wasn't standing there reciting facts. I want him beside me, holding my hand and telling me that he understands everything I went through. Everything *Devlin* went through.

"Defense of others? Don't even, Ellie. You know that wouldn't fly. He could have gone to the authorities. He could have hidden you away, gotten help. Instead, he took matters into his own hands. He did what his father wanted, and your uncle's dead because of it. Peter could still be alive. He could have served his time by now and be back with you. Your family. A man who loved and took care of you."

His eyes turn cold. So does my blood. "Instead, you have the man who killed him."

"Lamar, please. You have to understand—"

I glance at Brandy, who looks terrified.

Lamar runs his hand over his head. "Look. I get what you're saying. I do. But you've got to remember who I am. I'm not just your friend. I'm a cop. You have to know that I love you and that I would never hurt you. You know that, right?"

He's waiting for me to respond, so I nod, hoping that I really do know that.

"Good. But Ellie, here's the thing. This ... I didn't ask for this. I don't know how I can keep a lid on it. Or maybe I did ask for it. Maybe I asked for it by poking around. I don't know. But did you think about this? Maybe he's just playing me. Playing you, too."

"No way," Brandy says, speaking for the first time, and I think I want to kiss her, I'm so happy she's still on my side. "He's not doing that. What are you even talking about?"

Lamar looks from Brandy to me. "Maybe he's trying to make himself look like one of the good guys when he's really three steps ahead of me. There's no question the man's smart. Maybe he knew I would figure it out eventually. That you would either accidentally tell me, or I'd find out he killed Peter. That's the job, right. And eventually I would have found my answers."

He pauses, then continues before I have a chance to say anything. "Doing it this way—telling you to tell me everything so that I feel obligated to keep *your* secret, not his—is Saint's way of staying three steps ahead of me. Of making sure he's protected. And by a cop, no less."

"No. No way. Lamar, you can't believe that."

"I'm sorry, Sherlock. I love you. But I don't know what to do with this. I don't." He blows out a noisy breath. "I need some time."

"But—"

He takes my hand, silencing me. "I'll make you one promise, though. I won't do anything without telling you first. Okay?"

I nod, mute, my vision blurring from the tears that are filling my eyes.

"You guys go ahead and eat. I need to think. I'm sorry," he adds. "I know you wanted me to say something else. I know you wanted me to be someone else. But I can't right now. I can't process any of this. I have to figure this out for myself. And to do that, I really need to go."

CHAPTER TWELVE

Devlin was awake when the security system buzzed, signaling that someone had stepped onto the property. He checked the feed on his phone, unsurprised when he saw that the midnight visitor was Lamar.

After all, Devlin had been expecting him.

He moved to the entryway and opened the door as Lamar was lifting his hand to ring the bell.

"Detective."

Lamar met his eyes, said nothing, then stepped past Devlin and into the house.

Devlin casually closed the door, biting back the urge to say something. It wasn't worth the pissing contest. Not when the underlying issue was Ellie. Her relationship with Devlin. Her friendship with Lamar.

"Tell me why," Lamar demanded, without preamble.

Devlin didn't pretend to misunderstand the question. "Because I took enough from her when I walked away."

"After you shot Peter."

Devlin smiled, but neither confirmed nor denied. "I can't take away her friends now, too," he said instead. He'd meant every word when he told Ellie to tell Lamar the rest, but that didn't mean he was going to confess to a murder in his own home. "And that's what would have happened. She would never have told you my secrets. Not without my okay. And that would have put up a wall between you. You might not have realized it, but she'd know. And eventually, that invisible barrier would wear down the foundation of your friendship."

"So it's all about her."

He met Lamar's eyes. "It's always been about her."

Lamar made a harsh noise in the back of his throat. "I could believe that. Or I could believe you're a manipulative son of a bitch who's stacking the cards in his favor to make sure he has an ally in the police department while he's facing a murder charge."

"It's a theory," Devlin agreed. "Hell, it's not even a bad one. But do you really believe that's how I'd stack the deck? You know how much I'm worth. Do you really think there's no one in the LCPD—hell, in the mayor's office or even the governor's office—I couldn't have in my pocket if I wanted them there?"

Lamar's eyes narrowed. "I'm not sure you're actually making your case, Saint."

"I'm not trying to convince you, Detective. I'm only making sure you have all the angles to think about." They were still in the entryway, but now he headed for the living room. The doors were open to let in the cool breeze as a small fire burned in the corner fireplace. "I'm going to have a drink. Want one?"

"What the hell. Bourbon. Whatever you've got. Straight up."

Devlin poured him a glass, then filled his own before settling into a leather armchair and nodding for Lamar to take the sofa.

"So what's your angle?" the detective asked as he took a seat. "You said you were giving me all the angles to think about. Which one is yours?"

"I already told you. Ellie's my only interest."

"I don't buy that. She's going to hurt like hell if I arrest you for murder."

"I can't argue with that. I can only say that in my judgment, Ellie would be the most hurt by lying through default to her friends. It would hurt her soul. It would hurt her friendship with you. And ultimately, it would hurt us. Because it would be like an open wound in our relationship. Ellie knows the score."

"Well, you judged her wrong. Because she didn't tell me. Not about the murder, anyway."

Devlin tightened his grip on his glass, careful not to react as he admitted—only to himself—that he hadn't expected that. "I'm afraid you're going to have to explain that statement, Detective. I'm not quite following."

"She told me you were The Wolf's son," Lamar continued. "I asked if you knew who killed Peter. Since she's not looking for his killer anymore, it was easy to figure out the rest."

"Are you saying that she confirmed your assumption that I pulled the trigger?"

"Not overtly, no. She's protecting you, even though you told her to tell me all of it."

Devlin leaned back, realizing that he wasn't really surprised, after all. "And you think she underestimated you."

"But you won't."

"I make it a habit to understand my adversaries," Devlin said. "And my friends."

"Which am I?"

"I guess we'll find out."

"When I arrest you, you mean? I'll need to investigate. I know, but I don't have proof. Not the kind that will hold up in court, anyway."

"I'm afraid I can't help you there," Devlin said. "And I'm sure there are other investigations more worth your time. Peter's death may be an open case again, but it's old and not at the top of anyone's list—except possibly yours, Detective."

"And now you expect me to sit on it?"

Devlin almost smiled. "I don't know you well enough to have expectations. If you want to arrest me, I won't make a scene, but I'm sure my lawyers will have a field day. And if you want to sit down, have a drink, and talk this out, I'm good with that, too."

For a moment, Lamar said nothing. Just swirled his glass so the remaining liquid went round and round. Silence hung between them until he finally shifted his attention from the glass to Devlin's face.

"Do you expect me to believe that you weren't involved in the dirty side of Peter's business?"

"I don't expect you to take anything on faith, Detective."

"That wasn't my question."

Devlin sipped his whiskey, then smiled. "Actually, it was. But to get to the deeper query, no, I wasn't involved in that part of his business."

"Considering who your father was, how the hell was that possible?"

Devlin dragged his fingers through his hair, tugging out the tie that held it back from his face in the process. He bit back a sigh of frustration. He knew Lamar needed to be led by the hand. And he knew Ellie was worth taking the time to handle Lamar. But he didn't like being interrogated, and if he didn't watch it, he'd lose his patience. If that happened, Lamar really would start poking around in Peter's murder. And that was a headache Devlin didn't need.

"Peter was my boss and my mentor," he began. "He was embezzling money and selling drugs, and that shit didn't sit with me. But he treated me like a son, and he loved Ellie. You never knew him, of course, but he would have done anything for her. That car—Shelby? He probably lost a hundred grand just because he spent his time dealing with that car instead of running his operation."

"He could have asked you to step in and handle things."

"No. I told you I didn't touch that, and I meant it. My father sent me to learn, but I made it clear to Peter that I'd walk away if he made me get involved with anything more than the legitimate side of the business. I saw what he was doing, sure. But I didn't help."

"I'm supposed to believe that?"

"I don't care what you believe. It was another lifetime ago. Why would I lie about that?"

Lamar ignored the question. "What did you do after you shot him?"

"You mean after Peter was shot and I left town? I joined the Army."

"Did you go back to Nevada? To your dad?"

"Not then. I went later. Told him I'd joined the military. Was in Sniper School. Gave him a bullshit story about how I was learning skills that would help me when I took over his business. And that the military would give me credibility. He bought it, and I earned time away from the bastard."

"Then someone killed him."

"Yes, they did. If you're waiting for me to shed a tear about that, you'll be waiting a while."

"So why the identity change? Your father was dead."

"And being dead, his enemies had no one to come after. They would have turned to me."

Lamar nodded. "Yeah, okay, I get that." He took a sip of his drink. "On the whole, you've been remarkably honest. Giving Ellie *carte blanche* to talk with me was a risk."

"I'm disposed to trust you because Ellie does, and she's no fool. The jury's still out on whether I like you."

"Cheers to that," Lamar said, lifting his glass in toast.

"But this isn't about you, Detective, as much as you might like to think it is. It's not even about me. It's about Ellie. It's about a woman I hurt deeply once, and I don't intend to ever hurt again. Not being able to talk to you was hurting her. I'm sorry if that puts an unexpected and unwanted burden on you, but like I said, this isn't about you, and your burdens aren't my concern."

"They are if I decide to arrest you."

"No. That would be a different burden. An irritation that I'd have to fight. A waste of my time and my money. But I'd beat the charge. All things being equal, though, I'd rather not bother."

Lamar tossed back the rest of his whiskey in one swallow,

then put the glass on the table with a clunk. He stood, and for the first time in his life, Devlin couldn't read a man he was negotiating with. Probably because this wasn't a negotiation. Business was business, but emotions were something else entirely. And he had no idea how Lamar's emotions were going to play out.

"You hurt her, and all bets are off."

Devlin fought not to show his relief as Lamar continued. "I find out you're just a shined up version of your father, and I will take you down."

"I wouldn't blame you."

Lamar stuck his hands into the pockets of his jeans. "I liked you fine before Ellie came back. You seemed like a solid leader in the community. A guy who gave back and cared. So I suppose I can give you the benefit of the doubt now."

Devlin stood as well. "That's appreciated. Though I should probably tell you that before Ellie came back, I didn't think about you at all. I didn't even have a clue you existed."

Lamar chuckled. "Well, guess I fixed that problem."

"I'd say you did. Or, more accurately, Ellie did." He paused. "She loves you, you know."

Lamar shook his head. "Oh, hell, no. It's not like that. There was a time I wouldn't have kicked her out of my bed, but we are long past that. If we tease, don't think—"

"I know. What I mean is that she loves you. You're one of her closest friends. So whatever you choose to do with the information about me—well, you've got a pass there as far as I'm concerned. But if you do anything else that hurts her, be forewarned that the scar will go deep."

To Devlin's surprise, Lamar grinned. "If that's the way you think, Saint, then I guess we understand each other."

"I think we do." He extended his hand. "Detective."

A moment passed, and then Lamar's hand closed around his, a firm, solid handshake.

"Your life's a hell of a story, Saint. Now that our girl's part of it again, make sure it doesn't turn into a goddamn tragedy, okay?"

"Agreed," Devlin said, surprised and pleased to realize he was starting to genuinely like this guy.

He offered him another drink, but Lamar said he was getting up early to play golf with friends before going with Ellie to LA. "Does it bother you? The way she's doubling down to investigate Peter and how he got mixed up with your father and all of that?"

"A bit," he admitted. "Less now that you know the score."

For a moment Lamar looked puzzled. "You thought we might stumble across something and I'd make the connection. Figure out who you are."

"I'm afraid someone already has."

Lamar frowned. "What are you talking about?"

Devlin opened his phone and showed Lamar the copy of the text Ellie had forwarded. "Sent from a burner," he said. "Untraceable."

"Fuck," Lamar said, his eyes narrowing as he frowned. "I don't like seeing anyone harass our girl, but this may fizzle out to nothing."

"How do you figure that?"

"I'm guessing they think Ellie doesn't know who your father is. Their big reveal will go over like a lead balloon."

Devlin scoffed. "Don't be naive, Detective. They sent that text to Ellie because she and I are together. It's not about what they know about me, it's what they know about her. She's my weakness. If someone wants to get to me, the way to do it is through Ellie."

Lamar tilted his head, studying Devlin. "And that's another reason you're cool with me knowing the truth about who you are. Because now I know the kind of people who might have their eye on you two."

"And I'll take whatever help I can get making certain that Ellie stays safe."

CHAPTER THIRTEEN

D evlin watched Lamar head to his car, a sleek Lexus hybrid that looked like it was regularly detailed. He didn't wave, and Lamar didn't look back, but the air between them felt clear, and the tension that he'd lived with from the first moment they'd met was gone.

He'd always be a bit jealous of Ellie and Lamar's relationship, but he knew now it was only because Lamar had been her friend during those lost years when Devlin had been far away. The years when she grew into the woman she'd become—strong and smart and resilient—and he envied the time Lamar had shared with her.

He was about to go back inside when he saw the man standing there, leaning casually against a lamppost on the opposite side of the street, his blond hair gleaming in the light.

Ronan.

The moment Devlin saw him, he felt the pressure of a fury he'd been holding since Ellie had ranted at him on the sidewalk, and deservedly so. But his anger wasn't directed at El. No, the storm had swirled up around Ronan—around the things he'd said to Ellie behind Devlin's back.

Devlin had pushed the dark thoughts down, building a wall between himself and his emotions the way he'd learned to do when he was living with his father. When any sign of an unwelcome emotion could get him beaten. Or, worse, could get one of his friends beaten. Because hadn't Daniel Lopez learned early on that the best way to control his boy Alejandro was to threaten the people he cared about?

Now, he relied on that instinct once more, intentionally clamping down on his emotions as he signaled for Ronan to come inside.

"What was the detective doing here?" Ronan asked as he crossed the threshold.

"He knows," Devlin said simply.

Ronan's eyes went wide. "About you? About The Wolf? Or—"

"He knows who my father is. Who I used to be."

Ronan made a scoffing noise. "He's a hell of a lot better detective than I imagined if he knows all that. You should recruit him to your team."

"And he thinks he knows I killed Peter," Devlin added without missing a beat. "I didn't disabuse him of that notion."

"I see." Ronan nodded slowly. "You're sharing that little gem with everybody."

Snap. And there it was. The anger Devlin had been holding back bubbled over. "Do you want to tell me what you think you're doing?"

Ronan's brow furrowed, his head and shoulders moving back slightly as he studied Devlin, his posture tense even as his expression stayed casually neutral. Ready for anything, just like they'd been trained. Even through his irritation, Devlin had to admire his friend.

"Maybe you should tell me what you're talking about." Ronan's tone matched Devlin's. Flat. Hard. No nonsense.

"A distraction? You told Ellie to cut loose from me because she was a *distraction*?"

Ronan's hands rose as if in a gesture of surrender. "I like her. I do. And in case she didn't tell you, I said that before Vegas. Before you two were outed at the track. And before she'd learned who your father was and what happened with Peter. So back off and cut me a little slack."

Devlin drew in a breath, felt some of the tension drain from him as he nodded. "She thinks you could be behind that text I tried to trace."

"Oh, fuck no." Ronan shook his head. "That's not my style, and you know it. But I'll be honest, man, I've got my worries."

"You don't need to."

"Maybe you're standing too close to see the big picture, but I'm not. Think about it. She's a reporter. She was raised by cops. If she's not a distraction, she's a danger. Is she that good a lay that you're willing to risk everything you've built?"

Devlin took a step closer, reminding himself that Ronan *was* his friend, which was a damn good thing. If he was anyone else, Devlin would have already broken his nose. "One, don't ever speak about her like that again. Two, as far as I'm concerned, she's the only thing worth building anything for."

To his credit, Ronan didn't even flinch. All he said was, "Really?"

"Yeah." Devlin nodded slowly. "She's been the voice in my head for the last decade. Pushing me forward. Driving me to make a mark. To fight back against what my father set in motion."

"I get it, man, you know I do. But do you really think she's going to feel the same? That she's going to approve of the kind of mark you're making? You know the kind of woman she is. The way she thinks."

"I do. That's why I trust her."

"I guess you must. You didn't only tell Ellie your secrets, you practically threw a goddamn party and announced everything to all her friends."

Devlin dragged his fingers through his hair. "I made a judgment call."

"Her roommate. Now the detective. If that's the result of your judgment call, no offense, but I'm questioning your judgment."

"Fair enough. That's why I keep you around. But I trust them both."

"Why?"

"What about you? Are you going to rat me out? Spill my secrets?"

To his credit, Ronan looked appalled by the very thought. "You know I wouldn't."

"Even if I piss you off? Even if you think I've crossed a line?"

"You know the answer."

"Tell me the why," Devlin demanded.

"Because of who you are, you asshole. You and me, we've been through a lot of shit. Hell, we've walked through fire together."

"And you think those three haven't?"

Ronan's head tilted, and Devlin pressed on. "Even if they don't care a thing about me—even if they think I'm the devil incarnate—"

"And they might."

"They still won't say a word. Because if they do, it would hurt Ellie."

"The cop, too?"

Devlin hesitated, then nodded.

"Then I guess you're right. You don't have to worry about them." He met Devlin's eyes, his as hard as steel. "All we have to worry about is what'll happen when Ellie learns the rest of your truth. I hope she's worth the risk."

"She is," he said. But he couldn't deny that Ronan was right about one thing. As far as Ellie Holmes was concerned, Devlin was a selfish sonofabitch. Because even though Ronan didn't say it out loud, it wasn't just Devlin's neck on the chopping block.

If it turned out that Devlin had misjudged Ellie or her friends —if the decisions he'd made with his heart rather than his head caused everything he'd built to come crashing down around him— then Devlin knew damn well that he'd never, ever forgive himself.

CHAPTER FOURTEEN

I'm wearing PJs and in bed when Brandy knocks lightly on my bedroom door. "Are you awake?" Her voice is soft, barely a whisper.

"Come on in."

She pushes the door open and steps in, her damp hair leaving a dark spot on the shoulders of her nightgown. "I thought a hot shower would help, but I still can't sleep. You either?"

I shake my head and scoot over to make room for her on the bed. "It'll be okay. Lamar won't say anything. He wouldn't do that to me."

"Agreed." She squeezes my hand. "He just needs time to process."

I draw a breath. "You really believe that?"

"Do you?"

I shrug. "I've been asking myself that since he left. And I almost believe it. But like he said, it's an open case again. Ever since they realized Ricky Mercado gave a false confession, it's a mystery to be solved."

"You think Lamar's going to turn Devlin in to score cold case brownie points?"

"No," I admit. "But I went through the Academy with him.

And even though I didn't stay on the job, I know that world. So we talk about it a lot. Lamar has a code, and overlooking murder isn't part of it."

"Guess I know what you two will be talking about tomorrow." She yawns and stretches. "Ask him before you get out of town. It's going to be super awkward if you drive all the way to LA before he tells you he's going to rat your boyfriend out."

"Thanks so much for the comforting thought."

She laughs, then hugs me. "Gallows humor. Seriously, do you want to get drunk and watch a movie?"

"Want? Yes. But I should probably try to sleep."

"Me, too. I've got to be out of here by eight for a full day of meetings, and then Christopher and I are going for wine and appetizers."

"Nice," I say with a grin.

Brandy grins and blushes. "Yeah. It is." She leans over and gives me a hug. "It's going to be an early night for us, though. Christopher's knuckling down with his keyboard and writing tomorrow night. So shoot me a text and let me know if you're having dinner at home, because I'll—" She cuts herself off with a nod to my phone, the screen of which has just lit up with a text. "Gee. I wonder who that can be."

She slides out of bed with a little wave and a waggle of her eyebrows. "Be good. And tell him I said hi."

"Ha ha—*oh.*" I can only see part of the message on the lock screen, but what I see makes my stomach twist. "Lamar went to see him."

Her eyes go wide. "In that case, you better ask him where he buried the body."

I can't quite manage a laugh, and once she's out the door, I unlock my phone and read the entire message.

Had a guest tonight.
Lamar.
Did he tell you?

I frown. I'd hoped for more.

No. Do I need to
come claim the body?

I bite my lower lip as I wait for his response.

Touch and go there
for a while,
but all is good.

I read that twice, just to make sure.

Really?

He cares about you.
Can't fault him for that.

I close my eyes and draw a deep breath.

Thank you.

Feel free to invite me over.
You can express your gratitude
in a more tangible way…

**LOL.
If you send an
eggplant emoji,
you're never
living it down.**

*No emojis, baby.
Just the real thing.*

**The real thing is
very, very tempting.
But tonight's an
anticipation night,
remember?**

*Pretend I just used
a sad-face emoji—
and go check your door.*

My eyes narrow.

**You better not be standing
there wrapped in a bow.
Because we made rules,
and if I break them,
I'll feel terrible about myself,
and it will be all your fault.**

Do you trust me?

Always.

Then check the door.
And baby? Sleep tight.

I smile as I send him a heart emoji, then wait for the three dots indicating that he's replying. But there's nothing.

I frown, already sad the conversation has ended. But I do what he says and go to the front door. I open it to find a dozen roses on the doorstep. For a moment, I just stand there, my heart melting a little. Then I think to look out into the dark.

I don't see him, but I know he's there, and I blow him a kiss before taking the flowers inside, shutting the door, and sighing with such intense pleasure that I'm sure my heart will swell so much it will burst right out of my chest.

Brandy comes out of the kitchen carrying a glass of wine. She pauses, her eyes dipping to the flowers before she flashes an impish grin. "He may be complicated," she says, "but he's a keeper."

I cradle the flowers. "Yeah," I say. "He is."

"Hang on. I'll get you a vase." She puts her wine down on the hall table then hurries back toward the kitchen. I start to follow but pause when the phone I'm still holding vibrates in my hand.

I grin as I put the flowers next to Brandy's wine so that I can unlock the screen and read his message. Except it's not from him, and my body goes cold as I read the words: ***Don't you know you're fucking a dangerous man?***

Last night, I hadn't wanted to ruin the sweetness, but I also knew that the vile text was probably sent from a burner, and the only way for Devlin to track it was that weird Type-O thing. So I forwarded him the text and the number it came from. He'd replied in seconds, and though I'd hesitated before checking, I ended up laughing.

Our asshole texter says:
"You're fucking a dangerous man."
But technically, you're not.
At least not at the moment.
But if you want to let me
in your bed after all…

I'd laughed, and a few minutes later, he followed up.

I talked to Ronan. I talked to Lamar.
It's not either one of them, I'm certain.
We'll find the bastard. I'm on it.
In the meantime, sweet dreams.

I smiled at the kiss emoji and debated replying with an eggplant, just to be silly. But instead, I sent him back a single heart, then tried to do what he said and put the whole thing out of my mind.

I'd managed—finally—but now that it's morning, I'm thinking about it all over again. And I'm frustrated that I haven't heard anything more. Does his silence mean that, like last time, the number the text came from was a dead end? Or does it mean that Devlin's found the guy, is beating the shit out of him, and thinks I won't approve?

Since Lamar and I aren't heading up to LA until lunchtime, Shelby and I head over to the DSF so that I can not only thank Devlin in person for the roses, but so that I can also find out if he's learned anything about this latest disturbing text.

I hurry into the building, barely pausing to signal to Paul that I'm going to go on up.

He's on the phone, but I see him flash a thumbs-up as I hurry toward the elevator. I press the button to call the car. The indicator lights up, signaling its arrival, and I take an automatic step forward.

Then I stop cold as the doors open with a whisper to reveal none other than Regina Taggart.

"Ellie Holmes, right?" I can practically hear the smile in her voice as she thrusts out her hand in greeting. "Regina Taggart. Reggie. We met yesterday at the Inn."

"Great to see you," I say as we shake. "Are you here to see Devlin?"

Her brow furrows. "Well, he was supposed to be in the meeting—symposium planning—but since he's out of town, it was just me and Tamra."

"Oh. I didn't realize—he's where?"

"Sorry. I just assumed you knew. Anna mentioned you guys are dating. And, honestly, I've seen the pictures," she adds, and I cringe. "I only put it together after you came by the Inn."

"So where is he?"

"Oh, he had to fly to Vegas this morning," she tells me. "Did he know you were coming by?"

I shake my head. "I'm heading to LA today. He must have figured I was already on my way."

"He'll probably be back before you are. For Devlin, popping over to Vegas is nothing."

I nod, my spidey-sense tingling. She still looks so damn familiar, and I can't figure out why.

I only realize that I'm frowning when she says, "Is something wrong?"

"Oh, no, sorry!" My cheeks burn with mortification. "It's just that ever since we met I've been trying to place where I've seen you before. Or someone who looks like you."

The corners of her mouth turn down as she shakes her head. "No idea."

"Were you on Pacific Avenue last night?"

I'm watching her face, and though it's subtle, I'm certain her eyes widen with surprise. "I was, actually. But that can't be why I look familiar. You saw me at the Inn before that."

"I guess I'm just always surprised when I see a familiar face," I lie. "After so many years in Manhattan I forget what a small town this is."

She nods and smiles, and silence hangs awkwardly between us. Then she says, "Well, I should probably get back across the street. I've got two management trainees and no one with any experience on staff." She makes a face. "My right hand took a job in LA. But what can you do?"

With that, she offers me a finger-wiggle kind of wave, then heads across the lobby, her heels—Manolos, this fall's newest style —clicking on the floor. Apparently hotel ownership has a lucrative side. Even with my shoe-groupie ways, I rarely own a designer shoe when it's hot off the runway.

I consider following her out. After all, I only came to see Devlin. But I'm already here, and I really should apologize to Christopher for shooing him away last night. Since he's most likely in the Research Room, I get on the elevator and head to the third floor.

I push through the swinging double doors, then cringe when I hear whispers in this usually silent space. Apparently Christopher's not the only one using the facilities these days.

"Well, I don't know," a woman says in a hushed tone. "Some sort of accident, I'd think."

"Right, right," Christopher says. "But what? Traffic? Swimming? A fire?"

"Christ, how am I supposed to decide?" I recognize Anna's voice now. "That's what you're here for, isn't it?"

I consider staying where I am and eavesdropping. After all, I've never listened in on someone talking through the plot of a thriller novel. But that seems rude and invasive, so I clear my throat and make my way around the corner with an apologetic wave. "Sorry to interrupt."

Christopher nods, looking exactly like I'd imagine a frustrated writer. But Anna jumps about a mile. Her back is to me, and though I assumed that she'd heard me coming, clearly I was wrong.

"Plotting?" I ask as Anna twists to face me. Christopher's working on his second thriller novel, and since the story deals with organized crime and trafficking, the DSF resources are a huge boon. Or so he told me when we first met.

"I needed someone to bounce a plot point off," Christopher says. "And since Anna was here…"

She smirks. "I came in to get a file so I could polish a press release and got roped into doing his work."

"Better her than Brandy," Christopher says. "And if I don't work this out before seeing her tonight, she'll listen to me gripe about story points when we could be—"

"Ah, ah," I say, holding up a hand and trying not to laugh. "That's my best friend you're talking about."

"And my girlfriend," he says, looking very pleased with himself.

"I thought you two were only having drinks," I tease. "But if you're planning to come back to the house instead of going home to write, I can always make myself scarce. I figure I owe you. Sorry about last night. It's just that it was only supposed to be the three of us. Devlin crashed, too."

He nods. "Brandy told me. All the boyfriends got the boot."

I laugh. "Pretty much."

"So what are you doing here?"

"Christopher!" Anna sounds appalled.

Christopher holds up a hand. "All I mean is that Devlin's in Vegas."

"I get it," I say with a laugh. "The truth is, I didn't realize he was out. I was coming by to see him before I head to LA, then thought I'd search you out once I realized I missed him."

Christopher winks at Anna. "She's saying that I was just a second thought."

Anna scoffs. "Better than me. She didn't think of me at all."

"I'm not even going to try to dig my way out of the hole. I'll only make it worse."

They both laugh. "It's all good," Anna says. "At least you came before lunch."

"Why?"

"We're closing at noon," Anna says. "Devlin's orders. There've been some security breaches in Vegas. Minor, but Devlin takes every breach seriously. He's got Ronan heading up a security team on this end so they can make sure all the holes are plugged." She studies my face. "He didn't tell you?"

I shake my head, and Anna shrugs as if it's no big deal.

"Well, why would he?" she asks. "It's not as if you're actually part of the DSF."

I know she doesn't mean it unkindly—and the words are literally true—but I still feel the sting of being an outsider in Devlin Saint's world.

CHAPTER FIFTEEN

I'm stepping off the elevator into the DSF lobby when I see
Tamra Danvers standing by Paul's desk, looking perfectly put-
together in a pale pink suit. She looks up, then smiles widely as
she heads toward me, her three-inch Louboutin heels clicking on
the floor.

"I'm so glad to see you," she says. "Paul said you were in the
building."

"I was in the research room." I tell her, hurrying forward and
accepting her hug. Tamra is the DSF's publicity director, but
I've known her since high school when I was interning for the
police department and she was doing community relations work.
At the time, I didn't realize that she'd maneuvered herself into
that job to keep an eye on Alex, her friend's son. Bottom line,
she's known Devlin longer than I have. And I know she loves
him, too.

"I think Anna's helping him plot his book," I add.

Tamra smiles. "She helps him quite a bit. Maybe we have
another budding author."

"Maybe." I realize I'm grinning, happy to have bumped into
her. "I'm so glad to see you. I had the impression from Reggie that
you were busy."

"Always, but never too busy for you. I'm sorry you missed Devlin. He'll be sorry as well."

"I figure I need to get used to his jet-setting ways. Honestly, considering who he is and what he does, it's a wonder he has any free time at all."

"Things tend to come in spurts," Tamra says. She has dark hair with a single streak of gray, which she tucks behind her ear. "With you in the picture now, I'm sure he'll be more discerning when choosing what projects he'll travel for."

I smile, liking the fact that she so easily sees Devlin and I as a couple. "Reggie said he should be back tonight."

"Oh, good. But I'll move his interview to tomorrow afternoon, just in case."

"Interview? More coverage on the foundation? And my article's not even published yet..." I trail off, pretending to pout.

Tamra laughs. "Would he do that? No, this is a quick interview with one of the LA morning programs. Pre-taped, obviously. He'll talk about the foundation, of course, but mostly it's because of the award." I must look blank, because she continues. "He didn't tell you about the humanitarian award?"

I shake my head.

"Devlin's receiving the World Council Award for Humanitarian Services. It's a very big deal." She looks as proud as if she were his mother.

"This is wonderful," I say, meaning it. "Why on earth hasn't he told me yet?"

The corners of her mouth curve down. "Oh, I didn't mean to spill the beans. He must have been saving the news. The actual ceremony is a few weeks away in New York. I know he's planning to take you. Black tie, the whole nine yards."

"I can't wait," I say, already thinking I'll need Brandy's help picking out a dress. And this definitely calls for a shoe splurge in LA.

"He was joking to me me that you'll be most excited about the chance to buy another pair of designer shoes."

I burst out laughing, my shopping plans still lingering in my mind. "That man knows me too well."

"Well, of course," she says easily. "He loves you."

Shelby is more fun than Lamar's Lexus, so the plan is for me to pick up Lamar and then drive us up to LA. Since I spent less time at the DSF than I'd expected, I consider going back to Brandy's, then decide that I might as well head to Lamar's condo. I don't have a key—it hasn't occurred to me to ask—but the oceanside structure is impressive, with an incredible pool and spa, a full-service restaurant that will deliver to the units, a fine dining restaurant that boasts a celebrity chef, and a coffee shop that makes an amazing latte.

Lamar owns his unit as well as four others that he rents out, all bought and paid for with the money he earned by being a cute kid with acting chops and having powerful parents in the entertainment industry. "I couldn't have become a cop otherwise," he once told me. "I've got expensive taste."

I grab a latte, then take it out to the pool. The deck is built into the cliff, so that the pool itself is infinity style, the water appearing to fall off the edge and into the ocean. I settle at a table in the shade and open my phone, planning to clear out old emails.

Instead, I see last night's text, and the gulp of coffee I just swallowed feels like a stone in my stomach.

I know Devlin's busy, but I want an update, so I text him three question marks.

I don't expect a reply right away, so I'm pleasantly surprised when not only does he respond immediately, but actually calls me.

"Hey," I say. "I know you're busy. I didn't mean to interrupt."

"I've been meaning to call you all morning. I'm in Vegas. Some security issues I need to take care of."

"I heard," I tell him. "I popped by to see you this morning."

"I'm sorry I missed you."

"Me, too," I tell him. "I'm guessing you haven't had time to research last night's text."

"It was my top priority," he tells me, with the kind of ferocity in his voice that assures me that he means it. "But nothing to report. Same situation. Burner phone. Trashcan. Lamar's condo building."

I look around as if in reflex at the same time that I say, "Lamar didn't—"

"I know," he says, and with such certainty it makes me sigh with relief. "But someone wants to shed some doubt."

"They figure I'll choose sides? But why? What's the point?"

"Honestly, I'm not sure what the endgame is," he says. "Other than exposing me. But what do they know? Or think they know? Who my father is?"

"Or what happened with my uncle?"

"Exactly," he says.

I frown, then look around to reassure myself I'm alone on the pool deck. "Should we be talking about this over the phone?"

"It's secure. I've taken precautions."

"Right. Of course you have."

As he chuckles, I sigh. "I want to know who's screwing with us," I say. "And think about the timing of that text. It came right after you delivered the roses. Someone's watching us," I add, as much for myself as Devlin. "It can't be a coincidence."

"They said you were fucking a dangerous man. It's just as easily a general statement."

I hug myself. "I don't like it."

"There's nothing about it to like. But until we know who's doing this, there's not much we can do. Besides," he adds, his voice turning soft, "you already know I'm dangerous. I told you as much myself."

"And you know I get off on danger," I retort, forcing a tease into my voice because I know he wants to lighten the mood. "But that's not the point. What I don't get off on is someone harassing us."

"We'll get to the bottom of this," he says gently.

My thoughts go immediately to Ronan, but I hold my tongue. Devlin said last night that he talked to Ronan and all is well. And because I trust Devlin, I'm going to try to believe that.

Which, unfortunately, leaves my suspect list at exactly zero.

I frown, then turn my attention back to the question that's really on my mind. "When will you be back? Regina said by the end of the day."

"You talked to Reggie?"

"She's the one who told me you were in Vegas."

Vegas.

The word seems to stick in my head, and before he responds, I hear myself saying, *"Oh."*

"What?"

"Vegas," I say. "I think she's familiar because of Vegas."

"Baby, are you being intentionally cryptic or—"

"Sorry. I told you she looked familiar. Now I'm thinking maybe I'm remembering her from Vegas. Was she there when we were?"

For a moment, the line is silent.

"Devlin?"

"Sorry. Someone asked me a question. Honestly, I don't remember. She comes here frequently. She's on the volunteer board for the Phoenix Rehab Center. But I can't recall if she was in town then or not."

"I'll ask the next time I bump into her."

"She looks a little bit like that woman who stars in the new comedy series with the dog," he says. "Those billboards are everywhere."

"Yeah, maybe."

"Does it really matter?"

"Not at all," I admit. "Just one of those things that's bugging me."

"You know what's bugging me?"

I grin. "Tell me."

"Not seeing you until tomorrow."

"So she was wrong?" I hear the disappointment in my voice and wince. I don't want him to feel bad for having to work. "I'm sorry you're stuck there."

"Me too. Things are messier here than I thought. Looks like I'll be working through the night monitoring this bullshit."

"Do you want to talk about it?"

"I don't. I'd rather talk to you. I'd rather be with you."

"Yeah?" I add a sultry note to my voice. "What would we be doing?"

"Would it disappoint you if I said I just wanted to hold you? To take you out to dinner and talk about anything other than your uncle or my foundation or either of our pasts? I want to look to the future with you, El," he continues, his words making my heart swell and my breath catch in my throat. "I want to stand on the beach and look at the stars with the future laid out in front of us and think about all our possibilities. Just that," he says. "Just you."

"Yes," I say, my heart so full I can barely form the words. "I think that sounds wonderful."

CHAPTER SIXTEEN

"W ho are we seeing other than Cotton?" Lamar asks once we're underway.

"Longfeld," I correct. "Cotton was an alias."

"Right."

"The first appointment is with Leon Ortega. He's the guy who fixed up Shelby for Uncle Peter before he gave her to me." My dad had done much of the work, but Shelby had only been Daddy's hobby, and he'd never seemed to finish her.

After he was killed, the car remained on blocks, its interior and exterior only partially restored. I was young enough that it wasn't high on my list of concerns, and mostly forgot about the little car I'd spent so many hours beside during the years when my dad was alive.

It wasn't until I was sixteen—and saw the beautifully restored 1965 Shelby Cobra waiting for me in the driveway on the first day of school—that I truly fell in love. Not only was it an incredibly thoughtful gift from my uncle and guardian, but he'd also finished something my dad had always meant to not only complete, but to give to me when I was old enough.

Except, of course, that *he* hadn't done the restoration. Lacking the skills himself, Peter hired the work out.

"Apparently, he used Ortega for automotive work when he lived in LA, and then after he moved to Laguna Cortez, he drove all that way for the work on Shelby, too."

"Either they're close friends, or Ortega is one hell of a mechanic."

"That's what I figure," I say. "Check the glove box. The plastic folder in there has copies of all of Shelby's papers."

"You keep them with you?"

I shrug. "You never know. Ortega's shop issued most of the invoices. And it might be totally legit, but I'm thinking an auto repair shop is ripe for laundering money and moving stolen parts."

Lamar leafs through the papers, then puts the envelope back in the glove box. "Certainly possible. Got anything more solid than a hunch?"

"Not really. *The Spall* keeps a PI on retainer, so I had him pull a report on Ortega. Clean as a whistle. But that could just mean he's very good at what he does."

"Fair enough."

There are a couple of others on my LA list, and I have Lamar pull my notebook out of my satchel so he can skim through my notes. Most of the folks who were tied into Peter's drug network have already been convicted. I've put in requests at the various prisons for interviews, and now I'm waiting for the authorities to get back to me.

As for the people with whom Peter was doing legitimate business—or supposedly legitimate business—I haven't found too many leads in LA. There's a car wash he invested in, and we'll pop by to talk to the current owner. Same with the family who lived next door to him. You never know what people notice. They're on the way to Ortega's shop in Thousand Oaks, and though I don't have appointments, we're going to stop in unless we're running tight on time.

Other than that, despite scouring my mom's journals for more leads, most of what I know about Peter's less-than-legal business is

tied to Laguna Cortez. Which is why I'm really hoping that
Ortega or Longfeld have a solid lead for me. If I want to learn how
and why Peter got sucked into a criminal life, I need to find the
beginning. And that's somewhere here in LA. I just don't know
where or what.

I am, however, determined to find out.

"These folks—the neighbor, the guy from the car wash—may
not be willing to talk to you. And even though we got lucky with
Tom leading us to Cotton—sorry, Longfeld—the man himself may
be as silent as stone."

"I know. But I have to try."

"Do you?"

I slow as traffic piles up ahead of us, and I use the lull to shoot
him a questioning glance. "What do you mean?" My stomach
twists, and I wonder if now is the time to ask him about what
went on with him and Devlin. I know Devlin thinks they're cool
now, but I want to hear that from Lamar, too.

He adjusts his sunglasses. They're the reflective kind, which
means that even though he's facing me, I can't see his eyes. "I
don't know, Sherlock. It's just—I mean, I get before. You needed
to know your uncle, and you were shocked he was in with The
Wolf. But shock wears off, and that was all such a long time ago."

"He was my last living relative."

"I get that, too. But do you really want to taint all your memories of him? Because you're not alone anymore. You have me. You
have Brandy. And you even have Alex back."

Traffic has started moving again, and I tighten my hands on
the steering wheel and focus on the road. "I don't. I have Devlin."
I swallow, then continue. "And I'm surprised you're counting him
among my assets."

"Oh, hell, Sherlock." He exhales loudly, then tries to lean
back, though he's really too tall to stretch out much.

"Devlin said you guys ended up okay," I say. "Is that how you
see it, too?"

He nods slowly. "Okay? Yeah, I can live with that assessment."

"Even with ... everything?"

"What the hell is everything? All I know for sure is that he used to be Alex and that he had an asshole for a father." He turns and looks hard at me. "Whatever else I might think I know is just supposition. And," he adds, "from a long time ago."

"Right," I say as relief floods my body. "A very long time ago."

"Which takes me back to my point."

I frown as I shift my gaze from the road to him. "What do you mean?"

"Like you said—Alex is gone. Peter is too. You're spending a lot of time looking at the past, but you've got a pretty solid present in front of you. And if you keep searching, I don't think you're going to find anything good."

"Do you think I can't handle it?"

"I think you've handled enough. And you know what else? I bet Devlin agrees with me."

I don't answer because, of course, he's right. We drive for miles, supposedly in silence but it's not quiet to me. My thoughts are humming. Filling my head until I have no choice but to speak. "I need answers," I say. "That's the bottom line. I loved Peter. I mean, I really did. Not more than my parents, but different. My parents were *there*, you know? I never thought about loving them or how it would feel if I lost them. They just ... well, they were just my parents. I wish I'd thought about it more. Appreciated them more. But I didn't."

I draw a breath. "Uncle Peter was different. He wasn't the world's best parental figure, but he was a lifeline. And I thought about him being there every single day because I was terrified that I'd lose him, too."

I lick my lips, but the words keep rushing out. "I knew what I had in him because I'd lost so much, and he was an anchor in a very stormy life. I loved him. I respected him. Hell, I thought he hung the moon. And now I learn he was dirty. And not just a little, but a lot."

"Ellie..."

I keep my eyes on the road as I shrug. "I need answers," I repeat. "That's all. I just need answers."

He says nothing, but I hear acquiescence in the silence. He may not agree, but he understands, and a heavy quiet settles over us as we move inexorably toward Los Angeles.

We make good time, and I navigate us first to the car wash and then to Peter's old house in Beverly Hills. But the car wash has closed down, and though I've left a dozen messages over the past few days, I haven't heard back from either the current or the previous owner. I'm considering that a bust. At least for the time being.

We have more luck with Peter's former neighbors, but only in the sense that they remember him as a great guy who always said hello. Other than that, nothing. Which means Peter wasn't doing anything illegal from his house, or he was doing it very carefully.

We end up back in the car, both of us silent as the miles slide by. It's not until we're almost to Thousand Oaks that I'm tired of my own thoughts and want to lighten the mood. "Are you going to reschedule with Millie? I know she was bummed about not seeing us today."

He tilts his head, using his finger to pull down his glasses as he looks at me. "Are you psychic now?"

"What? I'm right? Have you already texted her? Did you set a date?"

"The opposite," he says. "I thought about it, but then Tracy and I had drinks by the pool last night." He shifts in his seat. "I don't know. I guess I lost my enthusiasm. I mean, Millie's great, but—"

"Well, well. This is interesting."

"Don't make a thing of it."

"How often do you two hang out by the pool?"

He scowls, but I can tell it's only to hide his grin. "Getting more frequent," he admits.

"Go on."

I expect him to protest that there's nothing more to tell, but then he says, "I broke a date with Carlton the other night so that she and I could watch *The Maltese Falcon* at The Prestige."

"I didn't even realize it was showing. Bummer." The local theater shows a few new releases, but mostly it specializes in classics. "Not that I would have crashed your party."

"We both thank you."

"You've seen that movie at least a dozen times."

"True. But she'd never seen it."

"Well, well," I say again. "And as for Carlton, isn't he your—how did you put it? Stress relief hookup? Are you telling me going out with Tracy, ah, relaxed you?"

"On the contrary. When I left her, I was still very tense. I look forward to working on that."

"Wow." I'm grinning as I grip the wheel.

"I know..."

"Me and Devlin. Brandy and Christopher. Now you and Tracy. Our little trio is spreading our wings."

"From what I know about me and Tracy, and what I've gathered about Brandy and Christopher, so far you and Devlin are the only ones doing any wing spreading."

"I'm just lucky that way."

"I wouldn't kick him out of my bed," Lamar says. "Not even when I thought he was a dangerous asshole."

I glow a bit, knowing that the cavalier remark betrays a new acceptance. "So what do you think of Christopher?"

Lamar shrugs. "He's a thriller writer whose hero is a detective. What's not to like?"

"Brandy's certainly happy. And he has the Jake seal of approval," I add, thinking about the way Jake pads after him, begging for head scratches and belly rubs. "So I guess he must be a good guy."

"He's smitten at least."

"Yeah," I agree. "I think it's sweet."

"So do—*shit*. That's the exit. I told you not to let me navigate. *Christ!*"

I cut across three lanes of traffic as Lamar belts out a string of curses.

"Next time I drive," he growls. But I just grin. My blood's pounding, I'm with one of my best friends, and I'm on my way to get answers.

Despite an absentee boyfriend, a bust at our first two stops, and last night's creepy text, I'm actually feeling pretty damn good.

The mechanic who fixed up Shelby, Leon Ortega, still works from the same Thousand Oaks location that's on so many receipts in the glove box. And from the look of the place, he's been at the same location since about the time that Henry Ford rolled out his first vehicle.

"So you're Peter's niece," he says, extending a calloused hand with surprisingly clean fingernails for someone who works all day on vintage cars. "Nice to meet you. Was sorry to hear about your uncle. He was a good man."

"I appreciate that," I say, wondering if he's really as clean as his fingernails, or if he's just managed to keep all his dirty deeds hidden. "To be honest, I was pretty young when he was killed, and now I'm trying to find out more about him."

He looks me up and down. "A little late, aren't you? He's been dead, what? About ten years?"

"About that," I say. "The truth is, I left Laguna Cortez soon after he died, and I've only recently returned. I guess you could say I checked out from my life and never really looked into what happened to him or why."

"I remember when he was shot. Wasn't too long after I'd finished working on your car here." He runs a hand along Shelby's hood "So your uncle was fresh on my mind when I heard the news."

I nod, then realize that I'm hugging myself.

"There was some talk that he'd been involved in some nasty criminal business." He glances at me. "Aw, hell. Did you know that?"

"I did, yes. That's what I'm trying to figure out. How he got wrapped up in all of that."

He frowns, deepening the furrows on his craggy face as he reaches up to rub his silver-gray stubble. "Doubt I can help you there. As far as I could tell, your uncle was a straight arrow."

I shoot a glance toward Lamar, who knows a cue when he sees one. He steps forward, his own hand outstretched. "Detective Lamar Gage," he says. "I'm with the Laguna Cortez PD."

Ortega looks between the two of us. "What's the police department doing looking into a man dead over ten years?"

"I'm not here officially," he says, which is true. But having a real live detective at your side can prompt some people into a nervousness that has them spewing truth left and right. "I'm just helping Ms. Holmes out. It turns out that Peter White got on the wrong side of The Wolf, and she's trying to learn more about that. Are you familiar with that name?"

"Somewhat. A bit off my radar, but now that I think about it, I remember some gossip after Peter was killed. Chatter with a few other customers who knew him. Said he'd gotten mixed up in drugs, prostitution, all that stuff." He shakes his head, looking truly baffled. "Honestly, that doesn't sound like the Peter White I knew."

"Didn't sound like it to me, either," I admit. "Do you have contact information for those customers?"

He shakes his head. "Sorry, not a thing. None of them come around anymore, and all my records from back then got fried when my hard drive did. That was before I backed that stuff up." He looks between Lamar and me. "Not sure what else I can tell you."

"Honestly, I'm not either," I admit. "He used your shop when he lived in LA, right? And he kept coming back to you even after he moved to Laguna Cortez?"

"Yeah, yeah. I restored an E-Type Jag for him and a sweet little '67 Corvette when he lived in LA. He didn't much work on cars, but he loved driving them. He had a few others he bought in decent condition. I didn't restore those, but I'd do regular maintenance. Always wondered how he got the money to buy what he did, but I figured construction was the business to be in. LA's always been a boomtown, right?"

"Pretty much," I agree. "Do you know if he sold those cars? I only remember a Suburban he used to haul stuff and a Mustang convertible. But it wasn't a classic." I wonder what happened to his other cars. Was it a hobby he abandoned? Or maybe he'd used refurbished cars in a money-laundering scheme that he stopped when he moved in with my dad?

I frown, not liking the fact that I'm coloring my uncle with illegal motives surrounding everything now.

"Don't know what he did with them, honestly. Never came up in conversation."

"What about after he moved to Orange County? Did he come back up here regularly after he moved? Or did he only come for work on the Shelby Cobra?"

"Couldn't say whether he came into LA other times," Ortega says. "But he didn't come see me unless it was about your car."

I glance at Lamar, who tilts his head in sympathy. This trail is going nowhere. And because of that, I decide to cut straight to the chase. "Listen, and, please don't take this the wrong way, but I was kind of hoping that he'd asked you to help out on the seedier side of his business. Like moving parts or laundering money."

"And that's not why we're here," Lamar says. "Whatever you tell us is off the record. I'm not going to breathe a word."

"Well, now, I don't know if I believe you or not about that, Detective. But it doesn't much matter because he never asked me to do anything like that. I wouldn't have, anyway. My pa and grandpa both worked in private security. And my great-grandpa was a Pinkerton agent."

I meet Lamar's eyes. A cop family doesn't guarantee someone's clean, but it sure doesn't hurt.

"Your uncle knew all that." Ortega grins. "Maybe that's why he never asked me. Probably knew he'd have to find another mechanic if I knew what kind of mischief he was involved in."

Once again, he strokes Shelby's hood. "You've done a good job keeping her up," he says. He gives me a nod as if we've known each other forever, and he's as proud of me as he would be his own daughter. "Glad you brought her by. It's always good to see one of my cars again."

"My pleasure. I'm glad you remember her." I glance at Lamar, at a loss for anything else to ask.

"Did you ever notice anything unusual?" he puts in. "Did Peter ever bring anybody with him who seemed shady?"

"Shady? No. I can't say I approved of his girlfriend—can't blame a man for dating a younger woman, but it never made much sense to me. Rather have a woman I can talk to. But I'm not sure I need to get into that kind of gossip with his niece."

For the first time, I realize that I rarely saw Peter date—just a few women he'd take to dinner now and then. And as far as I know, he was never married.

"Can you describe her?" Lamar asks.

"She came in with him twice, both times when he was coming to check on this Shelby Cobra. Young woman, blond and blue-eyed, very pretty." He grins. "I remember wondering if she was old enough to drink."

"That young?" I repeat, thinking that this girl couldn't have been much older than me. And now that Mr. Ortega has brought it up, I do have a vague recollection of seeing Uncle Peter once or twice with a blonde not that much older than Alex.

I'd been walking along the beach one time and had arrived home earlier than Uncle Peter expected me. I'd cut my foot on a broken shell, and I'd wanted to get home to disinfect it.

I didn't get a good glimpse of her, but she was standing on the back porch in a bikini top with a sheer sarong tied around her hips. She wore a floppy straw hat that shaded her face, but there was a blond ponytail. I could tell from her figure that she was older than me, but still young. I even wondered for a bit if she was there to see Alex, and I remember feeling queasy at the possibility that he was seeing someone else in addition to our secret romance.

By the time I got closer to the house, she was gone. When I asked Uncle Peter about her, he said she was a neighbor who had come by on some local business matter. I hadn't been interested enough to inquire further.

"Do you know her name?"

"Sorry. Not a clue," Mr. Ortega says with a regretful shake of his head.

Both Lamar and I ask him a few more questions, trying to jog his memory about any identifying detail, but he can't remember a thing.

Which means that as we climb back into Shelby and start toward Panorama City and Mr. Longfeld, I have one more question about Peter, and not a single answer.

CHAPTER SEVENTEEN

"I meant to tell you on the drive up," Lamar says as we wipe down the outdoor table where we'd each enjoyed a giant burrito from a local dive that Mr. Ortega recommended. Not exactly the fancy lunch that Lamar had wanted *The Spall* to pay for, but we were both starving. And depending on when we finish, maybe *The Spall* can buy us drinks at a nice hotel while we wait for the traffic to clear out. "I did some poking around about Ronan."

I toss a balled up napkin in the trash and turn back to him. "Did you find out anything?"

"Does Devlin know you're looking?"

I cock my head and shoot him a look, then head to Shelby. I wait until I'm behind the wheel and he's in the passenger seat before answering. "Devlin knows I have concerns," I say diplomatically. I start the car, then maneuver my way onto the street before glancing at Lamar. "He doesn't share them."

"Great. The guy and I have a shaky detente, and you have me sniffing around looking for dirt about his buddy."

I shrug, feeling a bit guilty. But not so much that I don't want the information. "I won't ask you for more, but you already did the poking. You might as well tell me what you learned. And where are we going? Can you map the way to Longfeld's job?"

He grabs my phone from where it's mounted to the dash, and I give him the code to unlock it. "The address is in the notes app."

He taps my phone, then navigates us back to the 101, where we'll stay for at least half an hour before changing to the 405. "He was in sniper school with Alejandro Lopez," Lamar tells me, once I'm in the far left lane. "So I'm assuming that's where they met."

I nod. "Devlin told me as much. The military."

"It gets interesting because Alejandro was discharged 'at the convenience of the government' after only two years of service." He makes air quotes as he talks. "Did you know that?"

"No," I admit. "But I don't think he's keeping it a secret. We just haven't really talked about his time in the service. What does that even mean?"

"I had to spend some time figuring that out. Apparently it can mean anything the government wants it to. Sometimes it's used when a soldier needs an out because of family issues. Sometimes it's used when someone's been recruited into intelligence services. Considering the timing, I think Alex—Alejandro—just wanted to disappear."

"The timing," I repeat. "What do you mean?"

"That was right about the time Daniel Lopez was killed. Devlin told me he made it a point of abandoning Alex and becoming Devlin then. As the heir apparent, Alex would have been in the crosshairs."

I glance sideways at him. "I thought you were poking around about *Ronan.*"

"I'm getting there. They're tied together, right?"

"Fine, fine. What have you got?"

"So about the time that Alejandro was magically dismissed, Devlin Saint shows up. Records show he signed up at seventeen, moved through the ranks, and ended up in special forces. Now we know some of that has to have been manufactured, but about the same time, Ronan Thorne transfers into the same unit. And after that, suddenly I can't find shit on either one of them."

"They must have ended up doing intelligence work." It's a guess, but I figure it's a good one. Devlin, of course, can tell me if I'm right.

"So that's what I know," Lamar says. "What I can assume is that if Ronan was special forces, he has bad ass skills. And that makes him dangerous. Which is great if he's fighting the enemy. Not so great if he thinks the enemy is you."

"Devlin's convinced that Ronan's about as much of a threat to me as you are."

Lamar makes a snorting noise. "Wish I could say I agree, but for me, the jury's still out."

I drive in silence for a while, letting it settle around me. "I trust Devlin," I finally say, my voice low. "I don't like being cross-ways with him." I glance sideways at Lamar. "We've come so far, and we're back on track. Thinking that Ronan may be the one harassing me—I don't know. It's starting to feel disloyal."

Beside me, Lamar shifts in his seat. "You're going soft, Sherlock."

I stiffen, because that is *not* how I want to be thought of. But then I relax, because it's not true. Not about everything, anyway. But where Devlin is concerned?

"Yeah," I whisper, with just the hint of a smile. "I think maybe I am."

Harold Longfeld, the former owner of Cotton Building Supply, lives in a studio apartment that used to be a storage shed behind the tiny grocery store where he works as a stock clerk. It has one window and a chemical toilet, and after taking three breaths, I suggest that Lamar and I buy him a cup of coffee at the diner we saw one block over.

He counters with a whiskey at the bar two doors down, and we readily agree.

"Vile, I know," he says once we're settled at a small table. "Where I'm living, I mean. But I deserve it. Life I led..." He trails off with a shake of his head. "I never wanted to hurt that woman, but what I did—running her down, taking her from her family—that changed me."

"I imagine it would," I say softly. I expect him to order coffee, considering he's talking about the woman he killed while driving under the influence, but he orders a whiskey. Under the circumstances, I order a Diet Coke. Lamar, who I'm sure is thinking about bonding with the guy, gets a beer.

Lamar pulled the information on Longfeld for me, and I skimmed over it yesterday, but there wasn't much there that I didn't already know. Longfeld had been charged with various financial crimes, but they hadn't stuck. Then he'd killed a woman, and everything changed for him. He'd regretted her death, but even more, he'd regretted the life he'd led before.

According to a memo Lamar found from the Parole Board, he'd started going to the religious services offered to inmates. And not, according to the board member, simply because that meant a weekly change of scenery in the chapel. Apparently Mr. Longfeld had become a believer, even going so far as to teach Sunday school classes to the other inmates, along with remedial reading and math.

There'd been no mention of my uncle in the file, and Lamar said he'd dug around in the evidence room and found nothing there, either.

But if Peter was as deep with The Wolf as we think he was, then surely I can track down some sort of proof that Peter was dirty. I know it's probably wishful thinking, but I have a feeling that Longfeld was dialed in. And that maybe, just maybe, his remorse and new perspective will push him to reveal whatever secrets he might hold.

I take a sip of my soda, then offer him what I hope is a

friendly smile. "I appreciate you talking to me. I told you I'm writing an article about Peter, but it's not a typical news story. He was my uncle, and I want to dig deep into how he got involved in crime. Unlike you, I'm not sure he ever felt bad about what he did. Maybe he would have gotten there eventually, but we'll never know. Can you tell me? Did you know he worked for the Wolf? Do you know anything about how he got involved with that world?"

"I know he sat at The Wolf's right hand," Longfeld says, and I try very hard not to react even though I'm positively giddy at having tracked down a solid source. "Told me they'd been friends for years. Never told me he was screwing Lopez—and thank God for that. I wouldn't have wanted to hear him say it. That would have put a target on my back. Me knowing it was dangerous enough."

"How did you know if he didn't tell you?"

Longfeld scoffs. "I was laundering hundreds of thousands for your uncle. That's not a mindless job. I knew what I was doing. Where the money was coming from, and where it was going to." He lifts his glass, signaling the waiter to bring another, then downs the watery dregs. "You're not gonna like what I have to say, but you asked, and I don't see no reason not to tell. You good with that?"

I glance at Lamar and find support in his eyes. Then I nod. "Yeah," I say. "It's all good."

"Your uncle liked what he did. He liked the danger of it. Daniel Lopez was his friend, sure, but Peter liked pulling something over on him. He liked looking at the devil and thinking he'd won."

My mouth goes dry and my hands are tight on my glass. So tight I have to make a conscious effort to loosen my grip or else risk shattering the glass. *He's describing me.* Not the illegal stuff, of course. But the dance with the devil. That thrill that comes from doing something dangerous and surviving.

I'd always thought it was survivor's guilt, and considering the life I've led and everyone I've lost, that makes sense. But now I wonder if part of it's in my blood, too. If there's a bit of Peter in me. More than simply the familial line, but some real shadow of the man he was.

Considering everything I'm learning about him, I'm not sure I like that possibility.

I do my best to mask my feelings, and since Longfeld keeps on talking, I guess I'm doing a reasonably good job. Lamar, however, knows me well, and when he presses his large hand against my middle back, I say a silent thank you to the universe for finding me such a good friend.

"As for your uncle not having the chance to make my choices," Longfeld says, "I gotta say you're wrong there."

I shake my head, frowning. "I'm sorry. I don't know what you mean?"

"To repent. He had the chance years before he was killed. But he didn't do a damn thing different."

My brow furrows in confusion. "What are you talking about?"

"Your mom." His voice is flat and even, and my stomach twists in anticipation of his words. "Peter stole from The Wolf, and The Wolf gave him a warning. Do it again, and Peter would pay the price." His shoulders sagged. "He paid, all right."

I glance at Lamar, who looks as befuddled as me. "I don't understand. How did he pay?"

Longfeld's eyes meet mine. "You really don't know? The Wolf had your mom killed in retaliation."

CHAPTER EIGHTEEN

I'm too numb, so Lamar takes Shelby's wheel on the way home.
I close my eyes and lean back, snuggling into the leather
seat as I let my thoughts drift over me in some perverse form of
meditation. Except that's the wrong word, because meditation
suggests peace and calm. There's nothing peaceful about the way
I feel.

On the contrary, I'm shell-shocked. Raw and empty and
ripped apart from the inside out. And as the traffic sounds whip
by us, I get lost in my own storm of emotions, everything from
anger to loss to betrayal. And, yes, to love. Because that's the worst
of it, isn't it? The fact that I'd loved my uncle, really and truly
loved him. And yet he did this. He'd put one foot in front of the
other, knowing perfectly well that the path he was walking would
end with my mother in a coffin.

Maybe he hadn't actually done it to me—hell, odds were he
hadn't even thought of me. For that matter, he probably hadn't
even thought of my mother.

But wasn't that the point? He'd thought only of himself, and
in doing so, he'd left a trail of destruction behind him. A trail that
culminated now in my broken heart.

There's a wreck on the 5 and traffic is a nightmare, which just adds to my malaise. I try to sleep in the car, and maybe I even succeed a little. But I don't think so, because the reason I wanted to sleep was so that when I woke up it would all be over, and I'd be left with nothing more than a bad dream.

But that's not the case. When we get to Laguna Cortez, everything is as real as it was when we left Los Angeles. And though I smile at Lamar and thank him for driving and let him put an arm around my shoulder as he leads me to the door, I know that he can see the pain as well.

And that he feels as helpless to fix me as I do.

"I'm okay," I lie when we reach the front door. "Really."

"I'm sure you are, but that doesn't mean I'm leaving you alone until you're settled inside." He presses a gentle kiss to my forehead, then releases me and punches Brandy's code into the keypad. I hear the familiar whirr of the lock, then the scrape of the hinges as he pushes the door open. Such familiar sounds in a world that doesn't seem familiar anymore.

He reaches for my hand, as if he's leading a child over the threshold. That's how I feel, too. Young and unsure and scared and lost. I don't like feeling this way. It doesn't seem like me, and yet maybe it is. Maybe I've finally reached that point where all the shit in my life bearing down is too much. Maybe it's finally broken me.

"I'm really okay," I lie again. He's my best friend, but I wish he'd go. All I want to do is curl up in a ball.

Except even that's not true. What I really want to do is curl up next to Devlin, letting him hold me while I sleep. Because if I can do that, maybe I'll wake up stronger simply by virtue of having him near.

But he's in another state, and while I love Lamar, it's not the same.

I manage a smile, and I'm about to kiss his cheek and push him out the door when I see a shadow move across the floor of the entryway. I freeze, because I didn't realize anyone else was home, then cry out in relief when I see that it's Devlin.

I don't realize I'm moving until I'm in his arms and he's holding me. It's only then that the dam breaks, and before I know it, tears are streaming down my cheeks and I'm clinging to him as he holds me tight. For a moment we stay like that, clutching each other in the hallway, with him whispering soothing things to me. Finally, I manage to gather myself, and I pull away enough to see his face. "How? You're supposed to be in Vegas. How are you here?"

"Lamar texted. Said I needed to be here when you got back. He said you needed me."

I turn, my eyes searching out Lamar who's standing in the entryway, the door now closed behind him. He lifts a shoulder in a shrug. "I wasn't wrong."

I mouth *thank you.*

"You flew back," I say to Devlin. "For me."

"Oh, baby, what else would you expect? Do you want to tell me what happened?"

With that, the tears start up again, simply from the knowledge that he came only because I needed him.

I bury my face against his chest again, and I'm clinging to him when I hear the door open once again at the same time that Brandy says, "—and when he went into the surf, I just about lost—Hello? What's going on?"

Immediately, Jake leaves Brandy and Christopher to bound forward and snuffle my rear. Despite everything, I laugh, then reach down to stroke his head.

"It's okay," Lamar says to the room in general. "I'll talk to you soon, Sherlock."

I nod, and then blow him a kiss.

He grins, holds my gaze for a moment, then turns to leave, his fingers brushing Brandy's shoulder as if to say that he'll fill her in later.

Brandy, of course, isn't willing to wait. She looks from me to Devlin. "What happened?"

"I had a shitty day," I say. "Lamar was sweet and told Devlin to meet me here."

I watch as Christopher tugs Brandy's hand before she can ask another question. "You know what I was thinking?" Before Brandy can answer, he continues. "I was thinking that it would be really fun to go to that movie theater on Pacific. What's it called? The Prestige? Go see a classic movie. Wouldn't that be a blast?"

It's clear from Brandy's face that she thinks that's about the weirdest request ever. But then she looks at me, and I see realization in her eyes. She turns to Christopher and gives him a bright smile and a quick nod. "That is a totally terrific idea. I wonder what's showing."

"Doesn't matter. Whatever it is, I'm sure we'll like it. There's got to be something starting soon, right? If not, we'll grab a bite first."

"*The Maltese Falcon*," I say, remembering Lamar's date with Tracy.

"A good movie," Devlin says. "And, guys? Thanks."

"Not to worry," Brandy says. "And we'll get drinks after the movie, so don't expect to see me back until at least one or two. Right?"

Beside her Christopher nods as Brandy gives me a supportive hug. I know it costs her something not to ask me for more details about what's going on. But I also can't deny that I'm glad she's leaving. Right now, I want only Devlin, and the fact that Brandy understands that is another reason why she's my bestie.

"Cocoa?" Devlin asks as the door closes behind them.

"What?"

"It's one of my quirks," he confesses. "When I've had a shitty day, I like to drink cocoa."

I feel the smile tug at my mouth. "In that case, by all means." He takes my hand and starts to settle me on the sofa that's a few feet away from where the kitchen opens into the living room. I shake my head, wanting to be able to see him and talk to him. So I shift our trajectory toward the kitchen island's bar. Then I settle on a stool and watch as he goes into the kitchen and starts to open and close all of Brandy's cabinets and drawers, finally ending up standing in the pantry looking more than a little befuddled.

"You don't look like you do this very often."

"*Au contraire*. I'm a man of many skills. This, however, isn't my pantry. And despite the fact that your roommate makes damn good muffins, she apparently isn't a connoisseur of fine cocoa. She does however have little paper packets. He pulls out a brand of powdered cocoa mix and shakes it. "Remind me to give her hell for this," he says. "I mean, fake marshmallows? That's just wrong."

Now my smile bubbles out into a laugh, and right then, I'm so damn grateful to Lamar for having sent for Devlin that I'm almost on the verge of tears again. I look down, not wanting him to worry about what are actually happy tears, and only look back up when I'm sure I have myself under control.

He's staring at me, his brow knit with concern.

"It's all good," I assure him. "I'm laughing at this unexpected domesticity."

"I'm a man of mystery."

I make a scoffing noise. "Yes. You are definitely that." I sit comfortably and watch him fill the kettle and heat the water, and then, with more aplomb than the making of powdered cocoa requires, he pours it into one of the fancy china cups he finds in the cabinet above the refrigerator.

He gently plates it on the matching saucer, then opens a box of Oreos and puts two beside the cup. "Is there anything else madam requires?"

My lips twitch, but I answer serenely. "No, thank you. That will be all."

"Then I'll leave you to it." He starts to turn away.

"Don't you dare go. Aren't you having cocoa too?"

"As m'lady wishes." He makes himself a cup with the still-hot water and comes to sit beside me at the bar. "Would you rather go to the sofa?"

I shake my head. "No. I like it here. This is where I sit when Brandy and I talk. It feels..." I trail off not sure what the word is. Not domestic? Homey? That's not what I mean either. "Right," I finally say with a shrug. "I guess it feels right."

He reaches over and brushes his thumb over my cheek. "As far as I'm concerned, baby, everything feels right when I'm with you."

I don't realize that I've started to shed tears until I taste the saltiness with my cocoa. "Thank you for turning around a really shitty day."

"Do you want me to ask what happened?"

I blink. "Lamar didn't tell you?"

"Only that you needed me. Do you want to talk about it?"

"Part of me does, and part of me doesn't." I take a sip of cocoa to give me time to think. "But you came all this way, you deserve to know."

"No, that's entirely up to you. You can tell me when you're ready, or never."

I take a sip of cocoa, then nibble at the Oreo, not breaking it apart because to me that just seems wrong. Why invent a sandwich cookie if they want people to take them apart? It's not like I take apart tuna fish sandwiches. Or peanut butter. The whole thing reeks of strangeness.

I tell that to Devlin, who nods with exactly the right amount of gravity. "Even so," he says, then proceeds to take apart his cookie and scrape off the frosting with his teeth.

"And here I thought I respected you," I say sadly, before taking a full, proper bite of my Oreo. Crumbs fall into my lap, and I wipe them off, then take another sip of cocoa.

I'm stalling, of course, but it's a nice kind of interlude. And when Devlin reaches over and takes my hand, it's as if he's turned a key inside me. I'm ready to talk now, but only so long as he's touching me. Sharing his strength with me.

He might as well have opened a floodgate. I start slow, but

soon the whole story pours out. About the threat to my mother, and how Uncle Peter didn't do a thing about it.

"He knew that if he didn't make it right with your father, that my mother would pay. He knew, he absolutely, one hundred percent knew, but he did it anyway. He loved that life—he loved taking those risks even more than he loved his sister. I don't understand how that's possible. And why did your father let him live afterwards? Peter stole from The Wolf, and yet he survived to do it all over again years later in Laguna Cortez. It doesn't make any sense. I don't know what he was thinking."

Devlin's face has gone completely pale. "Christ." He shakes his head. "I don't have answers for you, baby. Not really. As for why, my guess is that Peter didn't believe it. He loved your mom, and he was the kind of guy who got away with things. He had an inflated sense of his own importance, and he probably assumed he was enough of a friend to my father that he wouldn't get punished."

Devlin shrugs before continuing. "I think they were friends. But he wasn't punished by Daniel Lopez. He was punished by The Wolf. And most people in the fold—even those closest to him —never fully understood the difference."

"Not Uncle Peter," I protest. "He knew the score. He knew what The Wolf did to your mom, didn't he? Which means he knew The Wolf would hurt my mom, too, and he let it happen."

"I don't have an answer for you. Maybe he thought it was a risk that he could afford to take."

"That's the crux of it though, isn't it? He was willing to put the people he loved in danger so that he could take a risk." I take a sip of cocoa, wanting its comforting warmth, but it's already too cool. "That's what I want to understand. I want to figure out what made him that way. What changed him. And right now I'm so damn frustrated because I honestly don't have a clue."

I drag my fingers through my hair then wipe my damp eyes. "I don't know how to do this. I don't know what to do. What to feel. I want to hate him, but I can't. I remember him more than I remember her. I thought he was taking care of me because he loved me. But the truth is he felt guilty."

Devlin reaches out and takes a firm hold of both my hands. "He loved you."

I lift my head and meet his eyes. "Did you know?"

"That he loved you?"

I shake my head. "About my mother."

Devlin's eyes go wide as he slowly shakes his head. "No. I swear on my own mother's grave, I had no idea."

I nod, glad he hadn't been burdened with that truth. "Longfeld said Peter got off on the thrill. Thought that if he survived it meant that nothing could hurt him and so he was always flirting with danger. But in the end he got burned big time, didn't he?"

Devlin doesn't answer right away. Instead he studies my face, the silence lingering for so long that I start to squirm under his heavy gaze. Finally, he says, "You're not like him, El."

I make a scoffing sound, both hating and relishing how well this man can read me.

"People have facets. You can still love him, El. It's allowed. And you can hate him too, for what he did. Whatever you're feeling, give yourself permission to simply feel it."

"Is it horrible that right now, all I want to do is sleep?"

A sad smile touches his lips as he slides off the stool then reaches for me. He helps me down, then immediately picks me up, cradling me in his arms as he carries me to bed. He helps me out of my clothes, and I slide in naked between the sheets. It's only early evening, but I can already feel the pull of exhaustion drawing me down towards sleep. "Will you hold me?"

"You don't even have to ask."

He strips and gets in bed beside me. I move closer, craving the feel of his warm skin against mine. His arms go around me, and I close my eyes, letting the world fall away until the only thing keeping me tethered to this earth is his touch as I float free in memories, losing myself in the recollections of my mother, of Peter, of Alex...

I'm safe in this place where dreams meet memories, where Alex and my mother share the same patio looking out toward the ocean. Where I can stand between them, holding each of their hands in mine.

Then I realize I'm holding nothing at all. I'm standing on the beach with my arms outstretched and my eyes closed as I listen to waves crash against the shore.

I hear someone behind me, and I turn to face Peter, my heart skipping a beat when I realize that I'm looking not only at him, but right down the barrel of a gun.

My heart begins to pound. I want to scream, I can't. The pulse in my throat is too powerful.

I hear a click, but Peter's hand hasn't moved, and no bullet has been fired.

Terrified, I whirl around to see Devlin.

He's just cocked the hammer of a revolver.

And as I stare—as I scream—he fires.

CHAPTER NINETEEN

"El! El! Ellie! Baby, come on wake up!"

Devlin's voice pounds against me through the bitter haze of sleep, and I fight my way up through the fog, forcing my eyes to open and my body to stop screaming with the reverberation of the gunshot. I'm breathing hard when his face comes into focus. His eyes on mine, his brow furrowed, worry painted all across his face. He strokes my cheek and pulls me close and kisses my forehead, murmuring, "Hush, hush, baby. I'm here. It's okay, it's okay."

"Oh, God, I'm sorry." I cling to him, still trying to catch my breath, my pulse pounding in my ears. "Nightmare."

"Do you want to talk about it?"

I shift, trying to gather the lingering threads of the dream as I sit up in bed, pulling the sheet up and hugging it around me like a security blanket. "I was with Uncle Peter," I begin, then tell him the dream. Tears prick my eyes as I finish. "You killed Peter to save me," I say, as Devlin moves even closer, his nearness both comforting and sweetly enticing. He takes my hand, his thumb rubbing the tender skin at my wrist.

"You killed Peter to protect me," I say again. "That took courage."

"Courage is easy in a dream."

I laugh. There's no denying that's true. Even so...

I meet his eyes. "It wasn't only in a dream, though." A fist seems to tighten around my heart. "I came back to you because I need you. Because I forgave you. But I'm not sure I truly understood what you went through for me until now." I press my hand against his jaw, then lightly stroke my thumb over his lip. "What you did—Uncle Peter, I mean—that took courage."

When he starts to shake his head, I shift my position so that I can hold his head in place as I look into his eyes. "You told Brandy and Lamar the truth, too. That took courage as well."

"Technically, *you* told them the truth. And neither one of us told Lamar the full truth."

I lift a shoulder. "Yeah, well, he's smart. I think part of me knew he'd figure it out. And don't split hairs. You made the decision to bring them into our circle. I'm saying thank you."

"It's easy to be courageous if you have a reason."

"Me?"

"What else? *Who* else?"

The intensity of the statement acts like a charge on my senses, and I ease closer, wanting —no, *needing*—to touch him. The sheet has fallen, and we're both naked. My pulse speeds up and my nipples tighten as I brush a kiss over his lips, craving skin on skin, body on body.

But when I pull back to look in his eyes, I see not only a desire that rivals my own, but hesitation as well. "What is it?" I ask, confused and a little disappointed.

He glances away. "When you called out for me in your dream, you called me Devlin."

I shake my head, not sure what's remarkable about that.

"Uncle Peter was in the dream. When you knew me alongside Peter, I was Alex. Was I Devlin in the dream?"

It's already fading in the way that dreams do, and I try to grasp the threads of it, try to pull it back and take a closer look at the dream in my memory. "I think so. I don't know. But if that's what I said, then you must have been. Does it matter?"

He shrugs, almost boyish, and doesn't answer.

For a moment, I'm confused, and then understanding dawns. He's unsure. He's still not certain if I'm with him because of my lingering love for Alex or if I've truly accepted this new man—Devlin—in all of his facets. "You're crazy, you know that?"

"Do I?"

"I loved Alex," I say, untangling myself from the sheet and settling myself on his lap. The sheet is still a barrier—he'd tugged it to his hips as he'd slid up in the bed—but I can feel his erection teasing my core all the same. I can feel the tension in his body, too. It's costing him to hold back. To not take me as he wants to, claiming my body until he's conquered the nightmare for me. And this moment—this insight into the vulnerability of the man I love—makes my heart swell.

"I love you," I say, wishing there was an even bigger, more encompassing word. "You're the same as the Alex you were, but you're different, too, and there's room in my heart for both versions."

Gently, his hands rest on my waist. "I hope that's true," he says, and there's a harshness to his voice that I'm not expecting in such a tender moment.

I reach out and tuck a lock of his chin-length hair behind his ear. "Devlin? Tell me what's going on."

"That's the issue, isn't it? You don't really know the new me. Not completely. And honestly? I'm not sure you ever will."

His words chill me, but I do my best not to show it. "Well, that's true with anybody, isn't it? You can never know anyone completely." I press my hand to his chest, savoring the warmth of his skin. "But I know your heart. I know the core of you. Don't I?"

He meets my eyes and nods. One single tilt of his head. "Yes. You do."

I lean forward, resting my forehead against his as he strokes my back. I don't doubt that he loves me, but I also know that we're still finding our way together, like a toddler trying to walk. Our romance when we'd been Alex and Ellie had been like a bright flame, a Romeo and Juliet love that had ended appropriately in tragedy.

Now we're having to work through the remnants of that, but we still click, maybe even more than we did back then. But that doesn't mean it's not terrifying, and it doesn't mean we both don't know the real truth—everything ends. Nothing is permanent. And though I want to believe that we will be together forever, I know the dream can be ripped away from us in a heartbeat.

He knows that as well as I do, and I wonder if that's why he hasn't yet said he loves me. Not out loud. Not like Alex did.

He calls me El, yes, and I take comfort in that, but he's never spoken those simple words. I know he loves me—hell, even Tamra says he does. But I still long for the words. And I think that until I hear them, I'm going to keep protecting my heart, just a little, even when he's holding me close.

With a sigh, I force these melancholy thoughts away. I sit up straight again, the movement reminding me that he's naked beneath that sheet. Warmth floods my body, a sensual hunger, and I consider abandoning my question in favor of simply kissing him and letting us both get lost in oblivion. It's so tempting, and yet at the same time, I want more than physical closeness. I want to peer into the places that Devlin keeps hidden. I know that maybe he won't ever let me in, and I'll deal with that when I have to. Now, though, I'm going to keep knocking at that door.

I draw a breath. "Can I ask you something?"

"Of course," he says.

"What if we'd never found each other again? Would our time together as Alex and Ellie still have been worth it to you?"

I both see and feel his body go tense, and I know he's trying to discern the dark hole in my mind from which I pulled the question.

"How can you doubt that?"

"It's just a question," I say, trying to be casual.

I keep my eyes on his, as if I can see the answer before he speaks. But there are no clues in those sandy irises. Not until he says, "I'll tell you a secret—I prefer the woman who's with me now. She's all grown up and she's a force to be reckoned with."

Tears prick my eyes as he continues. "The Ellie I fell in love with as Alex was still a child in so many ways. I loved her, yes, but we were both too young to know what that meant. Now, we know what we have in each other, and I know what it is that I want to protect."

"Devlin—"

He presses a fingertip to my lips and doesn't miss a beat. "But I keep the El from my past locked in my heart, where she'll stay for my lifetime. Hell, she's the reason the foundation is here, she's the reason..."

"What?" I ask, my throat thick with tears.

"She's—*you're*—the reason I try to be a better man."

"What do you mean? You're about as good as they come. You're even getting an award for it in a few weeks." I add a teasing grin, deliberately trying to lighten this moment that is tugging so hard at my heart.

"You've heard about that?"

"Tamra told me." I lean forward and brush a kiss over his lips, full of pride in this man. "The World Council Award for Humanitarian Services. You deserve it."

"There are a lot of people who deserve it. They named me, but everyone at the DSF has a piece of that award."

"They do," I say. "And I'm still very impressed." I flash a flirty grin. "I might even want to be your groupie."

His lips twitch, and I can't help myself as I reach up to run my finger over the scar that bisects his upper lip. "Is that so?" he asks.

"Would I lie?"

He tilts his head, studying me, and I feel the subtle shift in the air, as if the electrons surrounding us have begun spinning faster, generating heat and creating a force that is leading us inexorably toward each other. Gone is my awe at his sweet words. Gone is the teasing. It's stripped away, leaving me and Devlin and the need laid bare between us.

"I don't want a groupie," he says as his hands lightly stroke my skin from the curve of my ass up the small of my back.

"Then what do you want?" My voice is husky, and it's taking all my willpower not to undulate my hips, rubbing myself over the sheet and the steel of his erection beneath.

"I want you," he says, making my core throb in anticipation. "I want to taste you. To sink inside you. I want you on your back beneath me, and, dammit, El, I want to know you're mine."

"Don't you already?"

"I know it," he says. "Now, I want to feel it."

"Yes," I whisper, my body craving him already, my skin alive with the anticipation of his touch. His hands go to my shoulders, and he easily shifts me onto my back. As he does, he throws the sheet aside, leaving us both naked, our skin bathed in the soft light through the window.

His knees are on either side of my hips and he casually strokes his cock as his eyes lock on mine. There's an eternity of desire in his eyes, and all I can think is *forever*. That no matter what, I will always belong to this man. I've been marked by him. Claimed by him. And as I feel that deep tremor of need, I know that what I want more than anything is to be touched by him. Used. Claimed. *Taken*.

I want everything. Soft and sweet. Hard and masterful. I want everything he has to give, and I would willingly spend my entire life in this bed to achieve that goal.

"You're smiling."

"I'm thinking of everything I want you to do to me," I admit. "I'm having some very naughty thoughts."

His brow rises. "Are you? Interesting." Slowly, he trails his eyes over me, his gaze lingering on my lips, my breasts. "Baby, you're so beautiful. Close your eyes."

I obey, then arch up in response to his hands on my breasts. He's bent forward, and I can feel his erection against my belly, teasing me as his palms slowly stroke me and his fingers tease my nipples, gently at first, and then harder until I'm biting my lower lip and my pussy is throbbing, the hot wire of sweet pain shooting from my nipple all the way down to my core.

"You like that." It's not a question. He knows me, after all. "Keep your eyes closed."

I do, and he shifts again. Now, his cock is between my legs, and I whimper, wanting him inside me, not teasing my clit and sensitive folds. I want him to fill me, and I'm about to beg when his mouth closes over my breast and he sucks, his teeth scraping my skin as his hand closes over my other breast while his free hand finds my mouth.

I draw him in, sucking on his thumb as if I was giving him head, gratified when I hear him moan. I want him to feel the way I do, as if every wondrous sensation is here for our enjoyment. As if we're the only two people in the world and we've inherited all the pleasure in it.

I cry out as he nips at my breast, my teeth scraping over his thumb as he slides down my body, his whiskers rough against my skin as he kisses his way down my belly. My cries turn to desperate whimpers as he reaches my mons, then uses the tip of his tongue to tease my clit mercilessly. I try to wriggle my hips. Try to buck against him. Try to move in a way that insists his tongue works harder, faster, deeper.

But I can't do anything. His hands on my hips have pinioned me to the bed, and I'm completely at his mercy as he sucks and laves my sensitive clit, taking me higher and higher, but never quite letting me go over.

"Please." I'm reduced to begging him. Pleading for him to give me what I need. "Please," I say again, this time opening my eyes as I beg. The view is beyond erotic. His face between my legs, his eyes tilting up to lock on mine as his tongue plays me so intimately—and so expertly.

He starts to lift his head, but I reach out, curling my fingers in his hair and holding him in place as I grind against him, knowing only that I want to reach that pinnacle and, more, that I want Devlin to be the one who takes me there.

"God yes," he murmurs against my flesh, the heat of his breath sending more shivers. With my free hand I tug on my nipple as I arch up and close my eyes. I hear his low groan and I whimper, knowing he's watching me.

So far he's been using only his tongue, but now he shifts his hands, lifting my ass with one palm and holding me in place as he slips his fingers inside me, curving them up to find that sensitive spot deep within.

I gasp, then cry out, "*Devlin*." His name is like an incantation, and I explode, my core tightening around his fingers, my body shaking, and all the stars in heaven seeming to fall down around me.

"Oh, baby," he says, sliding up my body to kiss me as I melt beneath him. Slowly he enters me, then buries his cock deep inside with slow, easy thrusts that become more desperate as I clutch at his ass, drawing him deeper, my hips rising to meet his thrusts as he pounds into me, a wonderful, wild claiming after the flurry of delicious kisses that had been our warm up.

"Yes," I cry, my fingers clutching him as I urge him in deeper and deeper until finally I feel that tremor deep inside him. It flows through him and into me, sending fresh waves of pleasure crashing through me as he cries out, emptying himself into me as I murmur, *yes, yes, yes*, not even certain if I'm speaking aloud.

He collapses beside me, and I twine my legs with him as I look into his eyes, wanting to lose myself in the way he's looking at me. As if I'm all that exists in the world to him.

For a moment we stay like that, breathing hard. Then I see the shadow cross his face.

"Devlin?"

"Baby, I'm so sorry."

I fight a pang of fear. "Sorry? Are you crazy?"

"We forgot to use a condom."

"Oh. Oh!" I push myself up and grin. "I totally forgot. With all that's happened it slipped my mind, but they left me a voicemail. The clinic I mean. Totally clean."

"Is that so?"

"All negative." I feel as accomplished as someone who scored an A-plus on a calculus exam with only an eighth-grade education. Considering the way I've lived my life these last few years, I hardly deserve to have aced this particular test, and I like to think it's the universe's way of saying it approves of me and Devlin being together.

Devlin is looking at me, with mischief in his eyes. "What?" I demand.

"Oh, nothing. Only that we need to celebrate."

"Mr. Saint, if you are prepared to indulge in more celebrating —" I make air quotes around the word. "—then I absolutely won't say no."

"Glad to hear it," he says, and I squeal as he flips me onto my back and straddles me. "Because with you, baby, I'm always in the mood to celebrate."

We make love again, slowly and sweetly, and when we are both spent, I spoon against him, then jump when the sharp ping of my phone startles me, signaling an incoming message.

"Sorry about that. I can't believe I forgot to silence it."

"I can't believe that's the first text message you've gotten," he says. "I consider us lucky."

"It's probably Brandy wondering whether it's safe to come back, or if we're having sex all over the living room floor. Or if I'm still a horrible mess."

"Damn. Living room floor. We missed another opportunity."

He rolls over and props himself up on an elbow. "And I'm very glad you're not a horrible mess."

"Thanks to you."

He lightly taps my lip. "You're okay?"

"Are you kidding? I'm perfect. Slightly sore," I add, taking his hand and sliding it between my thighs. "But that doesn't mean I want to stop yet. Shall we go for the gold?"

"Somebody's horny," he teases, then lightly strokes my clit, sending electrical sparks racing through me. "I like it."

My laugh turns into a needy moan—then a frustrated sigh when the phone signals again.

"You should check it," he says, and I reluctantly grab it off the bedside table.

The message box on my lock screen is blank, so I open the phone, then freeze when I see the text, which is decidedly *not* from Brandy.

Devlin frowns at my expression, then takes the phone. "Oh, fuck."

I look over his shoulder, this time taking a closer look at the text message that simply says, *Why do you even trust him?*

It's accompanied by a photograph inside the Las Vegas Phoenix Hotel. I recognize it, even though the image is nothing more than an open hotel door, because the sign on the wall next to the door reads *Sammy Davis Suite* in the now-familiar font.

It's the room we shared when Devlin took me to Vegas. And now the photo shows him exiting that same room with Regina Taggart on his arm, her skirt tight and her arm through his.

Beside me, Devlin spits out a curse. "That is not what it looks like. She's been my date to a couple of functions, but we haven't—"

"I know," I say, interrupting him. "I bet Reggie wasn't even in Vegas with you today. That's an old picture."

"Actually, she was. She flew in late afternoon. But you're right about the picture. I think it was from right before one of the foundation awards banquets. How the hell did you know?"

I shrug casually, then nod at the image on my phone. "Your glasses, for one. Different frames. And her shoes. Those Jimmy Choos are two seasons out of date." I lift my head, meet his eyes, and shrug. "Just one of my special skills," I say. "But it makes me certain that someone's fucking with us."

"Yeah," he says. "Someone definitely is."

CHAPTER TWENTY

I wake to an empty bed and the smell of bacon. Usually I have a hard time getting up in the morning, but not today. I roll out eagerly and follow my nose to the kitchen, and to Devlin.

"I was going to cook for you," I say, feeling slightly guilty. "You came back from Vegas to take care of me. I figured it was the least I could do." I shrug. "Although to be honest, I'm a terrible cook."

He grins at me. The stubble of beard is shaggier than usual since he hasn't trimmed it yet, and his hair is a tousled mess. He's not wearing his glasses or his green contacts and he looks sexy as hell in a rumpled, early morning sort of way. "I'm happy to cook for you. I was looking forward to it all night."

I laugh. "I sincerely doubt that, but I'm fine with being a spectator. I'm actually tempted to take a picture of you and post it on Instagram. Except I'd have to remember how to use my account." I'm terrible at using social media. Considering I can count my close friends on one hand, I don't really see the point. "Guess I'll keep it just for me."

I expect him to protest when I pull out my phone and start to take a picture, but then I laugh when he actually strikes a pose, pointing the wooden spoon he's using to stir the scrambled eggs to the *Kiss the Cook* apron that Brandy keeps hanging on the inside of the pantry.

"I think you look a lot cuter than Brandy does in that thing," I tell him. He's wearing the slacks he wore yesterday and a now-rumpled white button down. The office attire combined with the apron makes for an absolutely adorable picture. "By the way, is she here?" I never heard her come back last night, but it's possible I was asleep when she did.

Devlin shakes his head. "If she is, she hasn't emerged yet. Not Brandy. Not Christopher."

I make a noise in the back of my throat. "Interesting..." I close the photo app and check my messages but there's nothing from her. "She might've emailed, figuring I didn't need to be disturbed by the pinging of a text."

"And that's the reason she's your best friend."

I laugh, having thought the same thing many times myself. Sure enough, there's an email saying that she's staying over at Christopher's and not to worry. And that she'll give me full details when she gets back—but that *that* isn't happening and I should get my mind out of the gutter. The final is followed by a huge smiley face emoji. "Apparently it's just you and me," I tell Devlin.

"I'm happy for her. They make a cute couple."

"But not as cute as us?"

"Oh, definitely not."

I scoot around the bar and hook my arm around his waist so that we can take a selfie. But I end up making him do the hard work since his arms are longer, and I want the apron in the image alongside me posing to kiss his cheek. He protests, but takes the photo, and when I look at it, I can't help but grin. It's a little crooked, but totally cute.

"Too bad we didn't realize last night that she wasn't going to be here," Devlin says. "We missed out on living room sex. This morning we could have started on the kitchen counters, hanging from the light fixtures. You know. Taking full advantage of her absence."

I smirk. "Shut up and finish making me breakfast."

"It's great to see you smile," he says as he finishes the eggs and moves the bacon to a plate.

"Yesterday was hard. You made it easier. And even though it makes me sad, I'm actually looking forward to working on the article."

He looks at me, his expression dubious.

"Seriously. It'll be good to work through my emotions. I think —I hope—that even though Peter knew the risk, he was arrogant enough to believe that The Wolf wouldn't take my mom from him. But either way I'm coming to terms with the fact that I'll never know the truth." I shrug. "And that I'm a little bit like him."

He studies me, slowly shaking his head. "You would never put anyone in that position."

"No, but I flirt with danger all the time."

"Ellie..."

"I do." I tilt my head and offer him a smile. "I flirt with you, don't I?"

He grins. "You do indeed." He moves our plates to the bar. "So what else did you learn yesterday?"

"Nothing concrete," I say, "but I may have a lead you can help me with." He follows me as I move out of the kitchen and settle onto a stool at the bar. "Do you know if Peter was dating someone back then?"

He pauses, clearly not expecting that question. "Well, he went out occasionally, if that's what you mean. He was single and only in his forties. But I don't think he was ever serious about anyone."

"Do you remember anyone specifically?"

He shakes his head slowly, as if trying to remember. "Not really. He was pretty intent on spending his free time with you, actually. Why are you asking?"

I tell him about the blonde. "Ortega said she was young. Like, really young. Like, he didn't know if she could even drink young.

Did you ever see him with anyone like that? I'm thinking that if I can track her down, I might be able to find out more."

He doesn't say anything, but he doesn't look like he's thinking, either. Instead, he looks shocked.

"What is it? Do you have an idea? Do you know who I'm talking about?"

He shakes his head. "No, no, no. I'm just—it doesn't seem like Peter to date someone that young." He frowns. "That would have put his girlfriend at about my age. I never thought Peter was the type. Do you know how long it went on?"

I shake my head. Then frown when I look at him. "Are you sure you're okay?"

"Sorry. I guess like you, I'm realizing I never really knew Peter either." He stabs at his eggs but doesn't take a bite. "Listen, I need to take care of some things at work today. Are you sure you're okay?"

I cock my head. "It's sweet of you to want to take care of me twenty-four/seven, but I'm fine. I told you. Yesterday was hard, but I have the benefit of the healing powers of you. Honestly, I figured you'd have to go back to Vegas today."

He shakes his head. "I took care of what I needed to. The team can handle the rest." He cups his hand around the back of my neck and pulls me close to kiss my forehead. "Whatever you need, baby. Whenever you need it. You know that, right?"

He pulls his hand free, and I lean back so that I can see him. "Yeah," I assure him. "I do."

We eat in silence for a moment, and I finish before him. I move around the counter to set the water boiling for another cup of coffee, and as I wait for it to heat up, I open my phone and check out the selfie we took.

"I like this," I say. "The apron contrasting your super macho scar. Such dichotomy." I hold my phone out as if examining it from another angle. "I should enlarge it and frame it."

At the bar, he makes a snorting noise.

"Well, now I pretty much have to," I say. "And by the way,

you never told me how you got it. The scar, I mean. All you said was that it was a hunting knife. What happened? More important, what happened to the other guy?"

"I was ambushed during an assignment."

I cock my head, noting that he called it an assignment and not an operation. I've never spent much time around the military, but I have watched a lot of movies, and I'm thinking this wasn't during his regular service days. "You joined military intelligence, didn't you?"

His expression darkens as he says, "Lamar's research skills are solid. Or am I wrong?"

I shake my head. "Not wrong. He told me about how you were discharged and what that probably meant."

I stiffen, fearing the worst, but he takes it in stride. I'm glad. Technically, Lamar had been poking around about Ronan, but that's not a topic I want to veer onto right now.

"So you had some sort of spy-like assignment," I guess. "And you ended up in a knife fight with the bad guy."

Humor flickers in his eyes. "Something like that. As far as knives go, it was one-sided."

"You were unarmed?"

"Would you believe I had a whip?"

I laugh out loud, certain he's joking.

"No, it's true. He got the jump on me—trust me when I say that doesn't happen often. I had a whip. A full-on, Indiana Jones style whip. It was one of my more surreal moments, and it disarmed him just fine."

"Wow. I'm sleeping with an action hero. How's the other guy look?"

"Actually," he says casually, "he looks worse. Much worse."

I grin, strangely delighted by this bizarre story. "Good."

He lifts a brow—the one bisected by the scar. "Really?"

"A girl wants her boyfriend to be bad ass. Or at least this girl does."

He studies me so long I start to get fidgety. "I'm very glad to hear you say that."

"Why on earth did you have a whip?"

His expression goes flat. "That's classified. I could tell you," he says, "but then I'd have to kill you."

I burst out laughing, then blow off my boiling water to go back around the bar. I twist his stool a bit so that I can settle in between his knees and slide my arms around his neck. "So, you're telling me you're a bad ass?"

He grabs my hips and pulls me even closer, then kisses me hard. It's tongue and teeth and heat and lust, and when he pulls away I'm breathing hard and regretting the fact that I told him I was okay with him leaving for work. "Baby, you better believe it."

I laugh, enjoying the way he's teasing, even as some part of me wonders if it really is a tease.

"I need to get dressed," I say. "And you need to get to work. Because if you don't go to work now, I'm not sure I'm going to let you out of here." I start back around the island . "Go on and get cleaned up. I'll do the kitchen."

He shakes his head "Nope. Cooks clean their own messes."

"Do they?"

"But you can help. And then we can share the shower. Conserve water. Save the planet."

I grin, then bite my lower lip in anticipation of shower time. "You know what? I think that sounds like a very good plan."

CHAPTER TWENTY-ONE

Devlin moved on autopilot on the way to the office, his frustration growing and his good mood fading as he thought about the conversation he needed to have with Anna.

Surely, it wasn't true. Surely, he was wrong. Surely, he was crafting wild scenarios in his head.

Too bad he knew better.

Devlin wasn't the kind of man whose instincts tended to be off target. If he was spinning scenarios, it was because they were likely true and he'd missed seeing them.

He didn't like being wrong—who did? But with Devlin, his instincts were so rarely off that when he did miss something, it grated like fingernails on a chalkboard.

Today, however, he hoped he'd missed the mark by a mile. Because if the story he'd spun in his head was right...

He let the thought drift away as he pushed through the main door of the Devlin Saint Foundation.

"Good morning, Mr. S—"

"Where's Anna?"

Paul's eyes widened, but the young man didn't falter. "At her desk, sir, as far as I know."

"Thanks," Devlin said, wanting to kick himself for taking his mood out on his receptionist. "And good morning, Paul. Sorry for being short. It's going to be a busy day."

"Yes, sir. No problem, sir."

He kept walking, feeling Paul's eyes on his back as he climbed the four flights of stairs to his office. As Paul had said, Anna was at her desk, and she looked up in surprise when he reached the landing.

"You walked up? What? Did you skip your workout this morning?"

"As a matter of fact, I did. My office," he said, heading for the doors that were opening like magic for him. "Now."

She hurried in after him. "What's going on?" Her voice followed him. "You're supposed to be in Vegas. Did something—"

He rounded on her. "Were you fucking Peter White?"

She hesitated, her eyes wide. "What are you talking about?"

It wasn't a denial, and as far as Devlin was concerned, that was answer enough.

"Oh, Christ," he said, then rubbed his fingers against his temple against the start of a pounding headache.

For a moment, the only sound in the room was the electronic whoosh of his office doors closing. Then he heard that final *snick* of the doors shutting, and it was as if that sound was a signal.

"Tell me," he demanded as Anna shook her head.

"Devlin, come on. Where is this coming from?"

That was twice she hadn't denied.

"I'm serious," she pressed. "This is coming out of nowhere."

"The hell it is. You came to Laguna Cortez on your way to Chicago, heading for college. You delivered a message to me. Just like you'd delivered others before." He dragged his fingers through his hair, remembering how she'd been the harbinger of such horrific news and wishing he could block the memory of those days. Of all of it except the sweet hours with Ellie before he ran.

"I—well, yes." Her brow furrowed. "Your father sent me. You know that."

"How long were you here before you told me what my father had ordered? For that matter, how many times did you linger after coming to town to deliver other messages to Peter?" He stressed the word *messages*, filling it with meaning.

Her eyes went wide. "What does it matter? I had to come—you know I couldn't say no. So what if I played that to my advantage? You know what kind of life I had to lead."

He pinched the bridge of his nose, forcing himself to stay focused and unemotional despite her admission.

"And that last time, I was here for *you*. Not for Peter," she continued. "I could have warned him, right? But then you'd be dead, wouldn't you? Because your father would have assumed *you* warned him."

"Not necessarily. He might have thought you did," Devlin pointed out. "Especially if my father knew you were sleeping with Ellie's uncle."

"What is with you?" she snapped. "If I didn't know you better, I'd say you were jealous."

"I am *so* not in the mood for jokes."

"Fine." She crossed her arms over her chest. "Are you in the mood for walking down Memory Lane? Because I don't understand why we're talking about this. You didn't even clue in that I was sleeping with him back then, so why the hell do you care now?"

"You're right," he said. "I didn't know." There'd been a few rough months after the one time he and Anna had slept together, but after that, they'd slid into a solid friendship. Even so, he hadn't noticed that she'd been screwing Peter White. Probably because he'd been so focused on Ellie. And, honestly, even if he had noticed, would it have mattered? He might have said something to Anna because of the age difference, but in the end, it was none of his business.

Now, though...

"You were seen," he said. "It matters because you were seen."

"Gee, you think? Believe it or not, I figured that one out on my own, considering you marched into the office and started interrogating me. So what?"

"Do not be dense, Anna. It doesn't suit you. Peter White's murder is an open case again, and now not only Ellie but her detective know that he was sleeping with a girl about half his age. That's not good."

She pressed her lips together, for the first time looking a bit chastised. "No," she said. "That's not good. But do you really think the cops are going to pursue the case? It's so old, and it's so hard to get a conviction when someone has already served time for the crime."

"That's what I'm hoping," he admitted. "That it will fade slowly away. It's not as if Ellie's going to push the matter."

"I still can't believe you told her."

"Only that I killed her uncle." Both Tamra and Anna knew that Devlin had killed Peter. And he'd more recently told them that he'd confessed that truth to Ellie. He hadn't yet shared the revelation that both Lamar and Brandy knew as well.

Only Ronan knew that. And for now, that was enough.

"I told Ellie because I trust her," he said, pointedly meeting her eyes. "There aren't many people I trust. You know that."

She nodded, her hands smoothing her skirt before she stepped forward and took both of his hands in her own. "Yeah. I do. I won't second guess you. I like Ellie, too, but I worry about you. About all of this," she added, looking around his office.

"I know."

"We both escaped, Devlin. We have new lives. Good lives. I don't want anything to mess that up."

"Believe me," he said, "neither do I."

"So how much do you trust her?" Anna asked. "How much more are you going to tell her?"

"I don't know," he said honestly. "Everything? Nothing? Somewhere in between?"

"Can I give you some unsolicited advice?"

"Go ahead."

"Tread carefully."

He studied her. "You don't think I should say anything." The thought rankled. He'd carried his secrets for so long that he knew he could continue to do so indefinitely. But for the first time, he didn't want to stick with the status quo. He wanted Ellie to know the full man he'd become. A man with secrets and faults and deadly enemies. A man with a code and a purpose that both drove and defined him.

He wanted her to fully know him, because that was the only way for him to be sure that she was truly his. That she loved *him* and not the man she'd manufactured out of memories from the past and snapshots of the present.

He said none of that to Anna, though. Instead, he said, "You think she'll bolt."

"I don't know her well enough to answer that. But I know she was a cop. And I know she almost walked away after learning that you killed Peter. How's she going to feel when she learns that was just the tip of the iceberg?"

"Right." He swallowed. "Well, that's something to consider." He turned and moved to the window, then lost himself in the view of the ocean. He pulled open the door and stepped out onto the balcony. If he turned to face the ocean, he could just make out the tidal pools where he'd first kissed Ellie. And where, more recently, he'd let her see the old Alex hidden beneath the countenance of the man he was now.

She was his again, goddammit. No way was he losing her.

But whether that meant he had to tell her the truth or hold his secrets closer, he truly didn't know.

"Devlin?"

He turned back. "Ask Tamra to come in. I need to start working on the speech for the award ceremony."

"Okay. Sure. But aren't you going back to Vegas?"

"No."

"So it's all sorted out? Did you get the breach locked down? And what about—"

He held up a hand. "We can talk more later. Suffice it to say that everything's under control. I've got more information about the breach and Reggie's handling the rest of it."

"But what about—"

The buzz of the intercom interrupted them, followed by Tamra's voice. "Mr. Saint? Paul told me you were in the building. Do you mind if I come in?"

He pressed the button to open the doors, and Tamra walked in holding a folder, her expression tight. "I'm sorry to interrupt, but I thought you might want to know. This just came over the wire services."

Anna glanced at the printout as he took it from Tamra. "Is that—?"

"It's an article on the death of Adrian Kohl," Devlin said, referring to the man he'd grown up with. A man who'd recently positioned himself as the head of a criminal network in the Southwest. "Looks like I need to go back to Vegas this evening, after all."

CHAPTER TWENTY-TWO

After Devlin heads to the office, I settle in bed with my computer on my lap to check my emails. I haven't been able to get my work account on my phone for some reason, so I open up my laptop and check my account for *The Spall*. There's not much there, but one subject catches my eye right away: *Who shot Terrance Myers? Exclusive Tip.*

I recently covered the Myers story for *The Spall Monthly*. I'd attended the press conference in LA after the billionaire asshole who'd captured and tortured almost two dozen children was assassinated following an appellate court decision to overthrow his conviction.

My article had talked about Myers' history as well as some of the horror experienced by his victims. And, of course, I reported on the assassination following his release from prison—and that the police had no leads on the shooter who had fired from about a mile away from the roof of a bank building.

As far as I know, the LAPD is no closer to making an arrest. And while I expect that this email is going to be nothing more than spam or clickbait, it's my job to look. And who am I kidding? I'm crazy with curiosity. So I open the email, only to find that there's just two lines of text followed by those funky URLs with no words. Just letters and numbers.

I have an exclusive for you and
The Spall, *Ellie Holmes.*
Follow the link to find the shooter.

I hover the mouse over the link, tempted to go for it and click. But that would be beyond stupid. The odds that there's really information behind that link are slim. And the odds that there's a virus or some sort of worm that will let some asshole hack my computer are high.

But I really want to see...

I grab my phone and dial Roger in New York, then tap my finger on my desk until he gets on the line.

"Hey, kid. Are you calling to update me on the article about your uncle?"

"No. I've got some interesting leads, but I'm not ready to fill you in yet. I'll write up some notes soon and shoot them to you." That's been our process since I was interning for him while in grad school, and with this article especially, I think it will help to have someone without my emotional attachment reviewing the facts as I learn them.

"So what's up?"

"I may have a follow-up on the Myers article." I explain about the email, then add, "I'm not interested in fucking up my computer. Will *The Spall* pay for a cheap computer so I can follow this link?"

I'm thinking I can forward the email to a newly created Gmail account so that it's not tied to any of my other email addresses. Then I'll open the forwarded email on the cheap computer. That way, anything that might be spyware gets nothing except the information on an essentially empty computer.

"Can you manage with a three-hundred dollar budget?"

"I bet I can find something."

"Then you got it. Fingers crossed it's something interesting and not someone trying to hack your bank accounts."

"No kidding."

"Also, Corbin was going to call you today. Apparently he's got questions about the New York Transit Authority article. Mind if I put him on now?"

I hesitate, because in my book it's never fine to talk to Corbin Dailey. But I can hardly tell Roger that. "Fine."

Roger chuckles. "Don't sound so enthusiastic."

I roll my eyes. Of course, Roger already knows how I feel about Corbin.

I'm on hold for less than a minute, and then I hear Corbin's voice. "I hear you're writing a profile on your uncle. You should be writing yourself into an article about Saint. I covered the son-of-a-bitch once when he was giving a speech in New York right after he founded the DSF."

"I remember."

"Yeah, well, rumors are the guy fucks around. Never figured you to be that type."

"Corbin, honey, you don't know anything about what type I am. Other than the fact that I'm not a woman who goes for a guy like you, of course."

I hear the front door open then shut, and Brandy comes in grinning, then frowns as she mouths, *Who is that?*

I mouth back that it's Corbin, and then ask him to repeat the questions he had about my notes on the transit authority article, since I'd totally tuned him out.

Once I'm finished with the joy of talking with him, I hang up and hurry to Brandy for a hug. "All right," I say. "Spill. Now."

"Nothing happened. We just wanted to give you guys space."

"Nothing?"

"Nope," she says. "He even slept on the couch."

I tilt my head from side to side. "And was that a good thing or a bad thing?"

"Probably good," she says with a mischievous little grin. "The truth is, that we were both on the couch before he sent me to bed."

"Oh?" My voice rises with interest. "And was this a fully clothed couch experience?"

Her cheeks turn crimson. "Not fully."

"Brandy Bradshaw! Look at you. Tell me everything."

"I might have misplaced my shirt," she admits.

"And that was okay? You weren't feeling uncomfortable or—"

"Ellie, it was awesome." She squeezes my hand, then whispers, "I'm the one who pulled my top off. We didn't *do* anything—and honestly, he's the one who put on the brakes."

"Yeah?"

She nods. "He said that he knew I wanted to take it slow and that we should stop. And that's when he offered me the bedroom."

"Wow. Points for Christopher."

"Definitely," she says. "Except..."

I frown. "What? What's wrong?"

"Nothing with him," she says. "Only that I laid awake for awhile after. I kept thinking he might come in."

"But he never did."

"No," she says, then sighs. "But Ellie? I really kind of wanted him to."

"Sounds like he does, too," I say.

"I know. And now I'm nervous."

"I know," I say, squeezing her hand. "And it sounds like Christopher understands that, too." What I don't say is that I'm nervous on her behalf, as well. Christopher seems like a great guy, but what you see isn't always what's under the surface.

Still, sometimes all you can do is take a leap of faith.

"What were you talking to Corbin about?" Brandy asks, moving to sit on the edge of my bed.

I do likewise, then fill her in on the fact that he's covering my New York articles now that I'm based in Laguna Cortez. Then I catch her up on everything else, though it turns out that she already knows about what happened in Los Angeles yesterday, including the revelation about Peter, The Wolf, and my mother's death.

"Lamar filled me in," she says, as if in apology. "Sorry if we were gossiping behind your back."

"Are you kidding? You know I would have told you myself if I hadn't been such a mess."

"You're doing better? It was good that Devlin was here."

"It was, and I am. Right now, I'm focusing on work other than the Uncle Peter story."

"What's up?"

"I might have a lead on that Myers assassination."

"Myers. He's that pedophile who killed all those children?"

"Right." I fill her in about the strange URL. "Actually, I should call Lamar right now. He might be able to hook me up with a cheap computer."

Lamar answers on the first ring, and I give him the rundown of what I'm doing. "Does the city still sell refurbished computers?"

"I think so. Desktop or laptop?"

"Laptop if it's cheap, but I'll take whatever I can get."

I tell him *The Spall* budget then add that I'd be willing to kick in a few hundred on top of that if I have to.

"Sounds good. Let me get back to you."

"Thanks. By the way, I got another creepy text." I hear him make a little noise in his throat, and I'm glad I can't see his face. As far as being indignant on my behalf, he and Devlin are definitely in the same camp.

"What was it?"

"A picture of Devlin and Reggie coming out of a hotel room in Vegas. The text suggested it was from last night, but it wasn't. It's a couple of years old."

"And you know this because Devlin told you so?"

"Do not even. I know you like him now."

He chuckles. "Let's go with *accept*, okay? I'm not sure I know the guy well enough yet to truly like him. But seriously, how do you know when the picture was taken?"

I tell him that also, and he laughs at my shoe analysis, but he can't fault my logic.

"I'm worried about you," he adds. "First, I was worried that Devlin was going to break your heart. I'm mostly over that. Now I'm worried about the bigger picture."

"I know. I get it."

"Do you? Because Saint has secrets. He must."

I don't answer. Mostly because Devlin himself told me as much. But that's not something I feel inclined to share with Lamar, who's only recently come around to Team Devlin.

"Someone is obsessed with exposing whatever is going on with that man," he continues. "You're a reporter. They know he has a secret. And it sounds like they're starting to get dangerous."

"Yeah, but who?"

"I don't have a single idea, and that's what scares me the most."

"Me too," I admit.

"Shoot me the text," he says. "I'll poke around."

"Devlin's already poking around."

"Yeah, I figured he would be. But we have different resources. Let me do this."

I forward the text with the picture of Devlin and Reggie, but I don't have high hopes. As soon as he acknowledges that he got the text on his end, he tells me that he'll call later about the computer. We hang up, and I turn back to Brandy, who looks as concerned as Lamar sounded a moment ago.

"Were you planning to tell me any of that?"

"I wasn't keeping it—"

"Somebody has got it in for you. What does Devlin say about all this?"

"He's worried too." I shrug. "But what can I do? It's not like I'm going to hide under a log."

She grimaces but says nothing. After a minute, she gets up,

telling me she's hungry. I follow her to the kitchen, where she grabs one of her disgusting green smoothies as I climb onto a stool at the bar. She starts to sip it, then leans against the counter, her eyes on me. "I need to check in at a few of the shops on Pacific that stock my bags. Then I thought I'd surprise Christopher. He's doing research today at the DSF."

"He'll like that."

"Yeah, I thought I'd hit Brewski and get him a coffee. Want to come with? You could surprise Devlin."

"Not a bad idea," I say. "You can tell me the rest of the dirty details of you and Christopher as we walk."

"Yeah, if we'd actually worked up to dirty, I could. That's your department, remember?" She bats her eyes as she grins. "But you could maybe give me some tips?"

I snort with laughter. "Brandy, my naive friend, you have *so* got a deal."

For the next couple of hours, Brandy and I gossip our way from store to store as she checks stock, picks up order forms, and discusses pricing. I mostly window shop, though I do buy two silly T-shirts, and it's not until the last stop before we hit Brewski that someone finally recognizes me.

Or, at least, that someone tells me they do.

"You're the one who's dating Devlin Saint," a customer in The Escape says, hurrying up to me and then rummaging through her bag. "He is so hot. Is he as hot in person as he is from far away?" She's talking so fast I couldn't answer even if I wanted to. "I saw him once down the block, but he was gone by the time I got there. Is it cool having your picture everywhere? I bet you print out all the social media pictures. I'd have them taped to my mirror if it were me."

"Um," I say, as she finally pulls a pen from her bag and thrusts it to me. "This," she adds, "would you sign this?"

This is an envelope from a dentist's office with *Past Due* stamped on it.

"Um," I repeat, thinking how grateful I am that I never got hooked on social media. I know there are posts about Devlin and me, but I'm mostly oblivious, figuring that someone will give one of us a heads-up if the posts turn creepy.

"Oh, please," she says. "I swear I won't sell it."

I almost laugh, because the thought that anyone would pay for my signature is beyond funny. The owner, Inez, catches my eye, her head tilting in question. *Shall I get rid of her?*

I shake my head just enough to let her know it's fine. "Yeah," I say to the woman. "Sure, I'll sign."

I do, and she looks so ridiculously grateful that I think she must have mistaken me for a movie star. "That was weird," I tell Inez and Brandy after the woman's hurried outside, probably to go put my signature in her safe deposit box.

"People collect things," Inez says with a shrug. "That's part of why the line of turtle jewelry I sell does so well." She flashes a teasing smile that reaches all the way to her pale blue eyes. "When I read about Devlin Saint before, I used to think he collected women. But I guess I was wrong. He seems very content with only one trophy in his collection."

I do a fake curtsey and the three of us laugh. I've liked Inez since she saved my ass by finding me an affordable cocktail dress right after I'd arrived in Laguna Cortez. Now, Brandy and I invite her to come get a coffee with us.

"Rain check," she promises. "I have a stack of paperwork to get through. Running a business can be a pain in the ass. Plus, I'm expecting a delivery. But thank you for the offer."

"Any more stops?" I ask Brandy when we're back on the street.

"Not unless there's someplace you want to go."

I think about it, but shake my head. There are dozens of cute stores on Pacific Avenue, but we're working our way toward the Devlin Saint Foundation. Which means that right now, the only thing standing between Devlin and me is a short break for coffee.

Fortunately, she's just as eager to see Christopher, so we forgo sitting and chatting in favor of getting to-go coffees from Brewski and continuing on.

We cross the Pacific Coast Highway, then walk the short distance south to the DSF parking lot. I'm about to veer toward the main doors when Brandy comes to a stop, calling for me to hold up, too.

"What?"

"Who's that with Anna?"

I follow her line of sight toward the beach, then shrug. "I have no idea."

"He's hot," Brandy says.

I squint. "Maybe. They're too far away to tell." All I can see is that he has light brown hair and an ass that fills out his jeans. Not a bad start, but until I know more, I'm not calling him hot.

"Doesn't look like Anna cares anyway," Brandy says when I tell her as much. "She looks annoyed."

Brandy's right. Anna's arms are crossed over her chest, and her head is cocked to one side. I think they might be arguing, but between the sound of the ocean and the roar of traffic behind us, I can't make out a single word.

"Boyfriend?" Brandy suggests, then lifts a hand when Anna turns a bit in our direction.

She doesn't react, though, and Brandy lowers her hand as I say, "I don't think she saw us. And as for who he is, I haven't got a clue. You could ask Christopher. Maybe he knows."

"I guess," Brandy says as she shrugs. We turn away, and I know she won't ask. That's fine by me. I'm curious in the moment, but who Anna dates or argues with is very low on my list of things to worry about.

"I think I'm going to see if Christopher wants to blow off writing and go see a movie," she says as we wave to Paul and head toward the elevator.

"You just saw *The Maltese Falcon.*"

"No, we made out during *The Maltese Falcon,*" she retorts.

"Seriously?" I press a hand over my heart. "I'm so proud."

"I felt so naughty. You should try it."

"I have no trouble feeling naughty all on my own, but I can't say it's a bad idea. Look at you," I add with a grin. "You're turning into a wicked bad influence."

"Really?" She rolls her shoulders back. "I've never been anyone's bad influence before."

"Ha. Stick with me. I'll teach you all the tricks." I give her a quick hug as the elevator door opens on three, then watch her head into the Research Room before I continue in the elevator up to four. The doors slide open and I step out into the reception area to find Tracy sitting at Anna's desk.

"Hey! I'm so glad to see you." I hurry over and accept the hug she offers. "So?" I continue as we break apart. "A little bird tells me things are heating up at a certain condo building on PCH."

"Stop it," she says, but it's clear she's fighting a smile.

"I'm just teasing," I assure her. "But I am glad that you and Lamar hit it off."

"Me, too," she says, then settles back behind the computer.

"Covering for Anna?" Tracy is actually Tamra's intern in the PR department, but the DSF has a small enough staff that it makes sense that the intern would cover Devlin's desk when Anna's away. "Where is she?" I ask, feigning innocence.

Tracy shrugs. "She said she had to step out for a second. So here I am. He's in with Tamra, but I can buzz and let him know you're here."

"I don't want to interrupt. He's not expecting me. I'll hang with you for a while, and if he's not free soon I'll shoot him a text."

"Sounds good to me. And, hey, I've been meaning to ask. I'm going to drag Lamar to some of the Fall Festival events. I love perusing jewelry at craft fairs." She reaches up to flick a dangly copper earring. "I got these at a street fair in Santa Barbara right after high school."

"I forgot that that was even this month," I admit. The multi-day festival features music, food, arts and crafts. Pacific Avenue shuts down for car traffic, and booths line the street. It's fun and always draws a crowd.

"Do you and Devlin want to go? Brandy and Christopher, too, if they want."

"I can't speak for Devlin, but I'd love to."

"Fabulous," she says, with a little clap of her hands. "We can firm up plans later and—"

She's interrupted when the doors glide open on silent hinges and Tamra steps out, impeccably dressed as always in a linen pant suit and this season's Louis Vuitton flats. Her head is down, her eyes on the notepad she's reviewing. Then she looks up and smiles. "How are you doing, sweetheart? Devlin told me a bit about the texts, but he said you're bearing up."

"Texts?" Tracy asks.

I scowl. "Just some idiot harassing me. I'm surprised Lamar didn't tell you."

Tracy laughs. "No, you're not."

I shake my head. "No, you're right. I'm not." Lamar would never share my secrets without permission. "But tell him I said it's fine to share. I don't care if you know, but I don't want to be the one to talk about it."

"Where's Anna?" Tamra asks.

"She had to step away," Tracy says.

Tamra's mouth curves into a quick frown, gone almost as quickly as it arrived.

"Is he free?" I ask, nodding at the doors that had closed behind her.

"On the phone," Tracy says, and I glance down to see the lit-up line go dark. "But now he's free," she adds. She punches the intercom. "Ellie is here, Mr. Saint. Shall I send—"

She doesn't have the chance to finish the question, as the doors start to glide open again, apparently under Devlin's command.

I grin at Tamra and Tracy before I step through the widening gap, then listen to the subtle change in pitch as the doors change direction and begin to close.

Devlin's standing behind his desk, and I feel my muscles relax at the sight of him. I hadn't realized how tense I'd been, as if deep down I'd feared that he wasn't really in here and I'd never see him again.

He's glancing at something on his desk, but when he looks up at me, his entire demeanor shifts, his smile lighting the room and going straight to my heart.

"You are a sight for very sore eyes," he says as I hurry to his side.

"Bad day? What's going on?"

He brushes my words away. "Just a series of issues spreading out from Nevada like a spiderweb."

"Oh, no." Anna had mentioned the security breaches to me the day Devlin went to Vegas, but I'd gotten so lost in my own drama that I'd forgotten to ask Devlin if he needed to vent. "Do you want to talk about it?"

"Eventually," he says, "but not now."

"I'm here whenever you need me," I promise. "But that reminds me. I was checking my phone in the elevator and I saw this." I reach into my bag for my phone, then scroll to the news bite I'd seen after I'd left Brandy. "Some up-and-coming crime boss into drugs and trafficking was killed while you were there. Or later, actually. I guess you would have been on your way back to me. Anyway, his name was Adrian Kohl. Did you hear about it?"

"I did."

"Did you know about him? Through the foundation, I mean?"

"The foundation and my father." His expression is as hard as his voice. "I need to go back Vegas tonight. Will you be okay? I'll be back tomorrow evening at the latest."

"I'll be fine," I assure him, feeling both guilty and special about the way he left Vegas to come to my side. I'm sure he expects new residents at the rehab facility, victims of Kohl's enterprise. Devlin's very hands-on about the work The Phoenix does, and I assume he wants to greet the incoming survivors. I almost ask if I can come with him and help, but DSF volunteers go through rigorous training. I'm afraid I'd just be in the way.

So instead of asking to come, all I say is, "I hate that you have that kind of thing in your head all the time."

"Not all the time," he says, looking at me with such exaggerated heat that I have to laugh, lightening the moment for both of us.

Then again, why only laugh when I can play the game instead. "Poor you," I say, making my voice low and sexy. "Maybe I can make it better?" I move to sit on the edge of his desk. I'm wearing a flowy skirt, leather thong sandals, a tank top with a built-in shelf bra, and a light jacket. I kick off the sandals and shrug out of the jacket, pushing it off the desk behind me.

He cocks a brow, the one with the scar, and it's such a deliciously sexy look that I feel myself melt. I put my hands back on his desk blotter and spread my legs in what can only be interpreted as an invitation.

He moves closer, and as I arch back to emphasize my breasts, he puts his hands on my knees and pushes my legs even further apart.

"I never thought I'd be a cliché," he says, as he slides one hand slowly up my inner thigh, pushing up the material as he goes, "but right now, all I want to do is fuck you on my desk." His voice drops to a whisper as he says, "Want to pretend to be my secretary?"

I squirm a bit, my pussy already throbbing as I spread my legs even wider. "You *are* being a cliché. How about I be the boss? You can be my assistant. If you get the job, that is. I only hire the best. You'll have to prove yourself. I have a lot of applicants for this position."

"I bet you do." He slides his hands off my legs and repositions them on the desk at either side of my hips. Then he bends forward so that his mouth brushes my ear as he whispers, "What kind of duties does the job entail?"

"Well, I'm a difficult boss to satisfy. If you want to remain employed, you're going to have to work very, very hard."

"Hard work doesn't scare me."

"And I like my team to have initiative. If I have to tell my subordinates every little thing to do, that's definitely not going to win points."

His brow rises. "Good to know," he says, holding my gaze. He puts one hand on my thigh, but slides the other up my torso until he's cupping my breast through the tank. He uses his thumb to stroke the swell of my breast, and I bite my lower lip, trying very hard not to whimper. "I promise you want me. I'm the kind of man you can count on to get the job done."

I draw in a ragged breath as he tugs my tank down, freeing my breast. I close my eyes and arch back as he teases my nipple with his thumb. "I take very little on faith," I say, my voice breathy. "If you want to impress me, you'll have to show me more than just idle chatter."

"I admire an employer who values action over words." He rolls my nipple between two fingers, and I squirm, moving to draw my thighs together to quell the ache growing at my core. He defies me by stepping between my knees and ensuring that my legs stay spread.

He slips his hands under my skirt, his palms warm against my skin, then slowly slides up my thighs until his thumbs reach my panties. I bite my lower lip as he lazily strokes the soft skin where my thighs meets my sex, then gasp in surprise when he teases my clit through the thin cotton.

"Take them off. Please," I beg. "Take them off."

"Now?" The pad of his thumb moves in a small circle, the pressure and motion sending sparks shooting through my body. "You're not nearly ready."

"The hell you say," I protest, then gasp as his fingers slip beneath the material, teasing my entrance and making me crave more. So much more.

"Arch back," he demands, and I shift so that my arms are behind me and I'm leaning back, my eyes closed as his fingers continue to play and tease, making my hips move of their own accord. I'm so wet, my panties soaked, and he plays with me mercilessly, tugging the crotch aside as he thrusts into me.

At the same time, he bends forward, his mouth closing over my breast. His tongue dances over my nipple, and when he draws me in, sucking hard, I feel it all the way to my core, then gasp as he fingerfucks me, abandoning the lazy strokes for hard, deep thrusts.

I buck against him, wild with desire. Crazed with need. I want to be naked beneath him. I want to feel him inside of me. I want everything. Every stroke, every sensation, every pleasure. *Him.*

But I can't find the words. And all I can say is, "Now. Please, please, now."

I watch as he lifts his head and meets my eyes, the desire on his face so palpable I almost come right then. "Do you know what the best part of sex is?"

I shake my head.

"Anticipation," he says. And then, without warning, he steps back, leaving me untouched and very needy.

CHAPTER TWENTY-THREE

"Oh, God, Devlin," El protested. "Don't stop. Please."

He had no intention of stopping. But he wanted this moment. This certainty that she was completely his.

His greatest fear—maybe his only fear?—was losing her again. But here she was, his in every way. It was a gift. And damned if he didn't cherish it.

"Devlin, please." She'd shifted to the edge of the desk, and now she reached for his hand. "Screw anticipation. I want you now. My interview, remember? And if you think you're getting the job by leaving me hanging, you're not the man for this position."

She was teasing, of course, but it didn't matter. He took her hands and pulled her off his desk, taking some loose papers with her. They fluttered to the floor—contracts, reports, he didn't even care. He pulled her to him, then tilted her chin up. "I am," said. "Tell me."

He felt the shift in the air between them. The frustration in her melting into something dark and primal. "Yes. You are. You're the only man for me."

"You're mine."

"I'm yours. Devlin." Her eyes searched his face, but he knew she wouldn't see his fears there. With her, he could be vulnerable, true. But not now. Now, he only wanted her. Needed her. Needed to claim her and use her to help shift his world back onto its axis.

"Take off your clothes."

She took a step back, stopping when she hit the edge of his desk. "What? Here? Now?"

"Here," he said. He sat in his desk chair, then rolled it back a bit, watching her.

He expected her to protest, but when she reached back and unzipped her skirt, he realized he should have known she'd comply. This was El, after all, and the idea of submitting to him in his office where—at least theoretically—anyone might walk in, would be a new kind of temptation for her. A new thrill.

She matched him so well, even more than she knew. She was so strong, willing to face her fears. To take no shit from anyone except under her own terms. She was like lightning in a bottle, and the simple knowledge that he could have her completely— that he was powerful enough to compel a woman like her—that she would let him—made him harder than he'd ever been.

She kicked the skirt aside, then lifted the tank top over her head and dropped it on his desk. Now she stood in front of him in only her panties. Plain white cotton bikini style panties. Hell, he'd never seen sexier lingerie.

"Off," he said. He was so damn hard, and it took all of his willpower to stay in that chair, to not stroke himself as he watched her. Instead, he held onto the armrest, his fingers digging into the leather as his desire grew with every tilt of her head, every flash of her eyes.

She shimmied out of the panties, then tossed them onto his lap, raising a brow when she met his eyes. He held her gaze, then lifted the panties, still warm from her body, and breathed in her scent.

He heard the catch in her throat as she said, "Devlin."

"Tell me," he said. "Tell me what I want to hear."

"I'm yours." She tilted her head. "And you're mine, too."

"I am," he said. "And if I want you to prove it?"

She lifted her chin. "Whatever you want."

God how he adored her. He knew she meant it. Knew that, like him, she would bend to any whim. "Even if I told you to step out onto the balcony? Even if I said I wanted you to stand there naked, a thing of beauty for anyone to see?"

He saw the movement in her throat as she swallowed. Then she stepped toward him, veering slightly as if to go around his chair. He caught her hand as she was passing. "Why?"

"Because that's the game," she said, and damn him, he burst out laughing. She wasn't wrong.

With a wicked grin, she settled on her knees in front of him, her hands on his legs. Her eyes dipped to his cock, then she looked up at him, the question clear in her eyes. "I could be under the desk. You could be on a call. Or we could pretend Anna came in. Hell, she could come in. And your cock would be hard in my mouth, and you'd have to try to concentrate on what she was saying. What you needed to do, to sign, and all the while I'd be sucking, drawing you in deeper and deeper, and she'd be standing right there, never suspecting a thing."

"Christ, Ellie."

She pressed a hand over his cock, harder now.

"Is that what you want?" he asked.

She shook her head. "No." Her grin was impish as she stroked him. "But I like the fantasy."

He did, too, and that reality only fueled his desire. He stood, taking her with him. "Over my desk," he said, needing to claim her. Take her.

She did as he asked, her breasts on the polished wood, her hands gripping the far side. Her ass right in front of him. And his cock—well, his cock wouldn't wait any longer.

Roughly he forced her legs apart as she murmured, "Yes." He slipped his fingers into her, thinking to ready her, but there was no need. He'd never felt her this slippery, and right then he knew he couldn't wait any longer.

"I think you're hired, Mr. Saint," she said, and he fought back a laugh. Instead, he twined his fingers in her hair with one hand as he guided his cock with the other.

"Tell me you want this," he demanded, easing inside her. Just enough to tease. Just enough to make her whimper. "Tell me you want more."

"Yes." Her hips wiggled in demand, and he released her hair so that he could hold onto her hips and lose himself inside her. A primal claiming. A desperate taking. He'd never been with any woman in his office, but with El—

With her, he wanted—*needed*—everything.

Desire washed through him, erasing coherent thought. The scent of her, the memory of her. He wanted to take her everywhere, every way. More than that, he needed it.

He moved his hands, slipping one under her so he could tease her clit, his other hand on the small of her back as he buried himself inside her, each stroke taking him higher, each of her moans working on him like an aphrodisiac, taking him closer and closer to the edge. And when she lifted her head and twisted around, her eyes meeting his, it was as if she'd kicked him right over the cliff. He exploded inside her, her body tightening around his as they came together, their eyes locked, time stopping, until slowly, so very slowly, the world shifted back onto its axis, and his spent body went limp.

With a satisfied sigh, she started to get up. He helped her, then used a tissue from his desk drawer for a quick cleanup.

"Well," she said, settling on the edge of his desk. "I guess you're hired."

They shared a grin before he cupped her cheek and kissed her sweetly. "Come on," he said, gathering her clothes and leading her to the washroom.

"I'm glad you came," he said when she was dressed and they were both fixing their clothes.

She took his hand as they headed back into the the office. "Me, too. Busy day?"

"Always. What's on your agenda?"

It was the right question, obviously, because she lit up. "I have a lead," she said. "An anonymous source with a tip about the Myers assassination. With luck, it'll lead to identifying the shooter."

His entire body went stiff, the pleasure of the past moments shoved under by a wave of irritation.

His voice was as hard as ice as he said, "Why on earth would you pursue that? You met Sue. You talked to Laura. You know how broken they were, and Sue was one of the lucky ones. Whoever took that SOB out deserves a medal, not an indictment."

"Whoa, whoa, whoa," she said, her voice as tight as his. "Just hold on a minute. I might not give a flying fuck that Myers is dead, but that doesn't change the fact that whoever killed him committed a crime. The shooter was a self-appointed judge and jury, and that's not the way things work."

"Myers had already been convicted and sentenced," he reminded her. "He was released on appeal due to a technicality. *Not* because he was innocent."

"That may be so, but that doesn't give the shooter—"

He held up a hand, wishing they were on the same page about this. "Hang on. Just hang on." He knew that growing up with a father who was the Chief of Police and then working as a cop herself colored the way Ellie looked at the justice system. Still, he wished he could make her understand the way he thought.

"I get that we disagree," he said slowly, trying to gather his thoughts. "But with the position you're taking, you're essentially saying that whoever killed my father—whoever killed The Wolf—deserves to be prosecuted. Even though by killing that vile excuse for a human being, the shooter saved hundreds, probably thousands of lives."

"People can't just assassinate—"

"My father was one of the most notorious criminals who

walked this earth. He did horrible things to me and to everybody he stumbled across." Devlin felt bile rise in his throat along with the memories. Forcibly, he pushed it down, trying to keep his voice steady.

"He went out of his way to hurt people," he continued, "and one day someone took the son of a bitch out. If we go by the rules that you're advocating, that someone deserves to be put in jail. Possibly even sentenced to death. That's where your train of thought goes. You know that, right?"

She winced, his words obviously hitting home, and he had to wonder if she'd guessed the truth already. If she knew that he was the one who'd pulled the trigger and taken out The Wolf almost two years after he'd walked away from her.

Did she know?

And did she truly condemn him?

With sudden clarity he remembered one of the recent texts she'd received. *Don't you know you're fucking a dangerous man?*

A cold fury burned though him. Not because the words were a lie, but because they were true.

But he wasn't ready for her to know just how dangerous he truly was.

Not yet.

Maybe not ever.

CHAPTER TWENTY-FOUR

I want to bang my head against the wall in frustration. I get that we see things differently, but I can't understand why it bothers him so much that I'm pursuing the Myers story. I don't have the chance to ask, though, because the intercom buzzes, and Anna's voice fills the room. "I'm sorry to bother you, but I need to update you on a few things."

I see the muscle in his jaw tighten before he pushes the button to reply. "Traditionally, the Do Not Disturb light means do not disturb."

"It's time sensitive. And you might consider it urgent."

"Give me a minute." He turns to me. "Sorry. Work beckons."

"That's okay," I say glibly. "I've already had my way with you."

He chuckles. "Yes, you definitely did."

I grab his tie just below the knot and tug him down, as if for one, final quick kiss. Instead, I nip his lower lip with my teeth, then whisper, "Promise of things to come."

"So to speak," he deadpans, and I have to fight not to laugh. "Touché."

He grabs my chin, holding it firm between his thumb and

forefinger, the gesture so commanding that I feel the tingle of its intensity all the way to my core. "Stay with me," he murmurs.

"I think Anna would rather I get out of both your hair so that you two can get some work done."

"I mean tonight. Stay at my place. Be waiting for me tomorrow when I get back from Vegas."

I shake my head. "We both know I should stay at Brandy's. Someone's watching us. We talked about this. It's a little too intimate if I'm staying at your place even without you there."

He sighs. "My fear is that there will always be someone watching us."

I frown, then start to ask what he means, but he cuts me off.

"Ignore me. I'm just frustrated. I don't like being watched. And I don't like subtle threats. And I definitely don't like worrying about your safety. My place is more secure than Brandy's."

"Her place has an alarm, and I promise we'll set it. I'm armed. And I can take care of myself."

"You shouldn't have to. And yet you're in that position because of me."

"We're not having this conversation."

"Stay at my place," he repeats. "Tomorrow night I'll bring home take-out and we can watch a movie."

I cross my arms over my chest and cock my head. "Is that the best you can do?"

"Not even close," he says. "But you'll have to show up to find out how truly enticing my offer is."

"I think I should at least get a hint," I tease. "Something that lets me know how much you care?"

"Hmm." A slow grin touches his lips. "What can I do to make sure you're available at my beck and call?" His gaze roams over me, as predatory as a wolf. "Something to ensure you know how much I want you." His fingertips trace lightly over my neck and shoulders.

"Something to entice you," he continues, then brushes his

thumb over my lower lip. "Maybe something like your very own drawer."

His expression is as playful as his voice has become, and I fight an unexpected bubble of giggles as I press my palms over my heart. "Why, Mr. Saint, an entire drawer? I guess you really do love me."

He still hasn't said it out loud, and now I wait to hear those words, or even a simple *yes*. But all he says is, "Well, what do you think?"

It shouldn't bother me, but faith isn't my strong suit. He hurt me once, after all, and some hidden, broken part of me whispers that with Devlin Saint, maybe it's best if I'm always protecting my heart.

Anna's quick double-tap on the door has me sliding off the desk, and I'm standing beside Devlin when the doors sweep open and she walks through the gap. "Ellie, I'm sorry. When I first buzzed I didn't realize you were in here, and then when I realized..." She trails off, looking more than a little embarrassed.

"It's no big deal. I've stolen enough of Devlin's time."

"No, no. I don't mean to rush you out. I just wanted to let you know who tracked me down today," she continues, her attention shifting to Devlin.

He frowns. "Who?"

"Joseph Blackstone."

I see the slightest twitch in his muscles. I can tell the name has surprised him and he's working to keep himself under control. "Are you okay?"

Anna nods, but her face is tight, as if she's holding back intense emotions. She seems even more tense than she'd been on the beach, and I wonder what happened after Brandy and I left. Or maybe I hadn't gotten a very good look.

"You're sure?" The concern in Devlin's voice is palpable.

"Yes. Really. I'm fine. Just surprised. It's been a very long time."

I know this doesn't concern me, but I'm too curious not to ask. "Who's Joseph Blackstone?"

Devlin's eyes narrow as he says, "You know the security breaches I mentioned?"

I nod.

"Well, as far as we've been able to tell, Blackstone's been on the receiving end of some of the leaked information."

I frown, processing that. "So he's been stealing information from you?"

"That's unclear," Devlin says.

"But someone has," Anna puts in. "And even if Joseph isn't driving that cart, we think he's buying the goods."

I look between the two of them, now even more confused. "So why come to see you?"

She looks to Devlin when she answers. "No idea. He doesn't seem to have a clue that we know he's benefiting from the breaches. He said he learned that I was working for the DSF and that it would be *amusing*—his word—to come track me down while he was in Southern California."

"Does he know who I am?"

She shakes her head. "At least, I don't think so. Nothing he said made me think he knew."

"Why would he know?" I ask. "You're talking about Devlin being Alejandro, right? The Wolf's son? Why would he possibly know that?"

"Joe's about ten years older than me," Devlin answers, "and he was moving up fast in my father's enterprise about the time I came here to work with Peter."

"So he knew both of you." I say it as a statement, but Anna nods in affirmation.

"Yeah," she says harshly. "We knew each other."

Devlin moves to her side and gently cups her shoulder. "What else did he say?"

"Nothing. Just that we ought to grab a bite." She makes a scoffing noise. "As if. I told him that I'd left everything about The

Wolf's compound behind when I walked away, and that it wasn't personal, but that I was going to decline his invitation."

Devlin steps back, obviously studying her, as if looking for cracks in a porcelain doll. "And that was it?"

"That was it." She shrugs. "It's not—I mean, he didn't have any reason to track me down..."

"Tell our team to keep an eye on him," Devlin says. "Maybe it really was coincidence. Maybe he wants to get close to you to see if he can skim even more intelligence about our operations." He glances my way, and though it's probably my imagination, I get the feeling he wishes I weren't in the room right then. "And maybe he really does know more than we think he does."

"About you?" Anna shakes her head. "Nobody knows. Nobody could."

"Of course they could," Devlin says. "Nobody's ever really safe. You grew up the same way I did, Anna. You know that's the truth as well as I do."

"This is fun," Tracy says as we window-shop our way along Pacific Avenue. "Thanks for asking me." I'd bumped into her in the lobby as I was leaving, and we'd decided to make the walk to Brewski together, then do some window shopping.

"No problem." I check my watch. "I can offer you dinner, too, if you want. I'm aces at ordering pizza, and I'm not too bad at uncorking wine, either."

She laughs. "Truly, you have an amazing skill set."

"Well, I don't like to brag," I tease. "Seriously, though. Do you want to walk with me back to Brandy's? We can rent a movie or something? I can only offer my company. Apparently Brandy's got a hot date."

She wrinkles her nose apologetically.

"Right," I say. "That makes me the dateless one." I frown, then remember that I have a date with my computer, anyway. I want to put all my notes about Peter in order tonight. Because tomorrow I'm hoping to have a PC that I can use to open the creepy, anonymous URL, and then—assuming there's really a lead on the site—shift gears to the Myers story.

I shrug. "Well, maybe I'll get lucky and wrangle a little phone sex."

Tracy almost spits her coffee, and too late, it occurs to me that I'm talking about having phone sex with her boss. Not my finest hour.

Her lips narrow and her eyes bulge a bit as she tries not to spew the sip she'd just taken.

"Sorry. I'm so sorry."

She finally manages to swallow, then wipes her mouth, her eyes sparkling with tears of laughter. "Please, please, do not tell Mr. Saint you said that in front of me. I'd really like to be able to continue looking him in the eye."

"You got it," I say. "If you reciprocate and promise to share absolutely no details about your date tonight. Lamar is a very good friend. There are certain images I don't need in my head."

We shake on the deal, then chat for another block before she makes a right turn to cut diagonally back toward PCH and her condo. I continue straight toward the winding road that leads up into the canyons and to Brandy's house.

Pacific Avenue dead-ends at Sunset Parkway, and I pause long enough to make sure I have the walk sign. Then I step off the curb—right as a black Range Rover blows through the light and careens around the corner.

And it's coming straight at me.

CHAPTER TWENTY-FIVE

Time stops as my brain processes the danger—because even though I'm already stumbling backwards, my footing isn't solid, and there is no way in hell it's going to miss me.

I don't see my life flash before my eyes. Instead, all I see is Devlin, and all I feel is the tight pinch of loss and terror. I let my body go limp, trying to go down in a roll so that maybe, *maybe*, it'll miss me. But I can't, because there's suddenly a tight pressure on my shoulder and my neck, and I realize that someone's grabbed the collar of my zipped-up jacket, and I'm hurtling backward toward them, the force of the jacket pressing against my throat enough to make me gag.

I sprawl backwards, landing hard on the concrete, then whimper as I realize that tears of relief are streaming down my cheeks. I cough as I suck in air, then breathe in the pungent scent of burnt rubber from the squeal of the Range Rover's tires as it peels off, racing the hell away from the scene.

Everything's moving in slow motion now, and I realize that I'd looked for a license plate, but the SUV didn't have one. The windows were tinted, too.

"Ellie, are you okay? Can you get up?" The voice is familiar. But there's too much for my head to process, and so I just sit still for a moment, not able to do anything but assess the new reality that is racing through my mind. *That was on purpose. Someone tried to run me down on purpose.*

"*Ellie.*"

I hear it now—Lamar's voice, and I look up to find him kneeling beside me. "You're here," I say stupidly. "Why are you here?"

"I was trying to catch up with you." He runs his hands down my arms. "Are you okay?"

I nod. "Catch up?"

"I snagged you a computer." He nods at the padded laptop case on the sidewalk next to him. "Endo was going to give it to Goodwill. Said it's yours if you want it. I bumped into Tracy and she said you were walking home. It's only luck that I caught up to you when I did."

"Hell, yes, it was luck."

He helps me to my feet. That's when I tune into the hum of voices and notice the extent of the crowd around us, many of whom are snapping pictures with their phones. Some look excited —like they've just watched a parade—but most look shocked or horrified.

"That car didn't have a plate," a thin woman with a stroller says. "That's not legal."

"*That's* not legal?" I can hear incredulity in the skateboarder's voice. "The fucker tried to run her down." He flashes a crooked smile at me. "Probably some woman pissed off you're nailing Saint and she isn't."

"*Idiot,*" another woman mumbles, and I swallow a nod of acquiescence. Except, of course, he could be right.

"Come on," Lamar says. "I'm walking you home."

I don't resist when he takes my arm. We wait for the walk sign as the small crowd fawns over me, and I reassure them that I'm fine. I check and double-check the intersection before finally crossing the street with Lamar, then we start the slow climb up the hill toward Brandy's house.

It's dusk now, the area suffused with a hazy gray like a movie from the Forties. "Do you have any idea who that was?" Lamar asks.

I shake my head, but even as I do, I say, "Whoever's been sending the texts, I assume." I drag my fingers through my hair, then tell him about Joseph Blackstone.

He pauses by a lamppost as we reach the turn toward Brandy's house. "But Devlin doesn't think Blackstone knows he's Alejandro Lopez?"

"Right. As far as he knows, Devlin is just Devlin Saint to Blackstone."

"So what's getting leaked in these breaches?"

"That I don't know," I tell him. "But the DSF works with law enforcement and rehab groups to help shut down criminal enterprises. Maybe he's getting advance notice of raids?"

"Maybe," Lamar says. "Only way to find out is to ask Devlin. Is he going to be pissed you told me this?"

I shake my head. "No. For one, he told me I could talk to you, and he didn't put any parameters on that. And two, if that was Blackstone in that car, he'll be happy with any help you can provide."

"Fair enough. I'll see what I can find out."

"It might have been a drunk driver," I say, wishful thinking running amok.

He looks down his nose at me, but doesn't even bother to respond. Just starts walking again.

"I know. I know," I say, falling in step beside him. "But the bigger point is that there's no indication Blackstone knows who Devlin really is. But whoever is sending the texts clearly does."

"Are you sure they do?"

I pause. "What do you mean?"

"The texts only say Devlin is dangerous, right? Have any of them suggested he has a secret identity?"

I think back, then shake my head.

"So maybe this Joseph has it in for Devlin, and you seem like a good way to get at him."

I frown, but don't respond. It's an interesting theory.

"You carrying?"

I shake my head, gesturing to the tiny crossbody that holds my phone, a credit card, and an emergency fifty. I'd told Devlin I was armed, but I didn't technically mean at that moment.

He rolls his eyes. "You have a permit. Carry your damn weapon."

I don't argue since I don't disagree.

When we reach the house, I head inside, then set the alarm. Brandy doesn't always bother with it, often arming it only when we go to bed. Now, I want it permanently on.

"Brandy? You home?"

"Coming!" She appears almost simultaneously with the word. "Hey, I was going to meet Christopher for a drink later, but—"

She cuts herself off, frowning as she looks between Lamar and me. "What's wrong?"

I glance at Lamar. "Will you fill her in? I think there's a bruise on my ass. I want to check it out."

"Okay, now I really want to know," Brandy demands, her words directed toward Lamar as I head to my room. Sure enough, there's what's sure to be a doozy of a bruise rising on one ass cheek. Great. But as far as I can tell, that's my only injury. Even my palms are fine, despite aching a bit. I don't specifically remember, but I'm sure I must have used them—and my butt—to stop my fall.

When I come back, I bring my gun. As soon as I've put it down, Brandy tosses her arms around me. "You're really okay?"

"I'm fine. I swear."

"What's Devlin say?"

"I haven't told him yet."

She grimaces. "I'm new to the boyfriend thing, but even I know you're breaking the rules by not telling him."

"I know. I'm not keeping it from him, but he's in Vegas

dealing with some important stuff, and I don't want to distract him. You guys are here, and I'm safe." I can tell Brandy's about to argue, so I hold up a hand. "Really. He has shit to deal with. I'll tell him tomorrow when I see him. Right now, I just want that wine."

"Red or white?" Brandy asks, and I choose a Pinot Noir. "How about you?" she asks Lamar, who shakes his head.

"I completely forgot," I tell him, an apology in my voice. "You've got a date. Go," I say. "I'm fine."

He studies my face, as if looking for hidden signs that I'm about to break down. I cock my head. "Seriously? You know me. I don't get spooked easily. The house has an alarm, and I've got a gun. And whoever tried to run me down is a coward anyway. Tinted windows. No plates. That's not someone who's going to risk getting seen by the neighbors."

"I'll stay with her," Brandy says, as if none of my speech means a thing. "I was supposed to go out with Christopher tonight, but he had to bail."

"I'm sorry," I say. "What's up?"

She shook her head. "Not sure. He said he was having a bad day. I think he's having trouble with the book, so, you know, I figured I wouldn't bug him about it."

"If you're sure," Lamar says. "Because I can rearrange, too. Or I can have Tracy come here and we can all watch a movie. Seriously, whatever you need."

"I know," I say, moving close to give him a hug. "But I'm really fine. Now go. Brandy and I are doing girl talk."

Lamar flashes a toothy smile. "Oh, sugar, you know I can stay for that."

I roll my eyes. "Go. Before I tell Tracy what a pain in the ass you can be."

"You love me."

"Only because I'm an idiot."

He pulls me into a tight hug. "You be careful," he whispers.

"Thanks for saving my ass."

He kisses me on the forehead, looks me up and down, then backs away. "Take care of her," he says to Brandy.

"Always," she replies with a wave. "You do think it's safe, right?" she asks once he's out the door and we've re-armed the system.

"We're armed and locked in tight with 911 on speed dial. We're fine," I say as we settle on the couch. "And I don't want to think about it anymore, much less talk about it. Tomorrow, I'm doubling down to figure out who this fucker is. Tonight, we chill. Okay?"

"Sure. No problem." She bites her lower lip.

"What?"

"Is it okay if we talk about Christopher while we're chilling?"

"Of course! By the way, what does he drive?"

Her eyes go wide "Wait, what? You don't think—"

"No, no!" I hurry to reassure her. "I'm so sorry. I didn't think about how that would sound. I just have cars on my mind."

Her shoulders sag as she visibly relaxes. "An Audi," she says. "And, he always opens my door for me, which I like. I don't care if I'm a disappointment to womankind the world over."

"I like it, too," I admit. "But only because I also get to be on top."

She pretends to be offended by my crudeness, but I use it as a natural segue. "Well?"

She reaches over and grabs for her wine, then downs the rest of the liquid. I settle back, realizing this means the conversation is about to get real.

"You guys talked while I was in with Devlin," I guess.

She nods, then shakes her head. "We chatted, and I wanted to talk. About, well, you know. But it wasn't exactly ideal surroundings with all his musty boxes of research and his plot bothering him. He was so distracted—I mean totally in his head."

"Probably good you didn't bring it up. You need a cheese plate and a bottle of wine for that kind of talk."

"Exactly. I was going to talk with him tonight, but..." She

trails off with a shrug, then meets my eyes. "Actually, this is better. You can help me figure out what to say."

"That's what I'm here for." I shift on the sofa, tucking one leg under me. "So you want to..."

"Yeah," she says, after releasing a deep breath. "I want to. It's just..."

She trails off with a shrug, then visibly searches for words. "Okay, it's like this. He knows I've been hesitant, so he's not going to push. Except now I think maybe I want him to push." She meets my eyes, hers imploring. "So how do I make him push?"

I try not to let my smile grow too broad "You're going to have to actually talk to him, I'm afraid."

She groans. "I'm terrible at that."

"No," I assure her. "You're not."

She pulls her knees up and hugs her chest, mimicking my earlier position. For a moment she says nothing, then, "I'm nervous."

I take her empty wine glass from her and put it on the table before taking her hands. "I'm not surprised that you're nervous, but you'll know if it's right."

"I only—I mean I'm twenty-eight, and I've only slept with one guy. Two guys if you count the one I don't remember, which I don't. And as for Billy..."

I nod sympathetically as she trails off. The only guy she'd slept with willingly had been a terrible lover with no patience for her fears and issues. He hadn't hurt her, but it hadn't been good for her, either. "Come on, Brandy. You just have to find the one who's right for you. Who's patient and sweet and isn't in it only for sex, but because he wants to be with you." I study her face but see only a mixture of confusion and terror.

"Hey," I say, squeezing her fingers. "Christopher seems like a great guy, but you don't have to move fast if you don't want to."

"I know. And I do want to. But it's gotten so much bigger than it really is now that I've waited so long." She offers me a smile. "I would say you got lucky early on," she tells me. "But even with you and Alex, it hasn't exactly been easy. You have him back, except it's not really him. Except it is. And now you've got a freaky texter to deal with. It's like you two are cursed."

"Thanks," I say dryly.

"Yeah, I know. It sucks. But don't worry. In the stories, the girl always wins the prince."

I force a smile, but keep my thoughts to myself. Because even though it's nice of Brandy to say, my life has never been anything like a fairy tale.

CHAPTER TWENTY-SIX

"Did my notes come through okay?" I ask Roger. It's not quite noon, and I've spent the morning organizing my research on the Peter article and icing my sore rear end. I sent a summary over an hour ago, and since I hadn't heard back, I'd taken the initiative and decided to harass my boss.

Normally I wouldn't bother calling, but since I plan to focus on the Myers investigation for a bit, I want to make sure that he's set with the Peter project.

"I've skimmed them, but I'm going to read more closely later today," he assures me. "Meanwhile, you got a PC?"

"Lamar snagged a laptop for me. I'm going to set up an email account and forward that URL in a little bit. Cross your fingers there's something there and not a link to porn."

I make a face, because considering the creativity of spammers these days, that's probably a legit possibility.

"Crossed," he assures me. "And thanks for talking to Corbin yesterday. I got his article this morning, and he did your research proud."

I grunt, and he laughs. "I should lock you two in a room until you make nice."

"But we both get so much satisfaction out of our mutual dislike."

"Can't argue with that," Roger says. "And for the record, we miss you here. Or, at least, I miss you. Well," he continues, humor lacing his voice, "I miss Shelby."

"You realize that it's totally unfair that I can't call you an asshole since you're my boss."

"Pity that," he says. "We should talk about working out some sort of shared custody agreement. When I agreed to let you work from the West Coast, I forgot about Shelby."

"You wish." For the last three years, I'd been keeping Shelby garaged at his house since parking in Manhattan was well beyond my means.

"You can always do what my father did," I suggest. "Find yourself a '65 Shelby Cobra in need of some TLC and get to work."

At the other end of the line, I hear him chuckle. "Too bad I don't have your father's particular skillset."

"Ha. Even my dad didn't have that skillset. Or Peter. Read the notes. The mechanic didn't know much, but he mentioned a girl-friend. I haven't tracked her down—and I had no idea Peter dated anyone—but I'm hoping if I poke hard enough, someone in town will have a lead. And if it turns out that she was more than a side-piece—like if she was dealing or working for The Wolf or anything like that—the story will get that much more interesting."

"And you're okay with that?"

"The part about my mom knocked me for a loop," I admit. "But I'm trying to step back and look at it as a story. I'll add in the personal bits when I write it up, but if I'm going to keep a clear head while researching then I need to compartmentalize. You taught me that."

"And you learned well. I'm proud of you, kid." He pauses. "How are things with you and Saint?"

It's an interesting transition considering my relationship with

Devlin had almost gotten me fired and had definitely lost me a byline. "We're great," I assure him.

"No regrets about staying in Cali?"

"It's been about five minutes," I remind him. "But nope. No regrets at all. And I don't foresee any coming."

"I'm happy for you, kid. You want me to stay online while you set up that computer?"

"And let you hear me cursing at all the crap that'll go wrong when I try to set up an email account? No, thank you. I'll call or email an update later."

We agree that's a plan, and as soon as we end the call, I refill my coffee and settle in to work. I have the place to myself—and I'm locked down tight. Brandy's in LA doing stuff in the garment district, but she's checked in twice. Lamar came by on his way to his shift, and has texted three times. Devlin, who still doesn't know about the Range Rover, has pinged me twice to say he's thinking of me. And as much as I love my friends, it's Devlin's messages that make me smile the most.

Since I don't want to do anything related to the Terrance Myers email at Brandy's house or on her network, I head down to Brewski so that I can use their free Wi-Fi. I know Brandy and Lamar are going to be annoyed if they realize I went out, but I'm not inclined to be a shut-in. Besides, I'm in Shelby instead of walking, the seating at Brewski is outdoors and very public, and this time I have my gun in my purse.

All rationalizations, but the truth is that I like the idea of going out and then coming home safe. Because seriously, when have I not taken the opportunity to give danger the middle finger?

Within the hour, I have the new laptop set up and connected to Brewski's network. Next, I create a new email address for Nosey Parker, a name I picked because Gmail requires you to put in a name and other identifying information. Which, in this case, is absolutely fake.

The account has no ties to my name or any of my usual passwords. Then, because I'm seriously paranoid, I create a second fake email account. This one I call Flat Earth, for no reason other than an utter lack of imagination on my part. I write a few emails from Flat Earth to Nosey Parker, and they show up just fine.

When I open my real laptop, I glance around, expecting people to be looking curiously at the woman with two computers at a coffee shop. But nobody pays attention. That's the benefit of living in a tech-centric world. I could have two computers, a tablet, a cell phone, and a portable printer on this tiny table and no one would even bat an eye.

I pull up my work email on my real computer, then forward the anonymous Terrance Myers email to the Flat Earth address. Once it shows up there, I forward it on to Nosey Parker.

And then, when it arrives in Nosey's account, I finally —*finally*, click that URL, then cross my fingers as I hope that I didn't just jump through all of those hoops for nothing.

The connection is ridiculously slow, and I tap my finger impatiently on the tabletop as the bar indicating the site's loading moves with the speed of a snail across the screen

Finally, the site pops up. There's text above an embedded video, currently paused. All I can see is an image of the Hastings Bank building and the blue arrow I need to click to play.

I use the trackpad to put the mouse in place as I read the short note:

Drone footage caught something interesting. Check the time-stamp. Just a few hours before the assassination of Terrance Myers. Two figures rappelling down. Test run before the main event. Don't let the fuckers get away with it. That's not justice, it's murder.

I read it twice, then even though I took a table where my back would be against Brewski's exterior wall, I check for anyone looking over my shoulder. Because this is big—like holy fucking shit big—and there is no way in hell I'm going to lose a potential scoop of this magnitude.

Assuming, of course, that the video is what my mysterious benefactor says it is.

Please, I think. *Please be real.*

I draw a breath, then click play.

I watch, breathless, as the drone circles the bank building, finally focusing in on two figures rappelling down the side, just as I'd imagined it was done. As far as the police knew, there was only one person who descended the building at the time of the assassination, so I assume that the sender is correct and this is a test run.

The drone moves in closer, and I hold my breath, trying to get a look at the faces. I even put my finger on the trackpad, trying to zoom in, as if this were a map or something. I can't, of course, but if I take a screenshot...

I pause the video long enough to do that, then zoom in on the image. But it's far too pixelated. Frustrated, I let the video play some more. The two figures have almost reached the ground. They're neck and neck, and the winner hits the ground only seconds before the loser. The drone isn't recording sound, but something must have made a noise, because they both look up.

It would be a perfect shot for facial recognition, except for the fact that between the distance and the poor light, the images are terrible. There's too much visual noise and pixelation, and I don't have the skill set to fix it.

For a moment, I wonder if anyone does. Because surely whoever sent this to me would have tried. They want me to see the shooter, right? Does that mean that this is as good as the video gets? Or do they assume that reporters have magic powers, since in a movie, I'd probably tap a few arrow keys or write some code and get what I need.

As if.

I frown, trying to think of who I know with the skills to clean this up.

Or, correction, who might have the skills to teach me how to clean it up. I'm not ready to share this video. It's too hot, and a leak could mean that someone scoops me on the story.

What I need is someone who has software I can use. Someone

in graphic design or computer programming or, I don't know, just a tech savvy genius.

Unfortunately, I haven't got a clue, but I shoot a quick text to Roger asking if he does. Surely the magazine has needed to bump up the clarity of an image before.

His answer is both fast and unnerving.

We have someone on staff who used to code graphic design software. He says he wrote code back in the day that might help you. But you're not going to like it.

Not going to like it? Is he crazy? *Are you crazy?* I write. *Who?*

This time, the answer takes longer. So long, I almost call him.

Corbin, he finally says. *And he's agreed to send you the software. But in exchange, he says you owe him one.*

CHAPTER TWENTY-SEVEN

It's like making a deal with the devil, but if Corbin's software works, then I suppose it will be worth it.

Roger tells me he'll get all the wheels in motion, then puts Corbin on the line. He explains that he needs to do some tweaking so I can run the software myself. Right now, it only works on his system since it interfaces with other software he has installed. I'd have to share the video, and I'm not willing to do that. To his credit, Corbin doesn't argue. He promises to send me a list of additional software I'll need, and to call when it's ready so he can walk me through the installation and usage instructions.

He also mentions—every ten or so seconds—how nice it feels to know that I'm in his pocket.

I refrain from calling him an asshole, or worse. It's a testament to how much I want this story. And I figure if I can handle prostrating myself to my sworn enemy, then I can survive anything.

But when it's all over and I've paid my debt, I'm already planning a full-page ad in *The Spall's* competitor affirming that Corbin Dailey is a rare sort of prick.

Then again, maybe best not to. That would only add an all-new layer to his overinflated ego.

My mind is still spinning with anti-Corbin rhetoric as I pull into the garage. Usually, I park in the driveway or the street, but while I might be cavalier about my own safety, Shelby is my baby.

I enter through the garage door that leads into the laundry room. I drop my stuff on the dryer, then hurry through the nearby kitchen to grab a snack. I'm starving, which is ironic considering Brewski has food. But I'd been so wrapped up in work that my only sustenance had been a latte followed by a never-ending stream of black coffee.

I open the fridge, grab a container of vanilla yogurt, slam the door—and scream.

Because standing right behind the door where a horror movie monster would be is a man.

The scream dies in my throat when I realize it's Ronan Thorne, but I can't say that I'm relieved. Devlin may believe that Ronan doesn't have it in for me, but I'm still not convinced. Especially not now that Devlin is away and Ronan is inside this house that is supposedly well protected by an alarm system.

"What the hell are you doing here?" I demand, anger at his intrusion masking my runaway nerves.

"Sorry to scare you. Devlin gave me the code."

I bite back a curse and make a mental note to give my boyfriend hell. "Why would he do that?"

"He wanted me to check on you," Ronan says. "And I wanted to talk to you."

He moves casually to lean against the nearby countertop, but there's nothing casual about his demeanor.

When I first met him, he was smiling and charming and I thought that he looked a bit like a Nordic god with his blond hair and blue eyes and Thor-like body. He still does, but now there's a fury about him. He's like an angry god that has the ability to destroy the world.

I draw in a breath and tell myself that I'm not scared, but the truth is I am. Devlin may be convinced Ronan isn't behind the creepy texts, but the jury is still out for me.

Still, I've always been good at poker.

"Okay," I say, moving to get a spoon and then taking a bite of my yogurt. "What are we talking about?"

"I told you before that you'd be a distraction. It never occurred to me that you would be an actual danger."

I bristle. "What the hell are you talking about?"

"Devlin told me you got a lead on the Myers shooter. A link to some information. Is that true?"

"He had no right to tell you about that."

"Is it true?"

"What's your interest in it?"

"You are. Because Devlin's pissed, and he has reason to be."

My head is swimming. "What the hell are you talking about?"

"Are you trying to draw a target on your back? That news blast today on *The Spall* website about the video footage? About your exclusive lead on the identity of Terrance Myers' shooter? And how you're confident you'll be able to clean up the video to identify the shooter?"

"What the fuck? I didn't publish a news blast—*oh, shit. Roger.*"

After I'd first told him about the email, he'd published a tiny note on the website letting readers know that *The Spall* was investigating a possible lead in the Myers assassination. Today, of course, he must have posted an update mentioning the video. Ridiculous, since there's really no news yet, but even if I come up with zilch, just having that tidbit on the website will draw in readers—and advertisers. *The Spall* may be a quality print magazine, but per Franklin's edict, the website has a more sensationalistic slant, supposedly so that the magazine has more of a competitive edge in today's market. I can't say that I approve, but I also get that the magazine needs revenue.

"I had no idea," I tell Ronan. "I should have," I admit, "but my editor ran that piece."

"Well, tell him to take it down. Not that it'll matter. The damage has been done. Nothing disappears off the Internet."

He's right about that. "It can't have been live that long," I point out. "How do you even know about it?"

"Devlin subscribes to *The Spall*'s text alerts."

I blink, not expecting that. "Why?"

For a second, Ronan looks taken aback. "Because you write for the magazine, and it's important to you."

"Oh." I swallow, then take another bite of yogurt to hide my discomfiture. "Listen," I finally say, "I didn't realize Roger was going to run the blast, but so what? It's no big deal. I *am* writing the article, and I *do* have the video. Not to mention high hopes that I'll get a clear image soon. I get that Devlin thinks Myers was a worm who deserved to be taken out. And you know what? I don't disagree. But people can't just go around like this is the Wild West. And if I have a chance to use my job to reveal them, then I'm going to do that."

"At the risk to your own safety?"

"What are you talking about?"

He runs his fingers through his hair. "That news blast makes pretty clear that the footage was sent to the author of the original piece—you. If it's as damning as you think, wouldn't you expect that whoever was scaling that building will try to get it from you?"

I swallow, because he and Devlin are right of course. I've always been willing to take risks with my reporting, drawing out potential bad guys in the interest of building a story. It's never bothered me before because danger never bothered me before. Neither did death. All I was about was chasing the story. The rest of it could go to hell. In fact, the more dangerous the better.

But things have changed. I still don't understand why I'm here and my family isn't, but that deep need to take risks has faded. I want to stay. I don't want to leave this earth yet. Not when there's still time with Devlin.

"Honestly, I wasn't thinking about that." Now that I *am* thinking about it, I wonder if perhaps the Range Rover incident could be tied to the Myers story and not to the creepy texts.

"Well, then you're a fool. Does the video reveal the suspect's identity?"

I laugh, "No. I have a drone video that's pixelated as hell. I've got software that might be able to pull an image or it might not." I pause, thinking. "I'll have Roger post an update saying that the video is corrupt and we can't identify the shooter."

"Is that true?"

I shrug. "Hopefully not. If we do get an image and a story, then we'll update again. But maybe this way I throw off whoever's intent on harassing me."

He nods slowly. "How does the software work?"

I regurgitate what Corbin explained to me. "He said whether or not we can recreate a decent image depends on the quality of the original video."

"And how decent is the video?"

"I'm not a graphics person, but it looks fuzzy as hell to me." I don't tell him that I'm relying in part on Corbin's super-inflated ego. I don't think he would have offered his software if he didn't think we had a decent shot. The guy will want to be the hero, after all.

"Sounds like a long shot."

"Probably. Then again, reporting's all about following long shot leads. But I guess Devlin will be thrilled if I never get a clear image." I grimace. "I think he wants to be the personal cheering section for whoever took out Myers."

"I'm with him on that. Myers was scum. He deserved what he got."

I just look at him. This hard man. This man that Devlin respects and I fear. Not because I think he'll hurt Devlin—just the opposite.

Because I can't help but think that no matter what, in the end, he will always choose Devlin. That's a good thing. But to that end, I'm certain that he'd destroy anyone he thinks is in the way of Devlin's safety. Including me.

"I'll tell Devlin you're going to run the addendum to the article. But be careful. You never know who's read it and they might not see the update." I nod. And I watch as his facial features soften. "We just want you to be safe."

I stiffen with surprise. "We? I thought I was a distraction."

The corner of his mouth quirks. "I was probably wrong to say that. I've never felt for anyone the way Devlin feels about you, so I don't know exactly where he's coming from, but I do know that he would risk the world for you. And I will always have his back, so I guess that means I'm looking out for you, too. Whether I want to or not," he adds, but with a wink.

Which means that even as he's leaving, I'm still not sure if he's a turning into a solid friend or staying a dangerous foe.

CHAPTER TWENTY-EIGHT

It's dark when I wake abruptly, jolted out of sleep. I'm not sure what woke me, but after I glance at the clock and see that it's not quite two, I groan, start to roll over, and then see the figure silhouetted in the darkened doorway.

A scream catches in my voice, stopped only by the sudden recognition. *Devlin.*

He moves into the room, a shaft of moonlight illuminating him. He's breathing hard, his wild eyes on me. His hair tumbles around his face like a mane, and his beard needs a trim. He looks feral. Fierce. And though I know it's an illusion, his scar seems more prominent.

He emits danger like radio waves, and I can feel the force of his power from all the way across the room.

"Devlin?" I sit up. "What are you doing here?"

"Why the fuck didn't you tell me?"

I barely have time to process the question as he crosses to me in two long strides. He grabs my upper arms and tugs me out of bed. My body reacts immediately, my nipples tightening against the thin material of my tank top. My core throbbing as the loose sleep shorts brush my bare flesh. He's burning with heat and fury, and I've gone from a sound sleep to a desperate craving so quickly that I'm a little dizzy.

I know what he wants, why he's here. He's angry that I didn't call after the Range Rover almost ran me down. He's terrified of what could have happened. And he's translated that fear and fury into a need. To touch me. Claim me. To prove to himself and me and the whole goddamn world that I'm alive and I'm his and that I'm safe in his arms.

And oh, dear God, I want him too. So much that my skin burns in anticipation and my breath comes in shallow, stuttering gasps.

Except he doesn't touch me. On the contrary, he holds me at arm's-length, his gaze roaming over me as if he can't quite believe I'm whole.

I'm totally confused and completely turned on, and I hear the desperation in my voice as I ask, "Devlin, what are you—"

I don't get the question out before he yanks me against him, his mouth closing over mine in a kiss that leaves no question that I belong to him. I melt against him, lost in the pleasure of being taken. Claimed by this wild man. This savage lover. "Someone tries to run you over and you don't tell me?" His words are as bruising as the kiss he interrupts in order to force out the question. "What the hell were you thinking?"

"I—"

"No." He grabs my chin with one hand, another hard kiss silencing me as his other hand slips beneath the band of my shorts as he cups my ass. I moan, opening myself under the power of his desperate need. A desperation I share.

I rise onto my toes, my fingers sliding through his hair as I deepen the kiss, our teeth clashing as I pull his head closer, as if I could consume him. His fingers slide between my legs, finding me slippery and so, so ready. I moan against his mouth as our tongues battle with the same intensity as his finger fucks me. And though his kisses prove that he owns me, I still grind against his fingers, my body craving more than the release he can bring me. I crave the man.

I crave Devlin.

"You damn fool." His whisper is harsh. "I could have lost you. You could have been killed. Do you think I could stand it if I lost you again?"

His hands are tight on my shoulders, holding me in place.

"You won't," I say. "You didn't." I meet his eyes. "I can take care of myself."

"Do you think I don't know that?" He releases me, then goes to sit on the edge of the bed. He's wearing jeans, and they hug his thighs and accentuate the hard length of his erection. I take a step toward him, intending to tackle his fly, but he holds up a hand, silently ordering me to stop. "Take off your top."

I raise a brow, but I don't protest. I simply reach down, grab the hem, and tug the tank top over my head, then drop it on the floor beside me. My nipples tighten almost painfully in response, and my whole body fires from the way he looks me up and down. He's not smiling. On the contrary, I've never seen him look more serious. And though this is Devlin, the man I love, I can't help but feel a rush of trepidation mingling with the anticipation.

And, yes, I like it.

"The shorts."

I hook my thumbs into the band of my shorts, and wiggle my hips until they fall to the floor. Then I glance at the bulge in his jeans and, naked, take a step toward him. Then another. Then another.

"I think it's your turn," I say, expecting him to either strip off his jeans or invite me to tug down his fly.

Instead, he says, "No."

"No?"

He stands, then stalks toward me. Instinctively, I back away, but he comes closer until I'm pressed against the wall. He traps me there, his hand at my throat. "Dammit, El, do you think I could stand to lose you? Do you think I could bear it?"

"I—"

I cut off the word, as his hand tightens. "Is this what you need?" His lips are close to my ear. "Danger. Fear?" I have to struggle for breath as his other hand slides down my rear, his fingers thrusting into my pussy as his thumb rims my ass, sending a flurry of sensual pleasures skittering over my skin.

I moan, the sound silenced as he tightens his grip. His tongue traces my ear before he whispers. "No more chasing danger. You want danger, you come to me." His fingers fill me completely and I grind against him, understanding his need to control as much as I want to claim it, to surrender to it.

"You want to play rough? Fine." In one wild move, he releases my neck and twists me around, so that my bare breasts slam against the wall. His fingers are no longer inside me, and I cry out in surprise when his palm lands hard on my ass, the sting both sharp and sweet. He rubs the spot, and I bite my lower lip. No one's ever spanked me before—I've never let myself surrender before. But now...

Again, his palm lands hard, and again he rubs the sore spot. But this time he spreads my legs, his fingers going to my slippery core before moving back to my neck, holding me in place. Reminding me that right now, he is my everything. Even the air that I breathe.

"You like that." It's a statement, not a question.

I nod.

"What do you like?"

"All of it." My voice is raspy against the tightness of his grip. "You," I clarify. "I like what you're doing. I want this. I want—"

"What?"

"To surrender," I admit.

"You've always been in control," he says. "But not with me. With me, you surrender." He turns me back around as he speaks, then lifts me up. I hook my legs behind his back, then cling to his shoulders as he enters me. Each thrust pounds my back against the wall, and I curl my body against him, feeling the pressure build between us as he thrusts deeper and deeper inside me, claiming me. *Owning* me.

"Never again," he says as we're both on the brink of the explosion. "No more keeping me in the dark. What hurts you, hurts me. Do you understand?"

"Yes," I say, then, as the orgasm crashes over me, "Oh, God, yes."

I burst apart, taking him with me, and soon he's stumbling back to the bed, me still clinging to him until we break apart as we hit the mattress, both of us breathing hard. After a moment, he bends over me for a soft, sweet kiss. "Don't keep me in the dark again."

"I won't. I'm sorry. You're right." The words stick in my throat because they're true. I should have called. He deserves to know. Because even though he hasn't said it out loud, he loves me.

"I'm sorry," I repeat as I move on top of him with my cheek resting against his chest. "I didn't expect you to find out, though I should have," I add wryly. "And I didn't tell you because I didn't want you to worry. But that was wrong of me." I pull back to look at his face. "How did you hear?"

His expression suggests I've forgotten how to think. "There were dozens of people around, all of whom had camera phones and social media accounts. Only one person had to recognize you as my girlfriend, and—"

"*Shit.*" I let out a harsh breath. "Okay. I am an idiot. But so are Lamar and Brandy."

He makes a growling noise.

"No, don't even. They both told me I should text you. But none of us thought about Twitter." I make a face, then look up at him again. "I really am sorry."

"I know." He closes his eyes and draws a breath before looking at me. When he's done, I still see the lingering fear. "Dammit, El, don't do that again."

"Almost get run down? Trust me. Really *not* on my list."

"Do you have any idea who did it?"

"All I know is that it was a black Range Rover." I tilt my head. "Isn't that what Ronan drives?"

I know that it is. I'd watched him drive away last night, comforted only by the fact of his parting words and the fact that in Southern California you can't throw a rock without hitting a Range Rover. That and Devlin's unwavering trust in him.

Even so...

I meet Devlin's eyes. "He does, doesn't he?"

"He does. But he didn't—"

"I know you believe that," I cut in. "And I want to trust him— I really do. But he seemed pretty irritated that I was poking around in the Myers story. And I—" I pause to gather my thoughts. "The thing is, I trust my instincts. They're solid, and they're one of my tools as a reporter. Go with the facts, but don't ignore instinct, right? And there's something about Ronan that—"

"Trust *me*," Devlin interrupts. "Listen to your instincts, but at the end of the day, trust me."

"I do." My voice sounds small, and his bisected brow rises in response. "I do," I repeat. "About almost everything. And as far as Ronan goes, I really am trying."

He almost smiles. "I asked him to come see you because *I* was irritated about your Myers investigation. At the time, I hadn't heard that you'd almost been killed or I would have dropped everything and come myself."

I shrug. "Well, that made a great cover story for him, then."

He rubs his temples, clearly frustrated with me. And maybe I should drop it, but I don't understand why he can't see what I see.

"Ronan is not crosswise with this," he tells me. "I trust him with my life. And I trust him with yours, too. That should mean something to you."

"It does," I assure him. But what I don't say is that I still fear that his trust has been misplaced.

When he sighs, I know he understands what I haven't said. I

tense, expecting that we're going to continue this debate. Instead, he says, "Tell me about the footage. Have you found out anything yet?"

I shake my head and explain about Corbin and the software. "It's probably a dead end." I grimace as I meet his eyes. "And you think that's just as well."

"Yeah. I do."

I sigh, then sit up, the sheet wrapped around me. "We're not on the same page today, are we?"

He takes my hand. "We can disagree and still be together."

I swallow, my smile feeling a little watery as I fight tears. "You're right." I draw a breath and let it out slowly. "Okay. Convince me. Why are you so sure Ronan's a good guy?"

The mattress dips as he moves to sit up, his back against the headboard. "Other than the fact that we served together? That I've watched him work for years? That we've looked out for each other for a decade, and that he's kept my secrets without complaint?"

I sag a little. "Okay, I get it. I still think—"

"What?"

"I don't think he likes me."

Devlin laughs. "Does it matter?"

"Yes," I say, surprised by how much I mean it. "He's probably the closest person in the world to you—"

"No." He's looking right at me. "He's not."

My smile comes unbidden. "You know what I mean."

"I do. And you'll have to trust me that he likes you fine. But he worries about me. He knows I've never gotten serious about anyone since I was Alex. And he knows how much it will break me if..."

He trails off, and I take his hand. "There won't be an if."

"No," he says, his gaze burning into mine. "There won't."

For a moment, I lose myself in his eyes. It would be so easy to drop this. To slip away in forgetfulness in his arms. Maybe I should, but instead I say, "So what does Ronan do when he's not being an ambassador for the DSF?"

Devlin exhales with a sigh and a small shake of his head. "I adore you."

Laughter bubbles out of me. "That's good. Because I adore you, too." I tilt my head. "Well?"

He shifts a bit, getting more comfortable. "You know all those movies where the mysterious, quiet guy who worked in security is trying to live a normal life, then gets called in to save the day?"

"Sure. Those are my favorite kind. You're saying that's Ronan?"

"Pretty much."

"Independent security consultant," I say. "That's what he called it once."

"That sums it up pretty well. He protects politicians and celebrities. Investigates security breaches. Skills we learned in the service."

"You worked in intelligence, didn't you?"

He nods. "We both did."

"So he stayed in the same industry more or less, but you left. Why?"

"My path was different than Ronan's, but we're both doing good. I don't know why he gets under your skin, but you need to believe me."

"I do," I say, and it's not a lie because I really do believe that *he* believes it. As for me ... well, the jury's still out.

I am, however, done with this conversation. So I press my hand to his shoulder as I crawl onto his lap. I meet his eyes, then lower my voice. "Do you know what I want to do now?"

I see humor and heat flicker in his green eyes. "I'm guessing it's not sleep."

"Nope."

"Why don't you tell me?"

I slide my hands slowly up his bare chest as I bend forward to brush a soft kiss over his lips before teasing my way to his ear. I nip on his lobe, then whisper. "You've got me in the mood ... to watch an action movie."

His low chuckle reverberates through me as he squeezes my ass. "You're a tease."

I lean back enough to see his face. "Maybe," I admit. "But after the movie, I want a little more action of our own."

CHAPTER TWENTY-NINE

I'm awakened by a light tap on the door. Groggy, I clutch the sheet with one hand and prop myself up on my other elbow as I look over Devlin's shoulder. "Come in," I mumble.

The door bursts open, and Brandy pokes her head inside, her eyes immediately going wide. "Oh!"

That's when I realize that she's got an eyeful of Devlin, the sheet low on his hips so that all of his torso—and a bit more—is bare. He's still asleep, his face turned towards the door.

Sorry. I'm sorry. Brandy mouths the words.

I shake my head. "Don't worry about it," I whisper.

"I didn't realize he was here," she whispers.

"Give me two seconds, and I'll come out there."

Brandy nods and starts to back away, but is stopped by Devlin's voice. "Good morning, Brandy."

I bite my lip, stifling a laugh as her face goes entirely red. "Um, so, I was wondering if you wanted breakfast. Ellie, I mean. But that's only because I didn't know there were two of you here. Want me to make breakfast for you both?"

He pulls the sheet higher as he sits up, obviously fighting a grin and looking so deliciously sexy that Brandy is very lucky I don't jump him right then. "No, thanks," he says, the corners of his mouth twitching. "I'll be heading out soon."

"Back to Vegas?" I ask as he takes his phone from the side table and starts to tap out a message. I can hardly keep the disappointment from my voice, but I know he's got work to do.

He's silent for a moment as he taps a bit more, then sets the phone back on the bedside table. "Actually, no." He smiles at me. "In fact, I was planning to invite you out for breakfast." He turns to Brandy. "Would you like to join us? Assuming Ellie says yes."

"Are you kidding?" I say. "I'm totally saying yes. But don't you have to go back?"

"It turns out I did an excellent job picking my team. I'm utterly redundant."

I tilt my head and make a point of lasciviously looking him up and down. "Not to me."

He squeezes my thigh. "So, breakfast?" He looks back at Brandy. "What do you say? Join us?"

"I think three is a crowd," she says.

"I promise there will be no shenanigans."

"Oh, well, that's disappointing," Brandy quips.

Devlin laughs. "Sorry. That's not how I roll."

I bite the corner of his ear. "No? Because I've done a little poking around on the internet, and there's some interesting stuff about you and—"

He moves faster than I can deflect and pulls me onto him, somehow managing to keep the sheet in place so that Brandy doesn't get an X-rated view of either of us.

"Brandy," he says. "Please join us. I need backup."

She laughs. "I was about to tell Ellie that I had just enough time to fry some eggs before I head out. Although if you really don't mind, I'd love some business advice. I could move my first appointment...?"

She trails off, her expression hopeful.

Devlin looks to me.

I shrug. "I don't mind. If you two want to talk about business at breakfast while I sit there bored out of my mind, that's completely up to you."

They look at each other, exchanging an amused glance. "Sounds like a plan," Devlin says.

"Twenty minutes?" Brandy asks. "That should give me enough time to do some rearranging. Does that give you two enough time to get dressed?"

"Perfect. I thought we might take a walk on the beach after breakfast," Devlin adds to me. "Which means neither one of us needs to spend too much time dressing for the day. Sound good?"

I nod happily, and as soon as Brandy leaves, I decide to forfeit the first three minutes of our allotted time by straddling Devlin. That plan goes to hell, though, when he takes me by the shoulders, then makes me squeal as he flips me onto my back, his thighs on either side of my hips, and his cock as awake as both of us.

"We don't have time for that," I say. "But I really wish we did."

"Just a preview of coming attractions," he says, shifting as he bends forward to kiss me so that his erection teases between my thighs, making me crave a hell of a lot more than we have time for this morning.

"Maybe we can be late," I murmur, trying to spread my legs.

"That would be rude," he says, moving his hips so that his cock teases me even more, and little shivers race through me, both frustrating and enticing.

"*That* would be rude?" I counter, making his eyes crinkle with amusement.

He bends closer, his tongue teasing the curve of my ear. "Later," he whispers.

"Hell, yes, later. Later is when you're going to pay, mister."

He brushes a light kiss over my lips, then slides off both me and the bed. "We're going to be late if we don't hurry."

"Payback," I say, pointing a finger at him. "Soon."

"I look forward to it." He's trying hard not to laugh, and not doing a very good job. "I'll enjoy the anticipation."

I narrow my eyes, then turn toward the dresser, ostensibly to get my clothes, but mostly so he can't see my own effort at holding back laughter.

Since I'm dressing only in shorts, a tank top, and a lightweight hoodie, it takes me no time at all to get ready. Devlin takes a bit longer, since he came over in work clothes. But he keeps a gym bag in his car, and as he runs out to get it, I pull my hair back in a sloppy ponytail and put on sunscreen. And that is the sum total of my grooming for the day.

Soon we're all three walking down the hill together, with Jake galumphing in front of us on his leash. It turns out that Brandy's second appointment had to cancel so she's got a full ninety minutes before she has to be anywhere. We grab a table at the Omelet Tree, one of the restaurants on the ocean side of PCH with a huge deck, a pet-friendly policy, and an incredible view. As Devlin and I take long swallows of coffee, Brandy sips Chamomile tea and Jake crunches on a dog bone, courtesy of the restaurant.

Despite the name, the restaurant is famous for its pancakes. Brandy and I get banana, but Devlin goes for gingerbread. As we all dig in, he and Brandy talk about ways to not only increase her sales, but also her visibility and her public presence.

"I really want to do something like you do," she says. "Support something I believe in. Give back, you know? But I'm still all about making a profit. I started BB Bags on a shoestring, and it amazes me that it's doing well. But it is."

"That's because you worked hard, and it's paying off. There's nothing wrong with wanting to make a profit," Devlin says. "You're running a business. And the better you run it, the more money you make, and the more you can not only expand and prosper, but the more you can support causes you believe in."

I listen as they discuss the possibilities, outlining what Brandy wants to accomplish and what charities she wants to both support and promote. They also float the possibility of Brandy launching a nonprofit arm herself. Devlin tosses out a few more concepts, but mostly he promises to think about it and get back to her with some concrete ideas that they can discuss.

"I really appreciate this," Brandy tells him. "Especially knowing how busy you are. It really means a lot to me."

"I'm happy to do it." He checks his watch. "If you want to meet up after you're done with work, we can dig deeper."

"Can we wait a day or two?" She glances at me. "I don't want to interrupt your plans. And, to be honest, I think I need a day to process."

"Just say when," Devlin says. "I promise I'll make the time."

"Thanks. Right now my head is so full it's going to be hard to focus on today's meetings. Plus, it's a gorgeous day and I'm jealous that you guys are going to the beach while I'm going to Los Angeles."

"No, you're not," I tell her. "You love what you do. And I'm incredibly proud of you. You're building something truly fabulous."

The check comes and Brandy puts down her share, or tries to. Devlin waves her away saying that she can repay it by baking some muffins for him to freeze at his house.

He gives her a kiss on the cheek goodbye, and after she and I hug, Brandy heads back up the hill to get samples and her car. Meanwhile, Devlin and I keep Jake, who's settled into a nap beneath the table, his paws moving as if he's dreaming about chasing rabbits.

Although truly chasing bunnies is out of the question, a game of catch seems like a good plan. So while Jake and I watch the surf, Devlin crosses the street to the corner convenience store. Because it's near the beach, it also sells all the paraphernalia a tourist could want. I can attest to that, having popped in not that long ago to buy a pair of flip flops after I'd taken off running in bare feet, thrust into motion by the shock of learning that Devlin Saint was the boy I used to love.

Soon, Devlin emerges with a Frisbee, and the moment he pulls it out of the bag, Jake goes nuts. He tugs on the leash, practically yanking me off my feet as he bounds over the grassy area toward the sandy beach. I gesture for Devlin to take control of the crazy dog, but he's laughing too hard to be of any use to me at all.

We finally reach the surf and the sandy area where well-mannered dogs are allowed to be unleashed during the off-season. Jake has apparently forgotten the Frisbee, because he spends a solid five minutes chasing the foamy surf as I catch my breath. I lean against Devlin, my back to his chest and his arms tight against my ribs.

"Lot of help you were," I tease.

"You two were bonding," he counters. "How could I interrupt?"

I tilt my head back, just because I want to see him. "Hey."

"Hey." He bends close and kisses me. A quick kiss that soon turns heated, until I'm spinning in his arms, my own rising to go around his neck. The beach is mostly empty this morning, and I lose myself in the scent of him and the sweet ocean air.

I start to melt—for that matter, I start to regret that we didn't go back to the house—but I'm quickly cooled off when we are suddenly and unceremoniously showered with droplets. I squeal and jump back, only to realize that we're being sprayed by a thoroughly soaked Jake, now shaking himself dry beside us.

I meet Devlin's eyes, and we both start laughing. "Crazy dog," I say, kneeling in the sand to rub his ears. "You ready for the Frisbee?"

He perks up immediately, and Devlin tosses the disc, sending it sailing parallel to the water. Jake bounds after it, to the delight of two little girls building a sandcastle. Devlin and I kick off our sandals and hold them by the straps as we take off after him, splashing in the surf as we meet Jake coming back, his Frisbee-prey held proudly in his jaws.

"Good boy," Devlin says, taking the Frisbee, then rubbing Jake's neck. "Want to go again?"

The dog practically leaps with joy, and Devlin sends the toy flying again. We stroll that direction, hand in hand, until I come to a stop, suddenly realizing where we are.

Laguna Cortez is carved out of the hills, and as such, we have both sandy and rocky beaches. The beaches on the north end of town tend to be rockier as they approach the hills and cliffs that form into reefs that are great for divers and terrible for beach-combers and swimmers.

That's where Uncle Peter's house is, though it's not his anymore, of course. A house on the beachside of the Coast Highway tucked up near a rocky outcropping that rises up toward a cliff now topped with condos. The house is huge and modern with lots of glass on the ocean side, while the inland-facing walls are mostly solid for both design and privacy.

Jake is racing straight toward it. But I stop cold.

"I haven't walked here since I came back," I tell Devlin. "Every time I come to the beach from Pacific Avenue, I turn south." I shrug. "That's just the way I'm drawn. To you, I guess," I add with a smile. The DSF is a short walk to the south. And while it's certainly true that I will always head toward Devlin, we both know that it's not autopilot steering me away from Peter's house. It's loss.

Devlin takes my hand, then uses the fingers of his other to whistle to Jake, calling him back.

"No, it's okay," I say. "Really."

"It doesn't sound okay."

"Just melancholy. Can you blame me?"

"Not at all." He nods toward it. Whoever owns it now has kept it perfectly maintained. "Do you want to go closer?"

I shake my head. "Not today."

"Whatever you need, baby. Whenever you need it. All you have to do is tell me."

I flash him a smile. "I know." I sigh. "Is it weird that even knowing everything I do about Peter that I still miss him terribly?"

"Oh, baby. No. Of course not."

"Those years living in that house with him—and before, when

I would go there after school before my dad died—I mean, I grew up there. I grew up with him. I missed my house after Daddy died, but this place became my home. It was my sanctuary. It was where I met you," I add, meeting his eyes. "And you were my sanctuary, too."

"El—"

"You were," I say. "Even though you left. And I thought Peter was, too. But he wasn't. Not really."

"Wasn't he?"

It's a serious question, and I think about it. Because Devlin—Alex—really was my lynchpin. And he still is, even though he'd hurt me all those years ago. Because I understand why, and because I can live with the reasons.

With Peter, I can't grasp the *why*. Not yet, anyway. Maybe not ever. But I'm trying, and I don't know ... maybe it will make a difference.

I twine my fingers with Devlin's as I think about the duality of people. Who we are inside versus who we let people see. I think about Alex and Devlin, the same yet different. And me. Cop. Reporter. Lover. Survivor.

"Facets," I say, remembering something Devlin had said a while back about how I could still love Peter, despite the bad things he'd done. Beside me, Devlin nods.

"I guess it's not weird," I concede. "And the truth is, I really do miss that place. Not just the memories, but damn, that was an exceptional building."

"It was," he agrees. "For that matter, it still is." He hooks his arm around my waist. "My best memories are there, too. There, and one more place."

I look up, meeting his eyes. "Yeah," I say. "Me, too."

We turn south and walk there without needing words, Jake trotting beside us, the Frisbee in his mouth. It doesn't take long. It's a short walk down the beach to the tide pools near the DSF.

"You better be careful," I tease, as we get close. "It's Friday and you're playing hooky. If anyone in there sees you..."

"Lucky for us, I run the place."

"Lucky indeed." I grab his hand and tug. "Race you," I say, and we take off sprinting.

Jake makes it there first, Devlin second, and I come in a very pathetic last. "Your legs are longer," I complain.

"I love your legs," Devlin says, tracing his finger on the hem of my shorts so that his fingertip brushes my thigh.

"Careful."

His brow rises. "That was hardly a sensual caress."

"With you, everything is a sensual caress. Especially here."

Here is the place where he first kissed me, by the tidal pools formed by a collection of porous black rock.

"Come here," he says.

"Why?"

"Because I want to kiss you again."

"Oh." I slide into his arms. "Thank you for a wonderful morning," I say, as he tugs gently on my hair, angling my mouth up to his.

"What do you say we make it a wonderful day?"

"That sounds—" It sounds perfect, but I don't get the word out. Instead, I melt into his kiss as the waves break around our ankles and Jake frolics nearby.

And as I lose myself in this moment, all I can think is that I don't want it to end. Because somewhere beyond the veil of this fabulous morning is my mysterious texter. And he—or she—is determined to pop my hard-won bubble of happiness.

CHAPTER THIRTY

S ince it's Friday, we spend the rest of the afternoon with Jake on the beach and at the small park that abuts the south side of the DSF. Once the sun starts to set, we grab ice cream cones from the little store near Pacific Avenue before walking back to Brandy's house. She gets back from LA about the same time we get home, and we settle in for a movie marathon. It's Brandy's idea, actually, and she's also the one who suggests we watch the first two *Alien* movies.

"We were watching *Aliens* the night you two met," she says with a shrug. "I guess I'm feeling nostalgic."

Since I'm fine with both nostalgia and cuddling up with Devlin for the length of two full movies, I eagerly agree. Devlin doesn't hesitate either, and there's something about his immediate, no-strings-attached acceptance that tugs at my heartstrings. Because this is a man with Important Stuff To Do, and yet he's taking an entire workday to hang out doing exactly nothing with me, my bestie, and her dog.

With a sigh, I squeeze his hand, then lightly kiss his cheek.

"What's that for?"

"Just because. But there's a lot more coming."

He makes a show of looking me up and down, then comically leers. "I can't wait."

I bop him with a pillow. "Stay," I order, as Brandy and I pull together all manner of junk food to call dinner, then spread it over the coffee table along with two bottles of red and three glasses. And, of course, a chew toy for Jake.

As far as evenings go, it's just about perfect.

Brandy and I spend the next day in a flurry of domesticity. The plan is for Devlin and Lamar to come to the house so the four of us can share an evening together just hanging out. By evening, the enticing scent of homemade spaghetti sauce fills the air, making my stomach growl.

Though it was Brandy's mom's recipe, I'd done most of the labor under Brandy's direction. "Devlin really will be impressed," she says, testing it. "Careful," she adds, "or he'll think you can cook. Won't he be surprised when you move in together and all you serve him is coffee, toasted bagels, and cream cheese?"

I smirk. "First of all, he hasn't asked me to move in, just stay over. Second of all, I have pizza delivery services on speed dial, and I am a whiz at adding milk to cereal."

She wrinkles her nose. "I'm pretty sure Captain Crunch is candy, not cereal."

"Maybe. But it's tasty." I shrug. "This is why I have to continue living with you. The nutritional benefits of you being my best friend."

"How you survived in New York..."

"Take-out," I admit. "Lots and lots of take-out."

She looks at me, nodding slowly. "Well, I guess we'll hope that Devlin can cook. Do you think he will?"

"Cook?"

"Ask you to move in."

"Oh." I frown. "Moving a little fast, aren't you?"

"It's just a question," she says, innocently.

"Honestly, I don't know."

"Because he told you he has secrets. And that he's dangerous." She glances at the clock, then grabs a couple of tomatoes and passes them to me with orders to wash and slice. Meanwhile, she finishes topping the lasagna with mozzarella, then slips it in the oven. Honestly, I'm glad for the respite, because it gives me time to gather my thoughts. "I'm not concerned about danger," I say as I make a point of cutting the beefsteak tomatoes into uniform slices. "But the secrets ... if he's really worried I'll find something out, then why would he want me around twenty-four/seven?"

"Does it bug you?"

"That there's something he's not telling me?"

She nods.

"A little," I admit.

"Only a little?"

I tilt my head, then point to the clock. "We should both change. They'll be here soon."

"Ellie..." I can practically hear the frown, but I just lift my hand in dismissal and hurry to my room. The truth is, I don't want to think about moving in with Devlin. On the one hand, I want to be with him always. But on the other, I'm used to living alone.

But that's not the real reason I don't want to move in with him just yet. The real reason is that I want what was taken from us when The Wolf forced Alex's hand. When he had to run, meaning that we never got to be anything more than a secret, tragic romance.

I want dates on the beach and picnics in the park. I want him to call me and send flowers. I want to pop by his office and drag him out for lunch and have it be all the more special because he didn't see me in bed beside him that morning.

I want what other couples have. So far, there's been very little about our relationship that qualifies as average. And while I never thought I'd be the kind of girl who'd long for middle of the road, as far as dating goes—as far as *Devlin* goes—it's not only what I want, it's what I need.

Which, I think, is why I have to blink back tears when I open the door to him a few minutes later to find him standing there with a bouquet of roses for Brandy and a silver-wrapped box for me.

"Can I open it?" I ask as we move toward the kitchen so Brandy can put her flowers in water. "What is it?"

"The key to your heart," he says.

"To *my* heart. Not yours." I shake the box, which is small but has some heft. "That means I'm gonna assume it's not sexy lingerie."

There's a chuckle from the hallway, and we turn to see that Lamar has let himself in. "I didn't realize it was that kind of a party. I would have worn something pink."

"You're hysterical," I tell him, then hold up the package. "Brandy didn't have to guess. Devlin brought her flowers. I'm currently trying to figure out what's in my box."

"Key to your heart?" Lamar repeats, then holds out his hand. I meet Devlin's eyes, and when he shrugs, I put the box in Lamar's outstretched hand.

Lamar makes a show of bouncing it in his hand, as if testing its weight. Then he shakes it. Then he sniffs it.

After that entertaining production, he passes it back to me. "Easy," he says, looking from me to Devlin.

"You're saying you know what it is?" I ask.

"Like the man said—it's the key to your heart."

I shake a finger between the two of them, managing a mock scowl.

"This is why she quit the force," he tells Devlin. "Her detective skills are a little lacking."

"I see that," Devlin says. "It's been a few years, though. We should probably cut her some slack."

"You two are going to be in so much trouble," I warn, then turn my attention to Lamar. "So? What is it?"

"Isn't it obvious? It's coffee?"

I look to Devlin, but he has the world's best poker face. "Just open it," Brandy says, and so I slide my finger under the paper, open the plain cardboard box, and find a small, solidly packed brick of Dunkin Donuts ground original roast. Utterly boring, but my absolute favorite.

And, yeah, I melt a little.

"Ya done good, man," Lamar says, giving Devlin a friendly pat on the shoulder as I slide in for a hug.

"You just knew that?" I say, as Devlin's arms go around me. "That he got me coffee."

"The key to *your* heart? It was either coffee or a Pulitzer, and even Mr. Humanitarian of the Year here can't arrange the second one."

"Hell of a detective," Devlin says, with a mock salute in Lamar's direction as Brandy yells for me to come finish the caprese salad since the food's almost ready.

But I don't move. On the contrary, I just stand there, soaking it all in. Because the truth is, Lamar got it wrong. Coffee may be a weakness. But *this*—my friends laughing together—is the real key to my heart.

CHAPTER THIRTY-ONE

P acific Avenue is closed to traffic during the Fall Festival, and colorful booths fill the street. Fine art, crafts, jewelry, candles. Olives, salsa, cheeses, cookies. Things to buy, things to eat, and even a rotating line-up of local bands to listen to. It's organized chaos and absolutely wonderful, albeit way too crowded.

"How come you don't have a booth?" I ask Brandy as we check out a selection of sterling silver earrings. We've been at the fair since noon, and though it's already past four, we still haven't seen all the booths or visited all the shops.

"I was wondering that, too," Anna says, her eyes an especially vivid blue, as if she's channeling today's bright sunshine. Her red hair is gleaming, too, and for the first time I notice that her roots are darker.

She and Tracy caught up with us an hour ago, about the time that Lamar, Christopher, and Devlin decided to camp out by the bandstand and chow down on tacos and churros. Ronan and Reggie were around earlier, too, but I haven't seen either of them in the last few hours. I still haven't figured out why Reggie looks so familiar, and I've started to think it's just my imagination.

"Do you have an exclusive deal with The Escape?" Tracy

asks, then turns to show off her own BB Bags crossbody. "I got this about an hour ago. It's awesome."

"You are my new best friend," Brandy says. "Sorry, Ellie, but you had a good run."

"She's a lot of work," I tell Tracy. "But she's worth it."

"I am," Brandy says, laughing. "And nope, not an exclusive at all. In fact I was supposed to have a booth but I had to pull out last month." A laughing woman with a to-go cup of wine pushes past us. "We're blocking the booth," Brandy says, then leads us to the backside with less foot traffic.

"So why'd you pull out?" Anna asks, tucking her hair behind her ear.

Brandy's grin would rival the Cheshire Cat's. "Because I had to ship all my inventory to Chicago for my new deal with one of the boutiques there. Totally awesome and unexpected. And it's also why I'm going to spend the rest of the weekend sewing. And next week interviewing for part-time help."

"You didn't tell me," I say, giving her a hug so enthusiastic I almost topple her into the back of the jewelry booth's tent.

She shrugs, managing to look both modest and pleased with herself. "It's just business."

"At which you're excelling," Tracy says. "I want to be you guys when I grow up." Still in grad school, Tracy is the youngest of our little group.

"Well, let's go find out if you will be," Anna suggests. "I saw a Tarot card reader set up at the end of the block. Want to?"

Tracy checks her watch. "I'm meeting Lamar in thirty, but if there's not a line, sure."

"I should have told you to bring a date," I say to Anna since she's the only one who'd come unpaired to the festival.

"There's no one to bring, and right now, I'm fine with that."

I wrinkle my nose, wishing I'd kept my mouth closed. "Bad breakup?"

She waves my words away. "Not even a breakup really. More

like a clusterfuck. Turns out he didn't value what was right in front of him."

"I'm sorry."

"Don't be. His loss, right?" Her smile is tight and thin, and though I nod in agreement, I don't mention that I'm certain that the break-up was worse than she's admitting.

"You're doing the Tarot with me, right?" Tracy asks her. "We can find out if there's a new guy on the horizon."

"Or if my beloved is going to get his soon," Anna says wryly. "Sure. I'm coming." She looks at me. "How about you? Want to see what the cards say about you and Devlin?"

I shake my head. "Nope. Things are going fine right now. If anything bad is coming, I don't want to know."

Tracy frowns, and I immediately regret my words.

"Devlin and I are great," I assure her. "I was just joking."

"Oh, I know. I was thinking about what happened with the Range Rover. You're doing okay now, right?"

I nod. "I'm fine. Really. It was scary, and now it's over."

Anna's brow furrows. "You're lucky you weren't hurt."

"My ass was a little bruised, but that's all."

"It was freaking terrifying," Brandy adds. "I mean if someone really did it on purpose..."

"Do you really think the driver was trying to run you down?" Tracy asks.

"I don't know," I admit. "It might have just been random. There wasn't a license plate, so maybe it was a stolen car and I was in the wrong place at the wrong time."

Anna crosses her arms over her chest. "You don't honestly believe that."

"No," I admit. "But nothing else happened since. It might not have been directed at me at all. Or it might be tied to an article I'm writing. Maybe someone doesn't like me poking around."

"Occupational hazard, I guess," Anna says, then shakes her head with a sigh. "I don't know how you do it. I'd be looking over my shoulder every minute of every day. And now you're having to deal with all the social media, too."

"It's not that bad," I say, though I hate being in the public eye like that.

"Ellie avoids all the social media sites," Brandy chimes in, "but I've been paying attention. There were a lot of pictures right after the Range Rover thing, but that was a few days ago. It's mostly calmed down." She shrugs. "Considering you're dating Devlin, and he's both rich and very easy on the eyes, there've been fewer posts than I would have thought."

"Which is good," I say. "Because I really don't feel the need for my face to be plastered on everyone's phones." That's not a lie. But I'm mostly relieved that we're not the trending topic since any man with a secret identity should avoid too much scrutiny.

When I meet Anna's eyes, I have a feeling she's thinking the same thing. But, of course, we can't say anything because we're with Tracy, who doesn't know who Devlin used to be.

"How about you?" Anna directs the question to Brandy. "You want your fortune read?"

She shakes her head. "I want to get Christopher something." She points at Anna and then Tracy. "Do not tell him. It's a surprise."

"What is?" Tracy asks.

"Not sure yet. That's why I want to look around." She catches my eye. "Keep me company?"

I agree, and we wave the other two off, then start to meander through the booths again. "So what are we looking for? Anything in mind?"

"Maybe. I've already started on part of the present. I texted Tamra this morning."

"Tamra?"

Brandy nods, clearly pleased with herself. "The *Laguna Leader* is going to run an article about the thriller author doing research in our town, but since it's a surprise, I don't want them interviewing Christopher. So she's going to throw together some background research on him and his career they can use."

"That's a great idea. But if it's all in place, what are you looking for at the festival?"

"Maybe an engraved wooden fountain pen. I saw a booth a few blocks down. That seems authorial, right?"

"Very. But what's the occasion? Birthday?"

Her eyes light up as she shakes her head. "Nope. I just want him to know I appreciate him."

I pause, forcing the crowd to go around us as I tug her to a stop beside me. "You had the talk."

Her smile blooms. "This morning. We talked about the rape and giving the baby up for adoption. Everything. He was great about it. I mean, really great."

"I'm so glad," I say as we start moving again. "So the gift is a *thanks for being great* present?"

"Pretty much."

I press my hand to her shoulder. "And you? You're okay?"

"Yeah." She hesitates, then nods. "Yeah, totally."

I pull her to a stop, this time sidling up against the side of a booth selling honey and beeswax candles. "Why am I hearing a *but*? Did he get weird?"

"No, no. Christopher was great..." She trails off, the corner of her mouth turning down.

"Brandy?"

"Okay, okay. I know it's only my imagination, but after I told him, I thought I saw the guy."

"The guy? Walt?" We hardly ever use his name when we talk about him, but this moment calls for clarity.

She nods, her arms wrapped tight around herself. "I know I'm probably projecting. It's got to be fear, right? You know, that I'm worrying about having a flashback or shutting down or something if Christopher and I ... you know."

"Do you think you should see someone? Not about thinking you saw Walt," I hurry to explain. "But someone who can help you work through the sex part. You want it to be good. Special. And if you freeze up or get scared or—"

"No. No therapist."

"Brandy..."

She tilts her head, and I hold my hands up in surrender to the unspoken message—even with all my shit, I'm not seeing a counselor, so I'm hardly one to talk.

"Fine," I say. "Just make sure Christopher understands. And that he's patient. And I'm sure he will be. Billy didn't know your history. Christopher does. It'll all be good."

"I know." She looks around, as if scoping out the crowd. "And it couldn't have really been him, right?"

"It's your mind playing tricks. You were thinking about him, and so there he was. Totally natural. Don't worry about it."

"Right. Okay." She draws a breath. "Come on. Lots more browsing to do."

An hour later, we've shopped our way down another block when my phone vibrates. I pull it out of my pocket and see a picture of the sign from two streets over. The note from Devlin reads - *Plan is to meet here in ten minutes. OK?*

I text him back a thumbs-up, then tell Brandy, who immediately texts Christopher to make sure he knows the plan. Turns out he's still with Devlin, so all is good.

We start making our way through the throng to get to the slightly less crowded area one street over. The bar is easy enough to find, not only from the sign, but because Lamar is standing outside waving to us.

"Where are the others?"

"Devlin and Christopher went in with Anna to hold a table, but Tracy bailed," he says. "She'd already planned a video chat with her mom tonight."

"So you're out here being the greeter?" Brandy asks.

Lamar shakes his head. "I did some poking around." He turns his attention to me. "I have some news on the blonde. The one Ortega saw with Peter."

Brandy lifts a finger to pause the conversation. "I'll go on in so they know we're here, and you two can talk."

We give her our drink orders, then Lamar and I step further from the door. "So what have you learned?"

"Those archives you wanted from the original investigation into Peter's death came in this morning, so I did a quick flip through the files."

My stomach twists with anticipation. "You looked at the witness interviews?"

He nods. "The investigation closed pretty quickly. I mean, once Mercado confessed..."

He trails off as I twirl my hand impatiently. "Yeah. But you found something. About the blonde. What?"

"Might be nothing," he says. "But they talked with a guy named Cyrus Mulroy. Apparently, he and Peter were acquainted."

"Drugs?"

He shakes his head, then rubs his hand over his head, the way he does when he's stalling.

"Lamar, what?"

"I've busted Cyrus myself a time or two. He's pushing sixty now, served time. He's moved inland. Mission Viejo, I think. I never saw evidence of drugs."

"Then what—"

"Porn," Lamar says, flatly. "And he swore in interview that he'd done business with Peter."

I take a step back, feeling sick. "No."

He holds up his hands, shaking his head, and when he speaks, I hear the emotion in his voice. "I know it's not what you want to hear—and honestly, there might be nothing there. But you deserve to have all the facts."

"And what are the facts?" My voice is harsh and cold, and I don't want it to be. Whoever Peter was—whatever he did—I want to know the truth. And I feel like the worst of friends for lashing out at Lamar since Peter isn't there to field my pain and disappointment.

To his credit, he doesn't even flinch, and that sweet under-standing helps me settle myself. I square my shoulders and say more gently, "It's okay. Whatever it is, I'll deal."

"Like I said, it may be nothing," he says. "As far as I know, the department never had its eye on Peter for pornography."

I shrug. "That doesn't mean much. The LCPD didn't have its eye on Peter for drugs until after he was dead."

"Can't argue with that," Lamar says. "But there's also nothing in the Mulroy interview to suggest there was any sort of steady business. He said he dealt with him. That word specifically. So it could've been a one-time thing."

I nod, trying to process everything. "And you think the blonde..."

He lifts his hands. "It's only a hunch. Maybe I shouldn't have even said anything to you. Not until I had more, anyway."

I move close and take his hands. "No. Thanks. I'm glad you told me. I don't know what it means, but it's a solid hunch. But I doubt he'd have taken her up to LA and introduced her to his mechanic as his girlfriend if she was tied up in porn, too."

"Good point. Still, it's an angle. You want to find out more about Peter—what he was into, what motivated him to get dirty in the first place—you should talk to Mulroy."

"Can you get me an address or phone number?"

"I'll track him down," he says. "Maybe between him and the blonde—if you ever find her—you'll get more of a picture."

"I hope so," I say. Because the truth is, the more I learn about my uncle, the more I realize how hard it is to really know anything about anybody.

CHAPTER THIRTY-TWO

L amar holds the door open so that we can go in and join the others, but as I'm about to walk through, I hear my name.

I turn and see a woman with a vaguely familiar face behind us. "Carrie? Oh my God." I turn to Lamar. "I knew her in high school. Go on in. I'll be there in a minute."

He nods, and I hurry toward Carrie, who's hurrying down the sidewalk toward me. "Carrie Bartlett! You look amazing." Tall and blond with wavy hair, tight jeans, and as much attitude as she had in school, Carrie looks like she should be on a catwalk.

"Are you really fucking him?"

I stiffen, my body turning cold from the harshness in her words. "Excuse me?"

"Devlin Saint," she says. "He's a liar and a prick."

"What are you talking about? *Oh, fuck.*" Without thinking, I reach out and grab her upper arms. "Are you the one sending me those texts?" I demand, practically spitting with fury. "Is it you who's harassing us?"

She jerks free of my grasp, her blue eyes as cold as ice. "Texts? What the fuck? I'm trying to do you a favor, you idiot. Don't trust him."

I just stand there stupidly, my mind spinning as I try to

process where this is coming from. "Wait," I say. "I remember. You dated him. In New York, a few years ago. You were with him at some event he was speaking at."

I hadn't paid attention to Devlin Saint back then, but *The Spall* had covered the black tie event where Saint had announced that he was building a permanent location for his foundation in Laguna Cortez. It was a weird coincidence that my old high school friend was his date, but at the same time, it wasn't too surprising. God knows Carrie has the model-like looks of a woman often found on the arms of billionaires.

I might have even called the hotel and tried to catch up, but I'd been mugged that weekend, and after the attack, all thoughts of the rich philanthropist and his date from my past had fizzled from my mind.

Now I wonder how long they'd dated ... and what had happened to end it.

"Nothing he says is real," she continues, before I can ask. "Remember that, Ellie. Nothing he says is real."

I shake my head. "Whatever happened between the two of you—"

"You are so naive. Believe me, Ellie. I'm not some jealous twit. I'm trying to help you." Her eyes bore into me. "Get clear, okay? Because Devlin Saint is a fucking monster."

My heart is pounding so hard in my ears that I can barely hear my own voice. "I don't know what you're talking about, but I know you're wrong."

She doesn't answer. Just looks me up and down. Then she shrugs and says, "I tried. It's on you, now." She turns on her heel and pushes into the crowd. I start to follow her, but a tall man hurries past me into the bar, and in the time it takes for me to realize I've been blocking the door, she disappears.

"You okay?" the hostess asks.

"I'm fine," I lie, then point to the back corner. "I'm with them." I'm already walking before the words are out of my mouth.

Devlin sees me coming, his smile lighting his face as he stands and pulls out the chair next to him. I don't sit, though. Instead, I wrap my arms around him and press my face against his chest, breathing in his scent. He gently strokes my hair. "What happened?"

I shake my head, clinging to him for a moment longer before pulling back and tilting my head up so that I can see him. "Nothing. I ran into an old friend. Let's just say she's not in your fan club."

His brow furrows. "Do you want to talk about it?"

"Not now. Later." That's two things for us to talk about. Carrie and the revelation that Peter might have been involved in porn. For a day that started out light and breezy, it's fast turning into something dark and depressing.

No.

With a mental shove, I force the thought away. This is our day. A day to be out in the world with our friends. No worries, no demons, no responsibilities. "I'm fine," I say firmly. "Right now, I just want some food, a boatload of wine, our friends, and you."

"I think we can manage that," he says, before kissing me lightly. But I see the worry that lingers on his face as we sit. And I see that same concern reflected on every face at the table. *Fucking Carrie.* She always did love to grab the spotlight.

"I'm fine," I say. "Truly." I meet Brandy's eyes. "I bumped into Carrie. She was in one of her bitchy moods."

Beside me, Devlin stiffens as Brandy shoots a sideways glance at Christopher. "We went to high school together. We hung out together sometimes, but she straddled the line between us and the mean girls."

"It wasn't a big thing," I say, not looking at Devlin in case my face betrays the truth. "Just a weird reunion."

Anna, who's on Christopher's other side, leans around him, her hand pressed on his shoulder as if for balance. "I had friends like that growing up," she tells Brandy before shifting her attention to me. "Never liked running into them again."

She leans back in her chair, but I notice her hand lingers on

Christopher's shoulder. He doesn't seem to notice, though, and I remind myself that it's not a big deal. I know they've become good friends. I could tell that much from the time I walked in on them while they were going over plot ideas for Christopher's book.

"So what did she say that pissed you off?" Brandy asks. "Or was she just her usual charming self?"

I wave my hand dismissively. "Just catching up bullshit," I say. "Let's move on."

"Hear, hear," Christopher says, raising his wine. I have a full glass waiting at my place, and I lift my drink in toast, too, as does the rest of the table. For a good half-hour, we settle in to food and chatter, talking about nothing much and a little bit of everything.

Lamar stands to go to the restroom, and I consider heading that way, too, but I'm feeling more than a little relaxed after polishing off a full glass of wine, plus most of another. Instead, I stay put, listing a bit to the right and enjoying the feel of Devlin's hand pressed lightly against my back.

I'm sitting like that when Devlin lifts his other hand in greeting. I follow his line of sight to see Ronan and Reggie standing in the line at the bar for to-go glasses of wine, something that's allowed during festival days in the Laguna Cortez Arts District.

Ronan notices and raises his glass in greeting as Reggie turns, then smiles when she sees our group.

"Are they together?" I ask Devlin, keeping my eyes on Reggie's face as I try once again to figure out why she seems so familiar.

"You mean dating? Not that I know of. But they've worked together enough to become good friends."

"I think they went out once," Anna says. "I'm pretty sure there wasn't a second date."

Devlin chuckles. "Not too surprising."

"Why?" Brandy asks.

"They're both too strong-willed," he says.

I cross my arms over my chest and capture him in a hard stare. "And we aren't?"

He tilts my chin up and kisses me. "We are," he says when he pulls away, leaving me more than a little unsatisfied. "The difference is, I like it."

My guess is that Ronan likes strong women, too, but I don't say anything because I've finally realized what it is about Reggie that seems familiar—her deep set, Bette Davis eyes.

That's got to be it, I think as they wave goodbye and head back toward the festival. Uncle Peter was a huge classic movie buff, and Bette Davis was one of his favorite stars. I tell myself I've solved the problem, and yet the question still lingers. *Something else*, I think. More specifically, *somewhere* else. I know her from somewhere else.

But where?

I'm just about to share my frustration with everyone at the table when Brandy gasps, then knocks over her wine. "I'm sorry, I'm sorry," she says, but as she mops it up, I see that her hand is trembling.

"Bran?"

She lifts her head, her eyes meeting mine, and for a moment, all I can see is the fear reflected back at me. No, not fear. *Terror.*

"Brandy," I repeat, this time more softly. "What is it?"

Her lips move, but no sound comes out. It doesn't matter. I can discern the word from the movement of her lips and the fear in her eyes. *Him.*

I reach across the table and take her hand. "Him?" I repeat? "Walt?"

She's shaking, and I twine my finger with hers. "He can't hurt you," I say. "You're safe."

It's just Brandy and me, everyone else forgotten, and so I jump about a mile when I hear Devlin's voice, low and harsh. "Dark hair, blue shirt, nursing a Scotch?"

Brandy swallows and nods.

"It's him," Devlin says, and the words aren't a question. "He's the guy who—"

"Yes." The word is lower than a whisper, and no sooner does

it pass her lips than Devlin's chair scrapes back and he's crossed the room. Before I can even blink, he has Walt by the collar, lifting him up so that the guy's toes are barely brushing the ground.

I don't even realize that I'm out of my chair until I'm right beside them, and while the guy protests and the bartender threatens to call the cops, Devlin drags him toward the door, with Walt whimpering for help as shocked patrons stand by with their hands over their mouths or their phones out, filming it all.

I race that direction, pushing blindly through the crowd as I try to get to Devlin. Then I see Lamar coming out of the restroom, and I shift my trajectory toward him, calling his name and pointing toward Devlin. "It's Walt," I say, and to his credit, Lamar assesses the situation in an instant. Brandy doesn't talk about what happened with Walt much with either of us, but Lamar knows the basics. He's even spent some time over the years trying to track the guy down. Trying to find justice and closure for Brandy.

Now, I see his face harden as he flashes his badge, shouts for the bartender to call 9 1 1, then bellows for the crowd to get out of his way. It works, too. The bar's patrons scatter, as if he were Moses parting the Red Sea.

"Hurry," I cry, as I catch up with him on the sidewalk. "I've never seen Devlin so furious."

"Right there with him," Lamar says, his voice rough with emotion. "She's sure?"

He glances quickly over his shoulder, and I nod. "You would be, too, if you'd seen her face."

"Where the hell did they go?" We're beneath the awning, and from this perspective, everything seems like a normal night. People strolling. Laughing. Talking.

But about half a block down there's a small crowd, and a hell of a lot more lit phones than I'd expect. I take off with Lamar right at my heels.

"Police," he calls as he approaches. "Police. Clear the scene.

Coming through."

Devlin and Walt are behind a trash bin, and my first coherent thought is that Devlin looks unharmed. My second is relief that, considering the size of the bin, I doubt there will be many good pictures floating around. Only last do I consider Walt, whose face is swollen and bloody, with a split lip and one eye already swelled shut.

"He attacked me," Walt sputters, seeing Lamar. "This fucking cocksucker jumped me. You are going down, man," he says to Devlin. "My dad's gonna make your life fucking miserable."

"I think you're the one going down, my man," Lamar says, getting in close with his badge as I take Devlin's arm and pull him off the guy. "Maybe you weren't aware, but we don't really have a statute of limitations on rape in California."

"I don't know what the fuck you're talking about."

"Well, let me tell you, then. What's your last name?"

"I don't have to tell you shit," he says, then growls as Devlin pulls his wallet from his back pocket.

"William Alexis Tarkington," Devlin reads, then tosses the wallet on the ground.

Lamar snorts. "Guess that explains why I couldn't find a record of a Walt or Walter in town that matched the description." He clears his throat. "William Tarkington, you and I are going to have a little talk." As if on cue, the wail of police sirens fills the air.

"What the fuck? I didn't do any—"

He freezes, his eyes aimed not at Lamar or Devlin, but toward the end of the alley. I follow the direction of his gaze and see Brandy standing with Christopher beside two uniformed cops.

"I didn't do anything," he says again, but with much less conviction.

"No? Well, let's get out of this crowd and we'll talk about it some more." He signals for the uniforms, who leads Walt to the car. "I'm going with them," he says to me.

"You're not arresting him?"

"Not yet." He nods toward Brandy. "If we do, she'll have to

testify. I want to give her time to think about that. In the mean-time, Walt and I will have a nice little talk. And who knows? Maybe now that I know his name, other victims will come forward."

I nod, then hug him. "Thank you." I look to Devlin. "Thank you both so much."

Their eyes meet, but they say nothing. Lamar just shakes Devlin's hand, then gives Brandy a quick hug and a kiss on the forehead before sliding into the car next to the cuffed Walt.

Brandy runs to Devlin, who pulls her into a hug. "You're going to be fine," he says, and she nods, her sobs muffled from the way her face is pressed against his shoulder. After a moment, she pushes back. "You shouldn't have beaten him up. He'll probably press charges or—I don't know—drag you through the mud. It's going to be bad for the foundation."

Devlin shakes his head. "He got what he deserved. Call the cops first, and he doesn't pay. Not the way he should." His eyes go hard. "He still hasn't fully paid that debt."

I want to argue—to tell him that isn't the way the system works—but the words don't seem to come. Not now, with Brandy looking at him like a hero.

"Thank you," she whispers again, then kisses him on the cheek.

When she backs away, Devlin gently leads her to Christopher. "I froze," Christopher says. "Even once I wrapped my head around who that prick was, I completely froze." His eyes go to Devlin's face with something akin to hero worship. "Thank you so much for standing up for her."

"My pleasure," Devlin says. "You can repay the favor by helping me keep an eye on this one." He glances sideways at me, and I manage to restrain myself from rolling my eyes.

Christopher hesitates, probably feeling silly saying that he'll look after me when I obviously want to shout that I can look after myself. But then he extends his hand to Devlin's and says solemnly, "I owe you, Saint. You can absolutely count on me."

CHAPTER THIRTY-THREE

Devlin is silent on the drive back to his house. Christopher has taken Brandy back home, and Anna stayed behind to take care of the bill. Lamar, of course, had gone to the station.

Beside me, Devlin practically vibrates with energy, but whether it's fury, frustration, or something else altogether, I'm not sure. I stay quiet, too, though, knowing that he needs time.

Once we're through his front door, I can't hold back, and as soon as he's closed it and locked us in, I press against him, my arms going around his waist as I look up into his face. "You're an exceptionally good man, Devlin Saint."

He makes a low, guttural noise. "Am I? Sometimes I'm not sure. But every once in a while, I think I do a good thing." He takes my chin, then studies my face. "I didn't think you would approve of my method tonight."

I shrug, not quite meeting his eyes. "Maybe I shouldn't," I admit. "Maybe we should have let Lamar handle it. Told him about Walt and then watched as he arrested the fucker."

He tilts his head, his eyes narrowing just slightly. "But?"

I exhale. "But I'm not sorry."

He cups my cheek, his touch tender. "Because she matters to you."

I nod.

"She matters to me, too. Because you love her and because she's a good woman who doesn't deserve the shit she's been through."

"I know," I tell him. "It means so much to me that you like my friends."

He chuckles. "I've liked Brandy since I was Alex."

"Fair enough. It means a lot to me that you like Lamar."

"Tolerate him," Devlin says, but I can see amusement in his eyes and know he's only teasing.

He strokes my hair. "I do like Brandy, but that wasn't the only reason I went after that guy tonight." His hand fists in my hair, forcing me to tilt my head back and look straight at him. "I kept imagining that it could have been you."

There's an unfamiliar intensity in his eyes, and I try to shrug off his words. "I'm not Brandy. I can take care of myself."

"You can," he agrees. "Until the time you can't." He releases me, then turns away.

I watch him pace. I'm certain that he's thinking about the years when he wasn't around and couldn't watch over me. And even now, when someone is sending me harassing texts or aiming SUVs straight at me. "I'm fine," I say gently. "The Range Rover incident was scary, sure, but you can't be beside me every moment. And I promise to be vigilant."

"Sometimes vigilance isn't enough."

"Devlin, I—"

"I know you were almost gutted in New York. He had a knife. He could have sliced your throat. Or worse."

My blood turns to ice. "It was you. Oh, God, Devlin. It was you."

My legs are shaky as I walk into the living room. I feel heavy and sluggish, as if I'm pushing through the mire of those long, lost years. I settle onto his couch, then kick off my shoes and pull my knees up and hug them to my chest. "I looked right at you—at that larger than life man who'd rescued me—and I didn't even recognize you."

He sits on the table opposite me, then leans forward and presses his hand against my bare foot. "I didn't want you to."

"How often did you watch me?" We've talked about this a little, already. About how he kept an eye on me over the years. At first I'd been angry, because I'd been so alone, with no idea where he'd gone. But that anger faded to sadness and even a bit of sympathy. Because I'd been blissfully ignorant, whereas Devlin knew where I was and what I was doing. He knew if I was safe or in danger.

And yet he couldn't speak to me. Not if he wanted to keep me safe.

Not if he wanted to keep his secret.

"You shouldn't have done anything," I say now. "I might have recognized you. Someone else might have recognized me, then put it all together and figured out you used to be Alex."

He shrugs. "You're right. But do you really think I could stand by and watch you getting hurt and not do anything?"

I'd been looking down at my hands, but now I lift my head and meet his eyes. "You left, didn't you?"

"Ellie..."

I draw in a breath. "I know. I get it. I do." I mean the words, too. But that doesn't change the fact that I wish things could have been different. At the very least, I wish we could get back the ten years we lost.

We've talked about this before, too. What I do—or what I did before Devlin came into my life. The way I chased danger. But I was always in control. Like the guy with the BMW my first night in Laguna Cortez. That was me calling the shots.

At least, it was until Devlin showed up.

Until I came to Laguna Cortez, I took what I wanted. It was my game. My way of telling fate or death or whatever to go fuck herself.

"You wanted the thrill," Devlin says, understanding me well

enough to know where my thoughts have gone. "You wanted the danger."

"Always," I say, and I hear the defiance in my voice.

"But you didn't really want to die."

I pull my hands free and hug myself. "Didn't I?" It's a real question, because I'm not sure I know anymore. I don't want to die now; of that much, I'm certain. But back then? When I was all alone? When everyone I'd ever loved was either dead in the ground or dead to me?

"Not everyone," Devlin says after I tell him as much. "You had Brandy. Lamar. You were alone in New York, maybe, but you weren't alone."

"It was still too much," I say. "It was all too much. I remember going to the museums in Manhattan or the zoo and thinking that my mom would never see it. I remembered how much my tough cop father had loved opera. But he never went to The Met. And Peter—he'd been before, and he used to tell me that we'd go. That he'd show me all the cool places tourists don't see. But that wasn't going to happen, either."

"No," Devlin agrees. "It wasn't."

"So how the fuck can you know what I wanted back then? I was alone and lonely. I spent my days in a haze, and the only respite was school and the magazine and the nights I went out."

I'd been wilder in New York than I had been in California. Working as a cop had calmed the beast that lived inside me somewhat, but once I was in Manhattan, I was alone with no bad guys to chase. I was living in an incredible town, pursuing a life I truly believed I would love. I went home to a small but decent apartment, courtesy of Uncle Peter's financial planning.

On the surface, I had a good life. But my family was dead.

And, yeah, I thought I wanted to be, too.

"You didn't," Devlin says after I make that horrible admission aloud. "You wanted the danger, sure. But you wanted to win. You wanted to tell death to go fuck itself."

"That's now," I say. "Back then..." I trail off with a shrug. "I don't think so."

"I do."

I frown as his hand tightens on my leg as if he's using the connection as a buffer against an emotion too tense to go unchecked.

"I watched you, remember? You craved the danger. Survivor's guilt, right? And God knows I knew where that came from," he says. "But you never completely crossed the line. You never surrendered to the worst that would come. Never truly craved being powerless. You wanted to get close and say fuck you. But you never craved being a victim. That wasn't what you were about. Getting knifed? Maybe getting raped? Not even close to being on your agenda."

I swallow. "How can you be so sure?"

"I told you. I know you. And I watched you."

"Devlin..."

He draws in a loud breath. "That night—in an alley in Manhattan—I watched you fight for your life. I saw the terror in your eyes before you ran and I—"

"What?"

"I killed him, El."

I wait for the reaction. The protest to rise to my lips. The horror that he'd taken somebody's life.

But there's none. Only a hint of relief.

His forehead furrows. "You didn't know?"

I shake my head. "I wasn't working at the magazine that week. Meetings at school with our advisors. So I wasn't reading the news. Just working on school stuff."

That's a lie. Or almost a lie. The truth is that I always read the news, no matter how busy I was. But that week I hadn't. And now I'm certain it's because I knew what I would have found, and I didn't want to feel obligated to tell the police anything.

"The guy deserved to be dead," Devlin says. "And you were fine with his killer walking free."

"Stop reading my mind."

His lips twitch. "I'm not. I just know you."

I make a derisive noise, but I can't argue. He definitely gets me. He's the only person who has ever understood me so completely.

"You don't know everything," I tell him. "You don't know why I hooked up with him. Max," I add. "That was his name."

"Tell me."

I draw in a breath, then tell him a truth I haven't thought about in over five years. "It was because of you."

His hand tightens on my knee. "Alex, you mean."

He makes the words a statement, but I shake my head. "No. Devlin Saint. A billionaire philanthropist who'd just burst onto the scene."

I shift on the couch, tucking my feet under me and taking one of his hands in mine. I stroke his thumb as I talk, my attention on his perfectly manicured thumbnail instead of his face. "I probably wouldn't have noticed if you hadn't been in New York for some event with Carrie as your date. But I saw a picture of you two, and so I read the article. Do you remember what you announced while you were in town?"

"Of course. We'd just selected the site for the Foundation."

"*That's* what really caught my eye. Because it was our place. Mine and Alex's."

He makes a small noise in his throat. "The lot. Of course I built on that rundown old lot. Where else?" He lifts our joined hands and kisses my fingers. "Do you know what I did after they poured the foundation?"

I shake my head.

"I used a nail and wrote *El and Alex's place* in the cement. It's hidden under the reception area tiles now, of course, but I wanted it to still be there, even though the original chalk words you'd written had long since washed away."

It's only when his face becomes blurry that I realize I'm

crying. I brusquely wipe the tears away, then manage a smile. "I can't believe you did that."

"Yes, you can."

I nod. Now that I know how much our parting wrecked him, too, I do believe it.

"Go on," he says. "You paid attention to me in New York because I was prick enough to steal the lot you and Alex had christened."

"And one of my friends," I add. "Carrie was with you. Although to be honest, we weren't ever that close, and we'd lost touch years before. Still, she was a connection. I'd left Laguna Cortez behind, and then there it was, all in my face again."

"So you went out that night, planning to say fuck you to the past."

"Pretty much." I let the memory play out in my mind. I'd started first at bars, then moved to some of the more hardcore dance clubs. The underground kind with a seedier clientele. The kind you have to know someone in order to learn those hidden clubs even exist.

I hadn't known anyone. Not really. But you pick a guy up at a bar, and he'll tell you a few things. Maybe even take you somewhere to loosen you up before taking you home.

Not that I tended to let any guy take me home. I was more about dark alleys or the backs of cabs, depending on how hyped up I was on a particular night.

That night, I remembered a club that a lawyer I'd fucked had taken me to. I'd headed that way, determined to dance off some of my excess energy, then finish the night with the hardest man I could snag.

I found him lingering outside the club. Max. He wore tight jeans and a white button down. He looked like an accountant pretending to walk on the wild side, and I almost ignored him when he called out to me. There was something in his voice, though. Something hard. Commanding.

Something dangerous.

And so I'd gone to him. "Won't they let you in?"

He took a long drag on his cigarette and then tossed it onto the sidewalk. "They won't keep me out. But that's not where you want to be."

I heard the edge in his voice and felt my heart race. All too often, I was the one calling the shots on these nights, even though the guy invariably thought he was in charge. This guy, though... well, he promised a new kind of danger.

"Where do I want to be?"

"With me," he said. "I'm Max. You're Elsa."

I remember swallowing. I used my given name at clubs, but I hadn't shown my ID in this line yet. Which meant this guy had seen me before. He'd been watching me.

"You look like a girl who knows how to have a good time," he said before I could ask how he knew my name. "I think we have similar tastes, you and me."

"Is that so? Like what?"

"Like not this place." He jerked his head. "With me."

I'd told him that I wasn't going back to his place, and he wasn't going to mine, and he assured me that he had something else in mind. "You like clubs? Trust me. You can do better than this."

He'd led me down the block, his hand at my back as if he owned me. I let him because he had an edge about him, but something wasn't ringing my bell. Still, this was the way the game was played, and so I walked with him.

The street was dark, and I remember passing a few people, including one who had a familiar stride. A familiar shape.

I'd shivered, realizing that this was one more night when my mind was conjuring Alex.

"You cold?" Max had asked.

I shook my head. It was September, but the night was warm, and I forced myself not to think about Alex and concentrated on the guy beside me. A guy I barely knew but who wanted me. A guy I could fuck and leave, knowing that—once again—I'd be the one making the choice.

I'd be the one doing the leaving.

We ended up about half a mile from the original club. A seedier area, with dark, stench-filled alleys. "Down there," he said, nodding toward a metal door illuminated by a single, dim bulb. "Loud music, strong drinks, dark corners."

He pulled me to a stop and cupped my breast as he said the last, moving closer so that his hips brushed against me and I could feel his erection. "I think we'll have a damn good time."

"I guess we'll find out," I said. "But you're going to have to do better than that." I pushed past him and continued toward the door, wanting to take back some of the control. Needing that push, pull. I wanted him desperate for me. And I wanted to be the one who said when and how. Mostly, I wanted to be the one to end it.

Maybe Max was the best I'd get that night. Or maybe there was someone better waiting down in that dark, basement club.

My hand reached the handle, and I pulled, but it didn't give way.

"Fucking bitch."

He was right behind me, and I heard the words at the same time I felt the steel blade at my throat. "Do you think I don't know what you are, you little slut? Do you think I haven't watched you? Oh, don't worry, bitch. I'll fuck you just like you want it. I own you, bitch."

The blade pressed harder, and I tried not to swallow, because I didn't want my throat to move. I knew how to defend myself, but he was bigger and knew what he was doing. One wrong move, and he'd slice my throat.

Of course, he was planning to do that anyway. I was certain of it.

The ice-cold memory washes over me as I draw a ragged breath, my eyes on Devlin.

"Yes," I say. "I was terrified. And angry." I add the last with a shake of my head. "I was so, so angry." I hiccup, and it's only then that I realize I'm crying. "And then suddenly he was off me."

The other man in the alley stopped him. The man I'd noticed before who reminded me of Alex. A tall man, dressed all in black, including a black baseball cap, the bill slung low to cast a shadow over his face. He wore a bandana over his nose and mouth, but I could see his green eyes and just a hint of dark hair that gleamed under the dim light of the single bulb.

A man I now know was Devlin.

He held Max against him, the blade now at Max's throat. "Go," he'd said to me, his voice a low, raspy whisper. But even then, there was something familiar about it. "Run," he'd said. "You're strong, dammit. Get the fuck out of here."

You're strong. Alex's words to me. I knew they had to be a coincidence, but I wrapped myself in their sweetness anyway.

And, yes, I ran. And, yes, I knew what the stranger would do to Max. And I didn't fucking care.

Now, I feel the whisper of tears down my cheeks as I look at Devlin. "You were right there. *Right. There.*"

"Do you think it was easier for me? That close and not able to say a word? Do you think I walked away unscathed?"

I drag my fingers through my hair. "No. I think we're a goddamn Shakespearean tragedy."

"Not a tragedy," he says. "An epic romance. The kind that has a happy ending."

"Do epic romances ever end happily?"

"Ours does," he says firmly, then stands, holding out a hand for me. "Come to bed, El. I need you."

His words flutter against my heart. "Yes," I say, twining his fingers with mine. "I need you, too."

CHAPTER THIRTY-FOUR

M y body aches pleasantly after making love, and with a satisfied sigh, I roll onto my side and hook my bare leg over his torso. "You still haven't told me about Carrie. She was your date in New York, and now she thinks you're the devil."

His face hardens. "I think it's fair to say that Carrie qualifies as one of my regrets."

I ease my leg off of him and sit up, pulling the sheet up to cover me as I lean back against the headboard.

He shifts so that he can see me better, then slowly shakes his head. "No," he says gently. "There wasn't anything between us— not that way. I told you. There's only ever been one woman I've been serious about."

"I'm not jealous," I say, though I am a bit, and I'm sure he knows it. "Just feeling a little awkward. Carrie is Carrie, and we were never going to be besties. But she was still a friend, and—"

"I know. I knew it then, too. Believe it or not, that's part of the reason I took her to New York."

I cock my head. "Now you're really not making sense."

"She was the friend of a friend who lived in Manhattan. Jon. He knew I was coming up for the weekend. It was a conference for various non-profit organizations, and I'd been invited to speak. There was a formal dinner, and the expectation was I'd have a date. Carrie wanted to come visit Jon, and Anna was busy on-site with the final stages of construction. Seemed like a good idea at the time."

"You weren't worried she'd recognize you?" Though none of my friends except Brandy knew that Alex and I'd had a relationship when I was in high school, they did come to the house where Alex worked. Which meant they saw him—and often commented on how cute he was.

"I didn't worry about you, did I?" he counters. "And if anyone could see Alex beneath the mask of Devlin, it would be you."

"It's not a mask," I say, reaching out to stroke his cheek.

He catches my hand, holding my palm firm against his beard and the sharp angle of his jaw. "Not now," he agrees. "Back then, though..."

I nod. At that time, Devlin would have been about three years out of the gate from when Alex disappeared on paper and Devlin emerged from the shadowy past that Devlin's military and intelligence friends had created for him.

"Carrie was okay with it just being a friendly trip? She always thought Alex was hot. I have to assume she'd have been even more attracted to Devlin."

"She was," he says.

"Which?" I'm not sure if he means she was okay with the plan or that she was attracted to him.

"Both," he says, and we share a laugh.

"Well, I should have expected that." When he moves so that his back is against the headboard, I straddle him, letting the sheet drop away. He cups my breasts, and I bite my lower lip, my hips undulating in a way that's designed to entice both of us. And to signal very clearly that we're on a break and *not* done for the evening.

His fingers tease my nipples as he says, "You must not want this story very badly."

"On the contrary." I ease down, so that his cock is nestled between my legs, then lean forward at the waist, until I'm propped up on his chest, my head tilted to look at him. "Tell me the rest."

His hands go to my waist, then he slowly strokes the swell of my ass as he continues his story. "The first night was fine. We had dinner and appetizers with Jon. She went to her room after and I went to mine. They were connecting, but the door was closed. I spent the next day in seminars, and she spent it shopping. That night, she had drinks with a girlfriend from college. And while she was out, I did something I shouldn't have. Something I always did when I visited New York, even though each time I knew it was a dangerous mistake."

He meets my eyes, and my breath catches. *He'd gone to see me.* The realization hits me even as he says, "It was a compulsion. I couldn't have not searched you out any more than I could have willed myself not to breathe."

"Every time you came to New York?" My heart is beating so loud, I fear he won't be able to hear the words.

He nods.

"And I never saw you. Or, I guess, I never knew that I saw you."

The muscles around his mouth move, but I can't tell if he's fighting a smile or a frown. "I never wanted you to. But I watched you. Every time I came to the city, I found a way to watch you." His eyes lock on mine. "That night—with Max—you saw me, but you didn't really *see*."

"I had a sense of you, though," I tell him. "The way you moved. Walked. I don't know. I caught a glimpse of you before the alley, and Alex was on my mind. I thought I was a little crazy, actually, but—" I cut the words off, my mind back on that horrible memory of Max and what he tried to do.

I draw a breath, forcing myself to shake it off and continue. "Afterward," I say, then pause before starting again. "Afterward, I felt like the guy I'd seen was a guardian angel. It made sense, right? After all, for all I knew, Alex was dead."

He winces at that.

"It's okay," I say. "It wasn't then, but I have you back now." I flash a flirty smile. "So long as this story doesn't get too crazy, then all is forgiven."

I regret the words the moment I see the hard glint in his eye.

"Devlin," I say. "Just tell me. I already know she thinks you're the devil. I want to know why."

For a moment, I think he's going to stay silent. Then he says, "That night—after I saw you—after I stopped Max—I went back to the hotel. I was wired. I'd killed that man. That fucker who'd wanted to hurt you. But it wasn't enough. It wasn't even close to enough. I went into the room and had a couple of drinks. Slammed them back, one after the other just to dull every nerve in my body. Then I showered, wanting to wash it all away. The blood. The memories."

I tense, scared of where this is going, but not wanting him to stop.

"I told you our rooms connected, but we'd kept them locked at night. Earlier, though, we'd been talking, and it was still open. I was in a towel when she passed by the open doors between us. She'd been drinking—a lot. I had, too. I can handle my liquor, but I didn't want to that night. I wanted to get dead drunk. Blind drunk. I wanted to forget."

I feel the tears trickle down my cheeks, but don't wipe them away. Instead I sit perfectly still, wishing that things had been different, just as I'd wished so many times in my life.

"I don't know what she wanted other than sex. And after a few more drinks, I was happy to oblige."

I swallow, not sure I want to hear this, but at the same time hanging on his every word.

"I was ... rough. And she liked it that way. I—I had a lot of things to work out, and the alcohol was making it easy to get lost." He drags his fingers through his hair, then pulls me to him, resting his forehead on mine so that we're touching, but I can't see his eyes.

"I got lost," he said. "But I managed to pull out of it. I realized I didn't want that. Didn't want her. And so the next night, when she came to my bed, I sent her away."

"You've tied me up," I whisper. "And I like it rough, too."

He pulls back, then tilts my chin up, this time looking straight into my soul. "Because I want you. Want to claim you. To own you. And because I know what you like—that possibility of danger, even though it's only a fantasy, because you know I wouldn't ever hurt you."

"Yes." I swallow, not sure what he's going to say next.

"With her, all I thought about was you. I was punishing her—punishing myself—because I'd lost you. I was using her, just the way my father uses people. Hurts people."

I cringe. "You hurt her? It was an accident. She knew you—"

"No." He almost laughs. "I didn't hurt her." He draws in a breath. "She wanted me to. She wanted me to take her where we'd gone the night before, and then some. And when I wouldn't go there with her, she got angry. Explosive. Said I'd set her up. Used her. And she was right."

I lean forward and kiss him lightly. "That doesn't make you a monster, and you didn't owe her anything after." I press a palm to his cheek, holding his face steady as I look deep into his eyes. "You can use me, though. I want you to. You know there's nothing you can do that will push me away. Nothing you can want from me. Sweet. Rough. Whatever you need," I say gazing into his eyes. "Whenever you need it."

He smiles, recognizing his own words to me. "Baby, I know." He pulls me to him, holding me tight until, finally, he rolls me over onto my back, his arms on either side of me as he holds himself above me, those now-familiar green eyes studying me.

"What?" I feel the smile tugging at my mouth as I expect a flirty comment or a long, deep kiss.

So I'm not prepared when he says, very softly, "I love you, El. I've always loved you."

I blink, holding back tears as I try to speak through the thickness in my throat. "I know."

"I should have said it already. You did, and every time I heard those words, my heart swelled, and I felt like the luckiest man on earth."

"You've said it a thousand times," I tell him. "There's ways to talk without saying words."

"But you still like the words."

I laugh as he pulls me close. "Yes," I admit. "Very much."

We stay like that, our bodies touching, our breath mingling, for what feels like forever. Then he says, "She could be a problem."

It takes me a minute to shift gears and realize he's back to talking about Carrie. "What do you mean?"

"I didn't realize she was holding on to so much anger."

I nod. "When she first said something, I asked her if she was the one sending the texts. She didn't say yes, but she didn't say no, either."

"Do you think it's her?"

"Honestly, I'm not sure." I sit up, pulling my knees to my chest. "There's something else I have to ask you."

He shifts, too, his brow furrowing. "This is becoming quite the night," he says, and I laugh, grateful that he's lightening the mood.

"Did you know anything about Uncle Peter being involved with porn?"

I know before he answers that he didn't have a clue. "Are you sure?"

"No," I admit, then tell him what Lamar told me.

"Just because Mulroy was involved in porn doesn't mean that Peter was. That doesn't sound like the man I knew."

"Me either." But what I don't say is that working in organized crime and the drug trade wasn't the Peter I thought I knew either.

I've always known that everyone has secrets, but coming back to Laguna Cortez, that lesson has truly hit home.

Devlin has blueberry scone mix in his cabinets, and I watch as he stirs the batter. It's barely eight o'clock, but he'd slipped out of bed just after six. I'd felt the loss of his warmth immediately, and once I realized he was up for the day, I couldn't fall back asleep.

I'd pulled on one of his T-shirts, then gone in search of him. I heard him before I found him, and I spent a pleasant twenty minutes watching him beat the shit out of the punching bag on his back porch. He'd wrapped his hands, and I'm glad. I remember only too well the time I'd seen his fingers raw and red, along with the blood stains on the smooth, tan leather of that poor, beleaguered bag.

Last night, his knuckles had been red, but not raw and bleeding. He'd held back a bit with Walt, of course. Which is why the bastard isn't dead.

"Better now?" I'd asked when he turned toward me, sweat dripping off his brow into his eyes. He wore only shorts, and his entire body glistened like an ancient god's portrait spotlighted in a museum.

"Getting there," he'd said, then took my hand. "Talking last night helped. Showering with you now will finish the job."

"You have a one-track mind."

"If the track is you, then yes," he'd said.

Now, we're showered and dressed for the day, and soon enough we'll have scones together. Then he'll leave for the foundation, and I'll go home to check on Brandy and then dive back into my research about Peter, with reaching out to Cyrus Mulroy being the first order of business.

"Thirteen minutes," Devlin says, sliding the baking tray into the oven. "What can we possibly do in thirteen minutes?"

He fakes a leer and I laugh. "Down, boy. I'm dressed and actually wearing make-up. And you, sir, would smudge it."

"I can think of all sorts of ways to entertain ourselves that wouldn't disturb your make-up." He comes around the island and tugs me off the stool and into his arms. "Shall I demonstrate?"

I'm about to challenge him to do exactly that when we're interrupted by the sharp chime of his doorbell.

He frowns, then pulls out his phone to check the camera. "Brandy," he says, and my gut immediately tightens.

I hurry in that direction, Devlin right on my heels, then yank open the door the second he's disarmed the system. "Are you okay?" I demand. "Did something else happen? Shit, I should have stayed with you."

My words fall over each other, as she steps in, shaking her head and saying, "No, no. I'm fine. Truly. Christopher came home with me last night. I'm fine. Truly, I am."

"Then what's going on?" I ask, at the same time that Devlin invites her in and asks if she wants some green tea.

"That would be great," she says, and we both follow him, with me trying very hard not to spew out more questions. Devlin's right. Whatever Brandy's reason for coming this morning, she'll get to it in her own time.

He puts a cup of tea in front of her. "Would you like me to leave so you can talk to Ellie?"

"No. Thanks, but I came here to talk to you, actually."

"Oh," I say. "Do you want *me* to leave?"

A laugh bubbles out of her. "No. You can both stay." She draws in a breath, then lets it out noisily. "It's just that I feel bad about all the pictures. You haven't seen them yet?" she adds, apparently noticing the way my brow has furrowed in confusion.

"From the alley," I guess. "Devlin with Walt. How bad are they?"

"Some of them are quite vivid," Devlin says, and for the first time I realize that this isn't news to him. And, frankly, it shouldn't be news to me, either. But I'd been so caught up in the world of the two of us, that I'd let the world we have to live in slip from my mind.

The punching bag, I think. It wasn't about Carrie or Max or Walt or anything of it—or at least, it wasn't *just* about them. He'd seen the photos and was working it out the best way he knew how.

"Tamra sent them to you this morning," I guess.

He nods. "It's what she's paid to do. I'll be heading in as soon as we eat."

"Most of the comments are just silly," Brandy says. "Talking about you being a badass humanitarian. Tamra called me, too. She told me not to worry about it and said that the foundation was more than able to respond to unfortunate social media storms."

"Tamra is a smart woman," Devlin says. "She told you exactly what I'm going to tell you now." He looks at her hard. "Don't worry about it. And don't worry about me."

I watch as she swallows. "But I do worry," she says, standing up straighter. "That's why I came over. I'm going to go public. I'm going to press charges, and I'm going to tell the reporters what happened to me. I want them to understand why you went after him," she tells Devlin. "You do such good work, and something like this—if it looks like you randomly beat up some guy—that kind of publicity could be really bad."

I watch Devlin, who's looking at Brandy, his expression unreadable.

"Brandy," I say, my voice gentle. "Are you sure?"

"He can't get away with it," she says.

"Maybe he won't," I say. "Lamar has his name now. He can start an investigation. See if there are other women he drugged and raped." I move closer and take her hands. "It doesn't have to be you."

"Yes, it does. Maybe not for a trial, but now. For the reporters. For Devlin. Because otherwise they'll just publish that he's—"

"They'll publish that William Alexis Tarkington and I had a private dispute that's going to remain private, which is exactly the statement I had Tamra release this morning." He moves closer to Brandy. "Press charges if you want to, if it will help you sleep at night and give you peace. But you don't have to decide now. You know his name. Lamar won't lose track of him. And it may turn out that you won't be standing alone against him."

"But you'll be all over social media for something you didn't do. And with all your secrets..."

"I *did* do it, Brandy," he points out. "And I've been protecting my secrets for a very long time. But," he adds, "the choice is yours." He looks between the two of us as the oven timer goes off. "I'm going to pull the scones out to cool, then get dressed. I have a few things to take care of at the office today."

He brushes Brandy's shoulder as he turns to me, then takes my hand. "Will you stay here?"

I shake my head. "I can work better at home, and I have writing to do. Come by when you're done?"

"Like an arrow." He brushes a kiss over my lips, then turns off the timer and pulls out the scones before heading for the bedroom.

In the kitchen, Brandy sighs.

"I know," I say. "He's a keeper."

She laughs, and I pour myself a fresh cup of coffee, then lean against the counter, studying her. "Want a scone?"

"Always, but let them cool."

"So what do you think?"

This time, she understands I'm not talking about breakfast food. She draws a breath and lets it out. "I think he's right about waiting, but in the end, I'll talk to Lamar about making an arrest."

"You're sure?"

"Yes. No. I don't know." She twirls a strand of hair around a finger, then hops up onto the counter opposite me. "I don't want to testify. I mean, I *really* don't. I don't want to relive a moment of what happened." Her mouth twists ironically. "Even if I don't remember most of it."

"Brandy..." I trail off, unable to find the words to make it better.

She shrugs and sighs. "I don't want to," she repeats. "But I don't want Walt walking free. So I guess I'm hoping Lamar finds other victims with more backbone than me. But that's a horrible thought because it means he did it to more than just me."

"Bran..."

"I'm pretty screwed up, huh?"

"The situation, yes. You, never. And now you have time."

"It's not fair that Devlin's—"

"His choice," I remind her. "He didn't have to pummel the guy. Give him credit for making his own decision."

She nods. "Yeah. You're right." She draws in a breath, then lets it out slowly. "He really is a good man."

I feel the tickle of the smile that dances on my lips, then glance back over my shoulder toward the closed door to the bedroom. "Yeah. He is."

Brandy hops off the counter, then grabs a napkin. She takes a scone, then moves toward the living area. I grab one as well, then follow her onto the patio. We both look out over the hills and the rooftops beneath us until Brandy shifts just enough to look at me directly. "Christopher apologized to me. He said he should have realized who Walt was from my reaction. And that he should have done what Devlin did."

I don't say anything. If I were Christopher, I'm sure I'd have been thinking the same thing.

"I think he's a little in awe of Devlin. He even told me he didn't think he'd have had the balls to put himself in the line of fire like that. For a sec, I thought he meant because of who Devlin really is—you know, that the more public he is the more someone from his past as Alex might recognize him."

I start to speak, but she beats me to it.

"I almost said something—I almost screwed it up for Devlin because I was too shook up to think clearly."

Fear slices through me, but I press my hand over hers and

manage to keep my voice steady as I say, "But you didn't." I even manage to make it a statement, even though I desperately want an answer.

"No," she assures me. "I didn't. I realized before I said anything that he just meant he'd have been nervous about getting involved in such an explosive situation."

"Yeah, well, he doesn't know the kind of life Devlin really led. Between his father and the military, explosive situations must come pretty naturally to him." It's the first time I've ever really thought of it like that, and I frown as I wonder just what Devlin has done over the years. From the things he's hinted at—and from his flat out statement that he has dangerous secrets—I have to assume that from his perspective, last night wasn't really explosive at all.

"I'm pretty sure that all this time, Christopher has been thinking that Devlin is just some rich guy playing the role of benevolent savior," Brandy says. "But now he sees that Devlin's a genuinely good guy."

"Well, that's a bright spot," I say, and we both laugh. "Seriously, though," I continue. "I really like Christopher. I hope he's not feeling shitty about not being your white knight."

"A little shitty, yeah. But I think even that's good. Because we talked, you know? I mean, really talked. Like a whole different level of connection. As if we really got under the surface."

Her smile is a little shy. Mine is so wide it hurts my cheeks.

"Brandy Bradshaw, did you two—?"

"I'm thinking tonight. We're going out for dinner. In LA. I have lunch meetings in Beverly Hills tomorrow, and since he can write anywhere he has his laptop, it seems like a good idea."

"I'm happy for you," I tell her.

"I'm happy for me, too. And nervous. Tell me that goes away."

"About the sex? Totally. About the relationship...?" I trail off with a shrug. "You're asking the wrong person about that one. I still don't know what I'll do if I lose him again."

"You won't," she says firmly.

"He told me," I say. "He said he loved me. He actually said the words."

"Oh, Ellie." Emotion fills her voice, and I want to melt with pleasure. "See? He's not going anywhere."

I smile, because I desperately want to believe. But I know better than anyone that love isn't a magical shield, and that no matter how fervently you cling to it, that bitch Fate will rip away the people you love without even the slightest warning.

CHAPTER THIRTY-FIVE

"You have a house here?" Anna asks. "Where?"

I'm sitting on the bench across from Anna's desk waiting for Devlin to get off the phone. It's not even lunchtime yet, so I'm sure he's busy, but I'd come by in the hopes of grabbing a quick coffee with him. I'd been at the office of Sunset Realty and Management a few blocks down on PCH signing the documents needed to release them from the management contract that Peter had set up.

"Off of Sunset Canyon," I say. "So the north side of Pacific, opposite to where Brandy's is."

"It's where you grew up?" Tamra asks. She'd been deep in conversation with Anna when I'd arrived. Something about the Las Vegas security breaches.

"Only until I was thirteen," I say. "That's when I moved into Peter's beach house. And honestly, since I stayed with Peter after school, the beach house was pretty much home from the time my mom died."

Tamra gives my hand a sympathetic squeeze. "Still, it's a nice memory to have back."

I nod in agreement. "Unexpected, too. The same tenant has had the place since Uncle Peter put it up for lease." I don't know the man, but apparently he's moving to Virginia to take care of an elderly parent. Technically he gave thirty days' notice, but he told the management company that he'd be vacating in ten days. After which I can get in there and look around. Then start searching for contractors to update the place before I move in. I'll miss living with Brandy, but I'm excited to have my own place again.

I see the light turn off on Anna's phone, signaling that Devlin's off his call. I stand, only to see it light right back up again. I sigh, then look between the two of them. "So what *is* going on in Vegas, anyway?"

I see them exchange a quick glance before Tamra says, "You know how the foundation helps finance paramilitary support in rescue efforts against human traffickers and the like."

I nod, even though it wasn't a question. I'd learned from both Devlin and my own research about the scope of the foundation's work. Everything from helping victims with job-training to rescue efforts to cutting off the head of the monster at the source of the horrors.

"Obviously much of that work is planned in secret. But on at least three occasions, operations—and victims—have been moved before rescue forces arrive."

"Someone's leaking information."

Tamra nods. "It's possible the leak is from someone outside the foundation. One of the groups we partner with. And it's also possible that someone has hacked into our systems or has managed to get information through surveillance."

I make a derisive noise. "I can't imagine one of Devlin's operations would have that kind of a weakness."

"Which is why we think it's a person," Anna says. "Someone gathering and selling information."

I nod. "To that Blackstone guy."

She frowns. "We don't have proof. But yes. Devlin thinks he's selling information in advance of raids."

"Making a profit by warning people," I say.

"I've known him for years," Anna says. "I wouldn't put it past him, but I also didn't get the sense that was his game." She shrugs. "Not that anyone can really read Joseph Blackstone." Her mouth twists. "Or Devlin Saint, for that matter." She frowns, then studies me.

"What?"

"Sorry." She shakes her head, then leans forward, her elbows on her desk. "How are you two doing? With the social media storm, I mean?"

It's Wednesday, and Devlin's takedown of Tarkington was on Sunday. Devlin and I have both been working hard and spending our spare moments together. And neither of us has been spending much time online.

Still, we've gotten reports, mostly from Brandy and Tamra. Apparently Devlin had been a trending topic on Monday with some people flaying him online and others praising him as a protector of the people.

"We're fine," I say. "I don't get why people are even remotely interested in seeing snippets of the lives of folks they don't even know. But to each his own."

"And fame is such a fickle beast," Tamra says, scrolling through her phone. "Yesterday was much calmer and there's hardly any posts about you two so far today."

"He's off. Go on in before he gets on another call." Anna reaches for the button to open the door, but they're already in motion, and a moment later, Devlin strides out of his office.

As many times as I've seen him, and still my breath catches in my throat. He stands straight, wearing a suit as if he were born to it, perfectly tailored gray silk with a green tie that complements his eyes. He's wealth and power, yes, but there's more to him. The fire in his eyes. The wildness of his hair. He's a warrior, and I have no doubt that in the end he'll find whoever is fucking with him. And he'll completely destroy them.

He'd done as much for Brandy with Walt. What more would he do to save his foundation and the people it protects?

I shiver, thinking about the assassins who took out Myers. I remember what Devlin said—that he applauded them because they served justice where the system had failed. Those assassins were probably mercenaries for hire.

And right now, I'm certain that given the chance, Devlin would happily pay men like that to stop the leaks and protect the foundation.

"I'm glad you could get away," I say an hour later as we're walking barefoot on the beach, sharing the cup of ice cream we'd decided on in lieu of coffee.

"You're a welcome break in my morning. Believe me."

He's turned up the cuffs of his slacks, and while that might transform another man from corporate warrior to corporate beach bum, with Devlin, he looks just as powerful with the surf kissing his bare feet.

"From what Anna and Tamra were saying, it's not exactly the best time."

"Other than giving orders and making a few phone calls, there's not much I'm able to do at the moment," he says. "Which is why you're a pleasant break from the frustration."

I laugh. "It's nice to have a purpose."

He stops, then holds out a spoonful of mint chocolate chip for me. I take it, enjoying the sharp coolness on my tongue. "How is Brandy?"

"I haven't seen her since Monday morning," I admit. It's now Wednesday, and I feel the smile tugging at the corner of my mouth. "Christopher went with her to LA for some meetings, and she told me they were having dinner there and staying at a hotel. I'm thinking they decided to stay two nights. Either that, or they're holed up in Christopher's Airbnb."

Devlin chuckles. "I was wondering why I didn't see him in the research room yesterday. He's become such a fixture, I almost had Tamra call out the troops when he didn't show up."

"They seem good together."

There's the briefest of pauses before Devlin nods. "They do."

"What? You hesitated," I add when his brows furrow in question.

"Just thinking about how much I don't actually know about Christopher."

"He's a writer. Just Google him. Or go to his webpage. Pretty standard stuff. It's not as if you're putting him on payroll."

"True. But I like to keep a healthy paranoia about people. Especially when they're getting close to people I care about."

I take his free hand, squeezing gently, so grateful that he's watching out for Brandy, too.

"Last bite?" he says, and I shake my head.

"You go ahead. A treat before you go back to work." We've made our way back to the foundation, and I don't want to let him go.

"I very much want to play hooky today," he says, echoing my thoughts.

"You have work to do," I say. "And so do I. Lamar finally got an address and phone number for Cyrus Mulroy. I left him a message, and I want to be ready whenever he calls me back."

"*If* he calls you back."

"If he doesn't, I'll drop by his house. I'm intrepid," I tease, making Devlin laugh. "Bottom line, I'm doing a last minute push to find anything I may have missed about him or the connection between him and Peter so that I'm prepped." I release a breath. "I'm hoping he'll tell me that trafficking porn wasn't one of Peter's vices, but I'm steeling myself for the worst."

"In that case, how about dinner? We'll go someplace nice with a view of the ocean."

"How about we go someplace that's a dive with great burgers and fries. Also with a view?"

His arms slide around me as he laughs. "I think I can manage that. I'll change after work and then come get you."

"I like that plan," I say, then tilt my head back for a kiss that is significantly less chaste than I'd expected considering we're in full view of Paul and anyone else who happens to be standing inside the foundation's lobby.

"You're mine," he whispers, once again reading my mind. "And as far as I'm concerned, the whole world should know it."

CHAPTER THIRTY-SIX

I've just walked through the door to Brandy's place when my phone rings, and I pull it out of the back pocket of my jeans expecting it to be Devlin.

Instead, it's Corbin.

Normally, that would be a huge disappointment. Today, though, I'm eager to answer, and I hit the button to put the phone on speaker. "It's ready?"

"Yup. You at your computer?"

"I will be in two minutes," I assure him, kicking off my flats in the hallway and hurrying to my room. My laptop's on the unmade bed, right where I'd left it this morning, still plugged in, the screensaver admonishing me to *Sit Down & Work, Dammit!*

I throw myself on the bed, unlock the screen, and tell him I'm ready to go.

"Check your email. I'm sending you a link to a file-sharing server. Download it, then open it, then install it, then wait for me to get back before you do anything else. I'm going to grab a coffee from the lobby."

"Now?"

"It'll take about five minutes to download and another two to install. And nothing personal, but I doubt you and I can manage seven minutes of civil conversation."

I almost laugh. Despite myself, Corbin is starting to grow on me. "Good point," I say, planning to get my own coffee once the file is downloading.

Seventeen minutes and fifteen seconds later, I'm impatiently tapping my finger as I wait for Corbin to return. The file is downloaded and installed, and I'm staring at a screen that says *Welcome, Elsa. Patience is a virtue.*

And beneath that, an animated wagging finger while the sound blurts out "Ah-ah-ah" in a scolding tone.

I swear if this software is a bust, I'm going to make it my mission to bring Corbin down a peg. Or five.

"So we're good to go?" His voice slithers into my ear.

"Have been for over ten minutes," I say. "Did you get lost on the way back from the lobby? I know it can be complicated. There are so many buttons in an elevator to choose from."

"Not your best zinger," he says, and despite myself, I have to silently agree. "Okay, it's easy enough once you get the hang of it. You have the file you're trying to clean up saved on your hard drive somewhere?"

"Yes. Are you going to be able to see what I see on your end?"

"No."

I lick my lips. "How do I know for sure?"

"You don't," he says. "But in case you forgot, I'm a reporter, too. I won't fuck with your information or your sources, Ellie. You, absolutely. But not the job."

"Right. Sorry. I know you won't." I rest my fingers on the keys. "So what do I do?"

He walks me through uploading into the program, then takes me through the various controls that direct the process.

"Basically, the computer is looking for information in the pixels, and you're guiding it. So this only works if you have some idea of what the image is supposed to be. This is that bank building with the two rappellers, right? So you'll expect a building and human forms.

Possibly cars in the parking lot depending on the angle. Maybe the building equipment on the roof. It was a drone shot, right?"

"Right."

"All right. Let's try this." He guides me through some commands so that the program will focus on the building and the men and not the background. Then he tells me how to isolate the figures and give the computer instructions for clarifying their features.

"It'll take a few hours at least. Might even take a few days. But give it time before you start making adjustments. If you think you know who one of the images is, then you can upload their photo and let the computer decide if there's a match. But if you're flying blind, you just tell the program it should be a person. Got it?"

"Got it."

"Good. And call me if you need help."

"Really?"

"It's not like I'm inviting you to call and chat with me about your day. But if you get hung up, then, yeah. I want my software to work as much as you do. And it's not like either one of us keeps regular hours, right?"

"Thanks," I say, reluctantly admitting that while Corbin might be a prick, he may not actually be the biggest prick in the universe.

He wishes me luck, and as soon we've ended the call, I call Roger to tell him I'm set up and the program is working, and I'll let him know as soon as I do.

Then I sit there, watching pixels rearrange themselves on my screen. At first it's fascinating, but it soon becomes tedious. After ten minutes, I decide to clean the house. Not only will it keep my mind off the computer's progress, but it's a good way to say thanks to Brandy for letting me stay here, even though we're bending her landlord's rules.

I spend a few mindless hours cleaning the bathrooms and folding laundry, followed by vacuuming and mopping the tiled areas. I check in with my computer between tasks, and though the image isn't yet discernable, the progress bar indicates that it's moving toward something. I can only hope that something will be a recognizable image.

I tackle the kitchen next, and since I can see the television over the island, I turn on a classic movie channel as I work. I smile when I realize the current program is *All About Eve*, one of my favorite Bette Davis movies, and I've only missed the first ten minutes or so of the film.

My attention is split between the movie and putting away the dishes. I'd been thinking about Bette Davis the other day, realizing that's who Reggie reminds me of. But there was someone else, too, who'd reminded me of the actress. Someone else with deep set eyes.

I shake my head, frowning as I try to grasp the thread of a memory. That frustrating feeling when you're trying to hold onto a thought that keeps slipping through your fingers like smoke. It's right there, but it's completely impossible to—

The prostitute.

That was it. The prostitute in Vegas. The one whose picture I'd seen in the paper. She'd had deep set, Bette Davis eyes, too. And she's the one who'd been hidden in the back of my mind when I first met Reggie.

The prostitute who'd been with Lorenzo Bell when he'd been assassinated. The known kingpin of an established human trafficking ring who someone had taken out with a close range bullet when I'd been in Vegas with Devlin.

How could I have not seen it before?

For that matter, was I really sure now?

I leave the dishwasher open and the glasses on the counter as I race back to the bedroom. My computer's making progress, the Percentage Complete icon showing that it's already eighty-percent through the initial rebuild. And since that might be enough, I don't want to pause the program. I use my tablet instead, pulling up the browser and searching for the newspaper article that had reported Bell's assassination.

I find the image soon enough. It was picked up by multiple wire services. The picture is black and white, but it's obvious enough that she's blond with curly hair. Reggie has dark, straight hair. But both women have the same deep-set eyes. And while the photo is grainy, the prostitute's skin tone seems to match Reggie's. It's darker than I'd expect for a natural blond, although in black and white it's hard to really tell. But the cheekbones. The wide mouth. The thick eyelashes. And the tiny cleft in her chin.

Reggie.

I'm certain of it.

I toss my tablet on the bed and start to pace, trying to figure out what this means. Bell was assassinated, and she was right there. Had she gotten in close and pulled the trigger? Or was she a distraction, letting someone else get close? Someone like Ronan, who was friendly with Reggie. And who'd also been in Vegas, I'm sure, even though he had a cover story of being in Victorville.

Reggie supposedly runs a hotel, but that's an excellent cover for any sort of criminal operation, especially if money needs to be laundered.

And Ronan? Well, what exactly does an independent security consultant do, anyway? Hired gun, perhaps?

That's my best guess. And my second best guess is that he and Reggie were not only working together, but they were running their operation right under Devlin's nose, using the foundation's resources to get in close.

I drag my fingers though my hair, my thoughts spinning so fast I almost can't catch up with myself. Lorenzo was a shit of a human being. And while I can't abide the idea of those two deciding themselves to take him out, I also can't deny that the world is better without him. But that doesn't justify what they did and how they circumvented the law. More than that, who's to say that they're only going after bad guys? If Ronan and Reggie are guns for hire, then anyone could be in their sights.

I hug myself, hating the ramifications of what I've figured out. Because the bottom line is that it means that Devlin is wrong. For years, he's believed in Ronan, but that fucker has been using Devlin's friendship and foundation so he and Reggie can run their own criminal enterprise.

And, dammit, I have to let him know.

My fingers fumble as I dial his cell phone, and he answers on the first ring. "I was just thinking about you," he says. "Of course, I'm always thinking about you."

I open my mouth, but no sound comes out. How can I tell him this about his best friend over the phone? I should have waited. I should have—

"El? Are you okay?"

"It's Ronan," I say, my voice like sandpaper. "He and Reggie. They're dirty. They're using you."

There's a long silence, so long that I pull the phone back and look at the screen to make sure the call hadn't dropped. Then Devlin says, very slowly, "What are you talking about?"

I swallow, then take him through everything step by step. Everything from the prostitute with Bell to Ronan and Reggie being so comfortable together at the festival. "I'm right," I say when I'm finished. "I can feel it in my gut."

"No." Just one word, but it holds a world of certainty.

"Devlin, you can't just look away. Think about it. You know I'm right."

"You're not," he says. "Ellie, you have to trust me on this. I know Ronan. I know Reggie. I trust both of them, and they are not fucking me over."

I close my eyes, hating that I'm forcing him to look at his friends differently. And hating even more the fact that his friends betrayed him. "I know you don't want to see it," I say slowly. "I know how much the people in your life betrayed you. Do you think I enjoy telling you this? Do you think it's fun for me? But you have to open your eyes, Devlin. I'm staring at a mountain of facts. The least you can do is examine them, too."

"I know the facts. And I know you're wrong."

I sigh. This is not the way I wanted this to go, and more and more I'm wishing I'd waited to see him. "Come over," I say. "We can talk in person. And, honestly, I may have more proof by the time you get here."

"What are you talking about?"

"Corbin's software. It's doing its thing. I figure there's a good chance that Ronan's one of the figures on the bank building. And if that's the case, odds are good he's with Reggie."

"Christ, Ellie. What have you—" He cuts himself off, and I hear him take a deep breath. "You're telling me that software almost has a clear image of those people?"

"I can't tell how clear yet, but it's almost finished with the first rendering. The bank building is already cleaned up." It's true. The lines are crisp and clear now. Not that I care about the building, but it gives me hope for the software's progress with the people. "If the program's right, I might see their faces in the next twenty or so minutes."

I wait for him to respond, but there's nothing. And this time when I look at the phone, I see that the call has dropped.

I dial him back, but it goes straight to voicemail. I frown and check my signal, but it's strong. So I watch the software do its thing as I wait for Devlin to call me back.

Except he doesn't call.

Ten minutes later I hear the beep of the front door keypad. "Brandy?"

"It's me." A heartbeat later, Devlin steps into the bedroom. "Turn it off," he says. "End the program."

He couldn't have surprised me more if he'd slapped me. I'm cross-legged on the bed, and I just stare at him, my mouth hanging open, because I don't have a clue what to say.

"Shut it down," he says, coming to my side.

"Are you insane? No. Maybe you're right or maybe I am. Or maybe we're both wrong. But at the end of the day, I'm writing a story about the Myers assassination, and I am going to reveal who did it. And I'm sorry if the killer is your friend, but that doesn't change—"

"Ronan didn't do it." Each word is slow. Measured.

I let my head fall back in frustration. "For fuck's sake, Devlin. Can we stop this game? We'll know soon enough."

"I already know," he says, reaching past me to press the space bar and pause the program.

I slap his hand away, then freeze as he continues speaking.

"I know, because I'm the one who killed Myers."

CHAPTER THIRTY-SEVEN

"No." I shake my head, wishing I had the power to make his words disappear. "No. It isn't true."

I feel nauseous, and when he reaches for me—his fingers barely brushing my shoulder—I scramble away, almost falling off the other side of the bed in my attempt to get clear. "Don't," I say, my throat thickening with tears when I see the pain in his eyes. Pain I've inflicted with that one small word.

I shake my head, willing myself not to take it back. "I can't. Not now. I need to think. And if you're touching me—" My voice breaks on the words, and I try again. "If you're touching me, we both know that I won't be able to think clearly at all."

"Let me explain."

"Explain?" I snap the word at him, wanting him to snap right back at me. I want a fight. A battle. And yet every one of his movements is as gentle as his words, leaving me nothing to spar against.

I draw in a breath. "Explain?" I repeat, letting myself get lost in the mire of hurt and confusion. "Do you think I don't understand already?"

Even as I speak, it's becoming clearer and clearer. "Rappelling equipment. A trial run. That wasn't a spur of the moment decision because you thought the appellate court had screwed up. This is something you *do*." I hug myself. "This is part of who you are."

My throat is parched, and I hug myself as I pace the room. I stop at the window, then turn and look back at him.

"Yes." That's it. That's all he says.

"Was it a government hit? Did some agency hire you to take Myers out?"

He hesitates, and I see a flicker of something I think is hope cross his face. I feel it bloom inside me. If he still has that connection to the military ... if he was on a government mission...

But my tentative hope shatters like glass when he says, "No."

The fist around my heart tightens as a fresh wave of puzzle pieces rearrange themselves in my mind, coalescing into answers. I feel as if I'm in school, and I'd been stymied during a test. Then I'd looked at the question a different way and all the answers rushed into my head.

"You killed Myers," I say slowly. "But I was still right about the video. It's you, sure, in that video. But it's also Ronan."

His silence is all the acknowledgement that I need. "And Vegas. I was right all along. Ronan took Bell out."

"No. That was me, too. I told you. Ronan was in Victorville."

"But he's part of your team. He's the second figure on the building. You two did a trial run to see who was faster. You won."

He nods.

The air between us is deathly still. "In Vegas. The Glock I found in your drawer. That wasn't just for personal protection. It was a backup weapon. You killed Bell at close range, with a single-shot twenty-two, then tossed that pistol. Unregistered, no prints. But in case you got stuck getting out of there, you had the Glock on you."

"Do I even need to answer?" he asks. "You're doing fine on your own."

"Do *not* joke about this."

"No," he says. "I'm sorry."

I drag my hands through my hair and pace the room, part of my mind screaming that this conversation can't really be happening, the other part yelling that I should have known all along. That maybe I was ignoring it because I didn't want to face the truth that's now slapped me in the face.

I draw another breath. "And Reggie?"

"She's been part of the team for years."

"The team," I repeat. On the one hand, I'm fascinated. On the other, I'm repulsed.

Mostly, I'm drowning. And Devlin's proximity doesn't make it any easier to process all of this. How can it when I'm reeling, and all I want is for the man I love to hold me while I work it out? But he's the man who knocked me asunder in the first place, and I've completely lost my anchor.

"So ... what exactly does this team do? Are you guns for hire?"

"Sometimes," he says. "Not with Myers."

"Right. Of course." His short, to-the-point answers are starting to piss me off. I know it's his way of letting me pull out the truth at my own pace, but what I want is a battle. A fight.

"You already told me that, didn't you? He was released and you didn't think it was right. And so the great Devlin Saint decided to render justice."

"And you know why," he says. "You met Sue. You know what that child went through. And her mother. You talked with Laura. You know how broken that family is now. Broken, but at least they have the chance to heal. How many other families did he rip that chance away from?"

"That doesn't make what you did right."

"Doesn't it?"

"You aren't a god," I say. "You aren't even a saint. You're just a man and you can't play judge, jury, and executioner."

"Not always, no. But in some cases..."

"No," I say firmly.

He meets my eyes. "We're going to have to agree to disagree."

"Damn you, Devlin," I say, my voice hard and tight like a

whip. I want to strike him. To hurt him. "You've destroyed every-thing. Everything."

What I don't say is that he's destroyed me most of all. Because it's not the secret of the video that has gutted me, or even this horrible truth about what he does or this team of vigilantes he does it with.

That's bad, but what's worse is the deception. Because despite revealing himself at the tide pool—despite telling me he loved me—Devlin Saint never really showed me his secrets at all.

There will always be secrets between us, he'd said, and I shiver with the memory, my heart aching. *Things I'm not willing to talk about. Not ever. You should have stayed away,* he'd warned me. *I'm a dangerous bet.*

I let the memory wash over me, my body ice cold, like someone looking down into their own grave, for the first time acknowledging the inevitable darkness to come. Then I meet his eyes. "You were right," I say, lifting my chin. "You were a dangerous bet. And it looks like I lost."

He shakes his head. "This isn't over. You need time to think. I get that. You want more answers. I get that, too. But I know we're not done."

"You don't know anything."

His tilts his head so that he's looking me straight in the eye. "I know you once said that the only way I could lose you was if I was the one walking way. But I'm not walking anywhere."

My chest tightens, but I don't say anything.

"I know you still trust me," he continues "And I know that's a start."

"I don't," I say.

He turns and walks through the bedroom door, then pauses to look back at me. "Lie to me all you want, but don't lie to yourself."

Then he's gone, and I'm left standing there cursing him because he's right. I do trust him.

But that doesn't mean I know what to do now.

CHAPTER THIRTY-EIGHT

"And you just walked away," Ronan said, pacing in front of Devlin's desk. "Walked away and left her there?"

Devlin rubbed his temples and looked up at his friend. He'd called both Ronan and Reggie after leaving Ellie's house. He was certain El wouldn't do anything—wouldn't confront them, wouldn't tell Lamar or any other troublemaking official—but they still deserved the courtesy of knowing that the veil had been lifted.

That's what he'd thought when he made the call, anyway. Now, as Ronan's booming voice edged his already throbbing headache up a notch, he wondered if it wouldn't have been better to wait a day. He'd come here to his office in order to occupy his mind so that he wouldn't keep running the memory of El's shocked and furious face through his head like a damn gif, the same image playing over and over and over again.

But now that Ronan was here, his betrayal was all Devlin could think of.

Because he *had* betrayed her.

Not because of who he was or what he did. No, his conscience was clean. Devlin wouldn't ever lose sleep over taking out men like Lorenzo Bell and Terrance Myers.

No, his betrayal was in not trusting her from the beginning. Holding his secrets close because he feared that he'd lose her after only just getting her back. Fear that the gap between them would be too wide to breach.

And maybe it would be.

He dragged his fingers through his hair then pinched the bridge of his nose. *Maybe it would be.*

He'd made a judgment call by not telling Ellie the full truth earlier, and it had been the wrong decision.

He owed her the truth. The romance of their youth had been built on a lie, and he'd walked back into her life and done the same goddamn thing because he'd been a coward. Too afraid that if he told her the truth from the get-go, he would lose her right then. He'd been greedy, wanting time with her. Believing that the strength of their relationship would overcome his deception.

But how strong could that relationship be when he'd built it on sandcastles?

He'd fucked up. He knew that.

He'd made a huge mistake.

And now he was going to do everything in his power to get her back. To convince her.

He'd win—he had to win, because he couldn't bear the thought of losing her—and they'd move forward together in the light rather than the smoky mire of the secrets he'd been keeping.

He wouldn't lose her. He *couldn't* lose her.

And so he simply refused to acknowledge the possibility of failure.

Maybe she thought the gap between them was as wide as an ocean, but she was wrong. It was only a small stream, and she'd make her way across to his side. He just had to give her time.

"For fuck's sake, Devlin," Ronan said, once again interrupting his thoughts, "she has that video. Our pictures are on it. The goddamn FBI could come storming into the foundation any minute."

He looked up into his friend's stern face. "That won't happen."

"Really? You're so sure?"

"I am." The words hung between them. More than just a statement, they were a promise. A benediction. "I know her," he said. "I know who she is and what she believes in."

"She used to be a cop. She was raised by a cop. I think it's clear on which side of the line she falls."

"Our side," Devlin said. "Justice."

"In theory, maybe. But she's not the kind to break the rules. In case you hadn't noticed, breaking rules is pretty much our playbook."

"Do you trust me?"

Ronan's brow furrowed. "What?"

Devlin stood. "You heard me. We've worked together how many years? Gone on how many missions? One word from me, and I could have you behind bars for life. One word from you, and a cell would be my new home. So I'll ask again. Do you trust me?"

"You know I do. I trust you with my life. That's not the point."

"It is," Devlin said. "Because I trust her."

"One of her best friends is a detective. She's sitting on evidence that could fuck us in the ass. How are you not doing the math?"

"I trust her," Devlin repeated. "And you know I'm right."

"Do I? You're putting a lot of faith in her."

"Yeah," Devlin said. "I am. She won't turn us in."

"Us? Maybe not you, but—"

"*Us*," Devlin repeated.

Ronan put his hands on the edge of Devlin's desk, then leaned forward so that they were looking into each other's eyes. "Let's say you're right. She'll keep our secret. Where does that leave the two of you?"

"Now? I don't know," Devlin admitted. "She can push me

away. Hell, she probably will, and with both hands, too. But this isn't the end. I walked away from her when I was Alex, and it gutted me. And then she came back, and I tried to push her away again. I failed."

Ronan scoffed. "You could have tried harder."

"But that's the point, isn't it? I want her. No, I need her. And she can push me away all she likes, but I'm not letting her go without a fight. She's my heart, Ronan. She always has been."

"Do you think I don't know that? Do you think I don't envy you every single day for having found her? But this isn't a movie. Love doesn't conquer all. She is who she is."

"You're right," Devlin said. "And even though she may not realize it yet, she's of the same mind as we are."

Ronan scoffed. "Yeah, well, that's a lot for me to take on faith."

"But you will."

His friend nodded. "I trust you, just like I said. And I like her. She's got backbone. But goddammit, I hope you're right. Because if we're making the wrong choice, both of our asses are going to fry."

Devlin hit the button on his phone to buzz for Anna, then cursed softly when she didn't answer. She'd been away from her desk when he'd arrived. Apparently, she was still away.

A wave of irritation swept over him—she was his damned assistant, so why wasn't she there to assist him—but he tamped it down, immediately feeling like an ass for taking out his frustration on her, even if she wasn't in the room to shoulder his fury.

This was his loss, his problem, and he wasn't going to take it out on Anna.

Still, he needed to tell her what had happened. Ronan was right—Ellie was holding on to evidence that could destroy both of them.

Devin didn't believe Ellie would use it, but he hadn't gotten where he was by not covering his ass. And as much as it pained, him, he needed to let Anna know the score. If the worst did happen, and Detective Gage marched into his office with an arrest warrant, things would go south fast. He needed Anna and Tamra to be vigilant, because if that happened, they'd be the ones on the front line charged with making sure the operation was secure, the records safe, and the other team members shielded.

Tamra was back in Vegas. As for Anna...

He buzzed down to reception. Paul answered immediately. "Yes, sir?"

"Anna's not at her desk."

"Yes, sir. She transferred your calls to me. Can I help you with something?"

"Is she out of the building?"

"She's in research. Shall I have her come up to you?"

"No. It's fine. Thank you."

He started to buzz the research room, then decided to simply go there. He could use the walk. He was too tight, and the motion would calm him. He headed down the stairs to the third floor, then pushed open the door, stopping when he heard Anna's laugh.

He stepped further in, past the shelves of file boxes holding research material relating to current applicants for foundation grants. He rounded the corner so that he could see the large, oak table that he'd come to think of as Christopher's. And there she was, leaning close to Christopher as she laughed at something on his screen.

"Anna."

Her head jerked up, a lock of red hair falling across her expressionless face. Then she smiled. "Devlin, do you need me? Christopher was showing me the scene he just wrote."

"I'm surprised to see you, Christopher," he said. "Rumor has it you were in LA the last couple of days."

The other man's face turned nine shades of red. "Yeah. Well, we might have stayed an extra day, too. But Brandy got invited to present some stock samples to a boutique in San Diego. So she's heading that way. I think she's going to stay with her parents for a couple of days."

"Good for her. And good luck with your book. Anna," he added. "I need you in my office."

"Of course," she said, as he left the room to return to his office. To her credit, she didn't leave him waiting long, and when she entered, he was on the balcony, the doors open behind him as he looked out toward the tide pool.

He drew in a breath, then turned to face her. "What the hell are you doing?" he asked, working to keep his voice level.

"What do you—"

"Don't play games, Anna. Not with me or with him. He's dating Brandy."

Her eyes widened. "Is that what you think? That I'm interested in Christopher? Devlin, no. He and Brandy are great together. We were just plotting. It's fascinating. All the twists and turns. One branch leading somewhere, another going an opposite direction. And then it all ties back at the end."

"Plotting."

"He writes thrillers. Paid assassins. Undercover operatives." She shrugged. "He thinks my ideas are very creative."

Despite himself, he laughed. "Yeah, well, I imagine you would be a big help."

"That's not why you were looking for me. What do you need?"

He stepped back inside, then indicated the sofa, settling himself opposite her in the chair. "Ellie knows."

Her eyes widened. "Oh. You told her?"

"I should have told her a long time ago. As it is, she was about to learn too much on her own—the drone footage from the Myers trial run. From her perspective, I confessed to save my ass."

"You think she's going to turn us in." It was a statement, and the certainty in her voice—that revelation of disloyalty to the woman he loved—sliced through him.

"No," he said firmly, noting the surprise in her eyes. "No, I don't think so. But we need to be prepared if I'm wrong. And I want to amp up our efforts to find out where that footage originated. Who the fuck was operating that drone?"

"The team's on it," she assured him. "No leads yet."

He nodded. The moment Ellie had told him about the footage he'd told Anna to set the wheels in motion. So far, there were no leads, though if Devlin had to lay odds, he would guess that it was tied to the security breaches. Someone out there was watching not only the DSF, but his other operations as well.

"Who else on the team knows that Ellie's up to speed?" Anna asked.

"Ronan and Reggie. I'll tell Tamra today. The rest are out of town. So long as you do your job, no one will discover them even if the worst happens."

She nodded, and he was satisfied. They'd run through worst-case drills enough. He trusted her to keep her hand on the fuse—but not to light it until absolutely necessary.

"I've got your back," she said.

"I know," he said. "You always have."

"Right. Well." She pushed up off the sofa. "I'll go check in with Paul then get back to my desk."

"One more thing," he said, standing as well. "Did you ever hear of a man named Cyrus Mulroy? You have," he added, since the answer was clear enough from her wide, surprised eyes.

"Why on earth do you want to know about that scum?"

"What do you know about him?"

"He contacted Peter about using his business to move Peter's drugs."

"And you know this because you were working with Peter?"

She tilted her head, her eyes narrowing. "I knew because I was fucking him, which you already know. But I wasn't ever working with him. I was already walking the line with your father by sleeping with him, but I could justify that if I had to. Pillow talk, right? But getting in bed *that* way with Peter? The Wolf would have cut me to ribbons."

All true. And for the first time he wondered if she'd been sleeping with Peter on his father's orders or simply because she'd wanted the thrill of sleeping with an older, powerful man high in The Wolf's organization.

"Why are you asking me this?"

"Cyrus talked to the police."

"What? Now?"

"After Peter's death. One of the early interviews. Said they did business together. What do you know about that?"

"Nothing," she said. "His business was porn. As far as I know, that wasn't something Peter was into."

"So he was lying?"

"I don't know, Devlin. This is all news to me. But Mulroy did buy drugs from Peter on occasion."

"My info is that he wasn't a user or a distributor."

Anna shrugged. "Maybe it was for the girls he filmed. Maybe he considered that doing business."

He nodded. That made sense.

"Why is this coming up now?"

"Ellie's arranging an interview with Mulroy I want to know what he's going to tell her."

"Just about the drugs, I assume. What else is there?"

"That's always the question, isn't it?" The question, however, was rhetorical, and he pushed it away with a wave. "That's all. We're done here."

She nodded, then started toward the door again, but she paused after only a few steps, then turned back to face him. "I know you don't want to hear it, but maybe this is for the best. You and Ellie, I mean. She's never going to see the world the way you do. The way all of us who believe in you do."

She turned then, and left the room, leaving him to watch as the doors closed behind her.

She might be right, he knew, but that didn't mean he would give up on Ellie. On them. He wouldn't.

But maybe he needed to look at the world in a different way. Maybe at the end of the day, he and Ellie needed to find their own common perspective with which to view the world.

CHAPTER THIRTY-NINE

This isn't the way I thought it would end.

That's the thought I keep coming back to as I pace through the house, a stack of Oreos in my hand like poker chips. I've almost finished off the bag, and I feel no better. I feel no worse, either.

Mostly, I still feel numb.

Frankly, that pisses me off. We had everything going for us. Everything. Even with some horrible freak sending me creepy texts—hell, even with Range Rovers trying to mow me down—I've been happier than I can remember being since forever.

Since the last time I saw Devlin, though he'd been Alex at the time.

We're linked together, he and I, and after our hard-fought battle to get back to being *us*, he had no right to keep such a big secret from me.

I take a bite of an Oreo, then toss the part still in my hand across the kitchen, where it lands in the stainless steel sink with a metallic clink.

Part of me wishes that Brandy was here, but she's in San Diego with her parents for a couple of days. I'm sure her mother is thrilled, but Brandy's dad has been distant since she was raped. I told her to call me if she wants to talk, and there is no way in hell I'm going to dump my own problems on her right now.

And, honestly, I'll have to think long and hard before I tell her anything about Devlin's newest revelation.

I sigh, then grab a fresh cookie. I honestly don't know whether to laugh or to cry. Mostly because I don't know what I'm feeling. Am I angry that he's the kind of man who can take a life? A man who is arrogant enough to take on the responsibility of being judge, jury, and executioner, fully confident in the morality of his choice? Or am I angry that he kept the secret, not trusting me to either understand or stay quiet?

Or maybe I'm frustrated with my own hypocrisy. I knew Max would die in that New York alley all those years ago, and I felt only two emotions. Gratitude for the man who protected me and fear that some evidence would be left behind that either implicated me or my savior. More recently, I'd watched Devlin pummel Walt, and the only emotion I'd felt was fear that he'd get skewered by the press or sued by Walt for assault.

The actual attack? Well, that Walt had coming to him.

But unlike Max and the others Devlin has assassinated, Walt is still alive.

Fuck.

My thoughts are spinning, wild and fast. But there in the middle, like the eye of the storm, is Devlin. Always Devlin.

I love him. I do. And even knowing what I now know can't change that.

So the question is, can I live with what he's done? The secret he kept from me? The life he lives beneath the surface?

I don't know the answer to that. But I do know that there's only one way to find out.

I need to go talk to the man I love.

I don't call or text. I just go over and let myself into his house. I expect to be waiting a while, and I'm surprised when I hear the rumble of the garage door in under half an hour, followed quickly by the sound of the door into the house opening and closing and Devlin calling out, "Ellie?"

My breath catches as I rise from the couch, and I immediately feel like an idiot. Of course he gets notifications when someone punches in a code. And of course he has cameras surrounding the house.

I'm looking toward the hallway that leads to his garage, and my heart stutters the moment I see him. He freezes in place, his eyes on mine and full of hope. He takes a tentative step toward me, then stops. "Why are you here? Are we—"

"Don't ask me that," I say. "Not yet."

For a moment, I think he's going to argue. But then he nods before gesturing for me to sit down again.

I do, then point to the bag of Oreos I brought with me. "In case you need some chocolate, too."

A smile flickers on his lips as he sits opposite me, then reaches for a cookie.

"All right," he says, then draws a breath. "Say what you came to say."

Immediately, I feel stupid. "It's not that." I rush to reassure him. "I'm not here to tell you to go to hell. I'm not here to tell you I'm going to call the authorities or write a damn expose."

His jaw tightens. "That's good to know. Why are you here?"

"I have questions. Before—I wasn't thinking clearly. I am now." I lift my chin. "Tell me the details. How it works. How you're funded. Who's on your list."

The corner of his mouth twitches. "My list."

"You know what I mean."

"Yes. I do." He nods toward the cookies. "I need something to drink. Something stronger than milk. You?"

"Whatever you're having."

He gets up, then returns with two glasses and a bottle of bourbon. He pours, hands me a glass, then sets the bottle firmly on the table. "I have a feeling we'll both be wanting a refill."

I fight a smile. "I don't doubt it. Go on."

"You know I was in Sniper School after I joined the military. I was good. My father had trained me well."

"You were Alex then."

"Alejandro, yes. I was. Then he fell off the map."

"And that's when you became Devlin. And I guess you used shell companies or something to launder Alejandro's inheritance so Devlin could have it."

He nods.

"Okay." I nod, processing it all. "You said you're not working for the government. So what are you doing?"

"I said Myers and Bell weren't government operations, and they weren't. But I started in intelligence. So did Ronan. We were ghosts, sent in to take care of problems that needed a particularly deft hand."

I lick my lips. "Go on."

"After my father died—"

"After you killed him," I say, voicing what he hasn't told me, but what I'm certain is the truth.

"Do you blame me?"

I hesitate. "No."

"Would you turn me in for that? Should I be prosecuted for murdering that swine?"

"No." The answer comes immediately to my tongue, and I lift my chin defiantly, daring him to say that I've just proved his entire point.

"After that, I started the foundation. You know this part, too."

I nod. "But you use the foundation for more than charity work."

"No. I told you the truth about that. Saint's Angels was initially funded by me personally. Now it's self-sufficient."

"Saint's Angels." I can't help but smile. "Is that what you call it?"

"I'm not one for modesty," he says, and I burst out laughing. We share a smile, and I gesture for him to go on.

"I do use the foundation, though. I use it to find people who need to be taken out."

"People like Myers or Bell," I say.

"Exactly."

"Or Adrian Kohl."

His face goes hard. "No. My people had nothing to do with his assassination."

"Oh." I'm surprised, but it's not as if he and his team can take out every bad guy. "Okay. Tell me this—when you say it's self-sufficient..." I trail off, gathering my thoughts. "I thought you weren't a gun for hire."

"We're not. We step in when it seems necessary. Like Bell. Like Myers. But we don't advertise and we don't solicit. You're not going to find us on Yelp."

I take a sip of my bourbon as I roll my eyes. "Then where is the income coming from?"

"Those jobs weren't sanctioned, but we do take assignments from the government on occasion. Sometimes through private referrals as well. And we're paid well when we do, especially since part of the price includes the risk."

"Risk?"

He lifts his glass, then swirls the liquid. "The government jobs come with full deniability."

"They toss you to the wolves if you're caught."

"Which is why we don't get caught."

"How many. How often?"

"Maybe a dozen operations a year. Sometimes I'm in the field. Sometimes not." He meets my eyes. "Most of the time, I'm exactly what I seem to be. A wealthy man running a charitable foundation."

My mouth is dry, and my palms are sweaty. I run my hands over my jeans, then draw a breath as I look at him. "And the rest of the time you're a killer."

"I prefer sniper. Vigilante has a nice ring, too."

"Don't joke about this."

His expression hardens. "Never." He leans forward. "I told you I had secrets, Ellie. I made that perfectly clear."

"You did," I agree. "And you told me you loved me."

"I do love you," he says. "Probably more than you'll ever truly know."

"When you showed me Devlin, you said you were trusting me with the truth of who you really are. But you never did. Not really."

"No."

"You stayed silent," I continue. "You dangled the promise of a future in front of us, knowing full well that one day the gauntlet would fall."

He draws in a breath, then nods. "Yes."

For a moment, I simply sit there, soaking up the ramifications of that single word. Then I stand. "Thank you for being honest now."

He rises, too. "Ellie." He reaches for me, but I stay perfectly still, and he pulls his hand back, then slips it into his pocket. "I don't want to lose you."

I drop my gaze, my attention on the pattern in the hardwood floor. Only when I'm sure that I've erased all expression from my face do I lift my head. But I say nothing.

"What are you going to do?" he asks.

"I won't turn you in for what you've done," I tell him. "I understand your code, but it's not mine."

"For what I've done," he says. "Not for what I will do."

I stay silent, because the truth is, I don't know what to say or how to feel. Right now, it's taking all my effort to stand here and not cry. To see past this minute into the one after it, and the one after that until I'm out the door and can breathe freely. Anything beyond that is a blur.

"And what about us?" His words are level, but I hear the

emotion buried beneath them, and I force myself not to cry as I meet his eyes.

"Like I said, your code isn't mine."

He flinches, as if my words are a blow. "So how do we move forward now?"

"I don't know," I tell him. "I honestly don't know if we can."

CHAPTER FORTY

"You're surviving?" I ask Brandy when she calls the next day. "It's nice seeing Mom. She said to tell you hi. But Daddy..." Brandy trails off, and I can practically hear the shrug in her voice. "He's my dad."

"Sorry. I know it's never easy being around him."

"Yeah, well." Brandy had been Mr. Bradshaw's little angel growing up, but after she was raped—after she got pregnant—it was as if something had broken in him. Her mom, Sally, told Brandy that it wasn't her. It was her dad's self-loathing and regret that he hadn't been able to protect his little girl.

Maybe that was true and maybe it wasn't. All I know is that he pushed Brandy away, and as far as I can tell, he's never been much interested in fixing that.

"How did it go with the various meetings?" I ask.

"So great," she says, then proceeds to give me a blow by blow of the meetings she took and the orders she collected.

"I'm so happy for you," I tell her. "And for the record, I want to point out that I only asked about work. I figure you'll tell me the personal stuff in your own sweet time."

"I never realized you had such a dirty mind."

I laugh. "So you're saying that dirty things happened?"

"Not dirty. Wonderful." Her voice is singsong and I can imagine her smile.

I'm smiling, too. "I'm so happy for you."

"I'm going to bring him down here soon. At the very least, I want him to meet Mom. Maybe at lunch or something. But until then..."

"Until then there'll be a lot more Christopher at the house?"

"I think that's a fair bet."

"I'll be sure and only wear my PJs that don't have holes," I promise, making her laugh. "When is the article about Christopher coming out?"

"I'm hoping in a couple of weeks. I talked to Tamra yesterday, and she said she'd been dealing with some crises at work, but was going to set aside some time today. So fingers crossed. How's the romance of the century going?" she asks, changing the subject.

"Fine," I say, not managing to keep the unnatural pitch out of my voice.

"Uh-huh. So what's wrong?"

"It's nothing," I lie. "Just a stupid disagreement. It'll all be worked out by the time you get back." I immediately regret the lie. Devlin surely told Anna what happened. And Anna's become good friends with Christopher. If she tells him there's trouble in paradise and he tells Brandy...

I shake my head, forcing myself to stay silent. If Christopher spills my secrets, then I'll fess up. But Brandy's hours away and dealing with the fallout of being in close proximity with her dad. She doesn't need my shit on her mind, too.

"I got some more information about Peter," I tell her in a not so subtle change of subject. I fill her in on Cyrus Mulroy. "I've called twice, but he hasn't called me back."

"Porn," Brandy says. "Wow. I wouldn't have thought it of Peter, but we were just kids then, so maybe it's true. For that matter, maybe it wasn't just one blonde he was dating. Maybe it was several. Maybe he filmed them and then sold the tapes to this Cyrus guy."

I open my mouth to tease Brandy about this new cynical side of her, but then I realize she could be right. I don't like thinking it, but that's the thing about secrets. Most of them you don't see coming. And they're almost always unpleasant.

We wrap up the call, with Brandy promising to split a bottle of wine with me and give me all the details as soon as she gets back. Then, since he's on my mind, I try Cyrus Mulroy again. This time, however, I can't even leave a message since his voice mailbox is full.

I spend the rest of the day either avoiding writing or staring at the image on my laptop. Though Devlin had paused the process, I'd started it up again after he left out of spite or futility or just because I'm a glutton for punishment.

Now, the render is complete, and I'm staring at a slightly fuzzy but perfectly recognizable image of Devlin on the side of the building. Ronan's image is less clear, but I can still tell it's him. And I stand for a moment looking at the two of them, thinking that Corbin is a damn good programmer despite being an ass, and wishing I knew how I was supposed to feel about this.

Then, without really thinking about it at all, I sit on the bed and pull the computer into my lap. I shut down the program, then shoot off a quick email to Roger.

Render complete. Tell Corbin he may be a shit reporter, but he knows his way around a computer. Too bad the photo doesn't help us. The figures are facing the wrong direction. No identifying features.

Was worth a shot, though.

I hit send before I have the chance to talk myself out of it. Except that's not really true. I could have days to contemplate and engage in internal debate and self-reflection, but the result would still be the same. I'm not outing Devlin. Not like that.

Probably not ever.

I roll onto my side, then pull down a pillow and curl up against it as I wonder what kind of person that makes me.

More, I wonder what this tiny bit of help I just gave to Devlin and Ronan means for Devlin and me in the long run. Am I sliding back into his arms? Or am I simply doing what I can to clear a path so that I can walk away, leaving nothing behind except the status quo?

I wake to the sun streaming through the windows, my laptop's battery run dry, and me still in clothes and on top of the covers.

I sit up, groggy, then jump when my phone chimes, recognizing the sound that had pulled me from sleep. I grab the phone from the far side of the bed where I must have pushed it in sleepy protest, then fumble to connect the call, only half acknowledging Tamra's name on the screen.

"Um, hello?"

"Oh, sweetie, how are you?"

I sit up quickly, then put the phone on speaker as I rub my hands over my face, trying to eradicate the last wisps of sleep. "Devlin told you."

"He did."

I nod, expecting the answer. Of course he told Tamra. What I know now affects both Tamra and Anna deeply. But more than that, Devlin knows that Tamra cares about me, and that the feeling is mutual. He'd want me to be able to talk to her.

I smile a bit, appreciating that he'd thought of it even as I'd pushed him away.

"Do you want to talk about it?"

"Honestly? I don't know."

"I understand that. Sometimes a thing can be talked to death. Sometimes it's not about words at all, but feelings."

"I think it's always about feelings," I counter. "Right now, though, I'm still trying to figure out how I feel."

"And then trying to find the words to describe it," she adds with a laugh. "It all circles back again."

"Maybe. For a writer, words are failing me."

"I'm not surprised. Your head must be overflowing with emotions and facts and moral quandaries."

"Pretty much."

"Forgive me for adding to the morass, but I realized I never told you how I came to join Saint's Angels. And I think the story might interest you."

"It does," I say, then slide up the bed so that I can sit more comfortably.

"I've known of Devlin since he was very young. But he didn't know me until after he ran from his father. I told you that before, of course.

I nod, then say, "Right," since, of course, she can't see me.

"My husband led a military rescue mission. His team—they—they became trapped." Her voice breaks, and I pull my knees up and hug them, anticipating what was coming. "They were taken. Held hostage. Ransomed. And tortured. We know because their captors sent pictures." I hear her swallow. "We, however, sent no one. No rescue team. No support."

"Devlin's team got them out?" I hear the hope in my words.

"No. Devlin had no team. Not then. And soon I had no husband." She pauses. "Devlin came to me a year later. He told me what he was doing with the foundation. He told me that it was both real and a front. He told me about Saint's Angels. About the work he was doing on both sides. The foundation helping the kind of people his father's enterprise turned into victims. And his invisible team helping to eradicate men like his father in the first place."

I close my eyes, picturing it in my head. How it started. What Devlin had wanted to build, and why he'd wanted to build it.

"I joined on the spot," she says.

"Your husband doesn't fit either of those categories."

"No, but had the Angels been in place, my husband and his team would be alive. I believe that. Officially or not, the Angels would have gone in. That's why I do the work that I do, even knowing the risks."

I hear the catch in her voice and wish I could take her hand. "Because it's important," she continues. "Because we help people who might otherwise not get help. And because we dole out justice where evil walks unopposed."

"That's more hyperbole than I'd expect from you," I tell her.

"No," she says. "It's not. Think about it. That's all I ask. Don't give up on Devlin, and don't dismiss what he does—what he believes in—without giving it thought."

"I won't," I assure her. "Right now it's all I am thinking about. I love him," I tell her, voicing to my friend what I hadn't even told Devlin yesterday. "But is love enough to get us over this kind of chasm?"

"Maybe you're asking the wrong question."

"What do you mean?"

"The question isn't *is love enough*. The question is *how wide is the chasm*. If you really think about it, I think you'll find that it's more narrow than you thought."

I'm still sitting there, thinking about her words ten minutes later. She's right. I'm standing across a chasm from Devlin, and right now, I'm not sure if it's a crack in the sidewalk or the Grand Canyon.

And I don't have a clue how to figure that out.

CHAPTER FORTY-ONE

I'm still thinking about that damn chasm as I pace the kitchen waiting for my water to boil so I can have a cup of coffee. I'm hoping it will clear the cobwebs out of my head so that I can think clearly about secrets and Devlin. About what I want and what I believe. About what is right and what is wrong, and how to find that shimmering line that divides those two sides.

Five cups later the cobwebs are clear, but I have no answers.

I consider taking a walk on the beach, but Jake's in San Diego with Brandy, and I know that if I walk by myself I'll head straight for the tide pools.

Instead, I go back over my research on Uncle Peter. I've lost some enthusiasm about the article. The question of how he went from a middle class kid to a man who worked for and then betrayed The Wolf was interesting at one point. Now, though, it seems like a dull and petty story compared to the life and works of Devlin Saint.

But that's not a story I can ever share, not even with my reporter's blood screaming that it's a good one.

"Write," I tell myself. "Four paragraphs, and if you're stuck then you can stop."

It's a game I play with myself that works only about half the time. Today, though, work turns out to be a refuge, and by lunchtime, I've written three paragraphs and am poring over my notes, trying to think who else from Peter's past life might be around? Who else can I interview about finding the mysterious girlfriend?

Anna.

I want to smack myself on the forehead. Devlin told me that until she managed to extricate herself from The Wolf's organization and move to Chicago for college, she'd frequently been tasked with delivering messages to The Wolf's lieutenants around the country.

She'd even been the one to bring the message ordering Devlin to kill Peter.

She'd been around. She knew Peter. And if anyone had seen who he was dating, she probably had.

I grab my phone and dial the direct line to her desk. It rings twice, then I hear the click, followed by, "Devlin Saint's office."

I suck in air, then end the call, feeling like an idiot for not having seen it sooner.

Of course Anna knew who was dating Peter.

Anna had been dating him.

I'd bet money on it. She might not be blond, but she's not a natural redhead. I've seen her roots. So if she dyed her hair red, maybe she also bleached it blond.

But why not fess up? She knows I've been looking for Peter's former girlfriend. Either she didn't think she had any insight for my article or she was embarrassed. We're close to the same age, and it makes sense that she wouldn't want me to know if she'd been sleeping with my uncle.

For that matter, maybe she didn't want Devlin to know. She obviously hadn't told him back then. Did she think he wouldn't approve? Or was there something darker going on? Was Peter truly involved in porn? Had he sucked Anna in somehow?

I reach for the phone again, then yank it back when I realize

I'm moving on autopilot, reaching out to call Devlin to run my thoughts by him.

I don't have the right to do that anymore. Not yet.

Maybe not ever.

The thought twists me up inside all over again, and I shut my laptop and slide off the stool. I've been working at the kitchen island, and now I go and open the refrigerator, then stare inside as if I'll find answers along with a snack.

In the end, I don't find either.

All I know is that I don't want to think about Peter anymore. Not today.

I'm not sure when I make the decision, but soon I'm pacing the room with my earbuds in waiting for the person on the other end of the line to pick up. After five rings she does.

"Hello?"

"Hi, Laura? It's Ellie Holmes."

"Ellie," she says. "The article you wrote was lovely. It was nice to read about the rescue, and all the rest, too. It made my heart lighter to know that people understood even a little bit what my baby went through."

Laura's daughter, Sue, had been imprisoned in the mansion of a monster, Terrance Myers. She'd been one of the lucky ones, having survived to be rescued.

I know that the foundation provided support for the rescue. And I know that Devlin shot Myers after an appellate court ordered his release from prison on a technicality.

"If the article gave you even a little bit of peace, I'm glad."

"But I'm getting you off the subject," Laura says. "I don't imagine that's why you called."

"No," I admit. "I was wondering if you'd learned who killed Myers."

She makes a scoffing noise. "No. I wish I did, though. I'd give them a medal."

I feel the smile tug at my lips. "How's Sue?"

"Doing better. Her nightmares are less. She's playing more.

Laughing more. It's as if she has a guardian angel watching out for her."

"I think she does," I tell Laura, but even as the words pass my lips, I feel the regret wash over me. Because the truth is, that angel got there too late. Myers took the lives of so many kids, and once he'd walked free, he would have surely done it again had Devlin not taken him out.

A guardian angel? Yeah, that was about right.

I don't know that I'll ever be entirely comfortable with what he does, but I trust the heart of the man. More important, I love him. And I'll fight for him.

It's not the Grand Canyon that separates us. More like a bubbling brook, and that's easy enough to cross.

That's what I want to do right now, in fact. Cross it.

Cross it, and find myself in Devlin's arms.

I make my apologies to Laura, telling her that something came up and that I have to end the call.

Then I take a quick shower and get dressed, managing all of that in record time.

I hadn't put Shelby in the garage last night, so I leave through the front door and walk to the driveway. I have a view down the length of the street as I back out, and I see the black Tesla parked at the end of the block.

I smile. It doesn't have a front license plate, so I can't be certain, but I'd bet money that Devlin's in that car. And he's been sitting there waiting for me to finally realize what he already knows—that whether we have to cross the Grand Canyon or a bubbling brook, at the end of the day, we're supposed to be together.

And the sooner I get to his side, the better.

I hesitate by Shelby's door, then pass up the car and walk toward the Tesla. It's late afternoon now, and the sun is already hovering low over the Pacific, leaving long shadows to fill the foothills and canyons.

I squint as I approach, trying to make out who's in the car, but it's no use. All I can see is the glare of the setting sun reflecting back at me, and when I'm about ten feet away, the car silently backs up into a nearby driveway and disappears in the opposite direction.

Not Devlin.

I feel the weight of disappointment fill my chest, and that only confirms what I already know—that I'm making the right choice by going to him. By choosing us.

But now I'm all the more anxious to tell him so, and I hurry back to Shelby, fire up her engine, and roar backward out of the driveway.

The certainty of my decision overwhelms me—and I race forward, eager to see him and tell him that I should never have walked away. His revelations shocked and surprised me, true, but none of it changed the core of who he is or who we are together.

I was dead inside until I found Devlin again, and I know he was the same. He's the love of my life, the light in my world, and while there may be Big Things that we have to talk about, I know we'll get through them.

And the sooner I get to his side to tell him that, the better.

I race down the road, then whip onto the main stretch that leads higher into the hills. I'm pushing Shelby to her limit, letting the wind sing through my hair and sting my face as I urge her on, the speed and power reflecting the urgency of my need.

The roads become more narrow as I get closer to the cut-off to Devlin's and instead of cutting through the residential section, I choose the smaller canyon roads that are my usual route to his home, which sits isolated atop an abutment on a two-acre lot that assures his privacy. A canyon road extends from the southeast corner of his property up into the undeveloped section of the hills, and over to an intertwining network of smaller roads that ultimately find their way down to Sunset Canyon, the main thoroughfare through the hills.

That's the way I go now, as I know it will not only have the least traffic, but will let me open up Shelby. Not because I crave danger—not this time. No, right now, it's the joy I want. The joy of speed and power and the anticipation of soon being in Devlin's arms.

I whip to the left, turning off of Sunset and onto Sunrise Canyon. Right before I do, I catch a glimpse of black behind me. I check the mirror, again, and sure enough the Tesla is back.

I'm certain now that it's Devlin. I grin, my whole body thrumming with the sweet knowledge that he's not only behind me, but that he knows exactly where I'm going.

I consider speeding up and racing him to his house, but I'm already pushing a safe speed on this narrow road. There's no shoulder here, and the turns are tight. I've driven this route a hundred times, and, yes, I've even gone faster.

But I'd been taking a risk then. Saying *fuck you* to death and danger.

That's not my mantra today, and instead of speeding up, I slow down, allowing him to come up beside me.

He does, the silent engine making it hard for me to judge his speed and acceleration until it's too late and he's almost on top of me.

"Dammit, Devlin. What the fuck?" I don't know if he's misjudged the distance or is playing a game, but I scowl into the mirror then speed up, putting a bit of distance between us.

The next curve is tight, and I reduce my speed to take it. But, dammit, he's still on my ass. I'm cursing my boyfriend as an idiot when the horrible truth hits me—*this isn't Devlin.*

I've barely had time to process that reality when the Tesla slams Shelby's rear, pushing me forward onto the soft shoulder right as the road curves sharply to the left. I spin the wheel, but there's no traction, and the fucker taps my bumper again so that my front right tire is only partially on solid ground.

I gasp as the hood dips, and I realize that the packed dirt has fallen away. *Fuck.* I shift into reverse and try to inch backward, but the Tesla is doing the same thing, only with much more speed.

And then I watch in horror as it lunges toward me once again.

I don't want to abandon Shelby, but I don't have a choice. I shove open my door with one hand at the same time I work the buckle with the other.

But it's too late. The Tesla hits us again, and Shelby's entire front end falls over the cliff. We teeter for a moment, and then the cliff falls away and we're airborne, with me clinging to the door, half in and half out of the car, and knowing with absolute certainly that this time, I really am going to die.

CHAPTER FORTY-TWO

"Devlin! Thank God I caught you."

Devlin frowned as he paused in the foundation's parking lot, a few feet from his Land Rover. He could hear the worry in Tamra's voice, and though Ellie came first to his mind, he knew he was only being paranoid. More likely something had happened that required the foundation's assistance.

Either that, or she'd just lined up a new and urgent job for Saint's Angels.

"What's the matter?" he asked, moving to meet her, his concern growing as he got closer and saw the fear in her dark eyes.

"It's Ellie," she said, then took his arm as he stumbled back, cursing himself for dismissing his first instinct. "And it's Christopher."

"What are you talking about?"

"She's not answering her phone, and I think she's in danger. I was doing research on—"

"Get in the car," he said. "Tell me on the way."

"Where are we going?" she asked as she strapped on her seatbelt and he started the engine.

He tossed her his phone. "To find her." He gave her the password then told her to track Ellie's location. He didn't know where he was going, but if she'd had an accident, she was probably in the canyons. Damn her for driving too fast on those roads. She had skill, but that wasn't always enough, and—

He frowned, Tamra's words coming again to him. "What about Christopher?"

"The signal keeps popping on and off, but it looks like she's on Winding Hill Road."

"Terrible signal quality there. It'll be hard to pinpoint. But we'll find her. Hold on," he said, as he took off down Pacific like a rocket, veering through traffic until he was climbing the canyon roads. "Christopher," he pressed, his voice as hard as steel. "Tell me."

"I've been doing research for Brandy. She wanted the *Laguna Leader* to run an article on the author who's researching a book in our little town."

He could feel his pulse beat in his neck. "Go on." He didn't have a clue where this was going, but if Christopher was going after Ellie, then the bastard was a dead man.

"Christopher Doyle is a pen name. His real name is Christopher Morelli Blackstone."

Devlin slammed on the brakes at a four-way stop. "Say that again."

"He's Joseph Blackstone's half-brother. And maybe it's nothing, but with the threatening texts and now Ellie not answering her phone, I—"

"No," Devlin said. "It's definitely something."

How they got to Winding Hills Road without an accident, Devlin didn't know. He was driving blind, pushed forward with fear and fury, and taking the curves at a dangerous speed, especially in his Land Rover, and slowing down only when Tamra reminded him that they wouldn't be able to help Ellie if they went over themselves.

Her words were still hanging in the air when he took the sharpest curve, then gasped at what he saw up ahead—skid marks burned into the road. And terminating right at the edge of the cliff.

Bile rose in his throat, fear covering him like a dark blanket. She couldn't be dead. *She couldn't be dead.*

He didn't remember slamming on the brakes or killing the engine. He didn't remember running toward the cliff's edge.

There was nothing in his head until the moment he reached the edge. Until he forced himself to look over, then felt his knees give out as relief quickly shifted back to terror.

He could see her—but her position was ridiculously perilous and she was deathly still, half out of the car, with part of her body resting on the open door trapped in the tree's twisted branches.

He had no way of knowing if she was even alive, though he refused to believe she was dead. The car had gone over and Ellie must have been trying to get out before it bounced and rolled all the way down the sheer cliff face.

It was that attempt that saved both her and the car, he thought. The open door had caught on a deeply rooted tree that grew at an angle seemingly out of the rock. Its roots must go deep, Devlin knew, in order to have sustained the car and not been torn free.

Still, there was pressure and the force of the car's weight and the intense pull of gravity. Any moment, this precarious nest could come crashing down, and Ellie along with it.

"Oh, my God." Tamra had come up behind him, her voice a whisper "That's a miracle. If the car had gone all the way down. If it slips now…"

"I know." The drop beyond the car's resting place was deadly. And any tremor might send the car tumbling down into the canyon, and Ellie to her death.

"With me," he told Tamra, who followed him back to the SUV.

Devlin opened the back and scoured the few things he kept

back there. A jack. A crowbar. A length of chain and another of rope.

He took the rope, then hurried back, slowing his pace when he reached the shoulder, terrified that even the pressure of his footfalls could send the car skidding down.

He reached the edge, said a silent prayer, then looked down.

He didn't have much time.

"Don't move, baby," he called down. "I'm coming to get you."

CHAPTER FORTY-THREE

I'm coming to get you.

I want to cry when I hear Devlin's words. More than that, I want to call out to him. To tell him I want him. That I need him. And that I have to get out of this mess so I can show him just how much I love him.

But I can't say any of that. I can hear the tree branches creaking, and I know that's all that's holding me and Shelby in place. And when I look down, all I see is a deadly fall onto the rooftops far, far below. If I speak, I move. And if I move, I just might die.

"I'm coming down," Devlin says, and I bite back a whimper. "Don't move. Don't look. I've got a rope. It's tied off. I'm going to come down, get you, and we're going to come back up together."

I have to fight an ironic laugh. Devlin's rappelling down to save me. How poetic is that?

"Okay. I'm coming," he says. "All you have to do for me is absolutely nothing."

I close my eyes, wishing I could tell him that I'm unhurt. Just terrified. He's operating on faith alone. There's no way he can know that I'm conscious, much less alive. But he's coming for me.

I'm not surprised. I know well enough that Devlin will always come for me.

I hear the sound of his feet scraping the cliffside, his heavy breathing as he moves carefully closer.

And then, in the distance, I hear a siren growing louder and louder as Devlin moves closer.

"I'm right here, baby." He's so close I can feel the breath on the back of my neck. "Move slowly and let me loop this around you."

I swallow, then very slowly shift so that I'm looking up at him. I'm holding the steering wheel with one hand and the door with the other, and my body is hanging out over the void. I have to pull myself up toward the steering wheel, and as I do, I feel the car shift and hear the hard, brittle *snap* of the tree that's been holding me in place.

"Fuck," Devlin says, at the same time that the floor seems to fall out from under me. I hear a sharp, metallic clang, and at the same time Devlin's arms lock under mine.

He yanks me toward him, and my legs go free as Shelby drops away. I have only a moment to gasp—to mourn what will soon be a tangled mess of metal—when she comes to a sharp, violent stop, the downward motion stopped by the heavy cable now hooked to her bumper.

I sigh with relief even though Devlin and I are dangling over the abyss. Shelby's safe. I'm in Devlin's arms.

And right then, I know I'm going to be just fine.

"Jesus, Ellie," Lamar cries as he pulls me into his arms. I'm still tied to Devlin, and so he's yanked close, too, as Lamar captures him in a hug big enough to encompass us both. "You have to stop this shit—driving fast, taking wild curves. How many times have I told you—"

"I wasn't," I say, pulling back so I can look at them both. I shift my attention to Devlin. "I was being careful because I was on my way to see you."

I see the moment he understands my deeper meaning, and he lifts the hand he's been holding so tightly and presses it to his lips.

"So, what? You're saying you just lost control?" Lamar asks as Tamra joins us, her face still pinched with worry. "That this was a freak accident?"

"She's saying that somebody tried to kill her," Devlin says.

Lamar looks at me, and I nod in confirmation.

"Who?" he asks, his voice as steely as the metallic grinding coming from the slow engine of the chain pulling up my car.

"I don't know." I look between the two men. "It was a black Tesla. I thought it was you until—well, until they forced me over a cliff," I add, my eyes on Devlin. I draw a breath. "Now, my best guess is Joseph Blackstone. If you're getting close to proving he's behind the foundation's security breaches, then killing me makes for a quite a distraction."

"True," Devlin says, as Lamar taps something into his phone. "I happen to know that Blackstone's currently in Utah."

"Yes, but—"

Devlin rests a hand on Tamra's shoulder, interrupting her. "You're right, of course. He wouldn't have done this personally. One of his flunkies."

"Exactly," she says, though I can't shake the feeling that wasn't what she'd intended to say at all.

"I've got a forensics team on the way," Lamar says. "Take her home," he adds to Devlin. "I'll keep you posted."

"Thank you," I say, giving him another hug. "And thank you for calling Lamar," I add to Tamra, who holds me close and strokes my hair.

When she releases me, Devlin kisses my forehead and a paramedic with a kindly face, pulls me aside, insisting on looking me over. Since I'm certain that Devlin wants to speak to Tamra alone, I don't ask him to come with me. Soon enough, the paramedic tells me I'm good to go. I start toward Devlin, but see that he's now on the phone. So I shift direction and head to the SUV, then climb into the passenger seat. I put my feet on the seat and hug my knees. I give myself credit for not shaking, but there is no doubt in my mind that if my habit of flirting with danger was a death wish, I am well and truly over that.

I'm alive. I'm alive because Devlin found me.

A moment later, Devlin joins me, and the moment we're closed inside, he slams his hand down so hard on the steering wheel the entire vehicle shakes. "I could have lost you today, El. You could have gone down that cliff and been lost to me forever."

He turns, his eyes burning as he locks me in his gaze. "Tell me I haven't lost you anyway?"

"Never," I whisper, as the tears I've been holding in start to flow. "That's why I was coming to see you. I wanted—"

I don't get the words out. He pulls me toward him, my body crunched against the console as he cups my head and kisses me hard. I return the kiss with just as much ferocity, both of us finally letting go of the terror of what could have been and soothing our fears in each other's arms.

"Home," I say when we finally break away.

He nods, then continues up the hill toward his house, not even asking which home I meant.

"What about Tamra?" I ask as he pulls into his garage. I feel guilty not thinking about it before. We pretty much stranded her on the canyon road.

"Lamar's taking her home. And I told her to stay quiet about who was helping Blackstone."

"What? Who?"

"Christopher," he says, the name sending a fresh wave of fear through me. *"Brandy,"* I say, reaching for my purse, only to realize it's still in Shelby.

"I asked Ronan to oversee Shelby's recovery," Devlin says. "He'll get your purse, and he'll make sure they treat her well."

"Ronan? When did you talk to him?"

"I made a few calls while EMS was checking you over."

"Right. Okay. Tell him to send her to Mr. Ortega," I say. "He'll do a good job on her."

"Done," he assures me.

"But I need to call Brandy. I need to warn her. Christopher," I say, shaking my head as I reach for Devlin's phone, sitting in the console between us.

"Don't," he says. "I don't want to tip him off."

"But if he finds out I'm okay, he might take it out on her."

"I sent Reggie to San Diego. She's keeping surveillance on Brandy. If it comes to it, she'll tell her why. But I don't think it will. Christopher knows she's at her parents. He doesn't have a reason in the world to go down there."

He kills the engine as I turn to look at him more directly. "Why?" I ask. "Why would Christopher help Joseph Blackstone?"

"Because they're brothers," he says. "And that fucker has wormed his way into my life and my organization. He tried to kill you. And I swear on my life, I will make that sonofabitch pay."

CHAPTER FORTY-FOUR

I want time alone with Devlin, but Ronan arrives right on our heels.

"We need to talk," I tell Devlin, pulling him aside as Ronan steps into the kitchen to make a phone call. "There are things I want to say."

"Things I want to hear?" he asks, tilting his head slightly as he studies me.

"Yes," I promise. "And there are I things I want to know."

"I'll tell you everything," he assures me. "And I want to hear everything you've been thinking. Right now, though, I need to focus on keeping you safe. So I have just one question." He tips up my chin, then brushes a kiss over my lips. "Are you mine?"

"I'm as much yours as you are mine," I whisper, then sigh as his arms tighten around me.

"In that case," he says, "you're mine completely."

We pull apart long enough to come together for a kiss, long and deep. The kind that would usually lead to the frantic stripping of clothes and wild sex on the kitchen table.

Sadly, we have company. Not to mention a plan to work out.

We meet Ronan in the living room, and he nods slowly,

looking around. "There's a reason you live here. This place is like Fort Knox. That's good. I think this will work out well," he says, then lays out his plan.

Devlin asks a few questions, then nods. "That should work."

"I'd prefer having Reggie here with us, but I don't want to leave Brandy unprotected."

"And we do have three," Devlin says, looking at me. "You'll be armed, too."

"You better believe I will," I say. "But are you sure we don't want to pull Anna and Tamra into the loop?"

Devlin shakes his head. "Standard protocol for the Angels. Mission specs are need-to-know only, and neither of them work in the field. They don't need to know. Plus, they know the subject personally, and that's not something we've dealt with before. They're not tested in that kind of deception. If he talks to either of them and gets even the slightest wind of our suspicions..."

I nod. "I get it."

"With luck, this ends tonight," Ronan says. "You ready to make the call?"

I draw in a breath, then nod. I pull out my phone and dial Christopher, then curse when it rolls to voicemail. "Hey, Christopher. It's Ellie. Can you call me back? Thanks."

I end the call and look up at the guys, then shrug.

They exchange a look, then Devlin pulls out his phone and dials.

"Anna, hey. Are you still at the office? What, no, just one thing. I need to fly to Vegas. Can you call and let them know to get my plane ready? Thanks. Actually, there's one more thing. I was trying to reach Christopher. I thought he might be working late in the research room."

He meets my eyes, then Ronan's. Then he smiles. "Great. That's perfect. Give him a message for me. I just need to check something out. Okay. Right."

Another pause, and then he continues, his gaze shifting to me, hardness fueling his voice. "Someone tried to run Ellie off the road, and I don't want to leave her alone. But I have a theory I want to explore. Right—that's why I'm going to Vegas. Listen, I've been trying to reach Brandy, but I'm not getting an answer. Can you ask Christopher to get in touch with her and ask Brandy to drive up for the night? Yeah. My house. Give him the alarm code to pass on to Brandy. Yes. Be sure to tell him it opens the door and turns off the alarm. That confuses some people. And tell him that Ellie might be asleep. I gave her something to relax her. What? Yes—yes things are fine between us now."

He meets my eyes, his smile slow and sweet. *I love you,* he mouths.

I know, I reply, happiness flooding through me.

Humor dances over his face before he turns serious again. "Oh, yes. Yes, of course I will. Thanks, Anna. I knew I could count on you. I'll talk to you tomorrow."

He ends the call, then sits beside me. "She says to tell you she's sorry and hopes that you're doing okay."

"You're having them get your plane ready?"

"Got to make the illusion look good." He taps out a text. "Marci will make sure the log shows that I was on the plane. And I'm sure she and the crew will have a lovely night in Vegas."

I almost point out that faking the log is illegal, but I stop myself. Hardly the point.

"And now?"

"Now we wait," Ronan says. He looks at me, and there's so much concern reflected on his face, that I'm not sure how I ever thought he had it in for me. "You doing okay?"

"I've got the two of you here with me," I say. "I'm doing just fine. And thank you," I add. "Everything before is such a blur. If I didn't already say thank you for coming to help and for taking care of Shelby, then I'm saying it now."

"You did," he said. "And you're still very welcome."

I smile, then look to Devlin as a new thought occurs to me.

"What if Brandy calls to find out how I am? Or shows up at the door in ninety minutes, frantic about me?"

"Then we'll know Christopher isn't our guy."

I hug myself. "No, I think you're right. His connection to Blackstone. And I overheard him talking about ways to kill someone—supposedly in his book—and running them down in the street was one of them."

Devlin drags his fingers through his hair. "I should have seen it."

I shake my head. "None of us did. Hell, I like him."

"He's good," Ronan says. "Good at what he does. But so are we."

I swallow. "Should I keep trying him?"

"You don't need to," Devlin says. "I gave Anna the message. She knows it's urgent. She's never once let me down."

He stands up, then reaches out a hand for me. "Let's get you cleaned up."

I nod. I've got dirt on my clothes and dust in my hair, and I let Devlin lead me into the bathroom. He runs a bath, then helps me undress and get into the warm water. It feels delicious on my bruised skin. Miraculously, I don't have many injuries, but I'm definitely sore and banged up, and the water feels like heaven.

On the counter, I hear my phone ping a text, but I ignore it. Devlin is with me, and right now, that's all that counts. I close my eyes, sighing as he gently washes the lingering dirt off my face, then rinses my hair.

He's seated on a stool next to the tub, and as I lean back to sack, I open my eyes and take his hand. "Thank you for rescuing me. And for taking care of me."

"Always," he says. "I love you, El. I will always protect you. Always take care of you. You know that, right?"

"Yes," I assure him, my heart swelling from the love I see in his eyes. "Of course, I do."

We'd reached Devlin's house just after sunset and had called Anna with the message for Christopher about half an hour after that.

Now it's almost nine o'clock. Zero hour since we're assuming that Christopher will try to arrive about the time I'd be expecting Brandy.

I'm in the living room with the television on low and a 9mm Glock under the pillow beside me. Devlin is behind me, covering the entrance from the garage side door and the main front door. Ronan is on the opposite side in the utility room, giving him full coverage of anyone who gets past Devlin and the utility room, which has a side door that opens onto the yard.

These are the only entrances to the house, and they're covered.

"The patio can be accessed, too," Devlin had pointed out. "There's a spiral staircase that comes up out of the canyon. But you have to cut through the yard, then shimmy down the rocks to even get to it. And no one unfamiliar with the house knows it's there."

I'm watching *The Empire Strikes Back*, though I'm not really paying attention. Instead, I'm listening for the electronic beep signaling that someone is using the keypad to disarm the system. Disarming is only silent when it's done through the app, which, of course, Christopher doesn't have.

After a few minutes, I can't take it anymore, and I get up and pace, then sit and try again to watch the movie, but with no success. I move to the center of the room and turn my back to the TV and balcony so that I can speak roughly in their direction. "Guys, I don't think this is—"

I gasp, then curse myself, because my gun is still on the sofa, and I'm staring at Ronan, who's pointing his weapon straight at me.

I'm going to die.

The thought is so sure. So certain, and I hate myself for letting my guard down. I'd come to trust this man, and he'd not only fucked me over, he'd screwed Devlin, too.

"How could you," I whisper, but my words are drowned out by the sharp report of his weapon and the howling cry of pain from behind me.

I whip around at the same time I see Devlin bolt into the room.

Anna.

She's taken one panel of the sheer curtains down with her, and now the gauzy white is turning a chilling red from the wound in her shoulder. "Sorry," Ronan says to me. "She was just about to nail you."

I nod, mute, as Devlin rushes to embrace me.

After a moment, though, he lets go and moves to Anna.

"Why?" he says as he kicks her weapon away. She's slouched against the wall, the curtain panels that are still hanging now blowing in the breeze. "Why?" he asks again, and I cringe against the depth of pain and betrayal in his voice.

He grabs some of the curtain and wads it up, then uses it to staunch the blood. "Goddammit, Anna I need you to tell me why."

She looks at him, then shifts her gaze to me. "We could have been friends," she says, her voice breaking. "You took things that weren't yours."

"Devlin isn't a thing." I start to move toward them, but Ronan holds me back, a firm hand on my shoulder. "And this wasn't just about jealousy."

Devlin looks up at me. "What are you talking about?"

"I checked my texts earlier. Cyrus Mulroy is dead. That's why he hasn't returned my call. Anna killed him, didn't you? Because he had tapes of her."

The hatred in her eyes is enough to answer that question.

"Did you know Peter was filming you? Or did he have secret cameras?"

I see her throat move as she swallows. Then she turns from me, her face melting into warm goo as she focuses on Devlin. "He sold them," she says, her voice thin and her breath raspy. "He liked to tape me, but then he sold them to Cyrus and said he was done with me. *Done.*"

"Devlin, we need to call 911." My throat is thick with both fury and heartbreak. "She's losing a lot of blood."

"He was going to ... put those tapes out there," Anna rasps, as Devlin stands and pulls out his phone. "Your fucking girlfriend's fucking uncle ... Had you kill him ... That's why ... that's why I told you to do it. Pretended the order was from him ... from your father."

Her lips move and she struggles for words. "Had to ... Had to punish Peter because he—"

Her eyes go wide, her body stiffening as if she finally realized she said too much.

I'm in shock, the reality of her words coalescing in front of me into a picture I really don't want to see. The Wolf never ordered Peter's execution. Anna set Devlin up to murder her lover in order to get revenge for selling the tapes. And all along, Anna has been harassing me, trying to get rid of me. Until, finally, she decided to just kill me.

"She's poison," Anna says, her eyes drifting to me, her face twisting as a burst of energy seems to fill her.

She reaches behind her, and I drop to the floor, certain I know what's coming. I see her pull out the gun. I hear the *blam* of the bullet, and then I see her slump to the floor, her secondary weapon falling from her now-limp fingers.

I whip around to Ronan, but he hadn't pulled the trigger this time.

Devlin had.

He'd killed the woman he'd thought was his friend to save me.

I gasp, then run into his arms. This time, Ronan doesn't stop me. We sink to the ground, holding each other as Ronan dials 911.

"I'm sorry," I say, certain his heart must be breaking, his whole reality shifting. "I'm so, so sorry."

"I told you," he whispers. "I will always protect you. No matter what the price. No matter what the cost."

EPILOGUE

"Don't even think about it," I say, as Devlin's hand snakes up my thigh, taking advantage of the slit in the ballgown. "There is no way you're getting me all mussed up before you accept this award."

"And after?" he asks.

"After's a no-brainer," I say. "How many girls get to say they fucked the Humanitarian of the Year in the back of a limo?"

"Would hate for you to miss out on that," he says.

"Good. Because I don't intend to. Still," I add, taking his hand and sliding it up my leg. "Just a preview." I guide his fingers higher, until it becomes sweetly, deliciously, frustratingly obvious that I'm not wearing a single thing under this dress.

He groans in protest when I take his hand away. "We'll take the long way back to the hotel," I promise him.

"Yes," he says. "We will."

We smile at each other, then ride in silence for the next few blocks. We're almost to the Manhattan theater where the award ceremony is being held. I reach over and take his hand. "Are you okay?"

Since Anna died, we've talked a lot about what happened. We listened to Lamar chew us out for not getting him involved from the beginning. For flouting the law and for putting our lives at risk.

And we watched Brandy's shocked face as we told her everything, including how we'd suspected Christopher. Lamar had taken Christopher in for formal questioning, but there was nothing to suggest that he was working with Anna in her quest to get rid of me. Instead, the puzzle pieces seem to suggest that it was my investigation of Peter that started the ball in motion. Because sooner or later, I'd find out about the porn. And that would lead to Cyrus and the tapes of Anna. Tapes she wanted to stay hidden.

All because she loved Devlin. And in her mixed up mind she'd believed that she could win him if she just got rid of me and cleaned up her past.

As for whether Christopher was working with Joseph Blackstone on the leaked information, there was no evidence there, either. That's not something Lamar knows about, though. But Devlin and Ronan and the rest of his team are keeping an eye on the situation. And me? I'm just hoping it doesn't blow back on Brandy.

Most of all, I'm happy to be alive and with Devlin. We have work to do, of course. What couple doesn't? But I love him, and that makes it worth it.

"Devlin?" I press.

"I'm fine," he assures me. "I only—"

"What?"

"This award. What do you think of it?"

I hear the bigger question in his words. He's getting the award for the foundation side of his life. But he has other facets, too. Sides that use hard actions to solve scary problems. Methods that humanitarian causes the world over might find troubling, to say the least.

"I think it's wonderful," I tell him truthfully. "You deserve it. This award, and so much more."

He pulls me close and kisses me. "Thank you."

"Don't doubt yourself."

He laughs. "I rarely do." Gently, he strokes my cheek. "And if I show you my weaknesses, it must mean I love you."

"You do," I say. "But you're not weak." I tilt my head and smile as I recite the words he once left for me, printed on a note that he left as a talisman. "Always remember that you're strong."

"With you at my side, I can't be anything else. Now kiss me quick. We're here."

Our lips brush, the kiss lingering as we wait for the door to open. There's a red carpet and a throng on either side of it behind the velvet ropes.

As soon as the door opens, noise surges and lights flash as the crowd shouts out his name and questions. I almost laugh, because I've never walked among the paparazzi before, and though I avoid social media, I'll definitely be checking for pictures tomorrow.

Then I start to pay attention to the actual words. That's when my smile turns to plastic and my blood chills.

"Is it true?"

Devlin grips my hand harder.

"Is your name really Alejandro Lopez?"

"How have you managed to keep your identity hidden for so long?"

"Why the ploy, Mr. Saint?"

"Did you do wet work for your father?"

"How can you have the gall to accept the World Council Humanitarian Award under a false name?"

"Is your father really Daniel Lopez?"

"Did you really grow up with The Wolf?"

"Devlin, did you kill your father?"

Our pace quickens, and though it seems as though the walk took forever, I know that only seconds have passed from the limo to the inside of the theater. Now, the sound and the lights are gone, and we're inside with the Awards Committee, and my hand aches as if the bones are cracking.

I look down and realize he's squeezing my hand. "Devlin," I

say gently, my heart aching as much as my hand from the pain I see in his eyes. "Devlin, you're hurting me."

For a moment, nothing happens. Then he releases me so fast you'd think I had burned him. His chest rises and fall, and his face is completely expressionless.

"Mr. Saint." A man in a tuxedo steps forward. "I'm Arthur Packard, the committee chair. Do you think we can have a word?"

"Of course. I'd like Ms. Holmes to join us."

Packard nods, then leads us into a back room. "If you'll excuse me a moment."

He leaves, and Devlin meets my eyes. "They're going to withdraw the award. They'll focus on their other speakers, and I'll be tossed aside."

"Yes," I say, because of course that's what's going to happen.

"Goddammit." He pounds a fist onto his thigh. "God*dammit.*"

I want to touch him. To heal him. But I know there's nothing I can do, and a stab of terror cuts through me. He pushed me away before because he believed he was a danger to me. Now, with his world exploding around us, there's no denying that everything is about to change. God only knows what secrets will be revealed and what trials we'll have to face.

And, yes, I'm terrified that he'll push me away again.

Then Devlin's eyes open, and he looks right at me, his gaze full of strength and ferocity. But what I see most of all, is love.

Slowly, without a word, he holds out his hand to me. I take it, then hold tight. I don't know what's coming next for us.

But I do know that we'll get through this. Because together, Devlin and I can survive anything.

Devlin & Ellie's story concludes in
My Cruel Salvation
May 2021

He'll keep her safe, no matter the price.

Investigative reporter Ellie Holmes has uncovered billionaire Devlin Saint's dark and dangerous secrets, and he has both stripped away her protective armor and tamed the wildness within her. Bound by a shared past and the hope of a blissful future, they grow even closer, each exposing more of themselves as their love deepens.

But now that Devlin's true identity has been publicly revealed, old enemies appear, intent on destroying Devlin. And while he vows to enlist all of his resources to protect her, Ellie soon realizes that the only way to save them both is to take the last, final step to fully join Devlin in the dark.

My Cruel Salvation

CHAPTER ONE

A cool ocean breeze caresses my bare shoulders, and I shiver, wishing I'd taken my roommate's advice and brought a shawl with me tonight. I arrived in Los Angeles only four days ago, and I haven't yet adjusted to the concept of summer temperatures changing with the setting of the sun. In Dallas, June is hot, July is hotter, and August is hell.

Not so in California, at least not by the beach. LA Lesson Number One: Always carry a sweater if you'll be out after dark.

Of course, I could leave the balcony and go back inside to the party. Mingle with the millionaires. Chat up the celebrities. Gaze dutifully at the paintings. It is a gala art opening, after all, and my boss brought me here to meet and greet and charm and chat. Not to lust over the panorama that is coming alive in front of me. Bloodred clouds bursting against the pale orange sky. Blue-gray waves shimmering with dappled gold.

I press my hands against the balcony rail and lean forward, drawn to the intense, unreachable beauty of the setting sun. I regret that I didn't bring the battered Nikon I've had since high school. Not that it would have fit in my itty-bitty beaded purse.

And a bulky camera bag paired with a little black dress is a big, fat fashion no-no.

But this is my very first Pacific Ocean sunset, and I'm determined to document the moment. I pull out my iPhone and snap a picture.

"Almost makes the paintings inside seem redundant, doesn't it?" I recognize the throaty, feminine voice and turn to face Evelyn Dodge, retired actress turned agent turned patron of the arts—and my hostess for the evening.

"I'm so sorry. I know I must look like a giddy tourist, but we don't have sunsets like this in Dallas."

"Don't apologize," she says. "I pay for that view every month when I write the mortgage check. It damn well better be spectacular."

I laugh, immediately more at ease.

"Hiding out?"

"Excuse me?"

"You're Carl's new assistant, right?" she asks, referring to my boss of three days.

"Nikki Fairchild."

"I remember now. Nikki from Texas." She looks me up and down, and I wonder if she's disappointed that I don't have big hair and cowboy boots. "So who does he want you to charm?"

"Charm?" I repeat, as if I don't know exactly what she means.

She cocks a single brow. "Honey, the man would rather walk on burning coals than come to an art show. He's fishing for investors and you're the bait." She makes a rough noise in the back of her throat. "Don't worry. I won't press you to tell me who. And I don't blame you for hiding out. Carl's brilliant, but he's a bit of a prick."

"It's the brilliant part I signed on for," I say, and she barks out a laugh.

The truth is that she's right about me being the bait. "Wear a cocktail dress," Carl had said. "Something flirty."

Seriously? I mean, Seriously?

I should have told him to wear his own damn cocktail dress. But I didn't. Because I want this job. I fought to get this job. Carl's company, C-Squared Technologies, successfully launched three web-based products in the last eighteen months. That track record had caught the industry's eye, and Carl had been hailed as a man to watch.

More important from my perspective, that meant he was a man to learn from, and I'd prepared for the job interview with an intensity bordering on obsession. Landing the position had been a huge coup for me. So what if he wanted me to wear something flirty? It was a small price to pay.

Shit.

"I need to get back to being the bait," I say.

"Oh, hell. Now I've gone and made you feel either guilty or self-conscious. Don't be. Let them get liquored up in there first. You catch more flies with alcohol anyway. Trust me. I know."

She's holding a pack of cigarettes, and now she taps one out, then extends the pack to me. I shake my head. I love the smell of tobacco—it reminds me of my grandfather—but actually inhaling the smoke does nothing for me.

"I'm too old and set in my ways to quit," she says. "But God forbid I smoke in my own damn house. I swear, the mob would burn me in effigy. You're not going to start lecturing me on the dangers of secondhand smoke, are you?"

"No," I promise.

"Then how about a light?"

I hold up the itty-bitty purse. "One lipstick, a credit card, my driver's license, and my phone."

"No condom?"

"I didn't think it was that kind of party," I say dryly.

"I knew I liked you." She glances around the balcony. "What the hell kind of party am I throwing if I don't even have one goddamn candle on one goddamn table? Well, fuck it." She puts the unlit cigarette to her mouth and inhales, her eyes closed and her expression rapturous. I can't help but like her. She wears hardly any makeup, in stark contrast to all the other women here tonight, myself included, and her dress is more of a caftan, the batik pattern as interesting as the woman herself.

She's what my mother would call a brassy broad—loud, large, opinionated, and self-confident. My mother would hate her. I think she's awesome.

She drops the unlit cigarette onto the tile and grinds it with the toe of her shoe. Then she signals to one of the catering staff, a girl dressed all in black and carrying a tray of champagne glasses.

The girl fumbles for a minute with the sliding door that opens onto the balcony, and I imagine those flutes tumbling off, breaking against the hard tile, the scattered shards glittering like a wash of diamonds.

I picture myself bending to snatch up a broken stem. I see the raw edge cutting into the soft flesh at the base of my thumb as I squeeze. I watch myself clutching it tighter, drawing strength from the pain, the way some people might try to extract luck from a rabbit's foot.

The fantasy blurs with memory, jarring me with its potency. It's fast and powerful, and a little disturbing because I haven't needed the pain in a long time, and I don't understand why I'm thinking about it now, when I feel steady and in control.

I am fine, I think. *I am fine, I am fine, I am fine.*

"Take one, honey," Evelyn says easily, holding a flute out to me.

I hesitate, searching her face for signs that my mask has slipped and she's caught a glimpse of my rawness. But her face is clear and genial.

"No, don't you argue," she adds, misinterpreting my hesitation. "I bought a dozen cases and I hate to see good alcohol go to waste. Hell no," she adds when the girl tries to hand her a flute. "I hate the stuff. Get me a vodka. Straight up. Chilled. Four olives. Hurry up, now. Do you want me to dry up like a leaf and float away?"

The girl shakes her head, looking a bit like a twitchy, frightened rabbit. Possibly one that had sacrificed his foot for someone else's good luck.

Evelyn's attention returns to me. "So how do you like LA? What have you seen? Where have you been? Have you bought a map of the stars yet? Dear God, tell me you're not getting sucked into all that tourist bullshit."

"Mostly I've seen miles of freeway and the inside of my apartment."

"Well, that's just sad. Makes me even more glad that Carl dragged your skinny ass all the way out here tonight."

I've put on fifteen welcome pounds since the years when my mother monitored every tiny thing that went in my mouth, and while I'm perfectly happy with my size-eight ass, I wouldn't describe it as skinny. I know Evelyn means it as a compliment, though, and so I smile. "I'm glad he brought me, too. The paintings really are amazing."

"Now don't do that—don't you go sliding into the polite-conversation routine. No, no," she says before I can protest. "I'm sure you mean it. Hell, the paintings are wonderful. But you're getting the flat-eyed look of a girl on her best behavior, and we can't have that. Not when I was getting to know the real you."

"Sorry," I say. "I swear I'm not fading away on you."

Because I genuinely like her, I don't tell her that she's wrong —she hasn't met the real Nikki Fairchild. She's met Social Nikki who, much like Malibu Barbie, comes with a complete set of accessories. In my case, it's not a bikini and a convertible. Instead, I have the *Elizabeth Fairchild Guide for Social Gatherings*.

My mother's big on rules. She claims it's her Southern upbringing. In my weaker moments, I agree. Mostly, I just think she's a controlling bitch. Since the first time she took me for tea at the Mansion at Turtle Creek in Dallas at age three, I have had the rules drilled into my head. How to walk, how to talk, how to dress. What to eat, how much to drink, what kinds of jokes to tell.

I have it all down, every trick, every nuance, and I wear my practiced pageant smile like armor against the world. The result being that I don't think I could truly be myself at a party even if my life depended on it.

This, however, is not something Evelyn needs to know.

"Where exactly are you living?" she asks.

"Studio City. I'm sharing a condo with my best friend from high school."

"Straight down the 101 for work and then back home again. No wonder you've only seen concrete. Didn't anyone tell you that you should have taken an apartment on the Westside?"

"Too pricey to go it alone," I admit, and I can tell that my admission surprises her. When I make the effort—like when I'm Social Nikki—I can't help but look like I come from money. Probably because I do. Come from it, that is. But that doesn't mean I brought it with me.

"How old are you?"

"Twenty-four."

Evelyn nods sagely, as if my age reveals some secret about me. "You'll be wanting a place of your own soon enough. You call me when you do and we'll find you someplace with a view. Not as good as this one, of course, but we can manage something better than a freeway on-ramp."

"It's not that bad, I promise."

"Of course it's not," she says in a tone that says the exact opposite. "As for views," she continues, gesturing toward the now-dark ocean and the sky that's starting to bloom with stars, "you're welcome to come back anytime and share mine."

"I might take you up on that," I admit. "I'd love to bring a decent camera back here and take a shot or two."

"It's an open invitation. I'll provide the wine and you can provide the entertainment. A young woman loose in the city. Will it be a drama? A rom-com? Not a tragedy, I hope. I love a good cry as much as the next woman, but I like you. You need a happy ending."

I tense, but Evelyn doesn't know she's hit a nerve. That's why I moved to LA, after all. New life. New story. New Nikki.

I ramp up the Social Nikki smile and lift my champagne flute. "To happy endings. And to this amazing party. I think I've kept you from it long enough."

"Bullshit," she says. "I'm the one monopolizing you, and we both know it."

We slip back inside, the buzz of alcohol-fueled conversation replacing the soft calm of the ocean.

"The truth is, I'm a terrible hostess. I do what I want, talk to whoever I want, and if my guests feel slighted they can damn well deal with it."

I gape. I can almost hear my mother's cries of horror all the way from Dallas.

"Besides," she continues, "this party isn't supposed to be about me. I put together this little shindig to introduce Blaine and his art to the community. He's the one who should be doing the mingling, not me. I may be fucking him, but I'm not going to baby him."

Evelyn has completely destroyed my image of how a hostess for the not-to-be-missed social event of the weekend is supposed to behave, and I think I'm a little in love with her for that.

"I haven't met Blaine yet. That's him, right?" I point to a tall reed of a man. He is bald, but sports a red goatee. I'm pretty sure it's not his natural color. A small crowd hums around him, like bees drawing nectar from a flower. His outfit is certainly as bright as one.

"That's my little center of attention, all right," Evelyn says. "The man of the hour. Talented, isn't he?" Her hand sweeps out to indicate her massive living room. Every wall is covered with paintings. Except for a few benches, whatever furniture was once in the room has been removed and replaced with easels on which more paintings stand.

I suppose technically they are portraits. The models are nudes, but these aren't like anything you would see in a classical art book. There's something edgy about them. Something provocative and raw. I can tell that they are expertly conceived and carried out, and yet they disturb me, as if they reveal more about the person viewing the portrait than about the painter or the model.

As far as I can tell, I'm the only one with that reaction. Certainly the crowd around Blaine is glowing. I can hear the gushing praise from here.

"I picked a winner with that one," Evelyn says. "But let's see. Who do you want to meet? Rip Carrington and Lyle Tarpin? Those two are guaranteed drama, that's for damn sure, and your roommate will be jealous as hell if you chat them up."

"She will?"

Evelyn's brows arch up. "Rip and Lyle? They've been feuding for weeks." She narrows her eyes at me. "The fiasco about the new season of their sitcom? It's all over the Internet? You really don't know them?"

"Sorry," I say, feeling the need to apologize. "My school schedule was pretty intense. And I'm sure you can imagine what working for Carl is like."

Speaking of ...

I glance around, but I don't see my boss anywhere.

"That is one serious gap in your education," Evelyn says. "Culture—and yes, pop culture counts—is just as important as— what did you say you studied?"

"I don't think I mentioned it. But I have a double major in electrical engineering and computer science."

"So you've got brains and beauty. See? That's something else we have in common. Gotta say, though, with an education like that, I don't see why you signed up to be Carl's secretary."

I laugh. "I'm not, I swear. Carl was looking for someone with tech experience to work with him on the business side of things, and I was looking for a job where I could learn the business side. Get my feet wet. I think he was a little hesitant to hire me at first —my skills definitely lean toward tech—but I convinced him I'm a fast learner."

She peers at me. "I smell ambition."

I lift a shoulder in a casual shrug. "It's Los Angeles. Isn't that what this town is all about?"

"Ha! Carl's lucky he's got you. It'll be interesting to see how long he keeps you. But let's see ... who here would intrigue you ...?"

She casts about the room, finally pointing to a fifty-something man holding court in a corner. "That's Charles Maynard," she says. "I've known Charlie for years. Intimidating as hell until you get to know him. But it's worth it. His clients are either celebrities with name recognition or power brokers with more money than God. Either way, he's got all the best stories."

"He's a lawyer?"

"With Bender, Twain & McGuire. Very prestigious firm."

"I know," I say, happy to show that I'm not entirely ignorant, despite not knowing Rip or Lyle. "One of my closest friends works for the firm. He started here but he's in their New York office now."

"Well, come on, then, Texas. I'll introduce you." We take one step in that direction, but then Evelyn stops me. Maynard has pulled out his phone, and is shouting instructions at someone. I catch a few well-placed curses and eye Evelyn sideways. She looks unconcerned "He's a pussycat at heart. Trust me, I've worked with him before. Back in my agenting days, we put together more celebrity biopic deals for our clients than I can count. And we fought to keep a few tell-alls off the screen, too." She shakes her head, as if reliving those glory days, then pats my arm. "Still, we'll wait 'til he calms down a bit. In the meantime, though ..."

She trails off, and the corners of her mouth turn down in a frown as she scans the room again. "I don't think he's here yet, but —oh! Yes! Now *there's* someone you should meet. And if you want to talk views, the house he's building has one that makes my view look like, well, like yours." She points toward the entrance hall, but all I see are bobbing heads and haute couture. "He hardly ever accepts invitations, but we go way back," she says.

I still can't see who she's talking about, but then the crowd parts and I see the man in profile. Goose bumps rise on my arms, but I'm not cold. In fact, I'm suddenly very, very warm.

He's tall and so handsome that the word is almost an insult. But it's more than that. It's not his looks, it's his *presence*. He commands the room simply by being in it, and I realize that Evelyn and I aren't the only ones looking at him. The entire crowd has noticed his arrival. He must feel the weight of all those eyes, and yet the attention doesn't faze him at all. He smiles at the girl with the champagne, takes a glass, and begins to chat casually with a woman who approaches him, a simpering smile stretched across her face.

"Damn that girl," Evelyn says. "She never did bring me my vodka."

But I barely hear her. "Damien Stark," I say. My voice surprises me. It's little more than breath.

Evelyn's brows rise so high I notice the movement in my peripheral vision. "Well, how about that?" she says knowingly. "Looks like I guessed right."

"You did," I admit. "Mr. Stark is just the man I want to see."

Chapter Two

"Damien Stark is the holy grail." That's what Carl told me earlier that evening. Right after "Damn, Nikki. You look hot."

I think he was expecting me to blush and smile and thank him for his kind words. When I didn't, he cleared his throat and got down to business. "You know who Stark is, right?"

"You saw my resume," I reminded him. "The fellowship?" I'd been the recipient of the Stark International Science Fellowship for four of my five years at the University of Texas, and those extra dollars every semester had made all the difference in the world to me. Of course, even without a fellowship, you'd have to be from Mars not to know about the man. Only thirty years old, the reclusive former tennis star had taken the millions he'd earned in prizes and endorsements and reinvented himself. His tennis days had been overshadowed by his new identity as an entrepreneur, and Stark's massive empire raked in billions every year.

"Right, right," Carl said, distracted. "Team April is presenting at Stark Applied Technology on Tuesday." At C-Squared, every product team is named after a month. With only twenty-three employees, though, the company has yet to tap into autumn or winter.

"That's fabulous," I said, and I meant it. Inventors, software developers, and eager new business owners practically wet themselves to get an interview with Damien Stark. That Carl had snagged just such an appointment was proof that my hoop-jumping to get this job had been worth it.

"Damn straight," Carl said. "We're showing off the beta version of the 3-D training software. Brian and Dave are on point with me," he added, referring to the two software developers who'd written most of the code for the product. Considering its applications in athletics and Stark Applied Technology's focus on athletic medicine and training, I had to guess that Carl was about to pitch another winner. "I want you at the meeting with us," he added, and I managed not to embarrass myself by doing a fist-pump in the air. "Right now, we're scheduled to meet with Preston Rhodes. Do you know who he is?"

"No."

"Nobody does. Because Rhodes *is* a nobody."

So Carl didn't have a meeting with Stark, after all. I, however, had a feeling I knew where this conversation was going.

"Pop quiz, Nikki. How does an up-and-coming genius like me get an in-person meeting with a powerhouse like Damien Stark?"

"Networking," I said. I wasn't an A-student for nothing.

"And that's why I hired you." He tapped his temple, even as his eyes roamed over my dress and lingered at my cleavage. At least he wasn't so gauche as to actually articulate the basic fact that he was hoping that my tits—rather than his product—would intrigue Stark enough that he'd attend the meeting personally. But honestly, I wasn't sure my girls were up to the task. I'm easy on the eyes, but I'm more the girl-next-door, America's-sweetheart type. And I happen to know that Stark goes for the runway super-model type.

I learned that six years ago when he was still playing tennis and I was still chasing tiaras. He'd been the token celebrity judge at the Miss Tri-County Texas pageant, and though we'd barely exchanged a dozen words at the mid-pageant reception, the encounter was burned into my memory.

I'd parked myself near the buffet and was contemplating the tiny squares of cheesecake, wondering if my mother would smell it on my breath if I ate just one, when he walked up with the kind of bold self-assurance that can seem like arrogance on some men, but on Damien Stark it just seemed sexy as hell. He eyed me first, then the cheesecakes. Then he took two and popped them both in his mouth. He chewed, swallowed, then grinned at me. His unusual eyes, one amber and one almost completely black, seemed to dance with mirth.

I tried to come up with something clever to say and failed miserably. So I just stood there, my polite smile plastered across my face as I wondered if his kiss would give me all the taste and none of the calories.

Then he leaned closer, and my breath hitched as his proximity increased. "I think we're kindred spirits, Miss Fairchild."

"I'm sorry?" Was he talking about the cheesecake? Good God, I hadn't actually looked jealous when he'd eaten them, had I? The idea was appalling.

"Neither of us wants to be here," he explained. He tilted his head slightly toward a nearby emergency exit, and I was overcome by the sudden image of him grabbing my hand and taking off running. The clarity of the thought alarmed me. But the certainty that I'd go with him didn't scare me at all.

"I—oh," I mumbled.

His eyes crinkled with his smile, and he opened his mouth to speak. I didn't learn what he had to say, though, because Carmela D'Amato swept over to join us, then linked her arm with his. "Damie, darling." Her Italian accent was as thick as her dark wavy hair. "Come. We should go, yes?" I've never been a big tabloid reader, but it's hard to avoid celebrity gossip when you're doing the pageant thing. So I'd seen the headlines and articles that paired the big-shot tennis star with the Italian supermodel.

"Miss Fairchild," he said with a parting nod, then turned to escort Carmela into the crowd and out of the building. I watched them leave, consoling myself with the thought that there was regret in his eyes as we parted ways. Regret and resignation.

There wasn't, of course. Why would there be? But that nice little fantasy got me through the rest of the pageant.

And I didn't say one word about the encounter to Carl. Some things are best played close to the vest. Including how much I'm looking forward to meeting Damien Stark again.

"Come on, Texas," Evelyn says, pulling me from my thoughts. "Let's go say howdy."

I feel a tap on my shoulder and turn to find Carl behind me. He sports the kind of grin that suggests he just got laid. I know better. He's just giddy with the anticipation of getting close to Damien Stark.

Well, me, too.

The crowd has shifted again, blocking my view of the man. I still haven't seen his face, just his profile, and now I can't even see that. Evelyn's leading the way, making forward progress through the crowd despite a few stops and starts to chat with her guests. We're on the move again when a barrel-chested man in a plaid sport coat shifts to the left, once again revealing Damien Stark.

He is even more magnificent now than he was six years ago. The brashness of youth has been replaced by a mature confidence. He is Jason and Hercules and Perseus—a figure so strong and beautiful and heroic that the blood of the gods must flow through him, because how else could a being so fine exist in this world? His face consists of hard lines and angles that seem

sculpted by light and shadows, making him appear both classi-
cally gorgeous and undeniably unique. His dark hair absorbs the
light as completely as a raven's wing, but it is not nearly as
smooth. Instead, it looks wind-tossed, as if he's spent the day
at sea.

That hair in contrast with his black tailored trousers and
starched white shirt give him a casual elegance, and it's easy to
believe that this man is just as comfortable on a tennis court as he
is in a boardroom.

His famous eyes capture my attention. They seem edgy and
dangerous and full of dark promises. More important, they are
watching me. Following me as I move toward him.

I feel an odd sense of déjà vu as I move steadily across the
floor, hyperaware of my body, my posture, the placement of my
feet. Foolishly, I feel as if I'm a contestant all over again.

I keep my eyes forward, not looking at his face. I don't like the
nervousness that has crept into my manner. The sense that he can
see beneath the armor I wear along with my little black dress.

One step, then another.

I can't help it; I look straight at him. Our eyes lock, and I
swear all the air is sucked from the room. It is my old fantasy
come to life, and I am completely lost. The sense of déjà vu
vanishes and there's nothing but this moment, electric and powerful. *Sensual.*

For all I know, I've gone spinning off into space. But no, I'm
right there, floor beneath me, walls around me, and Damien
Stark's eyes on mine. I see heat and purpose. And then I see
nothing but raw, primal desire so intense I fear that I'll shatter
under the force of it.

Carl takes my elbow, steadying me, and only then do I realize
I'd started to stumble. "Are you okay?"

"New shoes. Thanks." I glance back at Stark, but his eyes
have gone flat. His mouth is a thin line. Whatever that was—and
what the hell was it?—the moment has passed.

By the time we reach Stark, I've almost convinced myself it was my imagination.

I barely process the words as Evelyn introduces Carl. My turn is next, and Carl presses his hand to my shoulder, pushing me subtly forward. His palm is sweating, and it feels clammy against my bare skin. I force myself not to shrug it off.

"Nikki is Carl's new assistant," Evelyn says.

I extend my hand. "Nikki Fairchild. It's a pleasure." I don't mention that we've met before. Now hardly seems the time to remind him that I once paraded before him in a bathing suit.

"Ms. Fairchild," he says, ignoring my hand. My stomach twists, but I'm not sure if it's from nerves, disappointment, or anger. He looks from Carl to Evelyn, pointedly avoiding my eyes. "You'll have to excuse me. There's something I need to attend to right away." And then he's gone, swallowed up into the crowd as effectively as a magician disappearing in a puff of smoke.

"What the fuck?" Carl says, summing up my sentiments exactly.

Uncharacteristically quiet, Evelyn simply gapes at me, her expressive mouth turned down into a frown.

But I don't need words to know what she's thinking. I can easily see that she's wondering the same thing I am: What just happened?

More important, what the hell did I do wrong?

The Runaway Bestselling Saga
Release Me
Claim Me
Complete Me
And Beyond...

ABOUT THE AUTHOR

J. Kenner (aka Julie Kenner) is the *New York Times, USA Today, Publishers Weekly, Wall Street Journal* and #1 International bestselling author of over one hundred novels, novellas and short stories in a variety of genres.

JK has been praised by *Publishers Weekly* as an author with a "flair for dialogue and eccentric characterizations" and by *RT Bookclub* for having "cornered the market on sinfully attractive, dominant antiheroes and the women who swoon for them." A six-time finalist for Romance Writers of America's RITA award, JK took home the first RITA trophy awarded in the category of erotic romance in 2014 for her novel, *Claim Me* (book 2 of her Stark Saga) and another RITA trophy for *Wicked Dirty* in the same category in 2017.

In her previous career as an attorney, JK worked as a lawyer in Southern California and Texas. She currently lives in Central Texas, with her husband, two daughters, and two rather spastic cats.

Stay in touch! Text JKenner to 21000 to subscribe to JK's text alerts.

www.jkenner.com

CPSIA information can be obtained
at www.ICGtesting.com
Printed in the USA
JSHW040206281220
10458JS00008BB/16